By Nicole Edwards

The Alluring Indulgence Series

Kaleb

Zane

Travis

Holidays with the Walker Brothers

Ethan

Braydon

Sawyer

Brendon

The Club Destiny Series

Conviction

Temptation

Addicted

Seduction

Infatuation

Captivated

Devotion

Perception

Entrusted

Adored

The Dead Heat Ranch Series

Boots Optional

Betting on Grace

Overnight Love

The Devil's Bend Series

Chasing Dreams

Vanishing Dreams

By Nicole Edwards (cont.)

The Devil's Playground Series

Without Regret

The Pier 70 Series

Reckless

The Sniper 1 Security Series

Wait for Morning

Never Say Never

The Southern Boy Mafia Series

Beautifully Brutal

Beautifully Loyal

Standalone Novels

A Million Tiny Pieces

Writing as Timberlyn Scott

Unhinged

Unraveling

Chaos

Reckless

A Pier 70 Novel
Book 1

Nicole Edwards

Nicole Edwards Limited
PO Box 806
Hutto, Texas 78634
www.NicoleEdwardsLimited.com
www.slipublishing.com

Reckless – A Pier 70 Novel is a work of fiction. Names, characters, businesses, places, events and incidents either are the products of the author's imagination or used in a fictitious manner. Any resemblance to actual persons, living or dead, or actual events is purely coincidental.

Cover Image: © Igor Chaikovskiy | 123rf.com (front cover image - 7338452); © Jasminko Ibrakovic | 123rf.com (back cover image - 36000609)

Ebook Image: © magenta10 | 123rf.com (formatting image - 14284060)

Cover Design: © Nicole Edwards Limited

Editing: Blue Otter Editing www.BlueOtterEditing.com

ISBN (ebook): 978-1-939786-54-8
ISBN (print): 978-1-939786-53-1

Gay Romance
M/M interactions
Mature Audience

Table of Contents

One

"DAMN IT, DARE! Is it too *fucking* difficult to do what we ask?"

Cam Strickland choked out a laugh when he walked into the dark office of Pier 70 Marina shortly after six in the morning to find Roan grumbling to himself. Cam didn't even need to look around because he already knew no one else was there.

Just Roan. And his pissy attitude. *Happy Friday, y'all!*

Smiling, Cam spared Roan a look. "Good mornin' to you, too, sunshine. Talkin' to yourself again?"

As though sensing he was overlooking her, Lulu—the two-year-old golden retriever who lived at the marina—came from behind the counter, tail wagging. "Mornin' to you, too, Lu." Cam dropped to his haunches to pet her while watching Roan.

Roan Gregory, Cam's longtime friend and business partner, cast a sideways glance at Cam, one dark eyebrow cocking beneath the dark, shaggy bangs that covered his forehead before Roan returned his attention to the printer/copier (or *office genius* as Dare liked to refer to it) in front of him.

Looked like it was definitely going to be one of those days.

Cam gave Lulu one last pat, then got to his feet. Flipping on the lights and turning the sign around to show they were open, Cam watched while Roan took out his frustration on the fancy new machine that one of their other partners, Dare Davis—the man Roan was clearly irritated with—had insisted on purchasing last month.

"Dare's not even here, so why're you yellin'?"

"He *should* be here," Roan muttered as he slammed the lid down and stabbed at one of the buttons repeatedly.

Well, the fancy machine *had* been new. At least until Roan had gotten hold of it.

Lulu barked once, clearly not happy with the loud noise. He felt her pain.

Cam didn't try to hide his amusement with the situation, even pretended not to notice when Roan glowered at him, evidently not as entertained as Cam.

"So is it Dare or the printer you have a problem with?" Cam offered a smile, flashing all his teeth.

Roan faked a laugh, then rolled his eyes, eyebrows shooting downward. Too soon for jokes apparently. Still, Cam couldn't help but laugh. He had to find entertainment somewhere. Might as well be here.

"Stupid printer," Roan grumbled.

Cam was beginning to feel bad for that *stupid printer*, taking the brunt of Roan's frustration and all.

Dare—always helpful, or so he claimed—had come up with the crazy suggestion for the ridiculously expensive machine after a huge falling-out with Roan on why they couldn't just get rid of paper altogether.

"Who even uses paper anymore?" Dare had asked, dead serious.

Roan's reply ... well... "We do, dumb ass."

Dare had even tossed out one of his statistics during his argument. Admittedly, Cam had been sort of impressed.

"Seriously, bro," Dare had argued, "I saw a report. Somethin' like eighty-four percent of businesses prefer Apple products. We don't need paper and shit. Just get a coupla iPads like the rest of the technologically advanced civilization. Make people sign with their fingers... Easy peasy."

Convincing Roan wasn't *easy peasy*.

Dare wanted to save trees; Roan wanted simplicity. Cam, well, he didn't give a fuck one way or the other.

Still, they'd ended up with the printer. Knowing Dare, he'd probably hoped Roan wouldn't have wanted to spend that much money, but Roan had shown him.

Roan was nothing if not stubborn.

As was Dare.

When Roan stabbed the button again, Cam stopped walking, coming to a halt on the customer side of the long counter that split the marina office. While his flip-flops froze on the rough slate floor, his full attention was focused on his friend.

Just ask what his problem is.

Don't have a death wish, Cam told the crazy voice in his head. Seriously. Cam saw what Roan was doing to that poor, unsuspecting printer.

It wasn't like Roan to get quite so pissy first thing in the morning. By the end of the day, sure, Roan was known to be a little frazzled from time to time. Not this early, though.

Unlike the rest of them, Roan *was* a morning person. Usually. Cam, on the other hand, didn't understand that concept whatsoever. Bright and chipper didn't make an appearance this early in the day for Cam. Blurry-eyed, yes. Cheerful, no. Then again, no one else at the marina—other than possibly Dare—was a bowl of fucking sunshine, either, until they'd had a little caffeine in whatever form they opted to take it. Cam's preference was coffee, and he could see the fresh pot sitting right there on the counter waiting for him.

Just. Out. Of. Reach.

With a heavy sigh, he accepted his fate. He had no choice but to confront his friend.

"What'd he do now?" Cam peered over at Roan, then back to the black liquid gold now calling his name. He was eager to answer, only he was mentally weighing the risks of getting too close to Roan at the moment.

Roan snorted. "We've got a huge group comin' in today. A freaking daycare, man. And he was supposed to do one simple thing. Get the waivers signed." Roan yanked the paper out of the machine. "I can't find 'em anywhere."

"I did get 'em signed, you asshole."

Speak of the devil.

Cam smirked at the sound of Dare's voice coming from behind him, followed by the annoying ding of the electronic door notification system that, no matter how much they fucked with it, still sounded on a delay.

"If you'd just open your eyes and look," Dare tacked on.

Dare Davis, the third owner of Pier 70 Marina, and another one of Cam's closest friends, stepped into the office looking as casual as ever with his white T-shirt that sported the marina logo, knee-length swim shorts, Dallas Cowboys ball cap on backwards, and as usual, was bare-footed. Oh, and carrying a Red Bull. Of course.

"Then where the hell are they?" Roan barked, pinning Dare in place with his heated gaze.

Cam took a step back and watched the exchange, as did Lulu, who appeared a little concerned. Cam patted her head reassuringly.

"Where y'all told me to put 'em," Dare countered, head cocked forward, as though pointing with his eyebrows. "That stupid rack you hung on the wall, remember?"

"Fine time for you to start listenin' to what we ask you to do," Roan groused.

Cam huffed a laugh, trying to cover it with a cough. With these two, he was always entertained.

"If I recall correctly," Dare said, flashing a mischievous grin at Cam before looking back at Roan, "I tried to get y'all to nix the paper and move to iPads, but *no*."

Roan shot a ball-shriveling scowl at Dare.

"No worries," Dare said, still smirking and holding his hands up in an *I surrender* gesture. "I'm cool. Just happy to chill in the Stone Age, rubbin' sticks together to make fire. Later, I'll take a break and go spear us a buffalo for dinner."

Rolling his eyes because he knew Dare was just looking to push Roan's buttons, which wasn't unusual, Cam made his way to the coffeepot, desperate to get his hands on a cup while Roan was distracted.

"You are such an ass—"

"Who's handlin' this party today?" Cam interrupted Roan's tirade, hoping to change the subject and keep the two of them from going head to head so early in the day.

As entertaining as this ongoing squabble might be, they had shit to do.

Pier 70 Marina was a full-service marina and boat storage that Cam, Roan, and Dare had opened nearly a decade ago with the financial backing from Cam's father. It'd grown to be one of the most exclusive, highly coveted marinas on Lake Buchanan. To the point that they'd acquired a staff of nearly twenty over the years, most of those people family or friends. Or family friends.

"Holly's handlin' the corporate event, and Teague's gonna run point on the water," Dare advised, tossing back what was left of his energy drink.

"Is she here yet?" Cam asked, referring to his younger sister, who'd recently taken over the position of party host.

Holly and her husband, Keith, had offered their services to Cam when the marina had been shorthanded a couple of summers back, and they'd stuck around ever since. They'd both adapted quickly to the prestigious party host role and now alternated between handling the off-water activities and taking care of their three kids. Holly was responsible for getting things set up for the large events—usually corporate or family reunion type—that took place in the fifteen-acre park adjacent to the marina, while the rest of them handled the watercraft.

"On her way. She just called before you came down," Roan said.

"Good. Where's Teague?" Cam asked.

Teague Carter was the recently added fourth and final partner in the marina. They'd brought him on board to help out with light mechanic work and some of the chores when Teague had still been in high school, and through the years, thanks to his hard work and dedication, they'd opted to give him stock in the place.

"Haven't seen him yet," Dare said. "He had a late night. Some party carried on until the early hours, and he didn't get outta here until around one."

That wasn't surprising.

Several years younger than the rest of them, Teague was the life of the party on a good day, always volunteering to go out on the party barges when a client requested. Sometimes Cam admired the kid's energy level, but Cam chalked it up to Teague still being young. Not that Cam was all that old at thirty-two, but he did have about seven years on Teague.

"What else's goin' on today?" Cam glanced back at Dare and Roan over his shoulder.

"You mean besides the heavyweight match between Roan and the printer?" Dare smirked, looking back and forth between Cam and Roan.

Roan shot Dare the finger. "Not a helluva lot," Roan griped, clearly still in a foul mood.

"So why so pissy?" Dare asked Roan directly.

Roan glowered at Dare but didn't respond.

Thank God for small miracles. These two … stubborn as mules.

Taking a sip of coffee and letting it burn all the way down, Cam turned around and leaned against the counter, watching the two of them carefully. Roan was frowning, Dare grinning like a fool.

Cam shook his head.

Sometimes, especially during the summer months when they spent so much time entertaining people for extensive periods of time, things started to heat up inside the office. Sometimes hot enough to rival the blistering three-digit temps. However, it was only the first week of June, the season was just now kicking off, so he hoped this wasn't indicative of what they had to look forward to for the next three months.

But it was that tension that had Cam seeking solitude—or trying to, anyway—in his own office whenever possible. It didn't help that he lived in one of the two private apartments above the marina office, either. Hiding out was nearly impossible in his line of work. And with Roan now occupying the other apartment, Cam never seemed to find a moment's peace.

Unfortunately, this morning he'd hit the snooze button on his alarm a few too many times and hadn't made it in before the others as he normally did, which meant he hadn't been able to sneak away.

Yet.

But he fully intended to rectify that now.

Sparing them both one more look, Cam pushed off the counter and glanced out at the parking lot.

Yep. Time to jet.

"You've got incoming," Cam noted as he took his coffee cup and headed down the narrow hallway toward his office, smiling as Roan greeted the customer with a chipper note in his deep voice that hadn't been there a minute ago.

Two

GANNON BURGESS HAD woken up that morning expecting a drama-free day. It was Friday, after all. A day most people traipsed into work still half-asleep—possibly still drunk—from the Thursday happy hour *slash* kickoff to the weekend party they'd indulged in the night before. Once they'd downed the requisite amount of coffee, they took care of the absolute necessities, then headed out as early as they could to pick up where they'd left off in kicking off the weekend.

Drama-free. Just the way Gannon preferred it.

Not today, apparently.

Granted, being that he worked seven days a week, no matter what, Gannon woke up with high hopes for smooth sailing every morning, and generally he didn't meet too many surprises along the way.

Did it always go the way he wanted? No, actually.

Since he owned and managed a multimillion-dollar entertainment software development company, there were some standard road bumps along with the occasional hiccup that arose—software glitches, viruses, employee issues, technical problems. Yadda, yadda, blah, blah, blah.

Those he anticipated, sometimes even predicted.

But today, it looked as though his crystal ball was a little cloudy because he hadn't seen *this* coming at all.

"What do you say? You up for it?"

As he stared back at his assistant/friend, trying to process what she was telling him—though he had to give her props, she had phrased it as a question, but he knew her better than that—Gannon knew this was not going to be fun.

In fact, he'd take a server crash over what Milly was suggesting any day.

"Seriously, Gannon." Milly's perfectly tweezed blonde eyebrows arched downward as she narrowed her baby blues at him. "It'll be good for us."

Us.

It never fared well for him when Milly used that one little word in a sentence.

Casually leaning back in her chair, long legs crossed at the knee, Milly Holcomb, the woman who kept Gannon and the rest of the Austin office organized and on track, looked more like a supermodel than a tenured administrative assistant for the president and CEO of Burgess Entertainment. Him.

But Milly was a different breed, Gannon would have to give her that. Not only was she his assistant, she was also his longtime friend, the keeper of most of his secrets, the woman who forced him to spill his guts when he had no desire to do so. So, yeah, he probably made a few exceptions for her, looked the other way most of the time. It was easier that way.

She was smart, driven, quick-thinking, even professional when the situation required her to be. Hell, he could list a dozen more things about her that he admired, because Milly had a lot of appealing qualities.

But subtlety wasn't one of them.

Perfect example … right now, her long, golden-blonde hair was haphazardly heaped on the top of her head like she'd just rolled out of bed—a style that had probably taken her an hour—held in place by some fancy clip. Her smooth, alabaster skin made her look closer to twenty-one than thirty-one. The knee-length black skirt showed off her legs, and the white, button-down blouse that was unbuttoned a little more than was probably appropriate for an office setting offered a glimpse of her generous cleavage, which was likely one of the reasons the game designers were always hovering around her.

And he knew for a fact that she enjoyed the hell out of giving the guys in the office something nice to look at. Hell, she'd told him so.

Leaning back in his chair, balancing it on two legs, Gannon placed his hands behind his head, elbows wide as he regarded her. "A boat?" he asked skeptically, still hoping he'd heard her wrong.

"Yes." The single word rang with an emphatic exhale, as though she was frustrated because he had a problem understanding. "A couple of hours out on the lake. Sunshine, conversation. It's just what the team needs."

"The team?"

Milly frowned. "Stop doing that."

"Doing what?"

She huffed. "Responding to me with two word questions. It's really irritating."

Smiling at how easily he could get her flustered, Gannon peered past Milly and through the wall of glass that separated his office from the rest of the floor. The place looked the same as it did on any Friday morning. A few people were wandering around, a couple of guys talking, several sitting in front of their monitors working diligently.

"They look happy to me," he said, nodding toward one of the designers who had snuck over to the open box of donuts to steal another one, flushing to the roots of his jet-black hair when he looked over to see Gannon watching him.

Gannon offered a small wave and a smile. With a mouthful, the guy waved back, then scurried back to his desk.

"You don't talk to them enough," Milly said firmly.

"You want me to go out there and chat?" Gannon frowned, his glasses sliding down his nose. Pushing them back up, he cocked an eyebrow, waiting for her to explain.

"No, I don't. I want you to get them out of the office for a little while."

"On a boat?" he repeated.

"Gannon."

He couldn't help but laugh at the admonishing tone she used with him. She should've been used to it by now; after all, she'd worked for him for nearly a decade, and shortly after that, she'd insinuated herself smack in the middle of his life, becoming his closest friend. She knew him better than most people, but there was still a lot she didn't know about him. And Gannon preferred it that way. The less people knew, the better off he was.

And one of the things she didn't know about him was that he hated water. Perhaps that wasn't a strong enough adjective. Loathed, abhorred, detested. Or … all of those to the power of infinity.

Yes, that worked.

Unless it was in a concrete bowl in someone's backyard or in his own bathtub, Gannon steered clear of it. A shower was his idea of a water sport, and he was content with that. The notion of spending an afternoon floating on the stuff… Let's just say he'd rather have someone pluck his toenails off with pliers, then feed them to him. The toenails. Or the pliers. Either way.

Clearly oblivious to Gannon's internal musings, Milly continued, "I already know the perfect place. It's about an hour away."

"An hour? Why not one of the lakes right here in Austin?" Not that he thought it was a good idea.

"Because they're too low right now."

He'd have to take her word on that.

"So why this particular place?" he questioned, not willing to give in just yet.

"I don't know," Milly huffed. "It looks nice."

"*Looks* nice?"

Milly pursed her lips. "Yes. On their website. And if you get your butt out of your chair, we can go right now. Get things set up."

Dropping his chair back down, Gannon leaned forward, resting his elbows on his knees as he regarded her once more. "Go *now*? What are you talking about? Why not just call them?"

"Because I don't know what I'm asking for." The tops of Milly's ears turned the same color red as her lipstick, and he realized she was embarrassed. "I was hoping we could go check it out, make sure it's something we want to do."

Gannon could've told her that *we* definitely didn't want to *do* any of it. Her, maybe. Him, nope.

Getting up, Gannon walked around behind his desk, getting ready to sit down at his computer so he could get some work done.

"No, don't sit down," she blurted, sitting up straight. "Come on. It'll be fun. And who knows, maybe there'll be a couple of hot guys there we can flirt with."

Gannon gave her his best *get real* look. "I'm not in the market for a guy right now. Hot or otherwise."

"Sure you are," she countered in that tone that said she knew him better than he knew himself. "And just think, it's easier for you to meet guys when I'm with you."

Gannon grimaced. "How's that?"

"Well, if they aren't checking *me* out, then we know they're gay."

Smiling, he rolled his eyes.

That was another thing about Milly, she certainly wasn't modest.

"Now get your shit together," Milly ordered as she stood. "We're wastin' time."

And there was the hard-headed, take-no-shit assistant he knew and loved. She was good at a lot of things, but ordering him around... That was something Milly had mastered years ago.

Shaking his head in disbelief, Gannon relented. He wasn't going to be able to convince her this was a bad idea, no matter how much he wanted to. Truth was, Milly did have the team's best interests in mind when she made her suggestions. If she thought they'd enjoy a day out on the boat, maybe they would.

He wouldn't.

But even he knew it wasn't about him.

Half an hour later, after Milly had tied up a few loose ends and allotted him fifteen minutes to check his email, Gannon was behind the wheel of his car, Milly riding shotgun.

"This is exciting," she said, bouncing in her seat like a five-year-old on the way to the toy store.

"Yeah," he mumbled. "Exciting."

"Oh, cool it." Milly smacked his arm playfully. "Seriously. I think the guys'll love going out on a boat. It's definitely better than sitting in that stale office all day."

"No," Gannon clarified, glancing over at her from behind his glasses, "I think *you'll* love going out on a boat. I think they'd prefer to be given the day off so they can go home and play World of Warcraft."

"Shush!" Her eyes widened as though he'd taken the Lord's name in vain. "How dare you speak of the enemy in my presence?"

Gannon laughed. She was incredibly loyal to Burgess Entertainment, insisting that any other gaming company paled in comparison.

"Fine," he conceded. "They'd rather be home playing Rise of Vengeance."

"Whatever," she interrupted. "They shouldn't be at home, period. They need to get out, experience life from the *other* side of those video game controllers."

No matter what she said, Gannon knew he was right. The people he employed were hard-core gamers. When not at work, they spent their time behind a keyboard, immersed in the video game underworld. Their lives were online, not out in a boat. But he knew he could never convince Milly of that. She insisted that no one could be that humdrum.

They could. And they were.

Gannon knew firsthand. He was one of them.

However, she refused to believe him. He'd had more than one heated discussion with Milly, usually over dinner and a bottle of wine, about how someone could get addicted to games. She didn't see it, and Gannon couldn't explain it, so he didn't bother to try.

"We should make sure they have sunscreen," Milly mumbled, staring out the window. "And maybe hats." Her head swiveled around, attention on him. "You, too. I think you need a hat."

Gannon frowned. "I'm not wearing a hat."

"What if your head gets sunburned?"

Gannon chuckled. "I go out in the sun all the time."

"Walking to your car from the office doesn't count," she countered.

Eager to get off the subject, Gannon asked, "Don't you have a date this weekend?"

Milly sighed, leaning back in her seat as though she'd been defeated. "Yeah. With Gary."

Was it him, or did she sound a little disappointed? "What's wrong with Gary?"

"Nothing," she told him, sighing dramatically. "You need to turn up here."

Gannon put on his blinker to exit the highway. "If nothing's wrong with him, what's the problem?"

"I don't know."

"Is he boring?"

"No. He's a musician. Nothing boring about that."

If she said so. "Is he ugly?"

"God no. He's freaking hot."

"Then what is it?"

"We have nothing in common," she answered. "He's a starving artist who craves the rock star lifestyle. While I'm ... not." Milly offered him a grin. "And while his stories are interesting, I don't really care for them."

"Then why're you going out with him again?" Gannon cast a sideways glance her way.

"Because I can't come up with a good enough excuse not to."

"Well, then, by all means, suffer through it."

23

Milly smacked his arm again. "Shut it. I'll figure something out. What about you? You have any plans to date in the near future?"

Gannon shook his head. The last date he'd had was... Shit. Probably a year ago? *Two* years ago?

Holy crap. Apparently time flies when you're ... not dating.

Damn, now that he thought about it, that did seem like a long time. Not that he'd even given it a second thought. At least not when Milly wasn't bringing it up. Dating wasn't the most important thing in his life. Burgess Entertainment took up most of his time and could technically qualify as his significant other.

"One of these days," Milly began, "you're gonna meet a guy who's gonna knock you right on that cute ass of yours."

Gannon frowned over at her.

"What? Just because you're gay doesn't mean I can't admire your cute buns."

"My *buns* are not cute," he blurted.

"Oh, they definitely are and so is—"

"Which direction do I go?" Gannon interrupted, desperate to cut her off. He'd heard this before, and as good as Milly was for his ego, he definitely didn't want to hear it again.

"Take a right," she told him, a wide grin splitting her face. "It's a few miles down this road."

Gannon was thankful they were close. The conversation had taken a weird turn, and he was more interested in getting this out of the way so he could get back to the office and do what he did best.

Work.

"I think you'll like this place," Milly commented. "And just wait till you see the guys who work here."

Gannon's head snapped in her direction. "*What? What* guys? You didn't mention anything about guys."

That smile.

Ah, crap. "Dammit, Milly."

Gannon knew that smile.

Gannon *feared* that smile.

Three

LOOKING UP AT the clock, Cam shook out his hands, then leaned back in his chair and spun around to stare out the window overlooking the smooth, glassy water that seemed to go on for miles and miles.

Damn, there wasn't a cloud in the sky.

He should be out *there*.

Spinning back around, he glared at his computer screen.

Not in *here*.

For the past two hours, he'd managed to focus on entering the monthly deposits into the system, comparing them to the rental agreements, and ensuring everyone was paid up for the month. It made his day when he only had to change the gate code for one renter who had yet to pay up. Hopefully, they'd see that person sometime this week and get squared away.

Handling the money and updating the books was a tedious task that he actually enjoyed doing most of the time. However, given the opportunity, he would've procrastinated in order to spend time outdoors.

It was what he did best.

Spending time outdoors, not the procrastinating. Although...

Okay, so sure, he wasn't above looking for something more enjoyable than paperwork.

Thankfully, this side of the company was not his main focus—or even something he was particularly good at—but on the flip side, Cam preferred to keep up to date on the state of the business, and this allowed him to do that. They had an accountant who handled the details, but Cam made a point to update the books every week—okay, every couple of weeks ... er ... once a month, but who was counting?

The handheld radio sitting on his desk chirped.

"Hey, good buddy," Dare announced in the crazy radio voice he loved to do, "anyone order up a side of bacon?"

Cam laughed.

"I repeat, we've got bacon."

Cam grabbed the radio and hit the button. "Roger that."

While he'd worked, Cam had listened to the radios chirp endlessly as Roan, Dare, and Teague bantered back and forth while they'd handled the incoming appointments and prepared the boats for the afternoon. And now, according to Dare's non-PC announcement, it looked as though Cam's father had arrived. Dare found it amusing to refer to Cam's father as bacon because he was a retired police officer. Michael Strickland was a good sport and he took it all in stride. It helped that Dare really did have the utmost respect for the man.

Hearing the delayed door alarm, Cam closed his laptop and looked up as his father appeared in his office doorway looking every bit the sturdy presence he'd always been in Cam's life.

"Is he still callin' me bacon?" Michael asked, his grin causing the skin beside his dark blue eyes to crinkle.

"He is," Cam confirmed. "Good mornin', Pop."

"Mornin'," his father replied, his rough voice reflecting years of smoking. His father's thick salt-and-pepper hair was slicked back, the white bushy mustache over his lip could've used a bit of a trim, and yes, he was smiling. He looked good, relaxed.

Leaning back in his chair, Cam studied him. "What brings you by?"

Michael propped himself against the door jamb, crossing his arms over his chest. "Just checkin' on you boys."

Cam smiled. At least once a week, sometimes more, his father stopped by to see how Cam, Roan, Dare, and Teague were doing. And not to talk business, either. Although Cam's father had fronted the money for the marina in the beginning, Cam had since paid him back and assumed full responsibility. So Michael's visits were always personal in nature, a chance for them to catch up. He would stick around for an hour, sometimes several hours, but he never left until he had a chance to talk to all four of them. Cam figured that was the cop in him. Sort of like a welfare check to ensure everything was kosher.

Not that Cam minded. He enjoyed spending time with his father, and these days, they didn't do enough of it.

"We're doin' good," Cam told him. "Gonna be busy startin' next week."

"Need any help?"

"Not yet, but if it comes to that, I won't hesitate to call. Why? Are you bored?"

Michael laughed. "Bored? Not a chance. I've got a boat and a fishin' pole. And three grandkids. What more do I need?"

Cam knew his father was playing up the whole retired fisherman routine. Michael had spent forty-five years on the force, every day a new adventure according to him. The fact that he'd retired at sixty-five had surprised everyone, but he'd insisted it was time. Now, not only did Cam's father visit the marina frequently, he'd been known to man the office, help Holly out with the events, even assist Hudson out in the repair shop. Rarely did he go out on the boat to relax.

"What more do you need?" Cam echoed.

The radio on his desk chirped and Cam reached over to turn it down.

"Well, I won't keep you," Michael said, glancing down at the computer on Cam's desk. "Looks like you're focused. But maybe we can have lunch one of—"

Before Michael could finish his sentence, a deep voice echoed down the hall, coming from the front counter. "Anyone here?"

Cam frowned. He hadn't heard anyone come in.

"Coming!" Cam hollered back as he pushed out of his chair. Looking at his father, he smiled. "And yes to lunch. That sounds good."

"All right then." His father grinned, clapping Cam on the shoulder. "I'm off. Gonna go find the boys."

"Give Dare hell."

"Oh, I plan to," his father said. "Don't you worry."

"See you, Pop," Cam said as his father led the way back to the front office, then maneuvered past the newcomers on his way out the door.

Cam followed behind, and after offering his father a casual wave, he pulled his attention to the two people standing at the counter. He did a double take after grabbing the appointment book and pulling it toward him.

Well. *This* was certainly new.

29

Reckless

He fought the urge to smile as he watched the well-dressed man and woman peering around as though they'd never seen the inside of a marina office before. Cam wasn't even sure they'd noticed him as they studied the rules they had posted on the wall.

Thro ugh the years, Cam had seen all walks of life come through that door, and these two ... they were clearly the corporate types, which made him wonder if they were lost. It wouldn't surprise him if they were. The way they were dressed, Cam doubted they'd seen much more than an office building in years.

The boyishly handsome man was suited up, sans the jacket, wearing a white dress shirt, buttoned at the wrists, along with a blue silk tie and—Cam peered over the counter—fancy black loafers. He looked kind of ... starchy. As well as completely out of his element in the small office.

As for the woman... Cam's initial assessment leaned more toward rich-girl chic. With her fancy ... er ... skirt-suit ... outfit ... or whatever it was called, her swanky though messy up-do, big hoop earrings, and bright red heels, she looked as though she should be in a boardroom, not in a marina office. She was pretty, in a New York law firm type of way. But he had to give her a little credit, she looked slightly more at ease than her partner.

"Can I help you?" Cam asked politely, trying not to think about the T-shirt and board shorts he was wearing. Then again, at least he had his shirt *on*. Most of the time they spent their days shirtless, because, for one, they were often in the water, and two, it was much easier to endure the ridiculous Texas summer temperatures that way. Even with his sun-faded Pier 70 T-shirt, he suddenly felt incredibly underdressed up next to these two.

The woman elbowed the man, and Cam noticed the guy's dark eyebrows dart down in confusion before he made eye contact with Cam.

"Gannon Burgess," he introduced, covering his grunt with a cough. "We're here to rent a boat."

Cam couldn't hide his amusement as he leaned against the counter after opening the rental book. "I'm thinkin' you're a little overdressed for the occasion, but to each his own."

When those dark eyes locked with his, Cam's body went on high alert. But then … Gannon smiled, and that slight curve of his lips and the dimple that formed in his cheek transformed his boyishly handsome face into something far more intriguing.

The man's smile was … mesmerizing.

Oh, hell. And now Cam was eye-fucking the suit.

Shit.

Shaking off the thought, he followed with, "What'd you have in mind?"

Gannon's spellbinding smile faded, replaced by an incredibly puzzled expression. It obviously *was* his first time at a marina.

Glancing over at the woman, Cam noticed the dazed look there, too.

"Okay, let's start simple," Cam said, taking pity on the couple. Twirling his pen between his fingers, he bounced his gaze between them. "How many people? Just the two of you?"

"Oh, God no," the woman said quickly, her take-charge tone telling him he'd pegged her accurately, though the sweetness of her face, and those bright blue eyes, didn't seem to match. She glared over at Gannon as though expecting him to do the talking. When he didn't, she released a heavy sigh. "It's for a party."

"A celebration?" Cam inquired, glancing down at the woman's hand to see if there was an extravagant engagement ring.

Nope. No ring.

Without permission, his eyes strayed to Gannon's left ring finger. No ring there, either. Huh.

"Not exactly," Gannon answered thickly. "Just a small get-together. Roughly ten people."

"Ten gives you plenty of options," Cam informed them, watching for a reaction. "Pontoon, yacht? Tritoons'll allow you to pull someone on a tube. What's the plan?"

Gannon glanced down at the woman, whose name Cam still didn't know. She simply shrugged her slim shoulders, looking somewhat bewildered. The man's penetrating gaze, framed by the thin, black rectangular rim of his glasses, came back to meet Cam's. While he waited for an answer, Cam did his best not to notice how those eyes were the color of espresso.

Deep, dark … devastating.

Shit.

Looking over at the woman, he spotted the slow smile that curved her full, red lips.

Fuck.

Busted.

Glancing down at the rental book as though that might help rein in his wandering thoughts, Cam took a deep breath.

"So, what'll it be?" the woman asked Gannon.

"Hell if I know," Gannon answered straightforwardly, making Cam grin as he lifted his head and stared back at Gannon once more. "I take it you're the expert. Maybe you can help."

"I can help," Cam confirmed, pulling his gaze from the intense mocha-brown eyes of the boyishly handsome, dark-haired executive standing before him. Peering down at the rental book, Cam skimmed the pages looking for an available time and date. "What day were you lookin' to rent?"

"Whatever day you've got," Gannon said. "Weekday, though."

Cam nodded. "Next week? Week after?"

This time the woman spoke up. "The sooner the better. Morale's down at the office, and a little relaxing time is just what we need to kick off a busy summer."

"Not sure how this'll help morale," Gannon added with a frown, his gaze lingering on Cam's face for several long seconds. "But if Milly says it'll help, I tend to believe her."

Milly. Good to know.

"You know what they say about all work and no play," Cam inserted, doing his best not to stare at Gannon.

"No, he doesn't know," Milly retorted, laughing. Her voice was husky, her eyes glittering with humor as she stared up at Gannon. "I don't think anyone ever enlightened him."

Cam liked her.

As for Gannon ... well, there was something about him that piqued Cam's interest. He was more pretty than rugged and looked fairly young, probably mid-twenties. And if Cam had to guess, the guy likely went to get manicures on a monthly basis. Perhaps pedicures, too.

And yet, for some inexplicable reason, Cam found the man appealing, although he certainly wasn't Cam's type.

He much preferred someone a little less ... well, pretty.

Not quite so starchy, either.

Reckless

Gannon's dark eyes seemed to capture everything, and his full lips didn't turn into a smile as much as Cam would've liked. Definitely all work and no play, evident by his expensive, tailored slacks and fancy navy blue tie.

Hmm. The things Cam could do to him with that tie.

His eyes immediately shot to Milly's. She was grinning back at him, teeth flashing.

Yep, she'd figured him out.

Crap.

This boat was sinking fast and Cam wasn't sure he could salvage it at this point.

Boat.

Right.

They were here for a boat. And a boat they would get.

Clearing his throat, Cam pulled his attention back to the task at hand. "All right then. Let's get it set up."

So Cam could send them on their way and get a grip.

Four

IT WAS A damn good thing Gannon had opted to leave his suit jacket in the car.

It was getting hot in here.

Even without the jacket, he felt more than a little out of place standing in the small, quaint office of the Pier 70 Marina. Not only was he clearly overdressed for the establishment, he didn't seem to have quite the amount of machismo required to blend in, either. At least not if he compared himself to the brick wall of a man staring back at him with those thickly muscled arms and beautiful cobalt eyes.

Yep, he was in so much trouble here.

Milly's comment from earlier echoed in his head.

It'll be fun. And who knows, maybe there'll be a couple of hot guys there we can flirt with.

Well, there was definitely *one* hot guy. The man Gannon couldn't seem to look away from.

Milly nudged his side again and he forced his gaze down to her.

"Quit flirting," she whispered.

Horrified, Gannon's face flamed.

"I'm kidding, big guy. Chill."

Reckless

Had he been flirting? It'd been so long since any man had held his interest for longer than a minute, Gannon wasn't even sure he knew *how* to flirt at this point. Yes, he'd caught and held the man's lingering gaze a time or two, making sure he saw Gannon's interest. At least that was what he'd *hoped* to portray with the lengthy stare. As rusty as he was with the whole flirting thing, there was no telling what he'd *actually* looked like.

But the guy hadn't looked away, which was a good sign, right?

Regardless, Gannon would be lying if he said he hadn't enjoyed the hell out of it. Right up to the point Milly had embarrassed the shit out of him. Now, he didn't want to look at the man.

Grabbing his phone from his pocket, Gannon pretended to be otherwise preoccupied, peeking up from beneath his lashes to see if the man was looking at him.

He wasn't.

Thank the patron saint of video games.

For the few uncomfortable minutes that he'd been there, Gannon had done nothing except eye the guy while doing his best to hide his instantaneous physical reaction—both from Milly and from the guy now skimming through the pages of what appeared to be an appointment book. And he thought he was doing a relatively decent job, up until he'd detected that knowing gleam in Milly's bright blue eyes. She'd busted them and she was enjoying the hell out of it. Which meant Gannon would probably die of embarrassment very, very soon.

Until that happened, Gannon needed to remember why he was there.

Rent a boat.

Yes.

So he could take his team out on the water—which he still hated, hot guy or not—and, according to Milly, boost morale. With a highly anticipated new video game scheduled to launch in less than three months, there was a lot that had to be done for them to be ready, so yeah, he understood her logic.

First part was out of the way. They were here. And they were ready to rent a boat.

Only Gannon couldn't focus.

He couldn't seem to stop ogling the thickly muscled, bronze-skinned guy with masculine hands and beautiful, intricate tattoos covering most of his forearms who was helping them. There was just something about him that Gannon couldn't ignore. Something that called to a very primal part of him that he'd kept under wraps for far too long.

Perhaps it was the man's rugged good looks with his firm, clean-shaven jaw, narrow nose, high cheekbones, and full lips. Or possibly it was his tousled dark hair or those pretty blue eyes and that smile… Fuck. That quick, easy smile that flirted with the corners of his eyes every so often made Gannon want to stand there all damn day.

Not that he'd noticed him. Much.

It wasn't professional for him to have such a visceral, primitive response to a man he'd just met, but he certainly couldn't deny the attraction. Hell, he didn't even know the guy's name at this point, yet his body was responding as though he knew him intimately. Or rather that he'd like to, anyway.

Damn dry spell.

"Will Tuesday of next week work?" the dark-haired man asked, pulling Gannon from his wayward thoughts.

Milly responded with a polite confirmation.

"Good. Morning or afternoon? I can get you out there at ten or one." The guy looked up at him.

"Morning's fine," Milly replied.

"And which watercraft do you prefer?"

"What's the difference?" Gannon inquired, feeling as though he should say something.

Funny how he could command an entire company but he couldn't do something as simple as renting a boat. Then again, he hadn't the slightest clue about boats. He didn't own one, didn't intend to. In fact, this trip would count for the second time in his life that he'd ever been out on the lake.

"We've got a thirty-eight-foot yacht, which is a little big for your party, but it'd work. Comes with a kitchenette, onboard bathroom, shower, and a bedroom."

"Sounds like too much for what we're hoping for." Milly peered up at him as though Gannon had the first clue about what they did or didn't need. After rolling her eyes and making Gannon grin, she turned back to Cam. "We're looking for something for a couple of hours. Small enough for people to talk to one another but not big enough for them to sneak off."

"My suggestion," the handsome man said, his attention directed at Milly, "is the tritoon or pontoon. If you're lookin' for water sports—tubing, skiing, that sort of thing—you'll go with the tritoon. If you're just lookin' to cruise the lake, the pontoon'll work best."

"Pontoon's fine," Gannon confirmed, hoping the guy would keep talking. Gannon was intrigued by that laid-back Texas drawl, the way he dropped the G on most of his words.

It was sexy as fuck.

Okay, not good.

Gannon clearly needed to get out of there because this man was proving to be too much of a distraction, and though Gannon was doing this at Milly's request, he didn't have much interest in the idea of taking his team out on a boat just so they could interact on a more casual basis. He'd rather order pizza in the office. They'd probably be content with that.

"Will there be someone who can go out with us?" Milly inquired. "After all, I'm thinkin' the big guy here can't drive a boat."

The man flashed that brilliant smile at Gannon once more, and he felt as though he'd been sucker-punched.

Twice.

"We'll have someone, sure."

"You?" Gannon queried, wishing he could pull the question back as soon as the word left his mouth.

"Not sure yet." Those full lips curved up in a knowing grin. "There're four of us. Someone'll be available."

"Perfect," Gannon said, hoping Milly hadn't noticed the sexual tension that had suddenly ratcheted the temperature in the small office up a few degrees.

"I'm sorry," Milly interrupted. "I didn't catch your name."

"Cam," the man replied. "Cam Strickland."

"Is that short for…?" Milly left the sentence hanging.

Cam grinned, a brilliant flash of straight white teeth. "Cam. It's short for Cam. My dad's a car nut."

Sexy guy, sexy name. Figured.

Gannon purposely looked away. The tension was coiling tighter in his gut, something he hadn't had to deal with in a while, and he wasn't sure how to handle it now.

"Thank you, Cam," Milly inserted. "We look forward to seeing you next Tuesday at ten. What else do you need from us to get it set up? Need us to sign something? A credit card? Want his phone number?"

Gannon choked, covering his mouth and praying he wasn't blushing.

Cam's eyes slid from Milly back to Gannon. There was something in that heated, inquisitive gaze. Those ocean-blue eyes casually raked over Gannon, but for the life of him, he couldn't translate what he saw there. Was it interest? Curiosity? Amusement?

Gannon didn't know, but suddenly he was hoping like hell Cam would be the one taking them out on the boat. A little premature, sure. But Gannon hadn't had this sort of reaction to anyone in a while, and although he knew better, he was having a hard time listening to reason.

At thirty-six—though most people thought he was far younger—it'd been a long damn time since Gannon had had any interest in a man. Sure, he'd had brief flings, but he usually kept those impersonal, using his company and the fact that he worked eighty or more hours a week as an excuse. The truth was, he didn't have time to date, nor the inclination. After years of trying to find the one person who would understand him, be able to cope with his drive to excel at everything he did, the fact that he sometimes traveled more than he was at home, Gannon had pretty much given up.

So, clearly, this instinctive reaction to Cam ... well, it meant Gannon's dry spell had reached the dehydrated stage. He was curious, sure, but the notion was illogical at the same time. There was no way they had anything in common, yet he still found himself fascinated.

And hell if he knew why that was.

Gannon watched Milly and Cam work out the logistics while he stole frequent glimpses of the sexy Cam Strickland and pretended to be interested in his phone.

"Yes, two hours," Milly confirmed.

Gannon felt a marginal amount of relief at the fact he'd only have to spend a couple of hours out on the water. Short, sweet, simple. Just the way he liked things.

He looked up at Cam again, felt that same thrill shoot through him.

Then again, he could probably tolerate a few more hours if it meant he got to spend it with Cam on board.

The insta-lust was new for him, something he'd never experienced before, at least not to this degree. And now, part of him wished that Milly wasn't there, and perhaps that this wasn't a marina but instead a bar.

Gannon wondered if he would've approached Cam if he'd seen him in a more relaxed setting.

He didn't know.

But one thing was for certain … if Gannon got to spend any extended length of time with Cam, they were both sure to find out.

Five

CAM WATCHED WITH subdued interest as Gannon and Milly left the marina office, and he didn't take his eyes off of them until the impressive black Lexus pulled out of the parking lot.

"Was that as weird for you as it was for me?"

Cam jumped at the sound of Dare's voice, spinning around to see his friend grinning from ear to ear. "Shit. You scared the hell out of me."

"He was hot, right?" Dare teased, coming to stand beside Cam at the counter.

Hot? Cam wasn't sure that was the word he'd use to describe Gannon. Attractive, sure. Nerdy, definitely. But hot?

Okay, he was fucking hot. In a nerdy sort of way.

"Whatever," Cam muttered. "He's now a client."

"I heard," Dare told him, glancing over at him. Then, in that irritating mocking tone of his, Dare continued to relay the conversation back to him, alternating voices. "*Can someone take us out? We'll have someone. Who, you?* Maybe. *You're hot.* You are, too."

Snorting, Cam elbowed Dare. "Shut the hell up."

Dare's grin widened. "No, seriously, man. That dude was checkin' you out."

Cam knew Dare could keep this up all day if he allowed it. "Aren't you supposed to be out doing something?"

"Nope."

Cam cocked an eyebrow.

"*What?* Seriously."

"Give Holly a hand. She's got that daycare thing today. I'm sure she could use your help getting the kids ready to fish in the cove."

Dare frowned. "I knew I should've stayed outside." That frown flipped almost instantly. "But yeah," he said as he backed toward the door. "I'll go help your sister. And I'll be sure to let her know you were eying some corporate hottie while I'm at it."

"Don't you dare," Cam snapped. If Dare told Cam's sister anything of the sort, Holly would give him hell. She was always trying to hook him up with guys. Once, she'd even tried to set Cam up with one of her husband's friends. The worst part about it, the guy wasn't even gay.

"Later, man," Dare hollered, laughing as he slipped out the door.

"Great. Just what I need."

"Talkin' to yourself again?" Roan asked, coming to stand beside him.

Cam jumped. The second time in five minutes. What the hell was wrong with these people? Didn't they know how to clear their throat or something? Let him know they were behind him?

"Who was that?" Roan asked, nodding toward the parking lot.

"Some guy and his assistant. They want to rent a boat next week to take out their work group."

"Cool." Roan didn't seem at all interested.

"Everything okay?" Cam asked, reaching for the coffeepot and pouring what was left of the three-hour-old coffee into his mug.

"Maybe."

Cam replaced the carafe, then faced Roan.

"It's my sister," Roan said.

"Cassie?" Roan had two sisters, one older, one younger. His older sister, Eva, was married with two kids, living in Ohio, while his younger sister, Cassie, was still in the area, though Cam didn't know for sure where that was. She moved around a lot.

"Yeah."

"What's wrong?"

Roan shrugged. "My stepmom called this morning. She didn't say much, just asked if I'd call Cass."

Before Cam could inquire further, the door chimed and in walked a group of people. A dull roar erupted as they chattered amongst themselves, obviously there to rent a boat.

"Mornin'," Cam greeted, then glanced over at Roan. "We'll talk later, yeah?"

Roan nodded, then disappeared out the back door, leaving Cam to deal with the incoming.

"THAT GUY WAS totally checking you out," Milly said when Gannon pulled out onto the road that would lead back to the office. "Holy shit. Did you see his tattoos? And those muscles."

Yeah, Gannon had seen them, all right.

"And I'm pretty sure his nipples were pierced?"

Gannon didn't take his eyes off the road, not wanting Milly to see the confusion on his face. "Pierced? Why would…? What makes you think that?"

"I could see the outline through his shirt. Sheesh. Pay more attention, Gannon."

Oh, he'd paid plenty of attention. Too much attention.

Milly continued. "He was hot, right? You thought he was hot?"

Gannon chuckled, amused by her excitement. It wasn't new for Milly. She was constantly attempting to set him up with someone, and on the off chance Gannon showed even the slightest hint of interest, she was all over it.

"You should call him," she said, still rambling incessantly. "Ask him out. Or maybe he'll call you. If he does, will you go out with him?"

"Take a breath."

Milly made a dramatic effort to inhale and exhale, giggling as she did. "That was so worth the hour trip," she told him.

"So does that mean we don't have to go out on the boat then?"

She leveled him with a glare.

Couldn't blame him for trying.

"I wonder if he'll be the one to take us out on the lake next week."

Gannon did, too. Part of him hoped he did; the other part, now that he'd had a chance to get his bearings, wasn't sure he could handle being close to Cam for any extended period of time. As it was, every time he blinked, Gannon saw him as vividly as though he were still standing only a few feet away.

That couldn't be good.

"When we get back to the office," Milly began, "I'm gonna send out a memo and let the team know this is a mandatory team-building event."

"Mandatory?" Gannon glanced over at her.

"If I give them an option, they'll stay right there in the office."

True, they would. He would, too.

Thankfully, Milly was silent for a few minutes. Long enough for Gannon to gather his thoughts about Cam.

He wondered if Milly was right. Maybe he should ask Cam out.

It'd been a long time since he'd felt this sort of attraction to a man; surely he shouldn't ignore it. If he did, who knew how long it would be before it happened again.

You'll see him on Tuesday, remember?

Okay, so the voice in his head had a point, but could he wait until then? What if he didn't get to see Cam on Tuesday? What if someone else took them out on the boat? Then what would he do?

What if Cam wasn't interested? What if Gannon made a fool of himself?

Gannon took a deep breath.

The pessimism didn't suit him. He didn't like to think negatively. Though he hadn't always had the easiest life, he had set out years ago to think positive. He attributed his success to that, the fact that he didn't look for doom and gloom around every corner.

So, yeah, what could it hurt?

"You're thinking about him, aren't you?"

Gannon shot a look at Milly. "I don't know what you're talking about."

Milly's husky laugh filled the car. "And now I know you're lying."

"What makes you think that?"

"Because you didn't answer my question with a question."

Turning back to face the road, Gannon smiled to himself.

This woman knew him too well.

Six

Sunday evening

CAM TILTED HIS beer to his lips, letting the warm breeze blow across his face, trying to relax as he sat on the edge of the pier, bare feet dangling in the water. Behind him, Lulu was snoring, zonked out after spending an hour leaping into the water to retrieve the stick Cam had tossed her.

He couldn't think of a better way to spend a Sunday evening.

"Tell me this…" Roan said quickly, his beer bottle dangling between two fingers as he sat on the edge of the pier beside Cam. "What made you think you could beat him in the first place?"

Okay, so maybe a little less chatter would be good, but he hadn't said it was a *perfect* Sunday.

Roan's question was followed by a laugh, and Cam smiled, staring down at the water. "I *did* beat him," he reminded his friend.

"It was close."

"Close only counts in horseshoes and hand grenades," Cam refuted. "I still beat him."

They'd been sitting on the pier as the sun started its slow descent in the sky, enjoying the solitude that only a Sunday evening could afford them. They closed the marina early on Sundays, which left them with a little free time for themselves. Dare and Teague had opted to go out, something Cam didn't much care to do these days. The gay bars that Teague was fond of didn't do much for Cam, but he knew Teague would likely never give up trying to get him to go. After the first time he'd mistakenly agreed, Cam swore he'd never do it again.

"One of these days, those young punks are gonna best you," Roan offered, tilting his beer to his lips.

"Probably," Cam agreed. "But I ain't ready to give up yet."

"Obviously. That's why we nicknamed you Reckless. So what's next? You gonna try skydiving?"

"It's on my list, so yeah, why not?" Cam spent most of his time on or in the water, whether he was working or not. And yes, as Roan had mentioned, Cam was somewhat wild, perhaps a little careless at times, never finding a dare he wouldn't take. It was the reason they'd started calling him Reckless.

That and a few years ago, he'd started a list of all the things he wanted to do, and once his friends had found out, they'd made it their mission to add more to it.

"You're gettin' a little old for that shit, aren't ya?"

"Old? Who're you callin' old, *grandpa*?" Cam laughed. He certainly didn't consider himself old; however, he didn't consider himself young by any means.

"Hey, watch it," Roan screeched. "I'm only eleven days older than you."

"And?" Cam took a long pull of his beer.

"Bro, that kid you beat today was twenty-one, max. *That* makes you old."

"Twenty-two." Not that it really mattered. "And I beat him, didn't I?"

Roan clearly couldn't let it go. Just that morning, Cam had rented out two of the personal water crafts to a couple of young guys. While they were out on the lake, Cam had opted to take his own jet ski out to check on them, make sure they were doing what they were supposed to. While he'd waited for the pair to finish a race they'd started, he'd floated in the general vicinity. And when they'd returned, the younger one had been hyped up on adrenaline, excited that he'd beaten his buddy. That was when the guy had offered Cam a dare, insisting there was no way Cam could beat him.

Well, Cam had easily accepted, as he always did, and twenty minutes later, the young punk wasn't quite as cocky as he had been. That short amount of time he'd spent out there had been fun, making Cam realize he didn't do nearly enough of it these days.

And now, as he sat on the pier with Roan, he thought back to all the crazy things he'd done up to this point in his life. He'd surfed the Pipeline in Oahu, gone zip-lining in Montana, swum with dolphins, once with sharks, been white-water rafting in Salmon River, went snowboarding every couple of years because he loved that shit. The list went on, but the list that remained was equally long. Sure, he was somewhat reckless by definition, but only in certain aspects of his life. When it came to recreation, he hadn't met a challenge he couldn't accept. However, in other areas, he was likely far too cautious for his own good.

Likely the reason for his nonexistent love life.

His thoughts strayed to Gannon Burgess, the pretty-boy executive who'd waltzed into the marina looking to rent a boat. Every time Cam closed his eyes, he saw the handsome face and dark eyes, not to mention the suit. Although Gannon was definitely Cam's opposite in every way, there was something about him, something that Cam couldn't quite put his finger on. Something that he couldn't stop thinking about.

For two days, he had spent far too much time thinking about the guy since he'd watched him walk out of the marina office and climb into his fancy Lexus. And for whatever reason, erasing him from his mind wasn't happening.

"Hand me another beer, would ya?" Roan asked, nodding toward the cooler of ice sitting beside Cam.

Retrieving another, Cam handed it over. He watched Roan for a moment, noticing the way his forehead pinched slightly.

"What's on your mind?" Cam inquired.

"Nada," Roan said a little too quickly, a clear giveaway that his friend was hiding something.

"Is it Cass?"

Roan shook his head, obviously not intending to elaborate.

Cam knew better than to push Roan to talk when he didn't want to. Roan was usually relaxed and calm, but when he was irritated, he was downright impossible to deal with.

Prime example was his argument with the printer a couple of days ago.

Rather than interrogate Roan, Cam sat silently.

"Is this enough for you?" Roan finally asked after several minutes of silence.

Cam looked over at his friend. That pinched look from before was replaced by what appeared to be confusion. "What? The marina?"

"Yeah, I guess."

Cam knew that Roan was a little restless these days, but he wasn't sure what was spurring it on. He didn't open up much, choosing to keep to himself most of the time, but he wasn't good at hiding it.

"Talk to me, man," Cam coaxed, but before he could encourage Roan more, his cell phone rang. Fishing it out of his pocket and seeing that it was Dare, he hit the talk button. "What's up?"

"Where're you at?"

"On the pier, why?"

"There's, uh … someone here who wants to talk to you. I'll send him down."

"Who is—" Cam's question was cut off when Dare disconnected the call.

"What's up?" Roan's curiosity had replaced his somberness from moments ago.

Cam shrugged. "Dare said someone's here to see me."

They both turned at the sound of footsteps behind them. Lulu lifted her head as well, but she clearly didn't see the stranger as a threat because she let out a soft snort and went back to sleep.

Suddenly grateful that the sun was setting low on the horizon, casting shadows around them, Cam prayed that his surprise didn't register as he watched the man approach.

"Who the hell is that?" Roan asked, his voice so low Cam barely heard him.

"A client."

"Well, that'd be my cue to go." Roan was up on his feet in an instant. "Come on, Lu. Let's get dinner." Without saying good-bye, Roan headed up the pier with Lulu at his side, stopping briefly to greet Gannon with a casual, "Hey, how are ya?" before casting Cam a smile, then disappearing toward the marina.

Not bothering to move from his seat, Cam took a deep breath as Gannon cleared the distance between them.

Clearing his throat, Cam found his voice. "What brings you down here? Doin' some research?"

Gannon's husky chuckle sent a chill dancing along Cam's spine. That was another thing he couldn't seem to forget about Gannon, that deep, sexy baritone.

"Actually…" Gannon began. "Mind if I sit?"

"Go for it," Cam told him. "Wanna beer?"

"Sure."

Cam retrieved another beer from the cooler and handed it over to Gannon. He had absolutely no idea what the guy was doing there. Had Cam somehow conjured him up from all the crazy thoughts he'd been having? Surely the guy wasn't lost. Whatever the reason, Cam prayed his confusion didn't show. It was bad enough he'd spent two days thinking about him and now he was face-to-face with his most recent fantasy.

Okay, no. Not fantasy.

More like…

Ah, hell.

His fantasy took a seat and… Wait, start over…

Gannon took a seat and Cam smiled to himself. Gannon had shed the suit, but he was wearing a navy blue polo, dark jeans, and … Cam fought the urge to laugh. Though he looked pretty damned irresistible, Gannon was wearing a pair of Vans that appeared to be brand new, which didn't work well with the water lapping beneath them. Not that Cam noticed for long. Gannon's intoxicating scent drifted past him on the breeze, and Cam's body hardened.

"Where's your lady friend?" Cam asked.

"My assistant?" Gannon twisted the cap off his beer.

"Yeah, her," Cam answered, needing to keep his mind from drifting to places it didn't belong.

"Knowing Milly, she's probably gettin' ready to go out."

"What is it with going out on Sunday?" Cam mused, thinking back to Teague's request for Cam to go out tonight.

"No idea," Gannon said. "I'm more of the stay-at-home kind, myself."

Cam was, too, but he didn't say as much. Instead, he settled for, "What brings you down here?"

What Gannon said next shocked Cam to the roots of his soul, and he knew for a fact there was no way he hid his surprise that time.

BEFORE HE COULD think better of it, Gannon blurted the first thing that came to mind. "I wanted to see you."

Well, hell. That had come out far too quickly, and the stunned look on Cam's face confirmed it.

Although it was true, Gannon hadn't intended to show up at the marina when he'd first set out from his house, but somehow he'd found himself there. Milly had attempted to get him to go out to a club tonight, but he'd turned her down, pretending he had work to do. When she hadn't believed him, Gannon had used the *it's Sunday, tomorrow's a workday* routine. She'd finally given up.

And after nearly two hours of driving around, desperate for something to take his mind off things better left alone—namely the man now less than a foot from him— Gannon had still ended up here, despite the voice in his head telling him this was a stupid idea.

Then, as though that weren't bad enough, for the last thirty minutes he'd been sitting in his car, staring out at the water, trying to get up the nerve to talk to Cam, wondering if he was even around.

Gannon had taken it as a sign when he'd seen another guy walk out of the marina office, locking up behind him. Figuring it was someone who worked there and he'd likely know where Cam was, Gannon had climbed out of his car, smoothed down his wrinkled polo, and made his way over, forcing his hands into his pockets in an effort to look casual.

He'd blown that all to hell when it'd taken him two tries before he managed to ask if Cam was around.

Although helpful, the guy had looked at him as though he were half out of his mind.

Perhaps he was.

And here he was, exactly where he'd told himself he shouldn't be, no matter how much he *wanted* to be. On top of that, Gannon wasn't sure what the hell he was supposed to say now that he'd revealed the truth.

"You wanted to see *me*?" Cam didn't sound at all as though he believed him.

"Yes," he confirmed. "I wanted to see *you*." There. Now that there was no confusion, Gannon felt… No, wait. It didn't help. He was still wound tight, maybe more so now.

Cam chuckled, the sexy, dark rumble reflecting what Gannon suspected was shock.

"He wanted to see me," Cam muttered, evidently talking to himself.

Gannon didn't say anything to that. He took a sip of his beer, then glanced down at the label. Not bad. Not exactly his thing, but tolerable. While he let the silence settle between them, Gannon peered over at Cam from beneath his lashes, trying to get a better look at the tattoos that covered the majority of his left arm, running from shoulder to wrist, revealed by the sleeveless shirt he was wearing.

"So, seriously?" Cam looked over at him, those pretty blue eyes glittering in the last of the sun's rays reflecting off the water. "You drove an hour to … *see* me?"

"How do you know I don't live here?"

Cam cocked an eyebrow.

"Fine," Gannon admitted. "I don't live here. I did drive an hour to see you. Wait. How did you know I live an hour from here?"

Cam turned back to face the water. Gannon grinned. Cam hadn't been the only one interested.

"Okay, fine. Don't answer that." Gannon didn't need an answer. "But is that hard to believe?"

Sure, it was a stupid question. And he already knew the answer because yes, it was apparent Cam found it hard to believe. As a matter of fact, Gannon still didn't know what had prompted him to come all the way down to the marina just to see a man he'd spoken to for all of fifteen minutes.

But here they were and he wasn't ready to leave.

Cam twisted around to look at Gannon, his bicep and tricep flexing when he planted his hand down on the wooden plank. "Has this worked for you in the past?"

Gannon smiled around the lip of his beer bottle. "Actually, no. But"—he took a sip—"this is the first time I've tried it. How's it workin'?"

"It's a little stalkerish, if you ask me," Cam said, a teasing note in his voice and a sexy smirk forming on his lips.

He liked that Cam was trying to hide his interest.

Slightly disappointed that Cam had turned back around, Gannon pondered the stalker reference for a moment. "I can see that."

Both of them sat in silence for several minutes. The gentle lapping of the water against the wooden beams that descended below was the only sound other than their breathing. Gannon really had no idea what he'd intended to accomplish by showing up unannounced. He didn't know what to say, what to do, what he even wanted from Cam, but he knew that he wanted to be there.

"Was it worth it?" Cam asked.

"What?" Gannon was confused.

"The trip down here?"

"Perhaps," Gannon stated honestly. "I had no expectations."

"Surprising."

"Why's that?"

"Most guys don't bother to show up unannounced without expectations. At least in my experience."

"I don't know you," Gannon conceded. "Maybe if I did, I'd know what to expect."

And that was the problem. Gannon wanted to get to know Cam. He'd thought of little else since he'd walked out of the marina office two days ago. Anyone who knew him would say that was way out of character for him. Gannon's entire life revolved around his work. He could spend endless hours working with developers, tossing around ideas, trying to come up with a newer, more advanced game that the gamers would go crazy for.

He definitely didn't sit around thinking about a guy he'd spent a few minutes in the same room with.

At least not until Cam.

"Are you at least flattered?"

From his profile, Gannon could see Cam smiling.

"I'm not sure that's the word I'd go with."

Gannon chuckled, remembering the argument he'd had with himself about coming here. At one point, Gannon had been so taken aback by thoughts of Cam he'd pulled up the marina's website just to see if there were pictures of him. And there had been. A lot of pictures. He'd learned some interesting things during the half hour he'd spent cruising the site, educating himself on the marina, its inception, who the men were who ran the place. And he had to admit, he'd been intrigued to learn that Cam was one of the owners.

After that, he'd managed to find Cam's social media pages, and he'd spent nearly an hour going through previous posts and pictures, soaking it all in.

Okay, fine. Maybe he'd been stalking the guy. A little.

Even after all that, though, it hadn't helped to alleviate any of Gannon's curiosity. So, he'd done the only thing he could do in this instance. Drive.

All the way here to see Cam.

Yes, Gannon could see the crazy in that.

Cam didn't say anything, and Gannon took that as his cue to keep quiet. There was a strange vibe coming from Cam, something that Gannon couldn't translate. He wasn't sure if Cam was pissed or happy. Maybe neither.

It didn't change the fact that he had done what he'd wanted to do and he refused to be ashamed of that fact.

Seven

POSSIBLY FOR THE first time in his life, Cam was at a loss for words. He didn't know what to say to Gannon, didn't really understand why the guy was there. Gannon had said it was to see him, but Cam wasn't sure what that even meant.

Yes, maybe Cam was being a little cynical, but he couldn't help it. This wasn't the first time he'd met a man who lived a good distance from the small town Cam called home. From his experience, relationships—sexual or otherwise—didn't work with long distances between them. An hour, in Cam's opinion, was a long distance. And that made Cam wary.

Probably not fair to Gannon, but it had been the first thing that had popped into his head.

So, what was Gannon really after? Did he want to ask him out? Was he hoping for a quick hookup? Did he simply want to talk?

He would've started pelting Gannon with those very questions, but silence had descended, and it wasn't as uncomfortable as he'd expected it to be. So rather than dig in to the man's reasons for showing up, Cam sat there, staring out at the water, sipping his beer, inhaling the sexy-as-fuck cologne Gannon wore, and listening to Gannon breathe.

All in all, not a bad way to spend a Sunday evening.

While his body hummed from their proximity, every cell aware of Gannon beside him, Cam told himself that this was definitely an interesting turn of events.

Yeah, he had dated clients before, once or twice, but usually he'd been the one to make the first move once he got the green light. In fact, most of the men he'd dated, he'd been the one to ask them out, not the other way around.

Not that Gannon had asked him out, but he got the feeling that was coming. Or maybe it wasn't, and now his cynicism was masquerading as optimism. Then again, how could he not think that when the man he'd been fantasizing about nonstop for two days just showed up out of the blue and was now sitting on the dock drinking a beer with him because he'd wanted to see him?

Cam still couldn't believe it.

"So, is this what you do on Sunday nights?" Gannon asked, that deep baritone sliding like warm water over Cam's skin.

"Sometimes," he said, not bothering to look over at him. "What about you?"

Gannon laughed, and again, the rough sound had a spark of awareness shooting through him.

"You mean do I show up unannounced and ask an attractive man if he'd like to go out sometime?"

Cam smiled, hiding it behind his beer bottle. "Is that what you're doin'?"

"Maybe. And if I was?"

Cam peered over at Gannon, lifting an eyebrow, waiting for him to continue. He damn sure wasn't going to make it easy on the guy. Not because he didn't like him. He did. More so because he was skeptical about anything that could possibly come from this.

"What would you say?"

Cam shrugged. "Depends on if it's hypothetical or not. I don't do hypothetical."

"What *do* you do?"

Ah, hell. A frisson of awareness streaked through him, attacking every nerve ending, lighting him up like a football stadium on game night, and instructing his blood to make a quick detour south. Cam's cock swelled, the obvious intent of that question making his blood heat.

Was this cute guy really hitting on him?

Then it occurred to him. Maybe Cam wasn't actually sitting on the pier. Maybe he was in his bed, sleeping. And this was a dream and when his alarm went off he'd wake up.

Reaching down, Cam pinched his hand. Ouch.

Nope. Not a dream.

He took another drink, trying to fight the smile.

He had to admit, Gannon wasn't what he'd expected. The man he remembered from the other day had been rather shy when he'd come into the marina with his assistant, but this guy … the one sitting beside him now was anything but shy.

"I don't do one-night stands," Cam finally told him.

"Good," Gannon said, but he didn't expand on it.

For a few minutes, the two of them sat like that, no one talking. With each passing second, the awkwardness seemed to be intensifying; however, it was rather nice. Cam didn't feel pressured to have to say anything, though there were plenty of questions running through his head. Yes, part of him was flattered that Gannon had come here looking for him. The other part was curious what the man had in mind. Based on his response to Cam's statement about not doing one-night stands, he had to think that Gannon wasn't looking for one, either, but he couldn't be certain.

Nor could he bring himself to ask.

"It wasn't hypothetical," Gannon finally said, drawing Cam's attention once more.

"No?" Another smile formed on his lips.

"Well, maybe a little."

Cam laughed. While he was entirely too buttoned-up, and a definite ten on the nerd scale, Gannon came off as confident and self-assured, but for some reason, the slight hint of insecurity in his tone was endearing.

Cam still wasn't sure what to think about all of it. He was enjoying the flirting, but he wasn't sure he wanted it to go further than that. Not yet, anyway. He'd met plenty of men, had a few relationships that had gone zero to sixty in three-point-five seconds, and that wasn't what he was looking for, either. In those cases, the fiery crash had been imminent, something Cam had absolutely no interest in repeating.

So rather than sit there and entertain the notion of jumping at the opportunity to go out with Gannon, he decided it was time to call it a night before things did get awkward.

Finishing off his beer, he tossed the empty bottle into the cooler and then got to his feet. It was impossible not to look down at Gannon, who was staring up at him. Heat infused him as Gannon's dark eyes slowly raked over him from head to toe, but he ignored it.

Okay, he *tried* to ignore it.

"It was good talkin' to you," Cam said, lifting the cooler. "But I better go."

"Me, too," Gannon said, getting to his feet.

Reckless

Rather than walk away, Cam found himself nearly face-to-face with the taller man. At five eleven, Cam wasn't short, but Gannon still had a couple of inches on him. And though Cam probably outweighed Gannon by twenty, maybe thirty pounds of muscle, he found he liked that for some reason.

"I guess I'll see you on Tuesday?" Gannon sounded uncertain.

"You'll see *someone* on Tuesday," Cam clarified with a small smile. He didn't plan to be the one to take Gannon and his crew out on the water, but he wasn't going to say as much.

He'd been tossing around the idea since Gannon had showed up at the marina on Friday, but now, with this strange attraction, he knew he needed to put some distance between them. He'd learned the hard way that rushing things didn't usually work in his favor. Add to that the distance thing...

Reckless or not, Cam wasn't interested in gambling with that area of his life. Not at this point.

Gannon's dark gaze searched his face and Cam felt a tightening in his groin.

"Well, I hope it's you I see," Gannon said softly.

Cam didn't know what to say to that, so he offered a smile and a casual tilt of his chin before forcing himself to walk away.

"Can I get your number?" Gannon called out after him.

"Maybe next time," Cam said, not looking back.

"So there will be a next time?" Gannon hollered, his deep voice following Cam on the breeze.

Cam shrugged and kept walking.

It wasn't that he didn't want to see the look on Gannon's face; it was that he didn't want Gannon to see the smile he couldn't seem to wipe off his own.

UNABLE TO STOP grinning like a fucking school boy, Gannon finally made his way to his car after standing on the pier and looking out over the water, replaying the strange turn of events over and over in his head. Once settled inside, relaxing against the cool leather with the air conditioner on high, he took several deep breaths to calm himself. His body was humming from the brief interaction with Cam.

There was no doubt about it, the man fascinated him to no end.

The attractive, tattooed bad boy had snagged Gannon's attention for sure. It had been a long damn time since he'd had to play the cat-and-mouse game, and he had to admit, it was better than he'd remembered. Especially with Cam.

Maybe it was the fact that Gannon could tell Cam was interested that made it worthwhile. Even though he seemed hesitant, Cam couldn't completely hide his reaction. And Gannon liked that. Or possibly he simply liked that Cam was making him work for what he wanted, something he was very familiar with. As far as Gannon was concerned, the best things in life didn't come free. And he'd learned that lesson well over the years.

When he pulled out onto the main road that would lead him back to Austin, Gannon's cell phone rang. He answered the call with the Bluetooth.

"Where are you at?" Milly asked. "I'm sitting in front of your house and you're not here. I thought you said you couldn't go out because it was a work night."

Ah, crap. "I'm driving."

"Where?"

"Burnet."

"Burn— Wait, what?" The high-pitched shriek in Milly's voice told him she'd put two and two together. "You went to the marina? Oh, my God."

Oh, my God was right, Gannon thought.

"Did you see him?"

"Yeah," Gannon said with a sigh, his eyes focused on the road in front of him.

"And?"

"And what? I saw him. End of story."

"There's never an abrupt ending to a story like that. Did you talk to him?"

"Yeah."

"Did you ask him out?"

"Kinda," he admitted, still grinning.

"What do you mean, kinda? Either you did or you didn't."

"I mentioned it, but I didn't come right out and say it."

"Gannon David Burgess, do *not* tell me you let that man get away without getting a date with him."

"I'm gonna see him on Tuesday," Gannon told her. "Boat. Lake. Remember?"

"I can't believe you went out there," Milly told him.

He couldn't, either, and now that he had, Gannon knew he wouldn't have a minute of peace. Not from his own thoughts of Cam and not from Milly's inquisition.

"So, how'd he look?" she asked, her voice resounding through his speakers.

Gannon thought about the way Cam had looked when he'd stood up to leave, that dark gray sleeveless T-shirt molded to his broad shoulders and wide chest, showing off the tattoos covering his muscular arms. The way the soft gray cotton had narrowed down over his slim waist. And the white and gray shorts that had hung down just past Cam's knees, giving Gannon a view of his impressive calves.

The man made Gannon's mouth water.

Not for the first time, he wondered what Cam looked like naked. Did he have more tattoos on other parts of his body?

"Christ," he mumbled to himself, ignoring his dick as it stirred to life.

"What?"

"Nothing. He looked … good."

"Liar. Did you check to see if his nipples are pierced?"

The question made Gannon choke, and while he sputtered in an attempt to catch his breath, Milly laughed at him.

"I'll take that as a no," she answered for him. "Okay, well, since it's obvious you're not gonna be back for a while, I'm going out. I was hoping, if I showed up, I could convince you to go with me, but I see you already had plans."

"Are you going out with Gary?"

"I don't know." She sighed. "Maybe."

"Milly, be careful," he said softly. "If you need anything, call me."

"I will, I promise. Bye for now," she said in a singsong voice.

"Later." Gannon disconnected the call and focused on the drive.

Reckless

An hour later, once he'd parked in his garage and made his way into the house, Gannon didn't bother turning on any lights as he went. There was no need. He was simply going to go to sleep. He had an early meeting tomorrow, and as far as he was concerned, the sooner he could get Monday over with, the faster Tuesday would arrive.

And that was the day he looked forward to most. Although he dreaded the idea of going out on a boat, he would get to see Cam. Maybe. And that was incentive.

Can I get your number?

Maybe next time.

So there will be a next time?

There would definitely be a next time.

Though Gannon had done something completely out of the norm by showing up at the marina tonight to see Cam, he knew he had to play it cool. He wasn't going to chase after the man. Putting himself in Cam's line of sight, sure. He wasn't above doing that. But he knew that desperation wasn't an appealing quality. In anyone.

"One day at a time," he mumbled as he made his way to the bathroom.

He thought back to those dark blue eyes and the heat he'd seen reflected there when Cam had been looking up at him, their bodies just a few centimeters apart. It had taken every ounce of control that Gannon possessed not to reach for Cam, to feel those muscles, to slide his lips over Cam's and taste the sexy maleness mixed with the beer he'd had while they'd sat there as the sun had gone down.

Tuesday was not going to get there fast enough.

For years, Gannon had put work first, rarely entertaining the idea of dating someone. And never someone like Cam. Now, it seemed to be the only damn thing he could think about.

Only he knew the key to getting Cam's attention was by taking things slow, being patient.

It would be worth the wait, he told himself.

And it was a damn good thing Gannon was a patient man.

Eight

Two days later, Tuesday

"I'M HEADIN' OUT," Teague announced just seconds after he stuck his head in the door.

Cam offered a two-finger wave but didn't look up from the appointment book he was reviewing.

Teague was one of the hardest-working men Cam knew. He never missed a day for any reason, and he didn't bitch and moan about the chores that needed to be done. However, Teague did have one serious downfall when it came to the office. According to him, he was allergic to paperwork, so he preferred to come in about the time the first customer arrived, which—Cam glanced over at his watch—would be sometime in the very near future. Between spending his day on the lake and helping out in the boat repair shop, Teague was a busy guy, but he never seemed to run out of energy, just as long as he wasn't asked to deal with paperwork. On the rare occasion that occurred, Teague was known to break out in hives.

Not that any of them had ever been witness to it.

But it explained why he opted to bolt rather than come inside.

Cam was doing his best to review the list of activities going on that day while ignoring the frequent interruptions. They were booked solid for the entire week, and although it was Tuesday, it felt like Monday all over again. Things were chaotic, and it was only nine thirty in the morning. Two cups of coffee in and he wasn't sure he was going to make it. Being that it was the first week of June, school was letting out, and more and more people were descending on the marina, hoping to get a few hours out in the sun. That would be the case for the next few months.

"Me, too!" Holly called out. "I've got the retirement home outing today at the park. Keith's helping Hudson on a repair."

Hudson Ballard was their lone boat mechanic. The guy was reliable and efficient, but there was only one problem. Well, technically it wasn't really a problem, more of an obstacle they'd had to learn to work with. Hudson didn't speak. At all. Not once had Cam ever heard a single sound come out of Hudson's mouth.

Though the guy had worked at the marina for the last year, Cam knew very little about Hudson, other than he was an ASE master technician, could identify a problem with an engine faster than anyone Cam knew, and he didn't speak, having been born mute. Since Hudson hadn't elaborated on the latter, Cam hadn't asked.

That hadn't stopped them from hiring him on, either. Hudson was good at what he did. Not only could he repair an engine in half the time it'd taken their last full-time mechanic, he was also good with a paint gun, which had helped Hudson build a rather lucrative little side business painting boats. And because they'd gotten along so well with Hudson, it had been Dare's idea for them to learn American Sign Language in order to communicate more effectively. The only person who'd been hesitant had been Teague, but Cam wasn't sure why that was.

"What about you?" Cam asked Roan, not bothering to look up from the appointment book.

"I've got one at eleven and another at three. Takin' some guys out this afternoon on the PWCs."

"PCWs," Dare corrected.

"There's no such thing," Roan argued. "It's PWC. Personal water craft. You can't just switch the letters around because you feel like it."

Dare lifted his eyebrows and smirked as Roan backed out the door. "I just did."

"Whatever, man," Roan grumbled, smiling as he left.

Ignoring them, Cam skimmed the book with his finger. That left... "Who's takin' the ten o'clock on the pontoon?"

"Which one's that?" Dare asked, darting into the room and then back out before Cam could answer.

"Corporate thing," he hollered. "Ten people."

"No can do, man," Dare replied, yelling from the other room. "I've got a lunch thing today. Will be gone from eleven to two."

Great. That meant Cam was going to have to pitch in and take the group out. As it was, he hadn't stopped thinking about Gannon Burgess since the moment he'd met the man, and especially not after the short time they'd spent together down on the pier. Spending a couple of hours in his presence didn't seem like a good idea—not for Cam's state of mind, anyway. But it looked as though he didn't really have a choice.

"Who's the lucky winner?" Dare inquired when he came back. "Who gets to hang out with you today?" Dare didn't wait for Cam to answer, he simply dragged the open appointment book away and peered down at it. "Holy shit. Is that *the* Gannon Burgess?"

"No idea," Cam answered. "Who is *the* Gannon Burgess?"

"Seriously? You haven't heard of Burgess Entertainment? The gaming conglomerate. Rise of Vengeance. Damn, dude, where you been? Hidin' under a rock?"

Apparently.

"Hold up," Cam said, glancing over at Dare. "Roan's the gamer. How the hell do you know about this shit?"

Dare shrugged, looking sheepish. "I might play. A little."

Until now, Cam had thought Roan was the only gamer in the group, spending a vast amount of his time with a keyboard. Not that anyone said anything about the man's video game obsession considering he made a nice chunk of change off those things. Who would've thought that they'd actually pay people to beta test and beat video games?

Dare smacked Cam on the back. "Looks like you'll be spendin' some time in the sun today, man. Good thing, too. You're lookin' kinda washed-out."

Cam laughed. If anyone looked washed-out, it certainly wasn't him.

Dare's tone turned serious. "So, you got an issue with this Burgess guy?"

"Not at all," Cam lied, feeling his face heat.

"Wait a minute." Dare's eyes narrowed, his mouth curling upward. "Was he the one who showed up on Sunday?"

Cam didn't get a chance to answer. As though summoned, Gannon opened the front door and, he and Milly walked in, the ding of the alarm not going off until after the door was closed, which meant it was quite possible that they'd heard Dare's question.

If they had, they were pretending they hadn't. And Cam was okay with that.

"Mornin'," Dare greeted the pair. "Y'all ready to get out on the water?"

"We are," Gannon confirmed, his gaze sliding over to Cam briefly before returning to Dare. "Will you be the one going out with us?"

Dare grinned and slapped Cam on the back. Hard. "Not me. Cam's your man today. You're gettin' the best of the best."

Cam's your man today? Seriously? He couldn't believe his friend had just said that.

If Cam wasn't mistaken, that was a slight blush that washed over Gannon's youthful features. Obviously he'd heard the double entendre the same way Cam had.

Hoping not to give away his own interest, Cam did a quick visual sweep of the man's body. Gone was the starchy suit, and in its place were a pair of shorts, a white T-shirt that reflected his company's logo, and yes, a pair of—wait for it—boat shoes. All of which looked as though they'd never been worn before, which amused Cam. The guy clearly spent too much time indoors.

Regardless, Cam still found him sexy as hell. Even the boat shoes. And the glasses.

Especially the glasses.

"The rest of our team'll be here in the next few minutes," Milly informed them. "I figured I'd give you a heads-up first."

Cam's eyebrows lifted as he waited for her to continue.

"They're a bit of a nerdy bunch," she relayed with an affectionate smile.

Dare nudged Cam's elbow, causing him to look over.

Milly continued, "Not that they'll attempt to hide it. They're gamers, and they don't get out as much as they should. And yes, don't worry, I advised them to bring a sufficient amount of sunscreen."

The corners of Dare's mouth slowly turned up as Milly spoke, his eyes dancing with amusement. "Well, they're in good hands," Dare told them before turning his attention to Cam. "I'm headin' over to help Holly set up. Then I'll be out for a couple of hours. Holler if you need me."

Cam nodded to his friend, then said to Gannon and Milly, "The boat's in slip fourteen. I'll meet you there in a few, if that's cool?"

Gannon didn't respond, simply turned and headed out the door. Cam watched as the couple walked outside, the door closing behind them.

Reckless

Instead of following them out, Dare took the opportunity to do what Dare did best. "Holy fuck, man. That guy's a helluva lot younger than I thought he'd be. And hotter. Please tell me he's single. And gay."

He was hot, all right. Cam couldn't deny that. And gay, as far as Cam could tell. As for single, Cam honestly didn't know, but based on their flirting, he assumed so. Still, he was also the polar opposite of Cam's type.

Then again, Cam didn't necessarily have a type these days. He spent most of his time working, the rest hanging out on the lake. He'd come to the conclusion that he'd entered a phase of his life where he wasn't interested in one night with a guy he'd likely never call again. He'd had more than enough of that shit when he was younger. Instead of serial dating, he'd become more isolated, although his friends had dubbed this new phase as his reckless phase. Instead of promiscuity, Cam spent his time testing his own limits, mostly taking on adventures that he'd added to his bucket list years ago.

Sometimes it was still hard to believe he even had a bucket list, but at his age, he figured it was time to start checking those things off. He wasn't getting any younger.

And nailing a young, hot guy wasn't on that list.

"Have fun out there," Dare said as he pressed his back into the glass door that led to the outside. "Don't do anyone I wouldn't do."

Cam barked out a laugh. It wouldn't have been so funny if Dare hadn't been as sexually inactive as they came. Seemed they'd all been going through a drought these days. All except Teague, but the guy was young and ... well, Cam tended to think of him as the reckless one, although he'd never be the one to tell Teague that.

"See ya," Cam called to Dare as the door closed behind him.

After unlocking the box that housed the keys for the boats, Cam grabbed what he needed, relocked the box, snatched his sunglasses from the counter, and headed out. He flipped the sign on the door to show they'd be back later before locking it behind him.

As he headed down the pier to the boat, Dare's words replayed in his head.

Don't do anyone I wouldn't do.

He smiled to himself as his eyes scanned the group for Gannon. When he found him, he had only one thought: *Houston, we might have a problem.*

WHILE HIS GROUP of geeky gamers—as Milly so lovingly referred to them—chatted about whatever it was that had sparked their interest this morning, Gannon kept his eyes trained on the pier, waiting for Cam to join them. He wasn't disappointed when the man appeared, either.

From the instant Gannon had stepped into the Pier 70 Marina office a short while ago, he hadn't been able to take his eyes off Cam. For the third time in less than a week.

Cam looked … just as he had last week. Only hotter. If that were possible.

His short, dark hair—cut a little longer on top than the sides and back—had been mussed as though he'd run his hands through it a few times. Gannon had initially wondered if it was due to stress, but when their gazes had collided, Cam's navy blue eyes had sparkled with mischief and curiosity. With his rugged good looks and massive physique, he was pretty damn irresistible, which was part of the problem.

And the tattoos on his muscular arms...

Yeah, those were sexy as fuck.

The mostly black ink curled over his sun-bronzed skin in various designs. Gannon had never been quite so compelled by tattoos, but on Cam, they only drew his attention, made him wonder what other parts of his body were tattooed and whether or not he'd get the chance to find out one day.

The hell of it was, Gannon couldn't stop thinking about him. About what it would feel like to slide his tongue past those smooth lips, about how Cam would respond from beneath him, begging and pleading for Gannon to give him what he needed.

As Cam came nearer to the group, Gannon did his best not to continue eyeing him. Not that Gannon had to worry much about anyone paying attention to him today. The people who worked for him tended to be centrally focused on one thing, and it definitely wasn't him. Thank the video game gods for that, because Gannon was positive his interest was written all over his face. He'd thought about Cam nonstop for days, half tempted to do a little more digging, find his number, and call him up just to hear the sound of his voice.

But he'd managed to avoid doing that for this reason. He'd wanted to feel—just to assure himself it hadn't been his imagination—that same powerful, gut-clenching punch that he'd felt the first time he'd seen Cam.

He hadn't been disappointed.

Today was going to be a test, though. As much as he wanted to draw out this stage, Gannon doubted he could keep his distance for too long.

"Y'all ready?" Cam asked when he approached. "I stocked the boat this mornin' with life jackets and supplies."

"Did you get my list?" Milly questioned.

Cam smiled at her, and for an instant, Gannon wished that grin had been directed at him, but he shoved the notion away.

"I did. The first-aid kit is all stocked up, and we've got nine Pier 70 hats waiting. We're all set."

Gannon glared at Milly, but she didn't look at him.

Instead, she made them both laugh when she offered Cam a fist bump that he returned with ease and then turned toward the boat. She was always telling them they were too nerdy for their own good, something Gannon couldn't dispute, but the trying to be cool part... Nah. He knew he couldn't pull it off, even if he'd wanted to.

Minutes later, they were all safely on board the large pontoon boat, filling the benches that lined the outer walls, pulling on the Pier 70 caps that were, indeed, waiting for them. Taking a seat in a chair near Cam, Gannon stared at the hat and pretended to relax while Cam masterfully steered the boat out of the dock, heading for open water.

The day couldn't have been nicer. Although there was a chance of storms in the forecast, you couldn't tell it based on the cloudless blue skies overhead. If they were lucky, Mother Nature would hold off for a few hours. Despite the fear of falling in, Gannon actually found himself looking forward to a little time on the lake. It'd been months since he'd taken any time off. Not that he considered today a day off with the top video game designers at Burgess Entertainment sitting less than ten feet away, but still. It was something other than his regular fourteen-hour day in the office, which was a nice change.

"So, Dare tells me you own a video game company," Cam prompted, a clear attempt to make conversation once they were in open water.

Gannon nodded, watching the way the wind blew Cam's hair back, those mirrored sunglasses reflecting the brilliant blue of the sky. Gannon was grateful he'd thought to bring his sunglasses, because it allowed him to watch Cam without anyone noticing.

"What's that entail?"

Gannon could tell Cam wasn't at all interested, but unfortunately for him, he'd asked the question, which meant he was going to get an answer. Eight of them, to be exact.

Listening with a smile, Gannon waited while his team gave Cam in-depth responses to the question, enlightening him on far more than the man obviously cared to know.

"The simple answer," Gannon said, motioning to the others when they'd finished talking.

Cam smiled in return, a flash of white against his sun-bronzed face, and a blaze of heat seared Gannon from the inside out.

"And you…?" Gannon prompted. "You and your friends own the marina?"

"We do," Cam said with a mischievous smile, likely realizing Gannon had done some digging of his own. "My dad fronted the money when I was twenty-four. Told me that he'd sign it all over to me if I graduated college. I started a little late, but I did." Cam's smile widened. "The rest is history."

"What's your degree in?"

"Sports management."

That definitely didn't surprise Gannon. It seemed to fit Cam. It would've contributed to his business acumen and had probably proven to be beneficial since he owned his own company.

The boat continued to cruise at a steady speed as they traveled farther out from the shore. Gannon watched Cam, impressed with how he moved with such ease. "So you spend most of your time on the water?"

"*In* the water," Cam corrected. "I'm not much for boats, unless one is draggin' me behind it."

Gannon peered out at the wide expanse of dark water surrounding them. He could picture Cam out there, expertly maneuvering behind the boat on skis or whatever people used these days.

"What about you? What do you do for fun?" Cam asked.

Glancing over at the others, Gannon realized they were in a heated conversation about a glitch they'd identified in their latest development, or more simply, they were ignoring him completely. Milly had taken to sitting farther away from them all, holding her iPad in her hands while getting a little sun.

No ears were paying any mind to their conversation.

"Work," Gannon replied.

"Not fun, Gannon."

Once again thankful for his sunglasses, Gannon locked his eyes with Cam's, wondering if the other man knew just how much Gannon liked the way he said his name. Cam looked away quickly as though reading Gannon's mind, and for the first time, he was convinced that this chemistry wasn't only one-sided.

Smiling to himself, Gannon once again glanced down at the hat he was holding.

"Put it on," Cam instructed.

Gannon looked up, watching Cam, holding his gaze though they were both hiding behind their sunglasses.

Fueled by the fact Cam probably didn't think he'd do it, Gannon pulled on the cap, situating it on his head while Cam continued to watch him.

"Nice," Cam said before looking away quickly.

His heart did an unexpected somersault, but somehow Gannon managed to keep his cool.

At least he thought he did, anyway.

The next two hours went by far faster than Gannon expected. After his initial conversation with Cam, he spent most of his time engaging his team in a more personal exchange. Asking about their families, what they did in their off time. Some of them, the few who'd been with him for a while, he knew well, others not so much.

Somehow he managed to keep the dialogue open between them as the minutes ticked by. After all, the intention of the outing was to boost morale and get to know one another. By the time they reached the shore, Gannon had chalked the day up to a success. He gave his team the rest of the day off, and they soon went their separate ways. Including Milly, who'd come up with a crappy excuse and opted to ride with one of the others back to the office.

Which left Gannon alone with Cam again, a situation that wasn't nearly as uncomfortable as he'd thought it would be. He helped Cam gather the extra life jackets and return them to a small wooden shed near the main building.

"Thanks for today," Gannon told Cam as they neared the main doors of the marina office after they'd finished unloading everything.

"Anytime."

Feeling bolder than he'd ever expected—perhaps a few hours outdoors wasn't such a bad thing—Gannon decided to do something incredibly forward. Cam had already blown him off once, but Gannon had seen it more as a dare than a rejection, so he was hoping if he was persistent, Cam would eventually give in.

"Have dinner with me tonight."

Cam's mouth slowly curved up as he kept his eyes on the ground in front of him, walking slowly beside him. "Is that an order or a request?"

"Which do you prefer?" Gannon asked, curious as to the answer.

Cam stopped, then turned to face him, pushing his sunglasses up on his head, that penetrating blue stare lifting to meet his. "I'm not sure you can handle my response to that."

"Try me," Gannon said, hoping Cam could see the challenge in his eyes.

Another smile tilted the corners of Cam's eyes as he looked at him, this smirk much more dangerous than before. Gannon held his breath when Cam pulled the hat from his head, fidgeted with it, and then put it back. When Cam's hand brushed Gannon's ear, the heat from his touch shot straight to his groin.

"What makes you think I'm even interested?" Cam's smile faded, and Gannon wondered if he'd felt it, too.

"You're still standing here," Gannon responded without hesitation.

"You're a customer. It's my job."

"You look at all your customers the way you look at me?" Gannon retorted, enjoying the easy banter. He could tell Cam was interested, but he could also sense that Cam was testing him, just as he'd thought he would.

"How's that?" Cam asked.

"You've been eye fucking me for the last two hours."

"I thought it'd been the other way around."

Unable to help himself, Gannon took a step closer, keeping his eyes locked with Cam's. "Is that a yes or a no to dinner?"

That obviously surprised Cam, because he didn't have a quick retort.

"I'll pick you up at seven," Gannon told him when it was clear Cam wasn't going to answer.

"I'm not big on going out," Cam informed him, his eyes searching Gannon's face.

"Then what's your suggestion?"

"Your place," Cam answered.

Gannon nodded. "Be there at seven." Not waiting for an argument, he quickly turned on his heel.

"I don't know where you live," Cam called out as Gannon continued to walk off.

Without looking back, Gannon said, "Show me how much you want to have dinner with me, Cam. You can figure it out."

With that, he made his way to his car, relishing the surge of adrenaline that coursed through his veins. It was another feeling he hadn't experienced in a long time. This one made him feel alive.

And he found that he enjoyed the fuck out of it.

Nine

"WHERE ARE YOU goin' all dressed up?" Dare asked when Cam came downstairs a few minutes after five.

Cam peered down the length of his body. "I'm not dressed up."

"Bro, you aren't wearin' flip-flops. For you, that's dressed up."

"Touché."

Cam hadn't expected anyone to be in the office, but he should've known Dare would be finishing things up after having taken a few hours of personal time. It wasn't that they had set hours, or even days—they did the job because it was what they loved to do—but generally, that late in the evening, they weren't hanging around inside.

"Date," Cam rumbled when it was clear Dare was waiting for an answer.

"Holy fuck, man. With that gamer guy?"

"His name's Gannon."

"Whatever," Dare remarked with a grin. "You asked him out?"

Cam smiled, remembering his conversation with Gannon. No, he hadn't asked him out; it'd been the other way around and a nice change of pace for Cam. Generally, he was the pursuer in the few relationships he had under his belt. He tended to go out with men who were looking for someone to take the reins. Granted, he hadn't had a clue what to expect from Gannon. Truth was, the man had surprised the hell out of him with his demand for dinner. It hadn't been a question, and had it been, Cam probably would've turned him down.

But the way Gannon took control… That had set off something inside Cam. Something that'd been dormant for a while, and he was strangely looking forward to whatever Gannon had in mind. Cam got the impression, although different, he and Gannon were matched pretty evenly.

"He asked," Cam told his friend. "I'm meetin' him at his house."

"He live around here?" Dare asked.

Cam shook his head.

"You sure you're good with that?" Dare's concern was evident. "I know how you are about the long-distance thing."

Yeah, Cam wasn't fond of it, but he'd come to a decision. Since Gannon had already come to the marina three times, it was only fair that Cam made an effort. He'd know more tonight, after they had a little privacy.

"I'm steppin' out of my comfort zone," he told Dare.

Dare responded with a long, slow whistle, followed by, "So, you'll be back … in the mornin'?"

Cam laughed but didn't answer. He wasn't sure when he'd be home, honestly. Hell, dinner could be hell and he could be home early. Or…

He didn't want to think about the other option. There was some serious chemistry between him and Gannon, strange as it was, but it came down to the fact that they were polar opposites and didn't know the first thing about one another. Although the sex had the potential to be spontaneous and fucking hot, Cam wasn't looking for one night of passion.

"You got condoms?" Dare asked teasingly as Cam pushed the door open.

"I'm good," Cam answered with a chuckle.

"Later, man."

Cam stepped outside, the evening sun sliding lower in the sky but still shining bright. As he walked to his truck, the gravel crunching beneath his feet, he realized he was still smiling.

It had taken him all of ten minutes to find Gannon's address, and another twenty to convince himself that he really was going to do this. He'd spent the next half hour getting ready, though he hadn't put too much effort into what he wore. At first, he'd considered going to Gannon's in what he'd had on for the day, but thought better of it at the last minute, choosing to jump in the shower.

It was one thing to enjoy the back-and-forth between them, but Cam was far more interested in Gannon than he was letting on. More than he cared to acknowledge. That didn't mean he'd dressed up for the occasion, but he had put on jeans and a T-shirt and dug his Nikes out of the closet rather than going with flip-flops. After he'd brushed his teeth, he'd even added a touch of cologne at the last second. He looked presentable, or at least he thought so.

Reckless

After programming the address into his truck's GPS, Cam set out for the hour-long drive. When he'd learned that Gannon lived in a house that overlooked Lake Travis, he had to admit, he'd been even more intrigued. Not because the homes in that area ranged from seven figures on up but because he was interested in the view.

Money didn't appeal to Cam the way it did to a lot of people. As long as he had what he needed to survive, he was happy. Granted, he wasn't hurting, by any means. The marina was thriving, continuing to remain in the black, and allowing them enough to grow to accommodate the steadily increasing business. But he had never been attracted by a flashy man with a big wallet. It just didn't do it for him.

By the time he arrived at Gannon's nearly an hour later, Cam's nerves were acting up. He'd tried everything from blasting the radio to rolling down the windows, but he couldn't stop thinking about Gannon and what this night might have in store for him.

First dates were hell.

Apparently he'd been even more worked up than he'd thought because he hadn't realized he was still sitting in his truck, parked in Gannon's driveway, until Gannon appeared at the window, tapping solidly three times to get his attention.

With an embarrassed smile, he looked over at Gannon and shut off the engine. Before he could open the door, Gannon was doing the honors.

"I see you found the address," Gannon said, his tone low, oddly seductive, as though he liked the fact Cam had put forth the effort to find him.

"I did," he replied, climbing out of the truck.

"So, what? Your truck having separation anxiety?" Gannon teased.

He caught the spark in Gannon's eyes as his heated gaze slowly perused Cam's body, down, then up again to rest on Cam's face.

"Somethin' like that."

"You look good," Gannon said, and the blatant approval in those dark, dark brown eyes had heat blooming deep inside him.

"Dressed up for the occasion." Cam kept his eyes on Gannon's face, his gaze dropping to those soft, smooth lips. Not for the first time, Cam wondered what it would be like to kiss Gannon, to feel those lips against his own.

"I can see that." Gannon flashed another smile. "Come on in."

Cam followed Gannon along the winding path that led up to the front door. Trailing behind him, he took stock of what he was up against tonight.

Faded Levi's that accentuated a very, *very* nice ass. Check.

A black polo that shifted over a well-muscled back. Check.

Bare feet. Oh, yeah. Something about the sight of Gannon's feet made Cam's blood pump faster.

Or possibly, that was just his increased heart rate from the long trek. Although doubtful.

Gannon's house was built on a hill, so it took a few minutes to make their way to the front door. When they did, Gannon stood there, waiting for Cam to come inside.

Taking a deep breath, trying to slow his rapidly beating heart—which he admitted had absolutely nothing to do with the walk—Cam stepped over the threshold and resigned himself for whatever Gannon had in store for him tonight.

And after that, he willed his nerves to chill.

As they'd done during the entire drive over, they ignored him once again.

GANNON HAD BEEN pleasantly surprised when he'd seen the big, black Ford Super Duty F250 Lariat—a truck that suited Cam to a T—parked in his driveway. Part of him had expected Cam to be a no-show, so when he'd looked on the security camera monitor and noticed he did have a guest, he'd actually felt a little light-headed with relief.

What it was about Cam, he still couldn't put his finger on, but Gannon was looking forward to the chance to get to know him better. He had absolutely no expectations for the night, other than a nice dinner, some conversation, maybe a little wine out on the deck overlooking the water.

"Smells good," Cam said as Gannon led him through the house toward the kitchen.

"Me? Or the food?" Gannon probed, casting a quick look at Cam over his shoulder.

The way Cam's eyebrow lifted casually, the corner of his mouth curling just a little… That was probably the sexiest look he'd ever seen on a man.

When Cam didn't answer, Gannon laughed. "It'll be ready in about half an hour. Thought we'd have a drink while we wait. Preference?"

"What do you have?"

"Beer, wine, scotch, iced tea, water."

"Beer's good," Cam said, his eyes scanning the room briefly before coming to rest on Gannon again.

Gannon nodded toward the double doors that led out onto the back deck. "If you wanna go out there, I'll bring it to you."

Their eyes locked for a brief moment. That same spark he'd felt earlier that morning ignited, sizzling in the air between them. Gannon was the one to turn away first, breaking the connection, the heat spiraling through his veins leaving him edgy.

The door opened and then closed, signaling Cam had gone outside. Without looking back to confirm, he made his way to the refrigerator and took a deep breath, holding it in, then letting it out slowly.

"Get a grip," he told himself.

"How 'bout I do that for you?"

Gannon's heart slammed against his ribs as he spun around to find Cam standing directly behind him, less than two feet away. Shit.

"I thought…"

Cam's slow smile was so seductive Gannon's pulse kicked into overdrive. "I know. You thought I went out, but I needed to do something first."

Gannon's brain scrambled, and he couldn't come up with words as Cam closed the remaining distance between them in less than two steps. When they were practically chest to chest, he mentally reached deep down and lassoed every ounce of his self-control, not wanting to touch Cam for fear if he did, he wouldn't be able to let go.

Ever.

God, the man looked so damn good. Smelled even better.

Gannon swallowed hard.

"Thought maybe we'd get this part outta the way," Cam mumbled softly.

This part? Which part was…?

Reckless

Cam's mouth brushed his, the warmth of his breath fanning his face, and Gannon no longer had questions. He knew exactly which *part* Cam was referring to, and though he admired Cam's aggressive nature, it went against everything he was to let him take the lead. So, before their lips firmly touched, Gannon reached for Cam, spinning him around so that Cam's back was against the refrigerator, trapped between Gannon's body and the stainless steel. Cupping Cam's face in his hands, he allowed his lips to brush against Cam's, slowly, gently, while Gannon maintained control.

"Definitely a nice change of pace," Cam muttered.

Gannon didn't ask what that meant. That control he'd lassoed threatened to snap when a deep rumble rose up from Cam's chest, followed quickly by a desperate growl. Always looking for an opportunity, Gannon took advantage, urging his way into Cam's mouth, their tongues sliding together.

A second later, Gannon pulled back, separating their mouths. "Your tongue is pierced." It wasn't a question; he'd felt it for himself.

Cam grinned but didn't say anything.

Wanting to feel the foreign glide of that barbell against his tongue again, Gannon put his lips back on Cam's, leisurely sliding his tongue in Cam's mouth. Curious, he licked the barbell, then Cam's tongue, mapping it out with his mouth.

Then, tilting his head so he could explore further, Gannon gave in to the intense desire that had left his breath lodged in his chest. Crushing their lips together, he slid his hand behind Cam's neck, holding him as he persistently drove his tongue against Cam's, licking, tasting. He fucking tasted good, like mint and the promise of sex. A heady concoction that had Gannon craving more.

When Cam gripped his waist, hands twisting into his shirt, Gannon slid his fingers into Cam's short hair, tugging his head back and plundering his mouth, taking all that was being offered.

The rough groan that escaped Cam, combined with the way Cam jerked him forward, their bodies aligning perfectly, had Gannon reassessing the situation. Given the opportunity, Gannon could easily let this get out of control. And as good as Cam's lips felt against his own, as much as he wanted to devour every delectable inch of him, Gannon wasn't going to let this move too quickly.

There'd be plenty of time for that later.

With his fingers twined in Cam's hair, Gannon separated their mouths, brushing a kiss over his lips, inhaling the intoxicating scent of the man as he stared into those mesmerizing blue eyes. "As far as first kisses go…"

Cam's mouth quirked as he filled in where Gannon left off. "Not bad."

Yeah. Not bad. Understatement of the fucking century.

Pulling back enough to study Cam's face, Gannon took a moment to catch his breath. He knew Cam was goading him, and he liked that about him. The constant push and pull was riveting, leaving Gannon desperate to see where this went. But that was part of the appeal. He enjoyed the chase as much as Cam clearly did, and he got the sense that Cam was still testing him.

"If you're nice," Gannon told him, drawing his hands back down to cup Cam's jaw once again, "we'll pick that up later."

"I'll keep that in mind."

Reckless

Taking a step back before he gave in to the nearly irresistible urge to see just how far he could push Cam, Gannon reached around him and pulled on the refrigerator door. When Cam stepped out of the way, he retrieved two beers, handing one to Cam.

Cam eyed the label and another smirk formed.

Yes, Gannon had purposely picked up a six-pack of the same beer Cam had offered him on the pier, hoping it might earn him a few points. From the lopsided grin on Cam's face, he'd accomplished his goal.

"Come on," Gannon said. "Twenty minutes till the food's ready. I'll give you a tour of the outside so you won't be eager to jump me again."

The bark of laughter that escaped Cam did strange things to Gannon's insides.

Yeah, he definitely liked this man. A lot.

Ten

PRETENDING NOT TO want to pick up where they'd just left off, Cam shook off the haze of lust that had consumed him the instant Gannon had taken control and nearly leveled Cam with a single kiss. He could still feel the intensity of that heated caress, the strength in Gannon's hands as he'd maintained control, the urgent, almost desperate need that had pulsed between them.

It'd been a long damn time since Cam had felt anything even remotely as powerful as that. And never during a first kiss.

Cam wasn't sure what had compelled him to approach Gannon that way, but the need to feel the man's mouth, to find out whether his lips were as soft as they looked had spurred him on. His feet had taken on a mind of their own, and the next thing he'd known, he'd been succumbing to the most deliciously enthusiastic kiss of his life.

As far as *first* kisses went ... that one was by far the best he'd ever had. Not that he would let Gannon know that, because he'd seen the glimmer of arrogance in Gannon's dark gaze. He knew very little about the man, but he knew that Gannon was used to getting what he wanted. At the same time, Cam also got the impression Gannon was familiar with having to work for it, as well.

And Cam intended to make the man work for it.

Following Gannon outside, Cam managed to pull his eyes away from the long, lean lines of his impressive body long enough to take in the view. "Very nice," he said, taking a sip of his beer.

"Me? Or the view?" Gannon teased.

Cam rolled his eyes, smiling. "The view, of course."

"Of course."

And what a view it was. The scene before him wasn't exactly what he'd imagined, but fairly close. High up on a cliff, Gannon's house was surrounded by massive trees that opened up enough to give an impressive view of Lake Travis far below. There were no neighbors on either side, nor anywhere below that he could tell. It was secluded and private, and based on the comfortable furniture, this was clearly a place Gannon spent some time.

Cam could imagine sitting out on the rustic deck, drinking coffee, and watching the morning sun peek over the horizon.

And he could imagine doing it with Gannon.

"Tell me somethin'," Cam said, sliding a sideways glance at Gannon. "If you're this close to Lake Travis, what took you all the way out to Buchanan?"

"Travis is down a little, so it gets crowded. Or so I was told."

"Not much of a water guy, huh?"

"No," Gannon said simply.

Cam nodded, surveying the beautiful expanse of water laid out before him. That explained why Gannon had a view when Cam would've preferred a house on the water.

"What do you think?" Gannon asked, coming to stand next to him.

"Eh," he said teasingly. "It's all right."

Gannon laughed, bumping Cam's shoulder with his own. "Looks like I'm gonna have to ramp up my game if I hope to impress you, huh?"

Cam smiled to himself. Little did Gannon know, but he was already impressed. More so than he wanted to be.

"So, how long have you been in the area?" Gannon asked. "From what I gather, I'd say you've been here your whole life."

Cam turned around to face Gannon, leaning back against the railing. "What gives you that impression?"

"You've just got that vibe," Gannon said with a teasing smirk.

"What vibe is that?"

"The *keep Austin weird* thing."

"That right?" Cam smiled. "Or did you read up about me on the website?"

"I plead the fifth," Gannon answered, tilting his beer to his lips.

Enjoying the playful banter, Cam dropped his eyes to the deck floor. "Yeah, I've been here my whole life. Couldn't imagine being anywhere else."

"And how many years would that be?"

"Subtle, Gannon. Very subtle."

"I thought so."

Lifting his gaze to meet Gannon's, Cam saw the *not-so-subtle* glimmer of curiosity. "Thirty-two."

"Well, I don't feel old now." Gannon's eyes slid away, his attention focused on the water below.

"Old?" Cam figured Gannon was close to Teague's age, though he wasn't positive.

Gannon lifted his eyebrows as though waiting for Cam to continue, so he did.

"Fine, I'll take a stab at your age," Cam said lightheartedly, wanting to draw Gannon back in. He liked the way the man looked at him, as though he wanted to figure out every little nuance. The feeling was mutual, because Cam wanted to know what made Gannon tick, what had driven him to become one of the most successful video game developers in the nation, possibly the world.

And yes, Cam had done a little digging of his own.

"Careful," Gannon said, his gaze sliding back up to rest on Cam's face.

"Sensitive about your age?" Cam joked. "Well, I'd say you're in pretty good shape, which probably hides a few years."

Gannon laughed. "Go on."

"And you've got the air of success that seems to come with age and wisdom."

"Is that right?"

That absolutely fucking adorable dimple formed in Gannon's left cheek, and Cam was suddenly riveted by it. "Only none of that matches up with the baby face. You still get carded for alcohol, don't you?"

Cam loved the way Gannon blushed, his eyes darting away quickly.

"Yep," Cam continued, "I'm gonna take a wild guess and say you're closer to twenty than you are to thirty."

"Wrong. But because you tried hard, you earn a participation medal, but that's about it."

Cam chuckled, once again transfixed on Gannon's handsome face. He was tempted to reach up and brush the lock of dark hair from Gannon's forehead, see if the strands were as soft as they looked. "I'm more of a first place kinda guy," he told him.

"I get that about you."

"Am I close?"

"On my age?" Gannon shook his head. "Try closer to forty than thirty."

Cam couldn't hide his surprise. Since the first time he'd laid eyes on Gannon, he'd thought he was in his twenties. Definitely thought Gannon was younger than him.

"I like that look on you," Gannon said with a grin. "I'm told I look a lot younger than I am."

"Okay, I'll bite. How old are you?" Cam was too curious now.

"Try thirty-six."

Thirty-six? Huh. He would've never guessed.

And oddly, that made Gannon even more appealing.

"How long have you lived here?" Cam inquired, curious to know more about this man with the nice house, impressive view, and more than kissable lips.

"Here? As in the house? Or here, as in Austin?"

"Both."

"I moved to Austin eleven years ago, right after I got my company off the ground. Bought the house three years ago," Gannon answered, glancing down at his watch. "Dinner's about ready. Hungry?"

Starving, but not for food, Cam thought. "Sure."

When Gannon turned to go inside, Cam followed, grinning to himself. He'd expected an awkward tension to have enveloped him by now. That was the way things normally went for him. Most of the time, it was his own fault because he'd gotten used to keeping himself distanced out of habit. Although he'd been on a few dates in the last couple of years, he'd yet to find someone he felt comfortable around. And strangely, despite the fact he and Gannon were definite opposites, and there was the whole long-distance thing, there was something about him that Cam connected with.

"Have a seat." Gannon motioned toward the table in the small breakfast nook.

Cam knew he should've offered to help but worried he wouldn't be able to focus enough to provide assistance. He was too busy staring at Gannon, taking in every inch of him. Lean and trim, it was evident Gannon took good care of himself. Unlike the clothes he'd had on that morning, the jeans he wore looked well-worn and soft, the black polo as well. But regardless of how he outfitted himself, there was an air of confidence to Gannon that said he was comfortable in his own skin.

Cam liked that about him. It was sexy.

"Do you cook?" Gannon asked Cam as he brought in a casserole dish.

"Only if I have to," he admitted. "If you're asking whether I know how, then yes. I can make enough to get by."

The deep rumble of Gannon's laughter echoed in the small space. "Are we talkin' Pop Tarts and chicken noodle soup from a can?"

"Maybe." Cam wasn't much of a cook, no, but cooking for one had never appealed to him. He didn't care for fast food like Dare and Teague, so he had learned to make a few things over the years.

"Hope you like lasagna," Gannon said when he returned, this time carrying two wineglasses and a bottle.

"Depends." Cam met Gannon's gaze. "Did it come from the freezer section?"

"Not this time. I knew Stouffers wouldn't impress you on a first date, so I pulled out all the stops."

"Smart man."

Smart *and* irresistible. Two things Cam figured he'd be hard-pressed to resist.

Although he wasn't sure he even wanted to anymore.

"YOU SAID YOU spent most of your time in the water," Gannon mentioned as they dug into the lasagna and garlic bread he'd made after pulling up a recipe online. "Is that all you do for fun?"

"I'm sure there're other things." Cam looked up at him, wiping his mouth with a napkin. "But not many."

"You have family here?"

Cam nodded, picking up his fork again. "One sister, she's younger. My dad's got a place on the lake, close to the marina."

"And your mom?" Gannon prompted.

He regretted the question when he noticed the sadness reflected in Cam's gaze.

"She died sixteen years ago. Brain aneurysm."

"I'm sorry," Gannon mumbled, wishing Cam would elaborate. It was obvious his mother's death hadn't been easy on him, and even all these years later, he was still dealing with it.

Cam's eyes dropped back to his plate.

Realizing it was a sensitive subject, Gannon redirected. "And your dad and sister? You see them often?"

Cam's face seemed to soften somewhat. "My sister, Holly, and her husband, Keith, work at the marina. Dad's a retired police officer."

Gannon took a bite, gave Cam a few minutes to eat as well. He didn't want to drill him with questions, but there were so many things he wanted to know about him.

"What about you?" Cam asked, using his fork to point at Gannon. "Family here?"

"No," Gannon said simply. He knew he should elaborate, but telling Cam that his parents, along with his straight-laced older brother, had disowned him years ago would only put a damper on the mood, and that was the last thing he wanted.

"There's a story there," Cam concluded, his gaze lingering on Gannon's face.

"There is," he admitted. "But not one that's worthy of a first date."

Cam appeared to understand, or so it seemed, when he nodded his head and returned his attention to his food.

They ate in comfortable silence for a few minutes.

"What's the craziest thing you've ever done?" Cam suddenly asked, his blue eyes glittering with interest.

"I started my own business."

"Not crazy, Gannon."

He couldn't help but laugh. It might not be crazy to Cam, but for Gannon, it was. "I wanted to be an astronaut when I was a kid. Then, when I was in high school, one year I wanted to be a chemist, another year I wanted to be a physicist."

Cam's grin widened as he took a sip from his wine glass. "I can see that."

"Can you now?"

"Yeah." The honesty in Cam's tone made Gannon relax again. "You're buttoned up pretty tight there."

"Is that code for nerdy?" Gannon laughed.

Cam laughed. "Maybe."

"And you like it?" Gannon prompted.

"What? The nerdy thing?" Cam nodded. "Yeah, it kinda suits you. So how'd you get into software design?"

"Fluke," Gannon admitted. "In case you couldn't tell, I've been a geek most of my life. Logged many hours playing computer games."

Cam's laugh released the last of the tension that had knotted in his chest when they'd gotten on the subject of family.

"Find that funny, do you?"

"A little bit, yeah. But I can totally see it."

"It's the glasses," Gannon told him.

Cam's nose twitched, as though he were considering it. "Nah, the glasses are hot."

Gannon's face heated, and he looked down at his plate, ignoring the crazy eruption that occurred in his stomach.

Cam's rough chuckle had him looking back up at him. Gannon grinned back. Lifting his wineglass to his lips, he watched Cam. "And you were a jock, I take it?"

"Definitely. Football mostly, but I played baseball for a few years."

"I can totally see that," Gannon said, throwing Cam's words back at him.

"Safe to say I would've picked on you in high school," Cam told him. "Or at the least, had you do my homework for me."

"Possibly," Gannon acknowledged.

"So were you a gamer like the guys who work for you?"

"Hard-core. Didn't even get my driver's license until after I graduated from high school. Had no need for it before then." Gannon didn't bother to tell Cam that he'd lived with a friend from the time he was sixteen until he'd graduated from high school. His parents had tossed him out after he'd told them he was gay. He hadn't seen them since. "Went right from high school to college, got a degree in media, animation, and digital arts."

"Where'd you go?"

"USC. Full academic scholarship," Gannon told him. "And I'd always had a knack for business, so I figured what the hell."

Cam's smile started slowly and took over his entire face. "I'd say 'what the hell' looks good on you."

"Thanks."

Cam lowered his fork to his plate. "I went to community college. I've spent my entire life on the water. For a while, I considered competing in water sports professionally, but when I was seventeen, I started workin' at a small marina on Inks Lake. Fell in love with it but knew I needed something a little more..."

"Ostentatious?" Gannon offered.

"Somethin' like that."

While they continued to eat, Gannon eyed Cam speculatively. As much as he was attracted to the guy, he was beginning to wonder whether or not they had anything in common. From the looks of it, that wasn't likely.

Then again, in theory, opposites did attract.

So that was certainly one thing they had going for them at this point.

Gannon only hoped it wasn't the only thing.

After dinner, Cam helped him clear the table before they went back out onto the deck with what was left of the bottle of wine.

The small talk continued until Gannon couldn't stifle a yawn. It had been a long day, and tomorrow would come early for him since he had a conference call with one of his teams in Singapore. Due to the time difference, in order for them to meet up, Gannon had to schedule calls for the early hours, three or four a.m., in order to catch them before they left for the evening.

"I guess we should call it a night," Cam said, getting to his feet. "Thanks for dinner."

Gannon placed his wineglass on the table beside him and forced his weary body up from the chair. "Thanks for coming."

"Didn't think I would, did you?" Cam asked as Gannon took a step closer.

Watching him for a moment, Gannon considered his words carefully. "Truth?"

"Yeah. Truth."

"No, I didn't." Stepping closer still, he added, "But I'm glad you did."

Cam's blue gaze met his. "Me, too."

Thinking back on that kiss they'd shared earlier, Gannon lifted his hand and touched Cam's cheek, the rasp of beard growth lightly abrading his palm as he watched Cam's face for any signs that he was being too forward. When Cam's Adam's apple bobbed slowly, Gannon knew this unruly attraction wasn't just one-sided.

Brushing his thumb over Cam's cheek, he leaned in, trapping Cam between his body and the railing. "I think maybe we should get this part outta the way."

That sexy smile tipped the corners of Cam's mouth, and Gannon leaned in, closing the gap between them as he reached around to cup the back of Cam's neck.

When their lips touched, it was a hesitant mating, but that lasted all of a few seconds before Gannon couldn't contain the driving urge to claim Cam's mouth with his own. With a ragged groan rumbling from his chest, Gannon crushed his mouth to Cam's, driving his tongue inside as he licked and teased. He could taste the wine on Cam's tongue, and he wanted to get drunk on it.

His hand still cupping Cam's jaw, he tightened his grip slightly, tilting his head as he explored the inside of Cam's mouth, licking against his tongue. The sweet gentleness of it all was driving him mad, but he refused to take too much too soon.

Reckless

But when Cam gripped Gannon's hips, jerking him forward, their chests colliding, lower bodies grinding against one another, he knew it was futile to resist. He needed this more than he needed his next breath, so he settled on plundering Cam's mouth, making love to him with his tongue until they were both breathless. Long minutes passed while they made out like teenagers. Hands groping, lips sliding together, grunts and groans escaping as they devoured one another.

As much as Gannon didn't want to, he finally managed to pull his mouth from Cam's.

"Not bad," Cam whispered, his breath labored, eyes glazed, and Gannon knew Cam was holding back as much as he was.

Although it would probably be fairly easy to progress this to the next level, Gannon wasn't ready for that. Well, he was and he wasn't. His dick was screaming and pleading with him to continue, but his brain told him he had to keep things slow between them. For both their sakes.

"Thanks for dinner," Cam said, his voice rough.

"My pleasure."

"Next time I'll have to cook for you."

Gannon lifted a brow in question. "So there will be a next time?"

"Maybe," Cam remarked with a mischievous smirk.

"Give me your phone number," Gannon stated firmly. It wasn't a request. He didn't want to let Cam walk out of his house without knowing he could call him just to hear his voice.

"Give me your phone," Cam countered.

Pulling his cell phone from his back pocket, he handed it to Cam. A minute later, Cam handed it back, still smiling.

Without hesitating, Gannon hit the button to dial the number Cam had just programmed. A vibration sounded from Cam's pocket.

"Now you have my number, too."

"I won't be calling you," Cam said.

"No?" Gannon loved the playful tone in Cam's voice.

"No."

Gannon waited for Cam to elaborate.

Rather than say anything, Cam leaned in and pressed his lips gently to Gannon's, a deliciously sweet kiss that made the hair on the back of Gannon's neck stand on end. But then, before things could get out of hand again, Cam took an immediate step to the side, slipping out from between Gannon and the rail as he headed toward the house.

Gannon pivoted around and continued to watch him until Cam turned the knob and opened the door, his blue eyes flashing as he peered back at Gannon over his shoulder.

"Show me how much you want this, Gannon," Cam said, his voice rough.

"How do I do that?" he asked, remembering he'd said something similar to Cam earlier in the day.

"You'll figure it out." With that, Cam left him staring after him.

And as he watched through the window as Cam made his way to the front door, Gannon couldn't wipe the stupid grin from his face.

An hour later, when he was falling into bed, his rock-hard dick in his hand, the smile was still there. And while he jerked himself off, images of Cam running through his head, the smile never wavered.

Not once.

Eleven

BY THE TIME Friday rolled around, Cam was exhausted. The marina had been slammed, far busier than even a couple of weekends before—Memorial Day weekend, officially their busiest of the year aside from possibly Labor Day.

"You seen Teague?" Dare asked as he passed through the front office.

"Not in a coupla hours. Why?" Cam tossed back what was left of the energy drink he'd retrieved from the small refrigerator in the break room.

"Need him to have Hudson take a look at one of the PCWs."

Cam laughed at the new acronym Dare was insistent to use.

"You do know that it's—"

"Oh, I know," Dare grinned. "But I've gotta bust Roan's balls somehow."

True.

"Why do you need Teague? Why not ask Hudson yourself?" Cam inquired, watching Dare as he went to the computer, bending over to tap his fingers over the keyboard.

"Wasn't there," Dare responded without looking back.

"Somethin' wrong?"

"Nope." Dare's matter-of-fact response was tossed out casually. "Got plans tonight. Wanted to get outta here."

"Can I help with something?" Cam offered.

"Nah, man. I know you're busy."

Cam looked around the office, frowning. It was empty, everything closed up for the night. "Unless you know something I don't know, I'm not busy."

"It's cool," Dare said, fingers flying over the keyboard before he took one final stab, lifting his head and smiling back at Cam. "All done."

The printer whirred to life, and Cam watched as Dare waited for the sheet of paper to slide out before placing it in one of the empty slots on the wall rack. Cam glanced up at it, then over to Dare, who was still grinning.

Save the trees, that was all it said.

"Yeah, I know, kinda defeats the purpose, but I got a coupla waivers signed electronically today. Let Roan figure that one out."

Cam shook his head. Great. Now he'd have to deal with a pissy Roan in the morning when he was looking for the paperwork Dare clearly didn't have.

"I'm out, man. But if you do see Teague, let him know there's a PCW waitin' for him."

"PWC," Cam corrected.

"Yep. Tell him?" Dare lifted an eyebrow.

"Will do."

Dare was leaning against the door, staring back at Cam, when someone else walked up. Cam instantly recognized the tall, lean form that sauntered toward him.

Surprised by the newcomer, Dare jumped back, spinning to face Gannon.

"What's up, man?" Dare asked coolly. "Keep hangin' 'round this place and we might just put you to work."

"I'll keep that in mind," Gannon said with a sexy grin.

"Later, man," Dare hollered through the open door, offering a quick wave.

Cam rested his elbows on the counter and studied Gannon as he stepped into the marina office.

"You didn't call," he said, trying to keep a stern face. Cam knew the fact that Gannon hadn't called him since they'd had dinner on Tuesday should've bothered him, but the truth was, he'd been so busy he wouldn't have had much time to talk to Gannon, anyway.

"No, I didn't."

"What brings you down here?"

"Feeling a little reckless," Gannon offered, his face serious.

Cam swallowed. The heat that churned between them stole his breath. There was no way Gannon could know that Reckless was the nickname the guys had given him.

"That right?"

Gannon nodded. "Have you eaten?"

"Not yet." Cam's stomach chose that moment to rumble as though to remind him of that fact.

"Wanna grab some food?"

Cam pushed off the counter. "The restaurant's still open, if you don't mind burgers."

"Sounds perfect." Gannon stepped back when Cam moved out from behind the counter.

Their gazes held for a moment, but neither of them said a word. Nodding toward the door, Cam led the way. After locking up behind him, he headed down the pier to the small restaurant they'd opened a few years back. It saw quite a bit of business but, as Cam had told Gannon, didn't serve much more than burgers and fries, the occasional hot dog.

"What's up, Reckless?" Jeremy Saunders, the forty-something cook who worked at the restaurant greeted when they walked inside.

Cam tossed Gannon a look, noticing his wide eyes as he glanced from Jeremy to Cam, then back again. Nope, he hadn't known.

"Hey, man," Cam greeted. "You still got the grill on?"

"Yup," Jeremy said with a wide smile that made his cheeks puff out. "What can I get you?"

"Couple of burgers and fries."

"Comin' right up," Jeremy called as he disappeared into the back.

"Let's sit outside," Cam told Gannon, grabbing two bottles of water from the refrigerator before making his way to the outdoor deck that sat over the water.

"Reckless?" Gannon asked, studying him intently.

"That's what I've been called, yeah."

"So, back there…" Gannon's gaze raked over Cam's face before his smile lit up brighter than the midday sun.

"Thought you wanted to feel me up. Tripped me up a little, yeah," Cam said. Dropping into one of the metal chairs, Cam propped his feet up on the rail and leaned back, watching the smooth water down below. "So, what brings you down here?"

"You," Gannon said bluntly.

Cam glanced over at him, unable to keep from smiling. "I'm glad you came."

Extremely glad, actually. Cam had thought about Gannon for the last few days, wondering when he'd get to see him again.

"Eager to serve up burgers and fries, were you?"

"Somethin' like that," Cam retorted. "Busy week?"

"Yeah." Gannon sighed as he leaned back in the chair, mirroring Cam's posture, only he crossed one ankle over the opposite knee.

"It's been hell here, too."

"You gotta get back to it in the morning, huh?" Gannon asked.

It sounded as though Gannon was fishing for something, but for the life of him, he didn't know what it could be. Rather than try to figure it out, he craned his neck and looked at Gannon. "Spit it out, Gannon. What's up?"

"Shit," Gannon huffed. "I'm just tired." He paused momentarily. "And I just wanted to see you."

"Well, here I am," Cam tossed back. "And last I checked, I didn't have a curfew, so let's make the most of it, shall we?"

Right before his eyes, Gannon seemed to relax a little. Then the door to the restaurant opened, and Jeremy sauntered out, carrying two red baskets, a handful of napkins, and a bottle of ketchup.

"Y'all need anything else?"

Cam looked at Gannon.

Gannon shook his head.

"We're good," Cam told Jeremy.

"I'm gonna shut it all down then."

Cam nodded. "Talk to you tomorrow."

"Yup."

With that, Jeremy left them alone.

Cam didn't mean to be a crappy host, but he was starving, so he dove into his food, watching Gannon as he did the same.

"So, you're not pissed that I didn't call?" Gannon asked, and Cam realized that was what was bothering him.

"Should I be?" he questioned, wiping his mouth with a napkin as he chewed.

"Hell if I know," Gannon blurted with a rough chuckle.

The vulnerability etched across Gannon's face made him want to wrap his arms around him. It was endearing, and oddly not what Cam would've expected.

"I'm not pissed," Cam assured him. Narrowing his eyes, he added, "But don't let it happen again."

"I'll do my best," Gannon said, his shoulders relaxing.

"Eat," Cam said, pointing at Gannon with a French fry. "Then I'll take you down to the cove for a swim."

"At night?" Gannon's eyebrows lifted.

Cam huffed out a laugh, trying to figure out if Gannon was serious.

He was.

Holy shit.

The laughter built in his chest and rumbled out.

"Ah, hell. You're not joking," Gannon said, his eyes dancing now as he clearly saw the amusement in it.

"Nope, I'm serious."

Gannon didn't say anything for a minute, still staring at Cam, that heated gaze lighting up the nerve endings throughout Cam's body.

"Okay," Gannon finally said, the minor reluctance in his tone quite charming.

Yep, Cam was suddenly looking forward to a nighttime swim.

Really looking forward to it.

"AREN'T WE SUPPOSED to wait thirty minutes before we get in the water?" Gannon asked Cam as they walked down the sandy beach toward the waterline.

"Scared?" Cam asked, bumping Gannon's shoulder.

Yes. "No," he lied.

When Cam suddenly stopped, Gannon did, too, turning to face him.

The look on Cam's face was one of wonder, but there didn't appear to be any judgment in his eyes, which surprised Gannon.

Truth was, coming here tonight had been a gamble in the first place. He'd feared what Cam would say since Gannon hadn't had a chance to call him all week though he'd wanted to. It felt as though he'd grabbed his phone a million times, intending to call or even text Cam just for the hell of it, but something had always tripped him up.

Figuring he'd already done the damage, he'd hopped in his car and made the hour drive to see Cam, intending to beg for forgiveness if necessary.

But Cam hadn't been pissed, and that had thrown Gannon for a loop.

Big, warm hands came up to cup Gannon's face and his breath lodged in his chest.

"I've wanted to do this since Tuesday," Cam breathed out roughly before his mouth met Gannon's.

An involuntary groan escaped him as he gripped Cam's thick wrists, holding tightly as the kiss consumed him. He'd wanted to do this since Tuesday, as well. Hell, for the last few days, he'd thought of Cam day and night, wishing like hell he had even a few minutes to spend with him. Which was why he'd forced himself to leave the office early and to ensure that Milly had cleared his calendar for the weekend.

A first for him. One that Milly had made sure to point out. Half a dozen times.

Although he would pay for taking a couple of days off, spending time with Cam seemed more urgent at the moment.

Cam's tongue was insistent, gliding against his own, yet somehow Gannon managed to keep from closing the distance between them. He feared if he touched Cam too much, he wouldn't let go until some of the lust that had consumed him as of late was sated. He'd been walking around with a raging hard-on since the last time he'd seen Cam. He hadn't had to deal with hormones the likes of these since he was a fucking teenager, a time when no matter how many times he'd jerked off, it'd never seemed to help.

And he doubted he'd be able to slake the lust until he'd buried himself deep inside Cam's delicious body.

When they broke apart for air, Gannon opened his eyes to see Cam staring back at him. He didn't look away as Cam pulled Gannon's glasses off his face. Cam folded the arms in and tucked them into Gannon's pocket.

"Definitely like the glasses," Cam whispered seductively. "So fucking much."

Gannon's cock thickened, intrigued by Cam's tone and the sparkle in his eyes.

"Not sure about you, but I need to cool off," Cam said, his voice low, rough. "Let's get in the water."

"Yeah, about that..." Gannon turned to look at the dark water before them.

Cam chuckled. "You're safe with me. I promise."

Gannon wasn't so sure about that, and he wasn't referring to the water.

"I didn't bring swim shorts," Gannon announced.

Reckless

Although it was dark, Gannon could still see the heat glimmering in those blue eyes that seemed intrinsically focused on him at the moment.

"Then I guess you better get naked."

Aww, fuck. A blazing bolt of fire shot through his body, lighting him up like a rocket at lift-off.

While his brain was on the fritz, Gannon could do nothing more than stare at Cam as he slowly worked his T-shirt off, giving Gannon the first look at his thickly muscled chest.

His breath caught in his throat as he read the script that looped across those beautiful pecs.

Reckless.

Interesting, because that was exactly how Gannon felt anytime he was around Cam.

A glint of light caught his eye, and Gannon's eyes trailed down to see a silver barbell pierced through Cam's nipple. Yep, Milly had been right. There was a matching one in the other nipple. Holy fuck. Another growl rumbled up from inside him at the sight. That was so fucking sexy... Shit, the mere thought of it made Gannon's dick jump.

He didn't try to hide his interest as he scanned Cam's smooth, muscled torso in the near darkness. He catalogued the other tattoos, several that ran down Cam's sides, one that ran from hip to hip beneath his navel, visible above Cam's shorts, which rode enticingly low on his hips. He wished there was more light so he could see Cam better, but if this was what he was being offered, he damn sure wasn't going to complain.

"Your turn," Cam said, amusement lacing his words.

Swallowing hard, Gannon reached behind him and grabbed a handful of cotton before tugging his shirt up and over his head.

"Very nice," Cam whispered, surprising Gannon.

Gannon definitely wasn't built like Cam. He wasn't rippling with muscle, though he was relatively toned, right down to the six-pack he worked hard to keep. The searing heat he felt coming from Cam made him grateful he'd worked so hard to keep up with his workouts, even though he could've easily allowed work to interfere.

Cam kicked off his flip-flops, shooting another beaming grin at Gannon before turning and walking toward the water.

"We're really gonna do this?" Gannon asked, speaking up so Cam could hear him.

"We are," Cam hollered back.

"What's in it for me?" The words were hardly out of his mouth before he was struck by the most beautiful sight.

Gannon stood rooted in place as he watched Cam shuck his shorts, allowing them to fall to the ground, his tight glutes and thick thighs the only thing Gannon could focus on. Hell, he wasn't even sure he was breathing.

"Come on, Gannon," Cam called out, still heading toward the water.

"Fuck me," Gannon breathed out roughly, keeping his voice low. "The man's gonna kill me."

He didn't look away until Cam's lower half was submerged in the water, and only then did he release the air that had been locked in his chest.

As hesitant as he was to get in the water, Gannon now had pretty damn good incentive.

Twelve

CAM DIDN'T BOTHER pretending not to stare when Gannon emerged from the tree line completely naked.

Seriously. Beautifully. Naked.

His body... Holy fuck. *Talk about taking someone's breath away.*

The spattering of dark hair across Gannon's chest caught his attention first, along with the sleek muscle that lined his entire body. Long, toned arms, even longer legs. Mmm. If he was being honest with himself, he hadn't expected it.

Truth was, although it was an adorable trait, Gannon really was a bit nerdy. So, naturally, Cam had assumed he was simply skinny. Nope. He was cut. From where he stood, Cam could even make out the washboard abs and that sexy V that arrowed down between Gannon's legs.

Definitely not skinny.

Not that it would've made a damn bit of difference. He liked Gannon. A hell of a lot more than he was willing to admit.

And now, watching him stroll down to the water, his fully hard, long, thick cock protruding up from his body, Cam fought the urge to grab his own dick and show it some five-finger love.

Sure, skinny-dipping with Gannon probably wasn't the greatest idea he'd ever had. If he'd been smart, he would've settled for sitting on the sandy shore with Gannon next to him—fully clothed—but when he'd realized Gannon had a fear of the water, Cam had wanted to help him to get over that.

That was when distracting him had come to mind.

Once Gannon made it into the water, he continued to walk toward Cam, his movements jerky and slow. As though he didn't trust the ground beneath him. Cam remained where he was, his body submerged up to his chest as he waited for Gannon to join him. Since it was early June, the water was cool but not too bad.

"I hope like hell those aren't fish I feel," Gannon muttered, his nose scrunched.

"Those are fish," Cam confirmed with a chuckle.

Gannon outwardly cringed but continued to make his way into deeper water until they were standing only a few inches apart.

"I'm proud of you," Cam told him, his tone sober.

"Well, if it weren't for the fact you were naked out here, you can bet your ass I wouldn't have left dry land."

"Whatever it takes," Cam answered, reaching for Gannon's hand. "You know how to swim, right?"

Gannon nodded.

"Come on."

Linking their fingers together, Cam led Gannon to deeper water, releasing his hand when they were deep enough to tread water.

"I promise, you're safe with me," Cam told him, swimming closer. "Relax."

"Easy for you to say." Gannon's words were choppy, as though he was still nervous.

Knowing he would never get Gannon to relax by forcing him, Cam reached for his hand once again as he swam backward, searching with his feet for the ground. Once he was able to stand up, he tugged Gannon toward him, wrapping his arms around his waist, his fingers kneading the tense muscles of Gannon's back as their bodies slid together.

Gannon hissed, his hands clutching Cam's biceps. "This is dangerous," Gannon whispered.

"Don't I know it," Cam said on an exhale, and like Gannon, he wasn't referring to swimming at night.

The sexual tension tightened substantially as they stood there neck-deep in the water, skin to skin, motionless, staring back at one another. Cam knew one of them had to make a move. And soon.

Something swam by his legs, and Cam felt a tremor race through Gannon. The man was terrified, but he was still out there, and that meant more to Cam than anything.

"Put your legs around me, Gannon," Cam ordered, pulling him closer.

Gannon hesitated only briefly but then allowed Cam to shift him so that Gannon's legs were wrapped around Cam's waist. He ignored his dick as it roared to life, sliding against Gannon's ass.

Who thought this was a good idea?

The buoyancy of the water allowed him to embrace Gannon easily, holding him tighter until Gannon understood what Cam wanted. When Gannon's arms wrapped around his neck and his lips came down over his, Cam dragged in a breath, allowing Gannon to control the kiss as he sucked Cam's lower lip. They remained exactly like that for what felt like hours, mouths fused, Gannon's hands sliding over Cam's back, shoulders, and arms.

"Brace yourself with your legs," Cam instructed, then released Gannon's back so that his hands were free. With ease, Cam slid both hands between their bodies, gripping Gannon's thick erection gently at first, watching those dark eyes widen.

Gannon hissed. "Cam..."

The single word sounded like a warning, but Cam didn't heed it.

"Kiss me," Cam demanded, continuing to double fist Gannon's heavy cock, stroking slowly beneath the water as Gannon's mouth returned to his. They were breathing too hard to maintain the kiss, though.

Gannon growled, hands clutching Cam's head, holding him still as he rested his forehead against Cam's. They were swapping air between them.

"We can't..."

"Just this," Cam whispered. "Just need to make you come for me."

"Aw, fuck," Gannon growled, his hips bucking forward, driving his dick into Cam's hand. "More."

Cam gave Gannon what he asked for, tightening his grip and stroking him more firmly. Faster. Harder.

He alternated, slowing his pace, thumbing the broad head of Gannon's dick, then stroking him once again. He continued to watch Gannon's face, enjoying the sexual tension that drew his mouth into a hard line. The distraction was definitely working.

"Cam." Gannon's breath fanned Cam's face. "Fuck. I'm gonna come."

"Kiss me while you come for me," Cam said softly.

Cam changed the angle of his hands, allowing him to tug Gannon's cock more insistently, jerking him beneath the water as their mouths crashed together, Gannon's tongue working against his. Gannon's kiss was unlike anything Cam had ever felt before. Powerful. Possessive. The way he used his teeth to pull at Cam's lower lip... It drove him fucking wild.

And though Cam was holding Gannon, jacking him off right there in the water, Cam knew without a doubt that Gannon had complete control over this situation.

Over *him*.

Gannon's arms tightened around Cam's head as he held on, his mouth hovering by Cam's ear.

"Fuck, Cam," Gannon whispered, his body tensing. "Feels so good. Don't stop."

Cam didn't stop; he worked Gannon's dick faster.

"Oh, shit," Gannon crooned. "I'm... Ah, fuck. I'm gonna come."

"Come for me," Cam insisted softly.

Gannon's entire body stiffened, every muscle going rigid as his dick pulsed in Cam's hand. Cam slowed, tightening his grip more, milking Gannon's seed from him. When some of the tension in Gannon's legs eased, Cam loosened his hand, caressing Gannon as he came down from his climax, arms still wrapped around him.

Although they were moving a little faster than Cam had intended, he couldn't say he was disappointed.

Not by a long shot.

THANKFULLY THEY WERE in the water, because Gannon's legs were shaky as he forced his feet back to the ground, arms still clutching Cam close.

"I didn't expect that," he admitted, sliding his lips against Cam's smooth, warm neck.

"Are you relaxed, at least?"

Gannon pulled back and met Cam's beautiful gaze. "A little."

Cam flashed that brilliant grin and Gannon answered in kind.

"I told you I'd keep you safe. Now swim with me."

Still trying to get his bearings, Gannon nodded. He suddenly realized he hadn't paid any attention to the water or what critters were likely lurking beneath the surface while Cam had given him the best hand job of his entire life.

Though he was still nervous, not exactly excited to be in the dark water, he decided to trust Cam on this one. Forcing his legs to move beneath him, he followed Cam out into the deeper water. They didn't remain out there for long before they journeyed back toward shore, and Gannon was grateful for that.

He trusted Cam when he said he'd keep him safe, but that didn't mean he was enjoying himself. However, he was trying because he knew this was Cam's world. The man was like a fish, moving with such masculine grace, body slicing through the water easily, effortlessly. Gannon was more like a fish *out* of water, flopping around, jerking wildly when something brushed against his leg. Quite frankly, it was embarrassing and he was glad it was dark.

"Come on," Cam said, tugging Gannon's arm as they began walking up toward the shore. "You did good. I won't torture you anymore."

Gannon's thoughts instantly drifted to that hand job Cam had given him. He'd take more of that torture any day of the week. Not to mention, he longed to return the favor.

After allowing the breeze to dry them off, they dressed and then made their way back to the marina office. Gannon thought Cam was going to send him on his way, so when he offered him a beer, he did his best to hide his surprise.

"Do you have to work in the morning?" Cam asked as they ascended a set of stairs on the side of the building.

"Took the weekend off," he answered. "You're working, though, right?"

"Bright and early," Cam said.

When they reached the exterior door at the landing, Gannon asked, "Should I go?"

Cam turned to face him. "No. Not unless you want to."

Meeting Cam's gaze, Gannon smiled. "That's the last thing I want to do."

"Good."

Gannon noticed Cam didn't smile, but he didn't get to ask him what was wrong because Cam turned, punched in a code on the electronic doorknob, and then they were inside. The second floor of the building seemed much bigger than the first. The exterior door opened to a hallway, which cut the floor in half, another door on the right and one on the left.

Cam moved to the door on the left, punching in another code, then opening it.

"It's not much," Cam said as they stepped inside. "But this is home."

They were greeted by a loft-style apartment, the space completely open. High ceilings, exposed brick walls on three sides. Very *Friends*-like. Only without the bedrooms and the fire escape balcony.

On the far side of the room, there was a king-sized bed with rumpled sheets. Beside it was a nightstand with a clock and a lamp, nothing else. A short six-drawer chest sat beneath a window covered with sheer black curtains. Closest to the door, though, a brown leather sofa sat facing a large flat-screen television mounted on the wall. In the corner opposite the bed, a sheet of opaque glass separated the rest of the area from what Gannon could only assume was the bathroom. And in the other corner, a small kitchenette.

"This is nice," Gannon said.

"Thanks."

There wasn't much in the space, but the things that were suited Cam's personality. At least the way Gannon saw him. Thick-planked hardwood floors lay out beneath the heavy, masculine furniture. Decorations were minimal, but there were a few pictures on the wall, most of them of the lake and what looked to be Cam and his friends.

Gannon walked over to get a closer look at a collage of pictures that took up nearly one entire wall. "Is that you?"

"Yep."

They were pictures of Cam doing various things—white-water rafting, hanging from a zip line with a brilliant smile on his face, snowboarding down a mountain—looking completely in his element.

Gannon peered over his shoulder at Cam.

"Have a seat," Cam said, nodding toward the sofa as he headed toward the kitchen.

Looking back at the images once more, Gannon tried to imagine himself ever doing any of those things. He couldn't.

Not wanting to think too hard on that, Gannon headed back across the room, dropping onto the plush leather sofa and relaxing back, still trying to take it all in.

"How long have you lived here?" he asked Cam.

"Going on eight years now. It took a couple of years for me to get the money to fix it up. There's another apartment on the other side that mirrors this one."

"Who lives there?"

"Roan."

Gannon took the beer Cam offered.

"Living here…" Gannon began. "Does it make it hard separating your personal life from work?"

"My personal life *is* my work," Cam said, tilting the bottle to his lips.

Gannon knew how that felt. His entire world was his company, but it wasn't simply a job for him. He loved what he did, so he understood what Cam was saying.

Glancing at the clock on the wall, Gannon realized it was late. Much later than he'd thought.

"I really should get going," he said, sitting up and resting his elbows on his knees. "You've got work in the morning."

Cam didn't say anything, but Gannon could feel his eyes boring into him. Turning slightly, he met the heated gaze.

"Stay," Cam finally said.

Gannon knew that was a bad idea. After what had happened at the lake, he wasn't sure he could spend the night with Cam. Not if he wanted to keep taking things slow.

The cushion shifted, and Cam took the beer from Gannon's hand, setting it on the coffee table, where he'd set his.

"I want you to stay," Cam said softly as he moved over him, forcing Gannon back on the sofa. "And not because I want anything. Because I want to spend time with you."

Sliding his hands along the firm muscle at Cam's sides, he worked his fingers beneath the hem of Cam's T-shirt, the warmth of his skin penetrating his fingertips, infusing his entire body with a blaze of heat.

Cam's knee eased between Gannon's legs, insistently pressing against his dick, which was quickly stirring to life as he stared up at the most beautiful man he'd ever laid eyes on.

"Let me see you," Gannon whispered, working Cam's shirt up and over his head.

Cam hovered above him, the muscles in his arms contracting as he held himself up. Once the shirt was out of the way, Gannon traced the tattoo across Cam's chest with the tip of his finger, his gaze sliding up to meet Cam's briefly before once again returning to take in the gorgeous body before him.

When Gannon tweaked the barbell piercing one of Cam's nipples, Cam groaned.

"Do you like that?" Gannon asked, his voice rough with his own arousal. He noticed the line of Cam's jaw as it tensed when Gannon applied more pressure to the steel bar.

"Fuck yes," Cam said through clenched teeth.

"Does it hurt?"

"In a good way, yeah," Cam muttered, eyes closed.

Gannon was tempted to put his mouth where his fingers were, but that choice was taken away from him when Cam draped his body over Gannon's, his mouth coming down over Gannon's.

Reckless

Sliding his hands up to cradle Cam's head, Gannon took control of the kiss, something he had already figured out that Cam wanted from him. Though he got the impression Cam was a switch, Gannon wasn't. Not usually, anyway. He'd bottomed a couple of times, sure. It hadn't been a bad experience, but he still preferred to be the one in control. Naturally, he was a top, and he longed to have Cam right where he wanted him.

But this worked for now. He certainly had no intention of rushing things, even if he wanted to repay Cam for the hand job from earlier. Truth was, he wanted to taste every inch of Cam's skin, to run his tongue over those tattoos, along the smooth lines of every muscle.

The kiss was pure bliss. Gannon focused on Cam's mouth, nipping his lip, sliding his tongue against the barbell that pierced Cam's tongue. When Cam began grinding his cock against Gannon's thigh, he encouraged him by adding friction, shifting his leg.

Cam groaned.

"Look at me," Gannon said, pulling back from Cam so he could see his face.

Cam's eyes opened, heavy-lidded as they stared down at him.

"Ride my leg," Gannon instructed. "I wanna watch you come apart."

Cam didn't slow, didn't appear at all embarrassed to be dry humping Gannon's leg. Not that he should've been, because quite frankly, it was probably the hottest thing Gannon had seen in his entire life. Every muscle in Cam's upper body flexed and shifted as he rocked his hips, grinding his cock against Gannon's leg.

Watching Cam was a pleasure he'd never tire of.

Gently brushing his fingers along Cam's ribs, he felt the shudder that tore through Cam's body as he continued to pump his hips, the thick, steely length of Cam's erection pressing into Gannon's thigh.

"That's it," he urged. "Beautiful."

Cam's eyes were glazed over, likely blinded by the lust that was coursing through him.

"Come for me, Cam. Let me see you let go."

Cam's groans intensified as he urgently pressed his hips forward and back, rocking himself.

A feral growl escaped and Gannon knew he was close. Reaching up, he twisted the barbells in Cam's nipples, watching as the pleasure ignited on Cam's face.

"Fuck... Ah... Fuck," Cam roared, his body stilling, his cock pulsing against Gannon's leg.

Cam dropped down, plastered against Gannon's body. Unable to move, he held Cam close, brushing his lips over Cam's jaw. "That was so fucking hot," he whispered. "I could watch you do that a million times over."

He felt Cam smile against his neck before he shifted. "I need a shower."

Gannon wasn't sure if that was an invitation, so at first he didn't say anything. When Cam got to his feet, he waited to see what Cam would do, and to his disappointment, Cam didn't reach for him, he simply moved across the room toward that opaque glass wall.

"Gannon?"

"Yeah?" he answered, staring up at the ceiling.

"Shower. Now."

Smiling to himself, Gannon got to his feet.

He definitely didn't need to be told twice.

Thirteen

CAM WASN'T SURE how he'd managed to survive the night.

Sleeping with Gannon—

Wait, scratch that.

Technically, they hadn't actually *slept* together. Not in the carnal sense, at least. They'd been in the same bed, beneath the same sheets, skin to skin. And yes, they'd both been naked.

But they hadn't … *slept* together.

However, sleeping with Gannon—while not *sleeping* with him—was a hell of a lot harder than he'd thought it would be. Sure, it had been better than good simply to close his eyes and drift off with Gannon's warm, reassuring presence beside him, curled up around him, those strong arms holding him. In fact, last night Cam had slept better than he had in years.

The sleeping had been the easy part.

After Cam had rubbed himself to orgasm on Gannon's leg like a horny fucking teenager, then showered with the guy *without* taking things to the next level, he'd fallen asleep with the mother of all hard-ons. But it had been the right thing to do. As much as he wanted Gannon, he had no intention of pushing this too fast. And he was pretty sure Gannon understood that.

There were a lot of things they had to work out between them. Sure, the chemistry was there. However, that couldn't be the only thing they based this on if they wanted it to work. They still had to contend with the hour drive between them, the fact that they both were married to their jobs, and then there was the actual *differences* between them—Cam liked water, Gannon did not. Gannon was a brainiac, Cam was not.

Although at this point, *too fast* ... well, they had obviously defined it differently.

So, when his alarm had gone off and Gannon hadn't so much as budged, Cam had left him asleep in his bed, loving the way he looked there.

And now that the sun was up and Cam was on his second cup of coffee, he was beginning to become somewhat coherent. He'd already had a brief conversation with Teague, who had come in early to take a group of feisty ladies out on one of the pontoons. They'd asked for Teague specifically. Not that it had been the first time a rowdy group of women had asked one or more of them to take them out. At least several times a year, they'd go through the motions of entertaining women, even harmlessly flirting. Cam merely found it highly amusing considering they could flirt with the best of them but had never so much as touched a woman.

Cam hadn't, at least. Not once. Never even experimented. He'd known from an early age that he wasn't the same as most of his friends. He'd always been attracted to the same sex. Always. He was fairly confident that Roan hadn't. As for Dare, Cam wasn't so sure. The guy was wild, crazy ... experimental. He didn't confirm or deny either way. And Teague ... well, the kid claimed he hadn't, nor did he have the inclination.

But that was all part of the job.

Reckless

Cam was getting ready to sneak back to his office, hoping for at least an hour to decompress before the day kicked into high gear, when his cell phone chirped.

Glancing down at the text message, he smiled to himself.

For some reason, this bed's not as comfortable as it was last night.

After grabbing his phone, he typed out a quick response: *Really? It was fine when I woke up.*

Less than a minute later, another text came in. *Where are you?*

Cam replied, *In my office.*

Hmm. Do you have a desk in there?

Confused, Cam typed, *Yeah. Why?*

Think I'll fit under it?

Cam barked out a laugh at the same time he heard the ding of the alarm on the front door. He looked up to see Roan watching him, a strange look on his face.

"What's funny?"

"Nothin'," he lied, dropping his phone into his pocket.

Roan's eyes scanned Cam's face slowly, intently before he said, "If I'm not mistaken, you had company last night."

Cam shrugged, not meeting Roan's eyes. "So?"

"That company's still here."

Cam wasn't sure where Roan was going with this, but he waited because he knew his friend would get around to it eventually.

Roan came to stand in front of him, and when Cam lifted his eyes, he realized Roan wasn't happy. Not a hint of amusement reflected on his face, and Cam knew instantly that he was going to get lectured. He could already predict where this conversation would lead, so he held up a hand, halting Roan before he could get started.

"Please don't."

Roan's dark eyebrow cocked. "Don't what?"

"I don't need a warning. It's cool," Cam said. "I'm not rushing."

"No?" Roan nodded his head toward the parking lot, frowning.

"No," Cam confirmed. "I know what I'm doing."

It might not be the complete truth, but it wasn't a lie. Cam was taking things slow. Mostly. But he understood where Roan was coming from. They'd been best friends since they were kids, and Roan had seen the harsh roller coaster ride Cam had been on for most of his life when it came to love. Not that this was love. He certainly wasn't jumping the gun where that was concerned.

Like most people, he'd been hurt a few times, but in his defense, he had survived.

"Just be careful," Roan finally said, his tone gentle, his eyes searching. "I don't wanna see you get hurt."

Cam nodded, not sure what to say. There was no guarantee that he would come out on the other side of this unscathed, even if he and Gannon continued to take things slow. Relatively speaking. But he couldn't deny that he wanted to see where it went.

It looked as though Roan was gearing up to say something else, but thankfully, Gannon chose that moment to show up, strolling in the front door looking like sex on a stick, his eyes darting between Cam and Roan as they stood nearly face-to-face.

"I'm cool," Cam reassured Roan. "No need to worry."

Roan's gaze slid to Gannon, then back before he nodded once and then went to check the wall for the waivers. The sound of rustling paper came from behind him. "What the fuck is this shit? Save the trees?"

Cam laughed, his eyes perusing Gannon as he continued to watch them.

"Did Dare do this?" Roan asked, waving the paper around.

Today obviously wasn't going to be Roan's day.

"What do you think?" Cam tilted his head toward his office. "Come on," he told Gannon, "I'll give you a tour."

Taking his lukewarm coffee with him, he led the way to his office. The instant he stepped inside, Gannon closed the door behind them, relieved Cam of his coffee cup, and then pushed him up against the wall.

All those pent up emotions released into his bloodstream when Gannon touched him.

"Waking up, alone in your bed…" Gannon's mouth brushed his roughly. "It was hell."

Cam smiled against Gannon's mouth. "But at least you were in my bed."

"Yeah? But you weren't there for me to do this."

Gannon cradled Cam's face in his hands, slanting his mouth over Cam's and stealing the oxygen from the room with a blazing kiss that had Cam's legs shaking by the time Gannon pulled back.

"I'll remember that next time," Cam said breathlessly.

Gannon's fingers stroked over his cheek, his eyes studying his face briefly. "Mornin'."

Cam laughed at the quick turnaround in Gannon's demeanor. Though he'd been playful, now there was a lightness that was contagious.

"Mornin'," Cam replied softly.

"So, what's on the agenda for today?" Gannon took a step back, his eyes scanning the room.

Hell, before that kiss, Cam could've easily answered that question. But now…

Now it felt as though all of his brain cells had been obliterated.

From one simple kiss.

Though, if he were completely honest with himself, there wasn't a damn thing *simple* about it.

ROAN GREGORY PRETENDED to be interested in the sheet of paper in his hand as Cam led Gannon down the hall toward his office. The moment the two men were out of sight, Roan leaned against the counter, took a deep breath, and attempted to calm his rapidly beating heart.

He felt sick. A twisting in his gut that made him nauseous. His legs were weak, his hands clammy, breathing labored. Only he knew he wasn't coming down with the flu and he didn't have a summer cold, measles, mumps … etcetera, etcetera. And he didn't need to go to the doctor.

Nope, none of that shit.

Unfortunately.

No, Roan felt off-kilter because it appeared that Cam and Gannon were actually … in a relationship.

Roan's gaze slid to the parking lot, and that fancy Lexus that was parked right next to Cam's truck. He knew it shouldn't have bothered him, that he didn't have any right to worry or be jealous. Only he did and he was.

A fucking lot.

But it was his own damn fault since he'd kept his mouth shut all these years, never telling Cam how he truly felt.

The sad fucking truth was, Roan was in love with his best friend.

And it sucked hairy donkey balls.

All these years he'd lived with the knowledge that the one man he loved beyond all else couldn't be his. Not like that. Cam was his best friend, his confidant, his business partner. The man he'd hoped he would spend the rest of his life with.

And yes, Roan was the king of all chickenshits. He'd never bothered to tell Cam straight out how he felt because … well, because he didn't fucking know why.

Instead of laying all the sappy emotional bullshit on his friend, he'd hoped that Cam would realize on his own.

Never happened.

And so Roan had sat by, watching Cam date various men, secretly hoping things wouldn't work out. Not because he wanted Cam to get hurt. That was the last damn thing he wanted. No, he'd been hoping Cam would wake up one day and realize he wanted to spend the rest of his life with Roan.

Not that Roan hadn't dated. He'd been out with plenty of men, experimented, sometimes even tried to convince himself what he felt for Cam was a stupid crush. Only none of his relationships had worked out, and he was pretty sure every failure had been his own fault.

"Ugghh."

Roan crumpled the sheet of paper in his hands and threw it in the direction of the wastebasket.

Missed.

Figured.

Story of his life.

And now, it looked as though Cam had actually found something good with Gannon. Roan couldn't remember the last time Cam had had an overnight visitor. Years, definitely. Which meant Gannon was more than just a passing fancy for Cam.

The worst fucking part about it all, Gannon was good for Cam. They didn't seem to have much in common, at least not from the outside looking in, but whatever they did have together had put a smile on Cam's face. As much as Roan wished Cam would look at him the same way he looked at Gannon, he knew it would never happen.

No matter how much he'd wanted it to.

The rumble of laughter coming from Cam's office made Roan's stomach lurch.

No way could he stand here and listen to the two of them. Cam was his best friend, yes. Roan wanted Cam to be happy, yes. But Roan didn't think watching Cam fall in love with another man was something he could deal with.

Not today.

Possibly not ever.

Reckless

GANNON HADN'T FELT this good in a long damn time. He'd spent a few minutes that morning shadowing Cam at the marina before making the hour drive back to his house to clean up because Cam wanted to take him out on the boat later.

After he'd shaved, showered, and dressed, Gannon had fought the urge to open his laptop to check to make sure there weren't any fires that needed his attention. Only the thought of getting back to Cam had kept him from doing so. Which was something he'd never experienced before.

Not once in his life had a personal relationship come before his work. When he'd been in college, he'd focused on studying. When he'd started out working as a video game tester, he'd focused on work. And when he'd started his own business, he'd never let anyone distract him from the most important thing in his life.

Until Cam.

Instead of giving in, probably finding himself in his office for hours on end, attempting to fix something that could've waited until later, Gannon had climbed back in his car, made the return trip, and even stopped to pick up food on the way back—making sure to get enough for Roan and Dare, since he'd heard they'd be in the office for a while.

That meal … well, he wished he could say that it had gone smoothly, but he got the impression Roan wasn't too happy with him for some reason. His first clue had been that morning when he'd walked into the marina office to find him and Cam in what appeared to be a heated discussion.

Gannon was pretty sure Cam had no idea that his friend had some deep feelings for him. More than friends. More than business partners.

He'd seen the way Roan looked at Cam when he didn't think anyone was watching. And he'd definitely noticed the evil eye Roan had shot his way throughout the day. Not that Gannon knew that for a fact, but it definitely explained why Roan was so standoffish toward him. Gannon wasn't sure what Roan had against him, if anything, but something was definitely off.

Had he done something to Roan? Had he inadvertently pissed him off? Was something else going on between Roan and Cam that Gannon didn't know about? Or was it simply because he was there with Cam?

Unfortunately, he didn't have the answers to those questions, but he was fairly astute. It seemed pretty clear to him. Granted, he didn't know Roan all that well, but if Gannon wasn't mistaken, Roan was in love with Cam.

"Gannon."

The sound of Cam's voice pulled Gannon from his thoughts, and he looked around to see that Cam had stopped the boat out in the middle of the lake, far from dry land.

"Please tell me you're not gonna make me get in that water again," he said quickly, his heart rate already soaring from the idea.

"Not tonight," Cam replied easily. "I thought we'd just chill for a while."

"That I can do."

"Then come here," Cam said as he dropped down onto the sun deck, leaning back on his hands and staring out at the water. The sun was lingering over the horizon, painting the sky pink and purple, which, in turn, made Cam's already bronzed skin even darker.

God, the man was beautiful. Every inch of his body was perfection, all the hard planes and angles, the smooth dips and valleys, right down to the scar beneath his jaw and that slightly crooked incisor. Those minor imperfections added character, made Cam all the more real. As far as Gannon was concerned, though, Cam was flawless.

Gannon joined him, taking a seat and soaking in the peace and quiet. "I can see why you like this."

Cam leaned back on his elbows, his head cocked toward him. "It's quiet. At least when you're not talking."

Gannon looked over to see a mischievous smirk on Cam's lips.

"You know the easiest way to shut me up?" Gannon retorted.

Cam's eyes blazed with heat, and Gannon realized exactly where Cam's thoughts had drifted. Gannon had actually been thinking about kissing, but yeah … that would do it, too.

"Slow," Gannon said, more to himself than to Cam.

"Slow is good."

Gannon leaned back, placing his hands behind his head as he stared up at the stars beginning to appear through the wispy clouds overhead. Cam mirrored him, lowering himself beside him, their elbows touching. The breeze off the water was warm, and the gentle rocking of the boat nearly lulled him to sleep. Before he allowed himself to be pulled under, he turned his head to look at Cam.

"Does Roan have an issue with me?"

Cam's head snapped toward him, forehead creased. "No. Why?"

"I'm pretty sure he's not happy that we're dating."

"Is that what we're doing?"

Gannon tried to see if Cam was teasing, but he didn't see any humor in the firm expression that drew his mouth tight and creased his brow. "That's what we're doing."

"Exclusively?"

Gannon rolled to his side, propping his head up with his hand as he stared down at Cam.

"Exclusively," he confirmed, trailing his finger over the rock-hard muscle on the underside of Cam's arm.

Cam's attention strayed back to the sky. Curling a finger beneath Cam's chin, Gannon forced him to meet his gaze again. "Is that not what you want?"

Cam shrugged. And for the first time since he'd met Cam, it seemed Cam didn't have anything to say on the matter.

"I'm not seeing anyone else," Gannon told him, sliding his palm over Cam's cheek, his thumb rasping against the shadow of dark hair that lightly lined Cam's square jaw. "And I don't want you to, either."

Again, Cam didn't say anything.

"Do you have something against exclusive?"

"No," he answered quickly, then sighed.

Gannon watched him closely, waiting for the extended version.

"Do you worry that we live too far apart?" Cam questioned.

"Not really, no." Gannon hadn't thought about it, actually. An hour drive seemed like nothing to him. At least not at this point. Sure, it meant he couldn't see Cam every day, and some days that bothered him. "It hasn't stopped us yet."

Cam opened his mouth, then closed it. Then, accompanied with a heavy sigh, Cam said, "I don't want to rush this."

"I picked up on that." Gannon had figured that out from the beginning, and he was okay with taking things slow. "But I plan to spend time with you when I can."

"I work every day," Cam stated, still facing him.

"I know. Usually I do, too. And a lot of the time, I'm not even here in Austin."

Cam's expression turned to one of question, but he didn't ask whatever was on his mind.

"Next week I'll be in California for a couple of days. And in two weeks, I'll be off to Singapore for a week. I'm not always here, Cam."

"You travel?" Cam pushed up on his elbows, watching him cautiously as though Gannon were going to pounce on him.

"Quite a bit, yeah," he admitted, trying to read Cam's face, to understand what he was really concerned with.

"To Singapore?"

"I've got a team of developers over there as well as IT support."

"So you go … often?"

"Yeah." Gannon was in the process of hiring someone he could put in place over there so he didn't have to travel as much, but he'd yet to find anyone qualified to do what he needed. The couple of candidates he'd had from the US wanted more money than Gannon was willing to pay, and there was only one candidate in Singapore who had the experience.

"To Singapore?" Cam repeated, apparently wanting clarification.

"I've got seven offices, three in the US, including the one in Austin."

"Where?"

"One here, two in California, one in Singapore, two in Europe, and we just opened one in Sydney."

"Australia?" Cam voice was slightly higher-pitched than before.

Gannon nodded.

"Good to know."

The way Cam said those words sounded almost final. As though the fact Gannon traveled was going to be a point of contention for them. "Does that bother you?"

"Nope," Cam said brusquely, dropping back down, resting his head on his hands once again. The move was meant to be casual, but Gannon could tell Cam was tense.

Leaning over, Gannon placed his hand flat on the boat beside Cam's head, staring down at him. "Just so you know, I'm not gonna let you push me away. I get that you've probably got valid reasons for wanting to go slow, and I respect that. So, we can either talk about it now or save it for another time. But I'm interested in understanding you better."

Cam didn't look at him.

"Last night, when I slept in your bed, holding you … I've never felt comfortable enough to do that. It's not easy when sex isn't on the table. It requires a certain amount of … effort. But with you, it's easy. I like that."

Before Cam could come back with a retort, Gannon lowered his head and pressed his lips gently to Cam's. He didn't take it further, just brushed his mouth over Cam's.

"I'm serious, Cam," he whispered. "We're gonna see where this leads us."

And that was a promise.

Fourteen

CAM REMINDED HIMSELF that he'd only known Gannon for a week. Exactly one week since Gannon and Milly had stepped foot in the marina, actually, but regardless, it wasn't enough time for him to develop feelings for the man. So, the fact that Gannon traveled, something Cam had a serious issue with, shouldn't have bothered him as much as it did. Yet his thoughts had drifted there, and he couldn't seem to reel them back in.

There was no way he could explain his concerns to a man he'd just met. Gannon would think he'd lost his mind. But he hadn't. He had very valid reasons for his concerns, for his fears. And knowing that Gannon traveled, well, that put things into perspective for him. Shit, the traveling thing made the one-hour distance between them nothing, at this point.

And still there was Gannon's revelation that they would see where this thing between them went. Despite everything, Cam wanted that. He wanted that with Gannon. The man was different than any man Cam had ever been with. The complete opposite of Cam's type. Hell, Gannon was scared of water. That in itself should've been a red flag, but Cam had convinced himself he could deal with it because Gannon seemed eager to want to fit into Cam's world.

But the traveling… He wasn't sure how he was supposed to come to terms with that. Or if he even could.

"Talk to me," Gannon urged softly, still leaning on one arm and staring back at him.

Cam turned his head and focused on Gannon's face, taking in every detail, his dark eyes, long, thick eyelashes that brushed the lenses of his glasses every so often, full lips, the arch of his brows when he was concerned. He was classically handsome.

Turning back to look at the darkening sky, Cam took a deep breath. "I don't have an issue with exclusive," he told Gannon. It was the truth. That wasn't what he had a problem with at all.

Gannon didn't speak.

Cam's gaze slid back to Gannon's face once again. He couldn't help himself. "I want exclusive with you," he admitted softly, the words coming out against his better judgment. "And the long distance … we can deal with that."

Gannon's smooth fingers trailed along Cam's jaw, a gentle, reverent touch that made it difficult for Cam to think. And when Gannon's long fingers slid behind Cam's head, his thumb pressing against Cam's chin, resisting became futile.

Warm lips came down to meet his, a soft sigh escaping him as he kept his hands folded against his chest. He wanted to reach for Gannon but forced himself not to. This would have to be enough for now, until he could sort through the myriad emotions that seemed to have bombarded him unexpectedly.

It was after ten when Cam docked the boat, then headed back to the marina with Gannon beside him. For nearly two hours, after Gannon had shocked him by his affirmation that they would see where this thing between them was going—exclusively—Cam had tried to relax.

Reckless

It wasn't easy. Even now, as he held Gannon's hand, making his way up the pier toward the office. His heart was doing a strange skipping thing in his chest. The most difficult thing for him to wrap his mind around was how effortlessly Gannon managed to maintain control when Cam could so easily allow things to get out of control.

Without saying too much, they'd managed to settle things between them and had enjoyed a couple of hours on the water. Cam had forced his more pressing thoughts out, refusing to deal with them until later, until he wasn't with Gannon. Gannon's presence overwhelmed him, made his brain fuzzy, and he wasn't sure that was a good thing. Not always.

So they'd enjoyed an evening with little conversation. And it had been nice.

Sure, there'd been some heated making out, but it hadn't made it past that. And because of that, Cam was pretty sure his self-control was all tapped out.

"Hey, Cam!"

Cam's head snapped over when he heard Dare's voice calling from the darkness. He scanned his surroundings, trying to see where it was coming from.

"Cam, get over here. Now!" There was a vibrating tension in Dare's tone, one that told him this wasn't a casual invite. Something was wrong.

With Gannon close on his heels, Cam jogged up the pier. When he rounded the office, taking in the scene before him, he came to a stop in the parking lot, feet skidding on the gravel.

"Fuck," he grumbled when he saw the group of guys facing off roughly twenty feet from the office doors.

"What's goin' on?" Gannon asked when Cam released his hand.

"Who fucking knows."

In front of him, backlit by the bright headlights from someone's truck, Teague was facing off against three guys, all of whom were bigger than him. Not that Teague couldn't handle himself. The guy might've been smaller—measuring in at roughly five nine, probably somewhere in the one sixty range—but he was fast. Cam knew firsthand that Teague could hand out a beating as well as any guy twice his size.

What he didn't know was what the fuck had started this confrontation.

"What's up?" Cam kept his tone firm as he approached the men. "There a problem?"

Dare was standing a couple of feet behind Teague, while two guys stood behind the one Cam assumed was the instigator. He'd never seen the guy before, but that didn't mean anything. When it came to the lake, people came and went as they pleased. And it wasn't uncommon for things to get out of hand once people started drinking and having a good time.

But this looked personal. Teague's hands were balled into fists at his sides, his chest rising and falling evenly, his eyes narrowed on the guy with the beer gut who was practically in his face. The other two behind him didn't seem to be worried about what was going on around them. They were also focused on Teague.

Awesome.

Three against one. How Teague managed to get himself into predicaments like this, Cam didn't know.

"What's up?" Cam repeated when it was clear no one was paying any attention to him.

"This little fucktard was flirtin' with my fiancée," the big guy grumbled.

"Bro, trust me, I'm not the least bit interested in your *fiancée*," Teague countered hotly.

"Oh, yeah? That's not what she fuckin' said."

Fucking fantastic.

While the verbal brawl ensued, Cam came to a stop a foot away, close enough he could insert himself between the two men if necessary. Not that he planned to, because he wasn't looking to get laid out in the parking lot tonight. But he damn sure wasn't going to let a fight go down, either. The last thing he wanted was the police to come out or for Teague to go to jail. They'd been down that road before and it wasn't pretty.

"So what can we do for you?" Cam questioned, letting his irritation reflect in his tone.

"Who're you?" the big guy asked, hands on his hips as he came to face off with Cam.

Great.

"I'm just a concerned citizen," he retorted.

"Well, you can go fuck yourself."

Cam rolled his eyes. This was not going to end well.

"Seriously, man," Teague said, "I'm not interested in your girl. Hell, I'm not interested in *anyone's* girl."

Shit.

As much as Cam respected the fact that they all lived openly gay, that they were lucky enough to live in a community that mostly supported them, he knew when not to flaunt that shit.

Now was a good example.

It wasn't going to help matters by taunting the big, burly guy who was itching for a fight.

"Dude, he's fuckin' gay," the genius in the group announced merrily.

Had to love smart rednecks.

"So you're tellin' me you're a queer?" Beer Gut questioned, eyebrows forming a V on his sweaty forehead.

"Fuck you, dumbass," Teague bit out.

"Teague," Cam reprimanded.

"No, fuck him. The fat fucker thinks he can come down here and start spoutin' bullshit. I don't have to take that shit."

No, he didn't. But making the situation worse by provoking him wasn't helping.

The big guy took a step toward Teague, and instinct had Cam stepping between them, coming face-to-face with the snarling asshole.

The guy was big, but Cam was bigger. Maybe not in height, but overall, Cam knew it wouldn't take much to take him down.

"Get outta the way," the guy spat.

Cam's nostrils flared as the smell of beer combined with the guy's foul breath blasted him in the face.

"Not gonna do it," Cam said calmly, trying to breathe through his mouth. "And I'm only gonna ask you once to leave. What happens after that is all on you."

The guy laughed, twisting around to look at his friends. "You hear that? The girly boys are threatenin' us." The man snapped back around, his face hard, his eyes narrowed on Cam's face.

"Trust me," Cam stated firmly, keeping his voice low. "You really don't want to do this."

"Oh, I do, ass-fucker," the man hissed. "I definitely do."

"Never heard that one before," Cam muttered.

The guy growled.

Damn it.

Cam fucking hated this part.

He knew he had to take the first punch—he had *no* intention of spending the night in jail, period—and that always hurt like a motherfucker. So, he stood right where he was as the guy reared back. He watched as the fist came directly toward his face, but before it made impact, the big guy was being rammed from the side, a pained sound escaping him as he went to the ground.

Lulu, who was at Dare's side, started to bark furiously, moving forward, then back.

Cam looked over to see Teague tumbling down on top of the guy, practically sitting on him as he wailed on him with both fists. Cam only had a second to stop one of the other two from interfering while Dare grabbed the third guy. He looked up to see Gannon watching them, his eyes scanning the area. It looked as though he was making sure no one else interfered while Teague laid into the guy, pummeling him.

Grunts drifted on the breeze as both men rolled a few times. When Teague was back on top, the sickening thud of fist against flesh sounding in the night, the guy behind Cam made another attempt to interfere. Cam stopped him with a shoulder, holding him back. Cam stood his ground while Teague let out some of his anger, but he knew he couldn't let it go on. He wouldn't put it past these assholes to call the cops and press charges.

Just as he was about to step in, he saw a blur out of the corner of his eye. Expecting to be blindsided by someone else, Cam prepared for impact, but it never came.

The next thing he knew, Hudson's big arms wrapped around Teague, yanking him off the redneck asshole, wrestling the smaller man back with ease. Teague tried to pull away, but Hudson held him in place.

"The fuck?" Teague hissed at Hudson.

Yeah. What he said.

In the thirteen months he'd known Hudson, never had he known him to get involved in anything like this. He kept his head down and his nose clean. Clearly, he'd had enough tonight.

Cam watched as Hudson stared off with Teague, his disapproval clear on his face.

Teague jerked away, spinning back to face the big guy, who was stumbling to his feet, but the guy wasn't a threat anymore. His nose was busted, blood pouring down his chin.

"It's time to go," Cam told the three of them. "Don't make me call the cops. Seriously."

Hoping his buddies could be more reasonable, Cam kept his eye on them as they helped their friend to the truck.

To his surprise, the guys climbed in, revved the engine a couple of times, then tore out of the parking lot, immersing them in darkness as the headlights moved in the opposite direction. Cam watched the truck leave, praying like hell they didn't come back.

"Why the fuck did you do that?" Teague snapped at Hudson.

Cam turned to watch as Hudson walked away, giving Teague his back. Lulu ran over to his side, trotting beside him faithfully.

Something was going on between Teague and Hudson, he just didn't know what.

Not that he had plans to stick around tonight to find out, either. He was suddenly exhausted and wanted nothing more than to go up to his apartment and spend a little more quality time with Gannon.

Reckless

"DOES THAT HAPPEN often?" Gannon asked when he followed Cam up to his apartment a few minutes later. His head was still spinning from how quickly things had gotten out of control. And the way Cam had attempted to keep things calm... Gannon had found that hotter than hell.

That commanding tone, the take-no-shit attitude.

Yep, hot as fuck.

"Fortunately, no," Cam said, punching in the code to unlock the door. "But it *has* happened before."

"With Teague?"

"With all of us, but yeah, mainly Teague."

Gannon had to admit, he'd been pretty damned impressed with how Cam had handled the situation. When the asshole had started dishing out hate comments, Gannon had been ready to punch the bastard himself. But it hadn't been necessary.

Granted, if it hadn't been for Teague launching himself at the guy, Gannon was pretty sure Cam would've taken a blow to the face. The thought of anyone putting their hands on Cam made him see red. It wasn't that he didn't think Cam could take care of himself, because it was clear he could, but that primal, possessive side of him made it impossible to accept.

As the adrenaline rush waned, Gannon followed Cam into the apartment, but he didn't sit down. He needed to go home. As much as he wanted to spend another night in Cam's bed, he knew they were taking a risk. If they weren't careful, they would push this too fast, and the last thing Gannon wanted was to put Cam on the defensive any more than he already was.

He'd managed to deflect one potential disagreement earlier on the boat. He didn't want to take a chance on another. It was obvious something had happened in Cam's past to make him wary of relationships, but Gannon wasn't ready to press him on the issue yet. They had all the time in the world.

"Beer?" Cam asked, turning to face him.

Gannon didn't need to answer, because Cam clearly realized he was about to leave.

"I could've just walked you to your car," Cam said, his tone lacking the casual confidence it usually had.

He was leaving because he wanted to give Cam some space, not because he wanted to. However, he didn't figure telling Cam that would do much good.

"I've overstayed already," Gannon said, moving toward Cam.

"Yeah. I've gotta work in the mornin'." Cam was shutting him out already.

Gannon closed the gap between them, forcing Cam back until he was up against the wall. Cupping the back of Cam's neck, he leveled him with his gaze. "It's not that I *want* to go," he said smoothly. "But I'm not gonna push this any faster than you want it to go. So I'll spend the night alone in my bed thinking about you."

There was a subtle vibration in Cam's body. It was as though he had too much pent up energy. Checking to make sure he wasn't imagining it, Gannon reached for Cam's hand, linking their fingers together. Sure enough, Cam was shaking, a very subtle tremor.

"You okay?" he asked Cam.

"Fine." Cam's curt tone said otherwise.

Unable to resist, Gannon captured Cam's mouth, allowing his tongue to slide past his lips. Just when he thought Cam would resist and force him away, Gannon felt Cam's big hands on his back, pulling him closer as his tongue met his stroke for stroke.

Cam groaned into Gannon's mouth, and the fire ignited, allowing them to pick up where they'd left off on the boat.

Releasing Cam's mouth, Gannon slid his lips over Cam's jaw, his neck, then lower. Letting go of his neck and his hand, Gannon slid his palms beneath Cam's shirt, sliding against warm skin. God, he felt so fucking good.

Dropping to his knees, Gannon peered up at Cam, then pressed his mouth to Cam's flat stomach, nipping the skin as he reached for the drawstring on Cam's shorts.

"Gannon." Cam's fingers dug into Gannon's hair, pulling roughly. "Can't."

"Can," Gannon said, loosening Cam's shorts before tugging them down.

"Fuck," Cam groaned, his head falling back against the wall with a thud as Gannon slowly eased Cam's shorts down his legs, freeing his cock.

Holy. Fuck.

Running his hands over the coarse hair on Cam's legs, Gannon found himself eye level with Cam's enormous erection. But it wasn't simply the length and the girth that stunned him, it was the ring that pierced through the head — a Prince Albert piercing, he thought it was called — as well as the row of barbells that pierced the skin. Three, to be exact.

Pierced.

Just as he'd suspected, Cam's dick was pierced—he'd thought he had seen the glint of metal in the shower, but at the time, he'd been trying to keep from pushing things too far.

His dick.

Was fucking pierced.

Not that he was hung up on that or anything.

Not that he should've been surprised, either. This was Cam. It was just that Gannon had never seen that before—only in pictures—but holy shit ... it was hot.

Yanking his eyes away, he looked up in time to see Cam watching him intently, his hand palming Gannon's head, gently urging him forward. Taking that as permission, Gannon leaned in and swiped his tongue over the engorged head, the metal ring, then down the shaft, over the ladder of piercings.

"Goddamn," Cam groaned, his hand fisting in Gannon's hair. "Suck me. I need to feel your mouth on me."

Gannon laved Cam's beautiful dick with his tongue, making sure to cover every inch before sucking the broad head into his mouth. His lips stretched wide. Cam's dick was bigger than he'd expected, far more than Gannon could take in his mouth, but that wasn't going to stop him.

The feel of the metal piercings against his lips and tongue was awkward at first, but Gannon quickly got used to it, bobbing his head up and down Cam's smooth shaft, taking him as deep as he could, even teasing the metal bars, loving the way Cam groaned when he did.

Cam's hands cupped Gannon's face, one hand on his forehead, the other sliding down beneath his jaw to hold his face right where he wanted him as Cam's hips began a slow thrust forward and back. Gannon allowed Cam to fuck his mouth, wanting to pleasure him any way that Cam would allow. And later, when Cam was ready, they'd kick things up a notch.

But for tonight, this would be enough for both of them.

"Gannon." Cam's strangled groan matched the tortured expression on his face.

Gannon never took his eyes off Cam's face as Cam used his mouth, fucking him slow and steady.

"Fuck," Cam bellowed. "So good. Never wanna stop."

Reaching for Cam's shaft, Gannon applied pressure, stroking him in time with his mouth, sucking him hard while using his other hand to knead Cam's heavy balls. He focused all of his attention on Cam's impending climax, pushing him higher and higher using only his mouth and his hands.

Cam released Gannon's jaw, lifting his shirt higher against his stomach, one hand still fisted in Gannon's hair as he watched the action between his legs. Gannon dropped his eyes to Cam's torso, admiring his beautiful body. The smooth ridges of Cam's abs flexed as he jerked his hips forward. The impressive muscles that arrowed down, forming a V, contracted and released with every move. It was so fucking sexy watching Cam come undone. Gannon was eager to do it again and again.

Another rumble escaped Cam's throat. "Gonna come in your mouth."

That was right where Gannon wanted him.

Eyes locked on Cam's, he felt the moment Cam reached that pivotal point. Cam's hips began to thrust harder; his hand pulled at Gannon's hair, sending shards of pleasure-pain darting down Gannon's spine.

Gannon's dick was like a steel rod, hard enough to pound nails, but he didn't reach for it, didn't take his attention off Cam for one single second.

"Gannon," Cam cried out. "Oh, fuck. Gannon, gonna … come."

Cam's dick pulsed against Gannon's tongue. Closing his mouth around the thick shaft, Gannon sucked him, milking every last drop from him until Cam leaned back against the wall, eyes closed.

Launching to his feet, Gannon plastered his mouth to Cam's, wanting him to taste himself, needing Cam to know that he was the one to control Cam's pleasure regardless of how it seemed from the outside.

Cam kissed him back fervently, his hands wrapping around Gannon's neck as he whimpered against Gannon's mouth. It was the sweetest thing to see Cam come apart like that. And he looked forward to the day he made Cam come undone while Gannon claimed him in the most primal, basic way possible.

Until then, this was enough.

It would have to be.

Fifteen

TEAGUE CARTER WAS so fucking pissed he couldn't see straight. His blood roared in his ears, a red haze obstructing his vision as he paced, trying to work off some of that pent up anger.

It wasn't helping.

Not only had that homophobic, redneck prick pushed him to the breaking point, but then Hudson had fucking stuck his nose where it didn't belong.

"Goddamn asshole," Teague bit out, kicking a box of tools that was sitting in the middle of the floor. Metal clanging against metal echoed in the room before silence took over once again.

The sound of squeaky hinges had Teague spinning around only to find Hudson leaning against the open doorway of the small boat shop office, staring back at him. Lulu came trotting out of the office, licking Teague's hand in an effort to get his attention.

Teague had thought he was alone, but he should've known Hudson would be lurking in the shadows. The man worked day and night, all the time, sometimes sleeping in the small office inside the boat repair shop rather than going home. Teague had caught him there more than once, his long, lean body passed out on the couch, feet hanging off the ends…

Not helping, Carter.

The last damn thing Teague wanted to do was to think about Hudson. Not like that, anyway.

"What the fuck do you want?" Teague snapped, knowing Hudson wouldn't say anything.

He *never* said anything. Ever.

Granted, that was partly because he was mute, but whatever. In the last year, ever since the man had started working at Pier 70, the guys had gotten pretty damn good with sign language, communicating with Hudson easily, but for some reason, Hudson chose not to talk to Teague. Not that Teague would've understood much of what he had to say, but he knew enough ASL at this point to get through the workday. As for a casual conversation, no, he probably wouldn't be able to keep up.

Since they didn't *have* casual conversations, it didn't fucking matter, did it?

"I can't believe you fucking broke up that fight," Teague said, addressing Hudson directly. "It was none of your goddamn business."

As he stood roughly fifteen feet away from him, Hudson's emerald-green eyes trailed every move he made, and Teague did his best not to admire the thick muscles of Hudson's biceps as they bulged beneath the white T-shirt he wore when he crossed his arms over his chest.

Hell, Teague had been trying *not* to admire a lot of things about Hudson as of late, and tonight's encounter should've made it even easier.

Fucking pissed, remember?

"Why'd you do it?" he asked Hudson, staring back at him, making sure to maintain eye contact.

The only answer he got was a shrug from those broad shoulders. Teague did notice a muscle flex in Hudson's rigid jaw, those green eyes locked on him. Something about the way Hudson watched him... It made Teague feel like prey being hunted.

And for whatever fucked up, masochistic reason, Teague fucking loved that shit. Something about Hudson— big, brooding Hudson Ballard—made his dick hard, made him want things he knew he could never have with a man like him.

They had nothing in common other than they were both pretty damn good with a boat motor and enjoyed the hell out of being on the water. Past that ... Hudson was at least six years older than Teague, somewhere around thirty-one, he didn't talk, didn't go out, and he worked too damn much. And Teague usually liked his men shorter, not quite so intimidating. He didn't mind that he had to look up at Hudson, that was actually quite sexy when he really thought about it, but Hudson made Teague feel... God, what was the word? Weak? Fragile?

Submissive?

Yeah, maybe.

Not that it mattered. None of it mattered.

"Well, you should learn to mind your own goddamn business," Teague ground out, turning away from Hudson and praying like hell the man didn't see the interest he was trying desperately to hide.

Hell, he'd been working double time for the past year fighting his attraction to Hudson. He didn't think the other man had a clue, but there were a few times he'd seen Hudson watching him. Only Teague could never read his expression clearly enough to know what he was thinking.

Balling his hands into fists, Teague fought the anger that surged through him. It wasn't only because of the prick who'd thought Teague had been interested in his fiancée or the fact that Hudson had practically tackled him in an effort to pull Teague off the guy. No, this had been building for months, ever since…

Nope. Not going there tonight.

Kicking another box, he growled, trying to fight the red haze that threatened to consume him. He was gearing up to kick something else when a callused hand wrapped around his bicep and spun him around. He turned to find Hudson behind him, staring down at him with a snarl curling his lip. And because he was a fucking idiot, the first damn thing he thought was how fucking hot Hudson was when he was pissed. The second thought was how he wanted to know if Hudson's lips were as soft as they looked, if the dark stubble that lined Hudson's angular jaw would leave marks on him if he did kiss him.

And the third thing Teague thought was how he wanted to punch the fucker in the mouth.

Hudson shook his head, clearly reading Teague's intention on his face.

"Then leave me alone."

Hudson glanced down at the tools now scattered on the floor, then back up at Teague, cocking one dark eyebrow as though to tell Teague he needed to clean the shit up.

Wasn't happening.

Not tonight, anyway.

Tomorrow morning, when he came back to work, maybe he'd be in a better mood. If not, Hudson would just have to deal with it.

Reckless

HUDSON WATCHED TEAGUE continue to unravel in front of him. He'd sensed the volcano slowly building inside the man for some time now, and he'd been waiting for that moment when Teague erupted. It had been part of the reason Hudson had interfered when no one else had bothered to jump in. Watching Teague wail on that guy in the parking lot... Hudson hadn't wanted to see Teague go to jail tonight.

That was why he'd interfered.

Or so he told himself.

"See you in the mornin'," Teague grumbled, not meeting Hudson's eyes.

He hated when Teague did that. It was hard enough for Hudson to communicate, but when Teague refused to look at him, it was impossible. Although Hudson could hear just fine, there was no way he could communicate anything to Teague in return.

But he knew when to leave well enough alone. As pissed as he was that Teague was taking out his anger on the tools, kicking them around like a recalcitrant child throwing a tantrum, he knew not to push the man.

What he really wanted to do was back Teague up against the nearest wall, crowd him with his body, and feast on his mouth until the fight drained right out of him. But he couldn't do that. They worked together, sometimes closely since Hudson was often needing help when the marina's small boat repair shop got overloaded. The last thing Hudson wanted to do was make things more uncomfortable between them.

"Sometimes I wish you could talk," Teague muttered as he walked away. "That way I'd know what the fuck you were thinkin'."

No, little boy, you don't, Hudson thought. The things that he thought about where Teague was concerned… Those were better left locked right there in Hudson's head where they belonged.

"Night," Teague called out but didn't bother looking back.

Hudson didn't even offer a wave as he watched him disappear through the side door and out into the night.

For the longest time, Hudson had wanted to get his hands on Teague, to thrust his fingers in that spikey blond hair and devour Teague's smart mouth with his own. Sure, the fantasies had gone much, much further beyond that, to the point Hudson's body would hum from arousal so strong, so powerful, he could hardly contain it.

But he knew better than to do something about it. Teague was too young, too immature. He was a player; he enjoyed going out to the clubs, spending the night with different men, and that was the opposite of what interested Hudson.

Admittedly, Hudson had difficulty establishing relationships with people because it wasn't easy to do when he couldn't speak, couldn't communicate how he felt. His inability to talk seemed to intimidate most people, and he'd spent most of his life alone.

He'd gotten used to being alone.

So, as always, he would pretend that Teague didn't affect him the way that he did, and he'd find a way to deal with the hard-on pressing insistently against the zipper of his cargo shorts. Maybe if he dealt with that, he'd have a better chance of dealing with Teague tomorrow.

Because he got the feeling this wasn't over yet.

Sixteen

Wednesday night

"HEY, BOY," MICHAEL Strickland greeted when Cam walked in his father's front door.

"What's up, Pop?" Cam replied, smiling as his father dropped the footrest on his favorite recliner, placed his newspaper on the table, and sat up straight. "Doesn't look like you cooked for me."

Cam's father's lips quirked beneath his thick white mustache. His wire-rimmed glasses slid down his nose, and he pulled them off, folding them and laying them on the table beside him.

"Didn't know you were comin'," Michael told him, hands resting on the armrests.

"Yeah, well…" Cam hadn't exactly known, either, but here he was. "How 'bout pizza?"

Michael reached for the phone. "Same as usual?"

Cam nodded, then flopped down on the worn sofa that faced the flat-panel LCD television hanging on the wall, stretching one leg out on the sofa. There was a baseball game on, but the sound was muted.

This would work.

He watched as the pitcher circled the mound, spinning the ball in his hand as he prepared for the inning. His father's voice sounded from beside him as he rattled off their pizza order, then hung up.

"What brings you by?"

"Just wanted to chill."

It wasn't unusual for Cam to show up at his father's house unannounced. They were close, usually spending one or two days a month out on the water, several more hanging at the house to watch TV or work on one of the old cars his dad was attempting to restore.

"Things good at the marina?"

Cam nodded, clasping his hands together and resting them on his stomach. "Busy."

"Not a bad thing, huh?"

"Not at all."

"How're the boys?"

"Keepin' it lively," Cam told him, turning his head to look at his father. "You know how they are."

Cam's father was close to Roan, Dare, and Teague, and he wasn't merely interested because of the fact he'd invested money in the marina years ago. Roan had been practically family since they were kids, spending as much time at Cam's parents' as Cam had at Roan's. They'd been inseparable. And then shortly after Cam had graduated from high school, he'd met Dare when he'd worked at the Inks Lake Marina. They'd worked side by side and had become quick friends. Before he knew it, the three of them were hanging out often, and as he had with Roan, Cam's father had welcomed Dare into their lives easily.

Reckless

It was the way Michael Strickland was. Ever since Cam's mother had died unexpectedly, Michael had made a point to show Cam and Cam's sister how much he loved them each and every day. According to Michael, life was short; not a second should be wasted.

And through the years, they'd developed a close relationship filled with mutual respect and love. Michael would even stop by the office just to chat with Roan or Dare or even Teague when Cam wasn't there. Rumor was, Dare was helping Michael to learn sign language so he could communicate with Hudson more effectively as well.

In turn, they'd all forged a bond with him as well.

"How's Teague? Still ornery?"

Cam smiled, turning his head back to face the television. "Not sure he knows how *not* to be ornery."

"I heard there was an altercation down at the marina last weekend."

Cam glanced at his dad again. "How'd you hear about that?"

"Dare. I stopped in to chat yesterday but you weren't there."

Heat infused Cam's face and he turned away again.

For a moment, neither of them said anything, and Cam had to wonder whether Dare had told Cam's father that he was out on a date. Gannon had called at the last minute and offered to take Cam to dinner, insisting they go to a restaurant rather than eat in. Cam had reluctantly agreed, meeting Gannon halfway at a small café.

"Did you have fun?" Michael probed, his gruff tone filled with amusement.

Well, that answered that question.

Cam choked on a laugh. "Yeah."

"Dare said he thinks this one's serious."

Cam shrugged. Serious or not, he wasn't going to explain the details of his relationship with Gannon to his father. Not yet, anyway. Hell, he wasn't even sure how things were going. The last thing he wanted to do was get his father's hopes up.

"I'll take that as a yes," Michael noted.

"I didn't say that," he argued.

"Didn't have to."

Cam didn't look at his father, not sure he wanted to see the concerned look on his face. He pretended to be interested in the television, but that was easier said than done when there was a commercial on.

"Tell me this, Cam."

Cam turned his head again, meeting his father's dark blue gaze, waiting.

"Is he good enough for you?"

Cam couldn't help but smile, turning back to face the TV.

Although they'd had their differences over the years—what parent and child hadn't?—Cam knew that he was lucky to have such a supportive old man. Cam's mother—rest her soul—had been just as understanding, possibly more so up until the day she'd unexpectedly died.

Cam fought the memories, not wanting to be overwhelmed by them. He missed his mother every single day, wished she were there for him to talk to.

"He's good enough," Cam confirmed.

"When do I get to meet him?"

Another smile curved his lips as he kept his eyes on the baseball game. "Don't know."

"Cam…"

Aww, hell. He knew that tone, knew his father was going to say something that would make him want to cry. That's the way it worked. Whenever it came to relationships, his father had his own view on things. It wasn't that Cam didn't understand it. He did. It was just too hard to listen to.

"Dad—"

"Nuh-uh," Michael interrupted. "You listen to me, boy."

Respect for his father had him turning his head once again, staring over at the man who'd spent his entire life taking care of his family, working his ass off, risking his life for the town he loved.

"Don't let one minute pass you by," his father said, tone soft but firm. "You never know what tomorrow'll bring."

No, he didn't. None of them did.

And that was the reason Cam usually kept himself distanced from relationships. He wouldn't survive falling in love with someone only to have them ripped out of his life unexpectedly. He'd watched his own father suffer for years, devastated by his loss. As far as Cam was concerned, his father was the strongest man he knew. His father had survived. How, Cam wasn't exactly sure. But Cam didn't think he could do it.

And with Gannon, Cam feared he was already falling. Much harder, much faster than he'd planned. The idea that one day Gannon might not be in his life, might not be there for Cam to talk to, to tell him how he felt… It scared the ever loving shit out of him.

As much as he wanted to get closer, he was petrified he'd be submerged into the darkness, having to live out the rest of his days alone.

And he damn sure wasn't equipped to do that.

A knock on the door had Cam bouncing up from the couch.

Saved by the pizza guy.

GANNON LAY IN his bed, staring at the ceiling.

It was after ten, and he should've been exhausted, but he couldn't get his brain to shut down. Having spent sixteen hours in the office, watching his engineers scramble to fix another issue found by some of their beta testers, he hadn't had much time to decompress.

The only thing he could think about now was Cam and how he wished he were there with him, sleeping beside him, keeping his mind from working overtime to fix something that was already being handled.

He'd texted Cam earlier, just to check on him, and had received a quick response, letting him know that Cam was having dinner with his dad. Not for the first time, Gannon had wondered what Cam's father was like. If he accepted Cam for who he was, whether or not they had a good relationship. He assumed that was the case since Cam's father had fronted the money for the marina, and from what Gannon could tell, Cam was openly gay.

That didn't mean Cam didn't hide it from his father.

Gannon squeezed his eyes shut, forcing out the thoughts that pummeled him regarding his own family and how they'd disowned him years ago, kicked him out on his ass because he was gay. He didn't want to think about them.

His phone rang, the ringtone he'd set for Cam's number. He lunged for it, snagging it off the nightstand.

"Hey," he said softly.

"Did I wake you?" Cam's deep voice sounded through the phone, calming Gannon almost instantly.

"Nope. Just lying here, thinking about you."

"Are you now?" Cam's chuckle made Gannon smile.

"Yep. How was dinner?"

"Good. Pizza and baseball. Can't beat that."

There was a rustling sound on the other end of the phone.

"What are you doing?" Gannon asked.

"Takin' off my shirt. Now, I'm climbin' into bed."

Gannon's body hardened, his cock twitching to life beneath the thin sheet. "Are you naked?"

Another chuckle from Cam. "Do you want me to be?"

"Yeah. I do." And he wanted Cam to be there with him, but he didn't say as much.

"Hold on."

More rustling, then Cam returned to the phone, his voice softer as he said, "Happy now?"

As happy as he could be without being in the same room with Cam. "Very."

"How was work?" Cam asked.

Gannon reached between his legs, gently caressing his dick, just enough to send a tingling sensation down his spine. "Busy."

"You get the problem fixed?"

"Not yet. Hopefully tomorrow."

"Can I do anything to help?" Cam offered.

Gannon's hand tightened on his dick. "Yeah."

"Tell me."

Damn. The rough, sensual cadence of Cam's voice was the most erotic thing he'd experienced in a long time. Lying in his bed, the room completely dark, with only the sound of Cam breathing through the phone … Gannon wished he were there.

"Talk to me, Gannon. Tell me what I can do." This time, Cam's tone was suggestive.

"Are you covered up?" Gannon asked him.

"Nope."

"Good. I want you to touch yourself."

"How?"

It was clear that Cam wanted Gannon to specify, so he decided to go all in. He'd never had phone sex before, but with Cam, he was damn sure willing to give it a shot.

"Reach down between your legs and massage your balls," Gannon instructed.

Cam's soft groan made every hair on Gannon's body stand on end.

"I wish your mouth was on me," Cam whispered. "I want to feel your lips wrapped around my dick, your hot tongue on my balls."

Fuck. Gannon wanted that, too. "Wrap your hand around your dick and stroke it for me. Slowly."

"Mmm."

"I wish I was there with you," Gannon told him. "Between your legs, my lips and tongue working your cock, teasing you while you watch me."

"Then what would you do?" Cam rasped.

"I'd push your legs up, slide my tongue in your asshole, fucking you. Slowly at first, then faster."

"Fuck," Cam sighed.

"Then, I'd slide my thumb inside you, working your ass open, preparing you to take my cock."

Gannon was stroking his dick insistently now, eyes closed, listening to Cam's rapid breaths through the phone. He could picture himself there with Cam, doing those things to him.

"I want that," Cam said. "So fucking bad."

"I know," Gannon told him. "Are you masturbating for me?"

"Yeah." Cam's breathless moan told Gannon he was close.

"Good. Stroke your beautiful dick for me, Cam. Do you like it rough?"

Cam grunted. "Yeah. Fuck."

"Imagine my lips on your nipples, sucking, biting, pulling them."

"Gannon... Keep talkin'... Don't stop."

"Imagine me kneeling between your legs, holding you open while I ram my dick into your ass, filling you, stretching you."

Another long, tortured moan escaped Cam. Gannon began fisting his cock harder, jerking himself as he thought about fucking Cam's ass, plowing into him, making him scream his name, begging Gannon to let him come.

"While you jack yourself off, I'm fucking you, Cam. Driving my cock deep. Deeper still."

"Goddamn," Cam whispered harshly. "Gannon ... gonna come. Fuck."

"Come for me, Cam." Gannon groaned, his dick pulsing in his hand. "Fuck. Come for me." As he barked the words, his dick jerked, his release barreling down on him. He came in a rush, harder than he'd expected when Cam's muted cry echoed in his ear.

It was the sweetest fucking thing he'd ever heard.

And now, sweating and sated, Gannon wished more than ever that Cam were there with him.

"You still there?" Gannon asked.

"Yeah," Cam whispered. "Still here."

"Have dinner with me and Milly tomorrow night."

"Milly?"

"Yeah," Gannon explained. "We have a standing date each week."

"A date with your assistant?" Cam sounded skeptical.

"She's my friend," Gannon admitted. "And my assistant."

"Sure she won't mind me taggin' along?" Cam inquired.

"She definitely won't mind. But I'm warning you, she'll probably interrogate you."

"I think I can handle her." Cam chuckled softly. "Where?"

"I'd say pizza, but…"

"I'm good with pizza," Cam said quickly. "*Always* good with pizza."

"Pizza it is."

"Not at your place," Cam added.

Gannon knew why Cam had said that. The same reason Gannon had insisted they go out last night. He knew that, given the chance, they would be taking this relationship to the next level. It was clear that Cam was still hesitant, and though Gannon longed to be inside him, to make Cam feel everything Gannon was feeling, he was going to be patient.

"No, not at my place," Gannon agreed. "Meet us in downtown Austin."

"Sounds like a plan."

Gannon hated to get off the phone, but tomorrow would be there before he knew it, and he needed to get a little sleep. Not to mention, tomorrow night, he'd get to see Cam, so that was incentive enough. "Good night, Cam."

Reckless

"Night."

With that, Gannon hung up the phone, cleaned himself up, and drifted off.

Still thinking about Cam.

Seventeen

CAM TUCKED THE check into the deposit bag and shoved it into the top drawer of his desk. He'd spent the last hour dealing with the hot-headed renter who'd insisted that he had paid his storage fee for the month. From the moment the guy had walked through the door, Cam had known he'd been itching for a fight, but Cam hadn't given him one.

Finally, the guy had given up, writing a check though he insisted he'd already written one and Cam had probably just thrown it away—because that was something Cam would do. Right.

Glancing at his watch, he realized he didn't have time to shower, but if he hurried, he would be able to change clothes. Grabbing his phone, Cam headed out, locking the door behind him and then double-timing it up the stairs to his apartment. He'd made it into the hall, was about to unlock his door when Roan stepped out.

"Where're you goin'?" Roan asked, following Cam into his apartment.

"Date," he said, heading to his dresser. He snagged a clean T-shirt, then shrugged out of the one he had been wearing.

"With Burgess?"

"Gannon, yes," Cam said, pulling the clean shirt over his head before pulling open another drawer and locating a pair of cargo shorts.

He dropped his shorts, then tugged on the clean ones, looking up in time to see Roan watching him. For the first time in all the years he'd known Roan, Cam suddenly felt strangely uncomfortable changing clothes in front of him. Was he mistaken? Or was Roan watching him with interest?

Not that Cam had time to question his friend. And he damn sure didn't want to put Roan on the spot if that hadn't been the case.

"Where're y'all goin'?" Roan inquired.

Cam headed for the bathroom, splashed water on his face, swiped more deodorant under his arms, and then returned to find Roan still standing in the doorway, leaning against the jamb. "Pizza."

Roan nodded.

"Did you need somethin'?" Cam asked, grabbing his wallet and truck keys off the coffee table.

"Nah," his friend said.

"I'll catch you later, yeah?" Cam herded Roan out the door, then turned to face his friend.

"Sure."

And as though that strange little encounter hadn't happened, Roan disappeared back into his apartment while Cam ran out the door, down the stairs, and to his truck.

An hour later, Cam walked into a small pizza joint on South Congress in downtown Austin. As soon as he walked in the door, he was assaulted by the delicious scent of garlic and tomato. Scanning the somewhat crowded space, he found Gannon and Milly sitting at a table near the wall.

"Sorry I'm late," he told Gannon, sliding into a chair beside him, across from Milly.

"Problems?" Gannon smiled at him, subtly touching Cam's hand briefly.

"Had to deal with a renter," he explained, glancing between Gannon and Milly. "Took longer than I thought."

"No worries," Milly said cheerfully. "Just means you get one less beer."

Cam smiled, forcing himself to relax.

"I already ordered," Gannon said. "Assume you like pepperoni."

Cam nodded, noticing Milly was looking at them intently, her smile widening.

"Care to share with the class?" he prompted, looking over at Gannon briefly, then back to her.

"Nope. I'm good." Milly's blue eyes glittered and she giggled.

Cam looked at Gannon. Gannon shrugged.

"So..." Milly prompted, wrapping her fingers around her beer bottle. "Gannon tells me you've got your nipples pierced."

Gannon choked on his beer, and Cam had to reach over and smack him on the back.

"Kidding," she said, laughing. "I knew before he did."

Cam stared at her, confused.

"I could see 'em through your shirt."

"Ahh."

"Wanna beer?" Gannon asked, his voice strained from his coughing spell.

"I can get it," Cam told him.

"No, no. I'll let Milly embarrass me while I'm *not* here for a change."

Milly winked at Gannon.

177

Reckless

When Gannon walked away from the table, Milly leaned forward, her expression morphing from carefree to serious. "What are your intentions with my friend?"

Cam sat up straight, trying to determine if he really needed to prepare an answer, but before he could, her smile returned.

"Gosh, you're easy. Or so Gannon says."

Cam laughed at that. He'd liked Milly from the beginning, but he liked her more now. It was obvious she cared about Gannon.

Leaning forward, Cam adopted a somber expression. When Milly leaned in close, clearly expecting him to lay something serious on her, he said, "Do you want to hear dirty details?"

Her laugh exploded from her, causing people to turn and look at them. Including Gannon, who was watching them from the counter.

"I like you," Milly told him. "I think you're good for him. Did you know he hadn't taken a day off for years? Not until last weekend. That, my friend, tells me a lot about you."

"Does it?" he asked, glancing over when Gannon returned to the table, three beers in his hand.

Cam took one and passed it to Milly, then took another.

"Yes, it does," she answered, winking.

"It does what?" Gannon's brow furrowed, as though he were trying to unravel a mystery.

"Oh, nothing. I was just telling him about your collection of sex toys. He wanted to know how one of them worked. I was just explaining."

Cam peered over at Gannon, watching as his cheeks flushed and the tips of his ears reddened.

"Why did I think this was a good idea?" Gannon mumbled to himself.

"Because you love me," Milly told him.

Gannon tilted his beer to his lips. "Or so you keep telling me."

Yep, this was bound to get interesting.

GANNON SPENT NEARLY two hours listening to Milly regale Cam with stories. Luckily, after her initial teasing, she'd stopped trying to embarrass him too much.

So, he'd spent most of his time listening to Milly and Cam talk about their ski trips. Apparently that was something Cam had done since he was a kid, and Milly's family used to go every year. Instead of feeling like a third wheel, Gannon had been relaxed, enjoying the easiness between them, the way Cam was frequently looking his way, sometimes brushing against him on purpose just to get his attention.

"No lie," Milly insisted, her eyes locked on Cam. "I was racing down the hill and ran smack into the tree."

Gannon frowned. "That's not the way you told the story to me."

Milly glared at him in a way that told him to be quiet.

Gannon laughed; so did Cam.

"Fine," Milly said with a huff. "I didn't so much ski down the hill. I kind of walked. And I didn't run into the tree. I hugged it to keep on my feet. But I was ten. Sue me."

Cam roared with laughter, making Gannon smile and Milly blush.

Going into this, Gannon hadn't known how it would go, but truth was, Gannon wanted Milly and Cam to get along. She was the closest thing to family he had, and over the past couple of weeks, Cam had become important to him, as well. Looked as though he wasn't going to have to worry about the two of them getting along.

"Thanks for putting up with me tonight," Milly told Cam as they walked down the sidewalk toward the parking lot behind the restaurant.

"Thanks for sharing all of Gannon's deep dark secrets with me," Cam replied, smiling down at her.

"Okay, I'm gonna hug you now," Milly said right before she walked up to Cam and put her arms around him.

Gannon grinned, watching Cam's surprise flitter across his face as he hesitantly embraced her.

"And now, I'm gonna go sit in the car"—Milly snagged the car keys from Gannon's hand—"while the two of you say good night."

With a small wave, she headed across the lot to Gannon's Lexus while he stood with Cam beside his truck.

When he turned back to face Cam, those dark blue eyes were locked on him. Thankfully, it was dark out and the single light post was on the other side of the lot, the yellow glow not making it to their part, which left them in the shadows. It afforded them a small measure of privacy, so Gannon urged Cam between his truck and the one beside it, backing him up against the driver's door.

"I had fun tonight," Gannon whispered. "But I can't walk away without kissing you."

Cam nodded but didn't say anything.

"Is that gonna bother you? Me kissing you in public?"

"Will it bother you?" Cam countered.

Gannon answered that question by leaning in and pressing his mouth to Cam's, placing his hand on the truck door on the side of Cam's head. He licked Cam's lips first, then urged him to open. A soft moan escaped Cam seconds before Gannon was crushing Cam's body against the door, his hips pressing against Cam's while their tongues explored.

Had they been anywhere else, Gannon would've pursued it further, but being in a public place, he knew he couldn't let it get too far. As it was, his cock was rock hard by the time he pulled back, breaking the kiss and pressing his forehead to Cam's.

"I want to see you again," Gannon whispered.

"When?"

Pulling back, Gannon moved back enough so he could see Cam's face fully. "I'm leaving for California in the morning."

And just like that, it was as though Gannon had poured a bucket of ice water over Cam's head rather than telling him that he had to go out of town for a couple of days. The heat he'd seen in Cam's eyes turned glacial in an instant.

"What?" Gannon asked, taking a step back when Cam turned to open his truck door. "What's wrong?"

"Nothing," Cam declared, his tone icy.

Gannon watched as Cam climbed into his truck, confused.

"I need to get home," Cam told him, turning his head toward Gannon but not meeting his eyes.

"Okay." Gannon didn't even know how to plead his case, because he had no clue what had just happened. One second Cam was melting in his arms, the next he was … Antarctica. "I'll call you?"

Cam nodded, then waited for Gannon to move out of the way before closing the door and starting his engine. Still trying to figure out where things had gone wrong, Gannon didn't move as Cam backed out of the parking space, then headed for the road.

When he finally made it back to the car, Milly was waiting for him, the radio turned up. Since he had no idea what had happened, or how he was supposed to explain it to her, he forced a smile as he slid into the driver's seat.

"That was fun," she told him, briefly looking at him before returning her attention to her cell phone.

"Yeah," he said, putting his hand on the gear shift. "Fun."

Eighteen

Friday night

"WHERE'S YOUR MAN?" Dare asked, pointing his beer bottle at Cam, clearly letting him know he was talking to him.

Cam didn't say anything, preoccupying himself by drinking his own beer.

"Uh-oh," Teague offered. "Trouble in paradise?"

Cam's gaze slid to Roan. He found his best friend studying him intently.

"No trouble," Cam said, merely to get them off his case.

"He's in Cali, right?" Dare asked.

Cam nodded.

He did not want to think about Gannon at the moment. Didn't want to think about him several states away, where Cam couldn't see him. Didn't want to let his fears get the best of him.

Last night, when Gannon had reminded him that he was going to California, something had broken inside him. One minute his switch had been on, the next ... off. He'd driven home in a fog, numb from the information. And most of the day, he'd attempted to process it, to no avail.

Reckless

He knew he owed Gannon an apology. His abrupt turnabout had been unfair. He couldn't deny that. But he couldn't bring himself to answer his phone or return any of Gannon's texts, either.

No one said he was acting rationally, but the only thing he could think about was Gannon in Florida. No. Not Florida. California.

Cam took a long pull on his beer, trying to dislodge the knot of emotion from his throat. He'd been choking on it all damn day while endless questions ran through his head.

What if something happened to Gannon?

What if he was sick?

What if he had a brain aneurysm and died while alone in his hotel room?

His throat was dry, his palms sweaty. He was choking on the hot ball of fear that seemed to be permanently lodged in his throat. Cam drained what was left of his beer, then grabbed another.

No, he wasn't going to think about any of that.

Hell, it was bad enough that he'd had a nightmare last night, waking up in a cold sweat. He'd dreamed that someone had called him to let him know that Gannon's body had been found in a hotel room. He'd died of a brain aneurysm.

The same way Cam's mother had died. Hundreds of miles away. Alone.

"When's he comin' back?" Teague asked.

"Tomorrow," Roan offered, meeting Cam's gaze.

"Can we talk about somethin' else? Seriously?" Cam didn't want to dwell on this anymore.

Sure, he'd missed a call from Gannon earlier, and he'd received a few texts, but at the moment, he wasn't in the right frame of mind to talk to him or about him. Shitty as it was.

"Dude," Dare began with a smile, "did y'all see that hot guy who came to talk to Hudson today?"

Grateful for the change of subject, Cam watched Teague's head snap over to Dare and had the urge to rub his own neck. That had to hurt.

"When?" Roan asked the question Teague clearly wanted to ask but didn't.

"This mornin' sometime. Holy fuck." Dare let out a long, low whistle. "Not sure what they were talkin' about, but Hudson looked happy."

Cam couldn't help but notice that Teague did not. Look happy. Not at all.

"Looks like the dry spell might be over," Dare added. "At least for some of us."

Cam looked away when Dare pinned him with his hazel gaze. He wasn't going to confirm or deny that. At this point, he didn't know how things stood between him and Gannon.

Sure, they'd rocketed out of the gate, hot and heavy, and he'd enjoyed the hell out of the time he'd spent with Gannon. But now … his fears had gotten the best of him.

As he'd always known they would.

And though he'd traveled himself, that didn't bother him. It was when the people he cared about ventured out on their own, leaving Cam at home to worry whether they'd ever come back again.

He could still remember that horrible day, sixteen years ago.

"When's Mom coming home?" Holly asked, passing the green beans over to Cam.

Reckless

Looking up at his father, Cam waited, trying to do the math in his head. She'd left yesterday? Or the day before? He wasn't sure. His mother took frequent trips for her job, so having her away had become the norm for them. Sometimes to the point that they didn't get the details of the trip.

"Tomorrow afternoon," his father told him, sipping his iced tea.

"Did you talk to her today?" Holly asked. "Is she having fun in Florida?"

Michael shook his head. "Not yet." The smile on his face said he looked forward to hearing from her. "She's having dinner with some colleagues."

"Well, hopefully she got to go to the beach," Holly said, stuffing chicken into her mouth. "I've always wanted to go to Florida."

For the next few minutes, Cam listened to his sister ramble on and on about how great Florida was and how cool it would be to visit. How one day, when she got married, she wanted to have her honeymoon at Disney World.

"Who's got the dishes tonight?" Cam's father asked when they finished their meal.

"It's my turn." Holly frowned.

"Good. Cam, help your sister clear the table. I'll be in the living room."

Cam nodded, then began stacking the plates. As he was placing them on the counter beside the sink, there was a knock at the door.

Glancing over at his sister, he lifted an eyebrow, silently asking if she was expecting someone.

Holly shook her head.

Wiping his hand on a dish towel, Cam went to the bar that separated the kitchen from the living room, watching as his father made his way over to the front door. After a quick look through the security hole, Michael glanced back, meeting Cam's eyes.

That was when Cam knew something was very, very wrong.

With his heart in his throat, Cam stood there as his father opened the door to reveal two uniformed officers standing on the porch.

Cam recognized them as a couple of guys his dad worked with. He couldn't imagine what they'd be doing there. It wasn't their regularly scheduled poker night, and not once had Cam ever seen them show up in uniform.

Afraid to move from his spot, Cam stood in the doorway, straining to hear what they were saying, but their voices were too low. When his father's legs gave out and the two officers reached for him, holding him up, Cam knew that the news they'd brought hadn't been good.

"What's going on?" Holly whispered, coming to stand next to Cam.

He shrugged.

Before he could stop her, Holly took off toward their father.

"Daddy, what's wrong?"

Michael muttered something, and when Holly turned to look back at him, Cam wasn't sure he wanted to know what he'd said. His sister's eyes widened, her chin trembled, and then she screamed, a horrible sound that had echoed through the entire house. When she crumpled into a heap, one of the officers managed to grab her, easing her down onto the couch.

Cam waited, his heart pounding in his throat. He didn't want to know what they'd said. If he didn't know, whatever it was hadn't happened.

"Cam," Bruce Derby said, moving toward him.

Cam shook his head adamantly. Whatever it was, he didn't want to know.

Bruce's eyes were sad. "It's your mom."

Cam's heart stopped beating at that moment.

"She didn't come into the office this morning. After a few hours, they got worried, so they sent one of her coworkers over to her hotel to check on her."

Cam's chest began to burn. He wasn't breathing.

"They found her—" Bruce swallowed hard, then cleared his throat. "They found her body. Medical examiner said she'd suffered a brain aneurysm."

From that point on, everything in Cam's memory was a blur. At least for the few days that followed.

His mother had been away on business.

Alone in a hotel room.

And she'd died.

They'd never gotten to say good-bye.

"HOW'S CAM?" MILLY asked, joining Gannon at the hotel bar. "Hear from him today?"

Gannon shook his head, wrapping his hands around the tumbler of scotch sitting in front of him.

The bartender strolled over and Milly rattled off her order before turning to face him.

"Talk to me," she encouraged.

That was when Gannon accepted that the woman sitting beside him wasn't his assistant, the woman who'd flown to California with him early that morning so they could spend a couple of days working on the marketing plan for the next game rollout. No, sitting beside him now was Milly, his friend. The woman who knew more about him than anyone on the planet.

"I tried calling, but he didn't answer," he admitted.

"Did you text?" she asked, thanking the bartender when he delivered her apple martini.

"Yeah."

"And?"

Gannon lifted his head, looking directly at her. "I think he's got an issue with me traveling."

"Why do you think that?" she questioned, sipping her drink and blowing her bangs out of her face.

"Last night…" God, he didn't even know how to explain what he didn't understand. "Last night, after you went to the car, I was saying good night. Things were fine. Right up to the point I reminded him I had to come here. To California. Then it was weird. He just shut down, retreating into himself. Just like the last time."

"*The last time*?" Milly's ice-blue gaze settled on Gannon's face.

"The first time I mentioned that I travel, he acted … strange."

"You think maybe he's just worried about you?"

Gannon shook his head. He tried to see that angle, but he didn't think that was it. It was more than that.

"Didn't you say his mom died?" Milly took another sip of her drink, crossing her legs and adjusting her skirt.

Nodding, he lifted his glass to his lips.

"How'd she die?"

Gannon shrugged. He didn't know.

189

"Ever thought maybe you should ask him?"

Of course he had. He'd wanted to ask Cam, but after that first night, when he'd seen the sadness that had dimmed the light in Cam's eyes, he hadn't wanted to risk seeing that again.

"Want me to ask him for you?" Milly's chipper tone said she'd do it in a heartbeat if he let her.

Gannon's head snapped up, his eyes slamming into her face. "Don't you dare."

The smile she shot him was mischievous.

"I'm never letting the two of you in the same room together again," he noted.

"Well, that's good. 'Cause I've got a lot of questions for him. Last night, I was just being nice."

"Like?" Gannon knew he shouldn't encourage her, but what the hell. He was sitting at a hotel bar in California, and he wasn't going back to Texas until tomorrow afternoon. Cam wasn't answering his phone, so there was nothing stopping him from getting blind drunk at the bar and hashing out his problems with his closest friend.

"For one, why the hell hasn't he jumped your bones yet?"

Gannon was grateful he hadn't been taking a drink. He would've shot it out of his nose.

"And I'd ask him if he has any hot *straight* friends."

"He doesn't," Gannon told her.

"And how do you know that?"

"Because I've met his friends."

"And they're all gay?" Milly didn't sound convinced.

"The ones I've met, yeah."

"Well, shit." Milly grinned, lifting her glass to her lips.

Gannon chuckled.

"Did you tell him about your parents?" Milly inquired a moment later, her tone less enthusiastic.

"Not yet."

"But you plan to, right?"

"Eventually."

"So, all this take-things-slow crap, I thought it meant with the sex. But clearly the two of you haven't shared some important details."

"We're getting there." At least Gannon had thought they were.

"Well, don't get all freaked out," Milly told him, patting his thigh. "You've only known the guy for two weeks. I'm sure he's just got something going on and that's why he hasn't answered."

He hoped she was right, but he didn't say as much.

"So, I think it's time you put that dopey grin back on your face and buy me another drink."

"Another?" Gannon grinned; he couldn't help it.

"Of course. You didn't think I was gonna buy my own drinks tonight, did you? Just because you're gay doesn't mean you get to take a lady out and let her pay her own way."

Gannon laughed, as he knew Milly expected him to. She was really something else.

And that was one of the many reasons he loved her.

Nineteen

CAM RUBBED HIS face, narrowing his eyes to look at his alarm clock.

Two twenty in the morning.

Who could possibly be calling him?

Grabbing his cell phone, he read the blurry information on the screen and swallowed hard.

Gannon.

For a moment, he considered not answering it, but his need to know that Gannon was all right won out, and he hit the talk button. "'Lo?"

"Cam?"

"Hmm?"

"Did I wake you?" There was a slight slurring to Gannon's words.

"Yeah," he told him, rolling onto his back.

"Sorry. I just needed to hear your voice."

Cam squeezed his eyes shut. He had no clue what to say to that. Ever since he'd come back to his apartment after having beers with the guys down by the lake, he hadn't been able to stop thinking about Gannon. Wondering what he was doing. Worrying that something had happened.

"Did I do something wrong?" Gannon asked, the concern in his tone making Cam's chest ache.

"No," he finally said, releasing the air from his lungs. "You haven't."

Silence greeted him, and they sat there like that for a few minutes until finally Gannon's voice filled his ear.

"I miss you," Gannon whispered.

Cam swallowed past that knot that was still blocking his airway. "I miss you, too."

He knew he should've told Gannon about his reason for being so standoffish, but the truth was, he didn't want to do it while Gannon was away on business. He didn't want to think about how fucked up his world would be if Gannon didn't come home.

He'd survived his mother dying in a hotel room, hundreds of miles away from home on a routine business trip. He didn't know if he could survive it again.

And yes, he knew it was illogical. Lightning didn't strike in the same place twice, or so the theory went, so surely Cam wouldn't have to endure it more than once. But still. His rational brain didn't hold a candle to the overpowering fear.

"Can I see you on Sunday?" Gannon asked. "Dinner at my place?"

Cam squeezed his eyes shut again, his chest feeling so full of emotion he wasn't sure what he was supposed to do with it. Somehow, he managed to force the words out, "I'd like that."

"Okay," Gannon said. "I'll let you go."

"'Kay," Cam agreed.

"Cam…"

"Hmm?"

"I really do miss you."

"Yeah. Me, too." *More than you know.*

After hanging up, Cam rolled over onto his side and stared into the darkness.

Over and over, his mind continued to replay Gannon's words, spoken in that smooth, sensual tone.

"He's coming back," he said aloud, trying to reassure himself, something he'd done numerous times throughout the day.

Well, that wasn't completely true.

For a few hours that morning, Cam had tried to convince himself that this thing between him and Gannon was over. That he could walk away now that they were apart for a couple of days and he wouldn't have to look back.

Only that was when he'd realized he was in deeper than he'd thought.

Much deeper.

Two weeks with Gannon had been like a lifetime. During that time, he'd felt so much for the man. Far more than he'd wanted to. But somehow, Gannon had broken right through Cam's defenses, and here he was, anticipating the moment he would get to see him again.

Closing his eyes, Cam gave in to the mental exhaustion, but not before he whispered once more into the darkness, repeating the words that were now imprinted on his brain.

"He's coming back."

WHILE GANNON LAY in his hotel room, staring at the ceiling, he was glad he'd finally given in to Milly's insistence that he try to call Cam again.

Hearing his voice... God, he'd never tire of hearing Cam's voice.

It had soothed something inside him, made him feel whole once again.

Truth was, he'd been tempted to go to the airport, hop on the first flight back to Texas, and go straight to Cam's to confront him. He still didn't know what was bothering Cam, but he honestly believed it had something to do with him traveling.

Was he worried Gannon was going to cheat on him?

He could easily assure him that would never happen. Not only because he didn't want anyone else but because that wasn't the way he was programmed. Perhaps that was because Gannon had rarely allowed anyone to get close to him. After he'd been shunned by his own parents, it hadn't been easy for him to get close to people. Other than Milly, Gannon hadn't had any close friends through the years.

And maybe that was why he'd buried himself in work. He could keep his relationships impersonal.

But then Cam had walked right into his world.

Well, technically, it was the other way around, but from the moment Gannon had looked into those blue eyes … he'd been lost.

He would never cheat on Cam. Never.

Other than that, though, he couldn't understand why Cam would try to push him away. They'd been doing well, or so he'd thought. Sure, he noticed that when things moved too fast, Cam started to back off a little, but Gannon understood that. Getting too close, too fast... That could easily blow up in their faces.

However, that didn't explain why Gannon thought the two were related. Cam distancing himself for fear of getting too close, along with his obvious distaste for Gannon traveling.

Somehow they were connected. But for the life of him, he didn't know how.

Reckless

Worse than that ... Gannon was scared shitless to ask. Because he had his own fears.

It all boiled down to the fact that he was hooked on Cam already. Probably had been since the day he'd met him. Falling deeper and deeper with every passing second.

And it was killing him now, knowing that Cam was pushing him away.

Sure, Cam had every right to be cautious, but what Cam didn't seem to realize was that Gannon had fears of his own.

His number one fear...

Gannon feared that Cam would abandon him.

And he'd have to live through hell all over again.

Twenty

SOMEHOW, CAM HAD managed to make it through the weekend. Work had kept him busy all day Saturday, which had helped. When Gannon's text had finally come in, letting him know that he'd made it home safe and sound, a boulder had been lifted from his chest.

If only things could go back to the way they'd been before Gannon had left for his trip. Unfortunately, Cam had fucked it up too much, and he knew he owed Gannon an explanation.

Which was why he was pacing his living room, counting down the minutes until he had to leave to go to Gannon's.

A knock sounded at his door and he stopped suddenly. "Come in."

Expecting to see Roan, Cam felt his heart miss a beat when the door opened and Gannon stuck his head in.

"Hey," Gannon greeted.

"What are you doin' here?" Cam asked, the words rushing out of him.

"I…" Gannon's smile seemed fragile. "I wanted to see you."

Cam nodded, processing those words. "But I was supposed to come to your house."

"I know, but I was impatient." Gannon held up a bag. "So I brought dinner to you."

Snapping out of it, relieved to see Gannon, regardless of where they were, he erased the distance between them. Without hesitating, he cradled Gannon's face in his hands and gently pressed his lips to Gannon's. He didn't try for more, content to feel the stubble along his jaw, his soft lips, his breath against his face.

Finally, after several seconds, he pulled back, keeping his eyes locked with Gannon's. "What did you bring?"

Gannon held out the bag for Cam to take, then closed the door behind him. Opening it, he peered inside. Laughing, he looked up at Gannon.

"You said pizza is always good," Gannon noted.

"I did. But this is frozen pizza."

For the first time since he'd walked in, Gannon finally smiled, and Cam felt the tension in his chest break.

"Look under it," Gannon instructed.

Moving the small box out of the way, he found a can of chicken noodle soup.

"You want *me* to make *you* dinner?" Cam inquired, grinning.

"I thought you'd never ask," Gannon answered, stepping forward. "But if you don't want to, that's okay, because I stopped down at the restaurant. Jeremy's making burgers and fries."

Of course he was. Gannon was always thinking ahead. Something Cam found incredibly attractive.

"You wanna eat down there?" Cam asked.

Gannon shook his head. "Not really. But if you want to get drinks, I'll run down there and grab the food."

"I can do that."

Gannon slipped out the door, and Cam headed for the refrigerator, his heart still racing. He still couldn't believe Gannon was there, that he'd come to see him. Even though he had every right to be pissed at Cam for how Cam had acted, he was there.

Cam swallowed hard.

He shoved the frozen pizza into the freezer, then set the canned soup on the counter before retrieving two beers. He placed them on the coffee table, then went to the bathroom to splash cold water on his face. He wasn't sure why he was nervous, but he was. Seeing Gannon … although it was a relief, there was still friction there.

Cam knew that the only way to move forward was to explain to Gannon why he'd reacted so irrationally. He'd never explained it to anyone before. Only his closest friends—Roan and Dare—knew what had happened. Reliving that day, it fucked up his head every time.

But Cam knew Gannon deserved the truth. He deserved to know that Cam couldn't change who he was and he couldn't promise he wouldn't freak out in the future. The panic attacks made him do crazy things.

The only thing he could hope was that Gannon understood and that they could figure out a way to move forward.

One way or another.

Reckless

A COUPLE OF hours later, after they'd had dinner and watched a sitcom on television, Cam had convinced Gannon to go back to the spot where they'd first gone skinny-dipping. Reluctantly, Gannon had agreed, but he'd been relieved when Cam promised they wouldn't be swimming tonight.

Now, as they sat on the sandy shore, drinking beer and watching the lights in the distance, Gannon managed to relax.

"I need to tell you something," Cam said softly, causing Gannon to look at him. He was sitting, knees up, wrists resting on his knees, beer bottle dangling from his fingers.

Okay, so Gannon had been relaxed. Now, not so much.

Rather than say anything, Gannon allowed Cam to continue.

"When you went to California…"

Gannon waited, his breath lodged in his chest. He had no idea where this was going or what Cam was going to say or ask, but he managed to keep his mouth shut, his throat working overtime as he swallowed past the dryness.

"I shouldn't've freaked out and I shouldn't've ignored you," Cam admitted, and Gannon released the air from his lungs. "I told you my mother died."

When Cam looked over at him, Gannon nodded, hoping to encourage him to keep talking.

"My mother worked for a local tech company. She traveled to other locations, training people. From what I remember, she was gone several times a month, sometimes a few days, sometimes a week or more at a time."

Cam lifted his beer to his lips and Gannon tried not to stare at him.

Bringing the bottle back down by his legs, Cam continued, "When I was sixteen, she went down to Florida. Regular trip, supposed to be gone a couple of days."

Gannon swallowed hard, fearing where this was going.

"She never came home." Cam paused, took a few breaths. "A couple of the cops showed up at the house to let us know they'd found her body in a hotel room."

"Brain aneurysm," Gannon said softly, remembering Cam's explanation of how she'd died.

Cam nodded, staring out at the water. "She died alone. And though they said it was probably quick, I still can't imagine what it would've been like to be alone like that."

So Cam's fear wasn't about Gannon cheating. It was about Gannon leaving and never coming back. Gannon could've explained to Cam that the traveling had nothing to do with it, that his mother had died of a brain aneurysm, that it had ruptured. It would've happened whether she was on a trip or at home. Either way, Cam would've lost his mother.

But he didn't say that because it wouldn't have helped.

Placing a hand on Cam's shoulder, Gannon squeezed lightly. He knew there weren't any words that could make it any easier, no matter how he tried to rationalize it. Even all these years later.

So, instead of offering empty platitudes or random explanations, Gannon decided to share his own secret. "A few weeks before my seventeenth birthday," Gannon began, taking a sip of his beer and swallowing hard, "I remember sitting in my bedroom, talking on the phone with this guy I'd met at school. His name was Chad. I'd met him in my math class that year.

Reckless

"We'd hung out after school a couple of times and had just started talking on the phone. Endless hours of conversation about everything and nothing. Thought I was in love with him. First boy I'd felt that way about and I knew I had to tell my parents. I wanted them to support me."

Gannon didn't look at Cam when he felt Cam's eyes sliding over his face.

"Chad had warned me not to say anything, but Chad was a senior, and we'd been talking about prom. I wanted to go to prom with him so badly that was all I could think about. Not that it would've been a good idea either way. It wasn't like either of us were out, but I wasn't thinking about that. Here was this guy who was giving me all his attention, and I was soaking it up like a sponge.

"Anyway, when I got off the phone with Chad, I went to the kitchen, where I knew my father would be reading the paper and my mother would be going through the monthly bills. I'd been so hyped from that phone call I didn't think twice about telling my parents why I was smiling when they asked."

Gannon drained what was left of his beer.

"God, I remember my mother's face. She was horrified. But my father… He went off the rails. I'd spent so much time thinking about that conversation, about telling my parents that I was gay. I guess I'd come up with my own ending to that story. A happy one, where they embraced me and told me that they were proud of me and that they loved me for who I was, no matter what." Gannon grunted. "I'd been a dreamer, because that night, my worst fears were realized. They told me that I was an abomination, that I needed some help. My mother mentioned treatment, and my father harped on religion.

"I told them there wasn't anything to fix, I wasn't broken. But when I refused to go to the church so they could try and exorcise the demons, they told me to get out and never come back. So, I calmly went to my bedroom, pulled out my suitcase, packed as much of my shit as I could take with me, and I left. Walked two blocks over to my friend's house and asked to sleep on his couch. Haven't seen my parents, or my brother, since."

In a sense, Gannon knew how Cam felt. He'd been abandoned by his parents, and though Cam's mother hadn't had the choice, from Cam's perspective, she'd left him. Different but the same.

"It's not easy for me to trust people," Gannon told Cam. He needed him to understand that it wasn't easy for him when Cam tried to push him away. "I'm not ashamed of who I am. From that day on, when I walked out of my parents' house, I made a promise that I'd be true to myself. No hiding. Not from them and certainly not from myself. But I had learned a huge lesson. I'd learned that even though some people claimed to love you for you, sometimes the version of you they loved wasn't real. It was merely the version they could live with. And it only took one revelation for them to turn their backs."

Clearing his throat, Gannon broke out of his thoughts and glanced down at the ground. "I try not to give too much of myself, for fear I'll be left to pick up the pieces again. Alone."

Cam didn't say anything, so Gannon stopped talking. He'd cut himself open and bled for this man at this point. If Cam couldn't deal with Gannon as he was, he wasn't sure there was anything else he could do to convince him. They'd taken things slow, and Gannon didn't have a problem with that. He didn't want to rush this. It was that important to him.

Cam was that important to him.

But he wasn't going to be with someone who cared about the version of him they could live with. He needed to know that when things got tough, he could depend on Cam.

Because at this point, Gannon was fairly certain he was in love with the man.

Twenty-One

One week later

WITH ANOTHER WEEK behind him, another Saturday under his belt, Cam was looking forward to an afternoon out on the lake. Sundays were usually busy enough to keep all of them working, but this one was slower than normal, and Cam had convinced Dare to manage the few appointments they had for the afternoon so Cam could get Gannon out on the water again.

It'd been a long week, and they needed to do something fun, to take some time to relax and enjoy. Without all the stress of work, without the constant friction caused by Cam's fears. Even though they'd talked it out, things had still been tense between them all week.

Reckless

Ever since the night Gannon had called him from California, letting Cam know that he missed him, Cam had been thinking about him often. About whether they should move forward, see where this took them. Whether or not it was time for them to take things to the next level, because if they did go forward, that was inevitable—seriously, the sexual tension between them was like a dry twig folded in half, ready to break at any second. But mostly, Cam had been thinking how relieved he'd been to share one of his deepest fears with someone and not be judged. Knowing Gannon had been in California, Cam had nearly come undone. And it hadn't been until Gannon had landed back in Texas a week ago that he'd released the breath he'd been holding for the two days Gannon had been gone.

Still, it was more than that. The fact that he'd been scared enough to run from Gannon meant he had feelings for him. This wasn't casual anymore.

"What's up, bro?"

Cam looked up to see Teague darting through the office.

"Where're you off to?" Cam hollered.

"Gotta go see a man about a thing."

Cam had no idea what that meant, nor did he bother to ask; instead, he pulled out the appointment book and scanned through the next week, his thoughts drifting back to Gannon.

It all came down to the fact that Cam missed him. More than he even cared to admit to himself, but more than he could deny. Although work had been hectic for both of them, they'd managed to spend several hours together over the course of the week since Gannon had gone to California. It had helped. Some. And when they couldn't see each other, they'd talked on the phone late at night when Gannon got home, even texted throughout the day, but still, Thursday night had been the last time Cam had seen Gannon, and he was ready for more.

Because they both knew their relationship was escalating rapidly, they'd opted to keep playing it safe during the week, going to dinner out rather than eating in. Gannon had taken Cam to an Indian restaurant on Monday—apparently one of Gannon's favorites—and Cam had been schooled on curries and spices. All in all, Cam hadn't hated it. It wasn't his favorite, either. Then, on Tuesday night, Cam had taken Gannon to Chuy's, his favorite Mexican food restaurant in Austin. And on Friday night, they'd agreed to compromise with pizza again.

Although that night had been awkward. Milly and some wannabe rock star she was dating had met them at a popular downtown Austin restaurant that boasted live music as well as good food. The guy had come off as a narcissistic asshole, and Cam was fairly certain Milly had decided she'd had enough of him.

Still, Cam had had a good time because he'd been with Gannon.

The *bing* of the door notification system had Cam looking up from the appointment book he was reviewing for the following week. A smile split his face as soon as he saw Gannon, looking pretty damn edible in shorts and a navy blue T-shirt.

"Are those…" Cam laughed as he looked at Gannon's feet.

"Flip-flops." Gannon lifted his foot, showing them off. "Like 'em?"

Cam moved around the counter so he could get closer to Gannon. He kissed him on the mouth, still smiling. "I'm impressed."

That adorable dimple in Gannon's cheek winked back at him.

"I thought you might be. So, what's the plan?"

"Jet skis."

The horrified look that took the place of the smile that had been there previously made Cam laugh.

"You're gonna be fine," Cam told Gannon. "Come on."

Taking Gannon's hand, Cam led him through the marina office and out the back door, then down to the slip where they kept their personal watercraft. He'd convinced Dare to let Gannon borrow his since Cam's was supercharged and likely too powerful for Gannon's first time out.

After a quick lesson on what levers did what, and helping Gannon into a life jacket, Cam mounted his own jet ski while Gannon got into position on Dare's. It was cute watching Gannon try to look calm when it was obvious his head was about to explode.

"You're gonna be fine," Cam assured him.

"Can I get that in writing?" Gannon retorted, his words terse.

Yep, he was definitely nervous.

For the first half hour, Cam took it slow with Gannon, helping him to learn how to navigate the wake, to speed up, slow down, make wide turns. He'd basically done the same for Gannon that he did for any of the clients who were new to the water sport. And because he liked the way Gannon watched him, Cam showed off a little.

But then, fueled by adrenaline, sunshine, and simply being close to Gannon, Cam could no longer contain the energy that throbbed in his veins. Telling Gannon that he'd be back, Cam opened the throttle and took off, soaring across the water, controlling the powerful machine between his thighs. Twice he encountered a couple of guys who wanted to race, but Cam shrugged them off. And when he returned to Gannon, finding him rocketing across the water on his own, he felt his spirits lift even more.

"Wanna race?" Cam challenged when Gannon made his way back around.

"Not a chance," Gannon said with a strained laugh. "I'm doing my best not to fall in the damn water as it is."

"Chicken," Cam teased.

He saw the spark in Gannon's eyes, a banked flame that flickered at the dare. Yeah, Gannon wasn't as level-headed as he wanted everyone to believe.

Cam pointed to a buoy far off in the distance. "Down there and back."

Gannon studied the distance, probably mentally calculating how long it would take to get there and back while Cam continued to tease him.

"Fine," Gannon huffed.

Feeling that renewed spark deep in his gut, Cam pulled up next to Gannon. "Loser cooks dinner for the winner."

"Deal." Gannon flashed a smile. "I'm a damn good cook."

Cam laughed, then counted down from three. He gave Gannon a slight head start, but once again, when Gannon was several yards in front of him, Cam opened the machine up and roared past the buoy and then back, leaving Gannon behind in his wake.

Slowing the machine, he coasted back to their starting point, smiling. This was what he'd been missing. A few hours out on the water, letting loose... It was just what he needed.

As he turned back around to watch Gannon, thinking about what Gannon would be making him for dinner and when, Cam's heart stopped beating in his chest. There, probably twenty yards in front of him, was the jet ski Gannon had been sitting on only seconds before, bouncing around on the waves.

Without a rider.

With his heart in his throat, Cam took off, scanning the lake for Gannon. The roaring of his blood in his ears finally stopped when he saw Gannon clinging to the life jacket near the jet ski, hair plastered to his head, a frown on his handsome face.

"You okay?" Cam called out to him as he moved closer, looking Gannon over to ensure he wasn't hurt.

"Do I *look* okay?" Gannon retorted, and the grumpy expression made Cam laugh.

As he sat there, preparing to help Gannon up onto his jet ski, Cam realized something: In the short span of nearly three weeks, he was pretty damn sure he'd fallen partially in love with Gannon.

And he didn't think it would take a whole hell of a lot more to get him in all the way.

GANNON WASN'T SURE how he'd let Cam talk him into this.

He hated the fucking water.

Granted, it hadn't been *too* bad when he'd been *on* the jet ski. In fact, there for a few minutes, he'd even enjoyed himself, getting the hang of it when Cam had taken off.

Perhaps he'd been a little overly confident when he'd agreed to race Cam, but he hadn't been able to tell the man no when he'd been smiling like that.

No, he hadn't thought he would beat him, but he had expected to be able to keep up, at least. He'd realized right away that Cam had given him a head start, but still, when Cam had shot past him, Gannon had laughed, a giddy feeling racing through him. But the moment he was launched into the water after bouncing over a wave, he'd remembered once again that he still hated the water.

Now, as he kept himself afloat—thankful for the life jacket—while Cam eased his jet ski closer, he was preparing to retaliate.

"Give me your hand," Cam hollered, reaching out to him.

Gannon clasped Cam's wrist with one hand, then the other, but instead of allowing Cam to pull him closer to the jet ski, he yanked as hard as he could, pulling Cam into the water with him. They both went under once, but when Gannon's head popped up again, he saw Cam glaring at him.

"Paybacks are a bitch," Cam growled, a mischievous smirk forming on his lips.

He was trying to think of a snappy comeback when Cam surprised him, going under the water and grabbing Gannon's foot.

"Shit!" Gannon held his breath when Cam pulled him under.

Reckless

He tried not to panic as he kicked his feet, but he had nothing to worry about because the life jacket propelled him to the surface once again. When he came up, he sucked air into his lungs, looking around for Cam. He found him directly behind him, grinning from ear to ear.

"Hold on to me." Cam instructed, chuckling as his arm banded around Gannon's chest.

Gannon threw his arm around Cam's neck, not because he feared drowning, more because he wanted to touch him. Holding on tightly, he slowed his breathing, trying to relax.

He wasn't sure how or when it happened, but Cam had positioned them so that he was keeping them both above water, one hand on the jet ski, his other hand on Gannon's hip while Gannon held fast to his neck.

"See how it feels?" Gannon taunted, staring into Cam's eyes, only a few inches separating their mouths.

"See how *what* feels?" Cam taunted with a sexy smirk.

"Ahh," Gannon groaned when Cam's hand snaked between them, sliding into Gannon's shorts and finding his dick. "Cam."

Afraid to let go and sink, Gannon tightened his grip on Cam's neck while Cam insistently jacked his dick, stroking firmly while they remained face-to-face out in the middle of the lake, the jet skis, still tethered to them, floating nearby.

"You like what I do to you, don't you?" Cam asked, voice rough.

"Yes," Gannon hissed, eyes locked with Cam's. "God, yes."

"You wanna come while I jack you off?" Cam asked, his voice a low, seductive rumble against Gannon's ear.

"Yes."

"Good. No. Uh-uh. Don't close your eyes," Cam commanded. "Look at me. I want you to watch me while I make you come."

Gannon managed to relax his hold on Cam just enough to give Cam more room to work between them. He could hear the rumble of boats in the distance, knew there were people in the vicinity, possibly even some who could figure out what they were doing, but Gannon didn't give a shit.

The only thing that mattered was Cam's firm, strong hand on Gannon's dick.

"Look at me," Cam insisted, and Gannon realized he'd closed his eyes again, succumbing to the overwhelming pleasure. While he continued to jack Gannon off, Cam kept up an endless rumble of dirty talk that had Gannon nearing the boiling point.

"I couldn't wait to get my hands on you again," Cam said. "I've dreamed about this. About making you come in my hand. Ever since that first night…"

Gannon kept his eyes locked on Cam's face.

"Know what else I've dreamed about?" Cam asked.

Gannon shook his head, unable to speak because his body was coiling tighter and tighter.

Cam's voice lowered. "I've dreamed about you fucking my ass. Just the way you said you would on the phone."

Yeah, well…

"You wanna bury your dick in my ass, don't you?"

Gannon nodded.

Cam's grip tightened, his hand smoothly working Gannon's cock beneath the water.

"Come for me, Gannon."

The stroking continued, and Gannon fought the overwhelming urge, wanting to savor every sensation that flooded him until he couldn't take much more.

"Fuck!" Gannon cried out, his dick pulsing as he came in a rush so violent he thought for a minute he would sink to the bottom of the lake, life jacket be damned.

"So fucking beautiful." Cam leaned forward and kissed him, his lips skimming Gannon's lightly.

Gannon continued to stare back at Cam in wonder. In such a short time, he found he was completely addicted to this man, desperate to spend every waking moment with him and then some. It was getting more and more difficult to hold back, to keep from claiming him the way he wanted to, the way Cam clearly wanted him to.

Then again, based on the heated glimmer in Cam's eyes, Gannon wasn't so sure that day was that far off anymore.

Twenty-Two

Two days later, Tuesday

CAM PULLED UP to Gannon's house at seven o'clock on the dot, just as he'd been instructed to do. This time, he didn't linger in his truck and he also brought a bottle of scotch with him. He made the trek up to the house only to find Gannon standing on the walkway near the porch waiting for him.

"Hi."

God, he loved the sound of Gannon's voice, the way those dark eyes lit up when he looked at him. "Hi back," Cam said, leaning in and offering Gannon a quick peck on the lips.

Gannon nodded toward the driveway. "I see the truck's over the separation anxiety."

Cam chuckled as they stepped into the house. "Yeah. Looks that way."

"Dinner's ready, if you're hungry."

"Starving."

He'd come straight from work after showering and changing clothes. He hadn't wanted to be late, eager to see Gannon again. Now that he was there, he hoped the night went on forever, because he already didn't want to leave.

Reckless

Cam followed Gannon through the house and into the kitchen, feeling more at ease this time around than the first time he'd been there three weeks ago. Hard to believe it had only been three weeks. It felt like an eternity had passed since that first kiss they'd shared that day in Gannon's kitchen.

Cam set the bottle of scotch on the counter. "Brought you something."

Gannon scanned the bottle, then looked up quickly.

Cam offered a smile. "You said you liked it."

"It's…" Gannon leaned in, clasped the back of Cam's neck, and pulled him forward, their mouths touching. "Thank you."

Whether it was the light brush of Gannon's mouth, the eagerness of his tone, or simply being there with him, Cam wasn't sure. But he knew tonight was going to be the turning point for them. He wasn't able to predict what was going to happen, but if things did escalate, he damn sure wasn't going to be the one to put the brakes on.

"Sit," Gannon said, nodding toward the table.

Cam sat.

"What is this?" he asked when Gannon brought a glass dish over and set it on the table.

Taking off the oven mitt and dropping it on the table, Gannon smiled. "Enchilada casserole. And no, it didn't come from the freezer section."

"I'm impressed."

"You should be. I usually stick to Italian food, but I know you like Mexican."

Cam watched while Gannon dished food onto his plate, then grabbed Cam's and filled it. He disappeared into the kitchen once again, returning with two margarita glasses and a pitcher.

"Are you plannin' to get me drunk?" Cam teased.

"Yes," Gannon said, his frank tone making Cam laugh.

"What if I told you that wouldn't be necessary?"

The heat that flamed in Gannon's dark gaze made Cam squirm briefly. They'd be lucky to make it through dinner at this rate.

"Eat," Gannon instructed, sitting down across from him.

Cam grabbed his fork, smiled at Gannon, then took a bite.

"How is it?"

Cam nodded. It was good. Really good. Rather than answer, he took another bite, which made Gannon laugh.

They managed to make their way through dinner with small talk. Gannon explained how they'd figured out the glitch in their recent game and they were pushing it back out to the beta testers. He seemed relaxed, which helped Cam to, as well.

It wasn't that he was nervous...

Okay, maybe he was a *little* nervous.

Sure, he felt entirely at ease with Gannon at this point, but the sexual tension hung in the air around them, thick enough to suffocate. And they both seemed to be waiting for the moment that it did.

"Want more of this?" Gannon asked, holding up the pitcher of margaritas after they'd finished dinner and cleaned up.

"No. I'm good." Truth was, he wanted to be stone-cold sober tonight. He knew what was coming as well as Gannon did, and he intended to remember every single second, every touch.

"Let's go outside." Gannon nodded toward the back door after he poured himself two fingers of scotch.

Cam led the way, shocked when he saw that there were kerosene lamps burning on the deck, giving it a soft, romantic glow.

"Why didn't we eat out here?" he asked, turning to look at Gannon.

"Didn't want to waste time bringing it out." The sexy smirk on Gannon's face told Cam they were on the same wavelength.

Gannon took Cam's hand, pulling him down to another level of the deck, where an outdoor cushion the size of a queen bed lay. Two pillows had been tossed down there as well.

"Don't worry, I'm not gonna jump you," Gannon told him when Cam hesitated.

Smiling, Cam shook off the nerves and took a seat, lying back and resting his hands behind his head, staring up at the stars. "What if I'm worried that you're not?"

Sitting down beside him, Gannon seemed to study his face briefly before looking away.

Cam knew exactly where this was headed, but he didn't want to stop it, not even a little. It had been a little more than twenty-one painfully long days since they'd first met. And three weeks exactly since their first … date, since Cam had gone to bed with a hard-on to rival all, desperate and aching as he pushed back his desire for this man. And now, as they sat outside, beneath the stars, he was eager to take this to the next level, only he wasn't sure Gannon was on the same page.

Sure, he knew Gannon wanted him. It was damn hard to ignore the steady hum of electricity that arced between them, the sparks that ignited whenever their eyes met. And though Cam had said he wanted to take things slow, he hadn't exactly meant turtle speed.

"What're you thinking about?" Gannon asked, his voice a throaty rumble.

"You," Cam admitted.

"What about me?" The roughness of Gannon's voice drew his attention up.

Cam tilted his head and met Gannon's eyes.

Gannon was sitting up, reclining against the rough stone of the house, his arm resting on one upraised knee, his full attention focused on him. He'd seen that look before, seen the way Gannon studied him when he didn't think Cam was watching. The intensity of it nearly stole his breath.

Going with the truth, Cam said, "About how fucking bad I want you."

"Cam."

Before he could say another word, Gannon set the tumbler of scotch on the ground beside them. Never breaking eye contact, Cam inhaled deeply when Gannon turned onto his side, lowering himself down to where Cam was. He could practically feel the heated caress of Gannon's gaze as it roamed over his face, smelled the rich scent of the alcohol on Gannon's breath. He knew what Gannon was looking for, some sort of encouragement, something to tell him that the time for waiting was now over.

He wanted to tell him, but he couldn't find his voice.

Cam swallowed hard when Gannon cupped his face with one warm hand, turning his head slightly so their eyes met, held. The smooth pad of Gannon's thumb brushed over his lower lip, and Cam instinctively opened his mouth, sliding his tongue over it before sucking it into his mouth. The rough rumble that resonated in Gannon's chest spurred him on.

Reckless

Reaching for him, Cam ran his hands over Gannon's face, feeling the bristle of his jaw against his palms before moving higher to remove Gannon's glasses, gently setting them on the deck behind him.

"God, Cam," Gannon whispered harshly. "Do you know how much I want you?"

He could guess and the feeling was definitely mutual. But he didn't say anything, didn't urge Gannon to kiss him, because he was content simply to touch him.

His heart was pounding against his ribs, his body hardening from the lengthy stare and the smoothness of Gannon's thumb against his tongue. When Gannon pulled his thumb from between Cam's lips, Cam turned and ran his lips across Gannon's hand, closing his eyes as he kissed the center of his palm.

A rush of heat whirled inside him combined with brilliant starbursts igniting behind his closed eyelids as Gannon's mouth brushed his. The heat intensified when Gannon flattened himself down, resting atop Cam. Their bodies touched from knee to chest as Cam forced his eyes open to stare up at Gannon, willing him to see how eager he was, how much he wanted this.

When Gannon's gaze dropped to Cam's mouth, he couldn't wait any longer. Sliding his hand behind Gannon's neck, he slowly pulled him down, never looking away until Gannon's mouth hovered just above his. Gannon was breathing hard, and the knowledge that Cam could get him this worked up with nothing more than a look had something in his chest erupting, a feeling so strong he was desperate to see what it would feel like once he got his hands on him.

"Tell me you want this," Gannon whispered, his eyes closed.

"I want this," Cam whispered back, his voice, rough from arousal, sounding strange to his own ears.

"Good," Gannon said, closing the gap and nipping Cam's lower lip. "'Cause I've waited a long damn time for this."

"Gannon?" When Cam said his name, Gannon put a few scant inches between them, releasing his lip and staring down at him.

Gannon's eyebrows quirked in question.

Squeezing the back of Gannon's neck, Cam lifted his head. "Shut up and kiss me."

"I can do that," Gannon said, his dark gaze glittering with heat.

And then—*finally*—Gannon's mouth was on his in a kiss so sweet Cam worried he'd disintegrate from the flash fire that erupted in his veins. Sliding his other hand down Gannon's back, Cam kneaded his ass, pulling him in so that their lower bodies ground against one another.

Warm and soft, Gannon's mouth melded with his. But beneath the gentle reverence, there was something powerful, something possessive in the way Gannon kissed him. It called to that place deep inside of him, the place he'd kept locked up for so long.

Gannon's hand trailed down Cam's arm, finding his fingers and linking them together before he did the same with his other hand, lifting Cam's arms above his head, holding him in place while he devastated him with a kiss fueled with weeks' worth of pent up passion.

"Cam," Gannon groaned as his mouth trailed down Cam's jaw, then his neck, his teeth nipping him gently as he went. "God, you smell good."

Gannon's lips trailed over the sensitive skin on the underside of Cam's arms, sending a tremor racing through him. He wasn't sure he'd survive the sensual assault, but he was damn sure going to try.

Helpless to do anything except succumb to the pleasure, Cam didn't try to move when Gannon took both of Cam's hands in one of his, then lifted the hem of his shirt, pushing it high up on his chest.

His back arched when Gannon's lips trailed over his right pec, then to his nipple.

"Fuck," he cried out, desperate for Gannon to ease the ache that was building inside him.

Gannon said nothing as he sucked one hardened point into his mouth, his tongue working the barbell that pierced him, teasing the sensitive tip with his tongue before raking it with his teeth. Cam was still groaning when Gannon attended to his other nipple, toying with the metal bar, pulling it gently as a blaze of heat shot straight to his dick.

He let out a disappointed grunt when Gannon lifted his head, meeting his gaze.

"Don't move your hands," Gannon instructed, releasing his wrists and grabbing his shirt, forcing it higher, then off completely.

When Gannon shifted positions, straddling one of Cam's thighs, he bent his knee, grinding his leg against Gannon's rigid erection, but Gannon wasn't deterred, leaving Cam helpless against the onslaught of Gannon's mouth sliding over his skin, teasing, tormenting, driving him fucking crazy with the need for more.

Blistering heat seared him, his body overwhelmed by sensation as Gannon did nothing more than run his lips, tongue, and teeth across Cam's torso, his warm hands spanning Cam's ribs as he held him there. A harsh grumble escaped Gannon, and he was back at Cam's mouth, devouring him while he rode Cam's knee, grinding against him. He was hot and hard and Cam wanted to feel him, skin to skin.

Unable to keep from touching him a second longer, Cam cupped Gannon's face, keeping him close, as a brutal mating of lips and tongues ensued. Gannon's hand trailed over Cam's chest, but he never ventured lower, leaving Cam aching and hard.

"More," Cam whispered against his mouth. "All of you."

Gannon lifted his head, staring down at him. "Not sure you can handle all of me."

The way he said the words … Cam knew they weren't simply the nonchalant dare Gannon obviously wanted him to believe they were. Still clutching Gannon's face, Cam met his eyes while they were both breathing hard, their mouths inches apart.

"*All* of you," Cam repeated.

"You know what you're asking for?" Gannon countered, an intensity in his gaze Cam had never seen before.

"Yeah," he answered roughly. He definitely knew.

"Fuck," Gannon muttered, slamming his mouth back to Cam's as his hands slid beneath him, arms banding tightly around him, their bodies crushed together. The kiss went from inferno to apocalyptic in a matter of seconds, sending Cam spiraling out of control.

Without offering Gannon a warning, Cam quickly switched their positions, Gannon's warm, willing body beneath him, mouths still fused together, tongues dueling for control.

This time, when he lifted his head and stared down into Gannon's flushed face, Cam knew exactly what Gannon had meant. Cam wanted him, there was no denying that. And right here in this moment, he wanted every fucking thing the man could give him.

Everything.

GANNON FELT AS though he'd waited an eternity for this moment.

A lifetime.

No, *ten* lifetimes.

It would've been so easy to rip Cam's clothes from his body and bury himself deep inside the man until neither of them knew what day of the week it was, but he didn't want that.

Okay, yes, he wanted that. But not this time. The first time he took Cam, he wanted to savor every moment, to pleasure him in ways Cam had never experienced before. It had been a long damn time since Gannon had been with anyone, so it wasn't nearly as easy as he wanted, but he knew it would be well worth the wait.

Pulling Cam's mouth down to his, Gannon ground his dick against Cam's, ratcheting his pulse up another notch from the friction alone. The weight of Cam above him was something he'd dreamed about, but the real thing was so much better.

Sliding his hands down Cam's back, he felt the thick muscle ripple and flex beneath his touch. He wanted to kiss him there, to see if Cam had any erogenous zones in that particular spot. But right now, it appeared Cam thought he was the one in control, and Gannon wasn't about to tell him otherwise. He loved the feel of him, strong, powerful, and melting for him.

When they broke for air, Gannon watched as Cam knelt over him, straddling his hips and then pushing Gannon's T-shirt up. Eager to feel Cam's mouth on him, Gannon worked his shirt off, tossing it to the ground beside them before reclining on the wide cushion once again.

They were both sweating, but he knew it had more to do with their attraction to one another than the oppressive Texas heat.

"Come here," Gannon instructed, reaching for Cam, needing to feel him closer.

Cam came down atop him once more, their bare chests sliding together. A rough whimper escaped him as the blazing heat tore through his body, rocking him to his very core. Winding his arms behind Cam, he once again dug his fingers into the rock-hard muscle, kneading and exploring as he held him close, their mouths uniting once more.

Cam's palm slid down his chest, squeezing his pec in his big, rough hand.

"Put your mouth on me, Cam."

Cam met his gaze briefly, then his head lowered and his lips seared Gannon's chest, licking, sucking, driving him higher and higher. That hot mouth trailed lower, straight down the center of Gannon's stomach, his tongue darting into his navel, then sliding lower, dipping into the waistband of Gannon's jeans.

Reckless

A broken cry escaped him as his cock pulsed behind his zipper. He needed to feel Cam's lips on his cock, needed to fuck that sweet mouth. The need was so great Gannon forced himself up to a sitting position, Cam moving with him. Though Cam was bigger, Gannon still managed to twist them until Cam was once again beneath him. Only this time, Gannon didn't go down with him.

Getting to his feet, he jerked the button on his jeans open, then lowered the zipper while Cam stared up at him. With Cam's help, Gannon got his jeans off, forcing his boxers down with them.

Their eyes met again as Cam sat eye level with Gannon's dick, his tongue sliding out to stroke the sensitive tip. Gannon lovingly stroked the top of Cam's head, the short strands soft against his palm while he took it all in. It seemed almost too good to be true. But they were really doing this.

When Cam parted his lips and sucked Gannon into the furnace of his mouth, the air escaped him in a rush.

"Cam," he said on a ragged breath. "Suck me, Cam."

Cupping Cam's jaw, Gannon rolled his hips forward, controlling the pace as he fucked Cam's lips, his breaths rushing in and out of his lungs. He was mesmerized by the sight, the yellow glow from the candles dancing over Cam's golden skin, wonderstruck by the way Cam's eyes stayed locked with his as Gannon maintained a slow, steady pace, heavenly warmth enveloping him.

Cam's eyes dropped as his mouth opened wider, taking Gannon all the way to the root. Not-so-gentle fingers kneaded Gannon's balls, and a streak of pleasure-pain shot through him. His head fell back as he fucked Cam's mouth, faster now. Holy fuck. He could so easily come right then, could fill Cam's mouth and watch him swallow everything he gave him, but he didn't want to. Not yet.

Despite the overwhelming desire to continue basking in the raspy warmth of Cam's tongue against his throbbing dick, Gannon found the willpower to pull back. Dropping to his knees, he forced Cam onto his back, then worked open the button on Cam's shorts, watching Cam's eyes as they glazed over when Gannon lowered the zipper and brushed the backs of his fingers over his thick shaft.

"Need to taste you," he said as he helped Cam out of his shorts.

Cam helped, shoving his shorts and underwear down his hips, clearly as eager as Gannon was.

"Have I mentioned how much I love this?" Gannon whispered harshly as he licked the ring piercing the head of Cam's dick. "And these?" He used his tongue to trace the silver bars that pierced Cam's thick cock, lifting his eyes to meet Cam's. "So fucking much."

Cam's smile was wicked, and Gannon could only imagine what was going through his mind.

Once Cam was naked, Gannon knelt between his spread thighs, admiring the beautiful cock before him. Thick and long, with a wide crest, Cam's dick was as powerful as the rest of him. The engorged head rested against Cam's stomach as Gannon stroked one finger down the length, trailing over the ladder of barbells.

Although he had a million questions for Cam regarding what compelled him to get pierced, Gannon was too preoccupied to ask them. He'd prefer to explore. With his tongue. Slowly. The first time he'd taken Cam in his mouth, Gannon had been eager to drive Cam out of his mind. This time, he wanted to enjoy him.

Reckless

Lying between Cam's muscular thighs, Gannon gripped Cam's cock with his fist, sliding his tongue down the steely length, feeling the metal bars beneath the stretched skin. It was a strange sensation, but one that intrigued him. He briefly wondered what it would feel like with Cam buried deep in his ass.

A shudder tore through him.

Not that he would find out tonight, because Gannon had every intention of being lodged balls deep in Cam's beautiful ass.

Cam's hiss had Gannon meeting those dark blue eyes, enjoying the way they watched as Gannon took the bulbous head in his mouth, circling his tongue over the smooth skin, through the ring.

"Aww, hell," Cam growled, his hand sliding into Gannon's hair, tightening just enough to send a bolt of electricity firing down his spine. "Ahh, yeah. Just like that."

With every murmur of encouragement, Gannon continued to blow Cam's dick, caressing him with his tongue, sucking him into his mouth, forcing him to the back of his throat. He pleasured him for long minutes, kissing the backs of Cam's thighs as he forced him to fold his legs back against his body. He trailed kisses down the pulsing shaft before licking Cam's heavy sac, sucking his balls into his mouth with care, his intention to drive Cam to the point that he was begging for more.

He continued lower, palming Cam's ass, forcing his hips upward, dragging his tongue across sensitive flesh, then spearing Cam's ass with his tongue.

"Oh, fuck... Gannon..." Cam's words were breathless, reflecting the pleasure Gannon was intent on giving him. Continuing to watch Cam's face, Gannon tongue fucked him, rimming his asshole, while Cam gripped his cock, jerking roughly. He speared Cam with his tongue, ruthlessly fucking him until Cam was groaning, his hips rocking as he begged Gannon to continue.

Sucking Cam's balls into his mouth once more, Gannon swiped his thumb across Cam's ass, pressing against Cam's puckered hole gently, applying just enough pressure to let Cam know what was coming but not giving him more than that.

"Gannon," Cam groaned, his heavy-lidded eyes focused on him.

"Like that?" Gannon teased, running his tongue along the barbells once more.

"Need ... more..."

"I know you do." Gannon studied Cam's face momentarily before slamming his mouth down over Cam's cock, taking him all the way to the back of his throat and swallowing, allowing the muscles of his throat to work over the wide head, the ring scraping him as he did. He bobbed up and down, licking, sucking, enjoying the taste of Cam against his tongue.

Releasing him quickly, Gannon crawled up Cam's body, his mouth trailing the intricate artwork that decorated his stomach and chest, stopping briefly to flick his tongue over one pierced nipple. When Cam's muscular thighs clamped around his hips, Gannon continued up over his chest, then once again found Cam's mouth as their sweat-slicked bodies writhed against one another.

Cam's hands gripped the back of Gannon's head, holding him to him as their tongues dueled. His shaft slid against Cam's slick asshole, eager to find its way inside.

Blindly reaching out, Gannon managed to find his jeans. Searching, he found his wallet, yanking it from the pocket and sifting through until he fingered the condom and the small packet of lube he had there.

He'd been prepared for this moment, he wouldn't lie.

"Fuck me," Cam whispered against his mouth. "Gannon, I need to feel you inside me."

"Getting there," Gannon assured him, brushing his lips over Cam's chin as he got to his knees once again.

As much as he wanted to prolong this until they were both delirious, Gannon knew he couldn't take much more. He needed to be inside Cam now.

And he couldn't wait any longer.

Twenty-Three

CAM WAS PRETTY sure his head was going to fucking explode.

Both of them.

It had taken everything within him to keep from coming when Gannon had taken his cock in his mouth and laved him with that skilled tongue. And when he'd tongue fucked Cam's ass, it was a wonder he was still in one piece.

Now, as he watched as Gannon rolled the condom over his cock, he was trying his best to keep from reaching for him. But then, as though something had snapped inside him, Gannon was forcing Cam's thighs back against his chest, nudging the head of his cock against Cam's asshole.

No more foreplay, no preamble.

Their eyes locked again, as Gannon pushed inside, his face flushed as pleasure coursed through them both. Cam dropped his head to the cushion, closing his eyes as Gannon pierced him, forcing every glorious inch deep inside, a ripple of pain rocketing through him as the fullness intensified. He forced himself to relax, holding his legs back as he spread his knees, taking everything Gannon was willing to give him.

Reckless

Forcing his eyes open because he didn't want to miss a second, he focused on the beautiful man kneeling between his legs, buried to the hilt inside him. Gannon stilled, staring down at where they were joined together before his eyes lifted to meet Cam's. They remained like that for several seconds, breathing deeply. Cam was ready, aching, desperate for more, but he didn't want to rush any more than Gannon did.

So he waited.

Patiently.

And then heaven rained down on him when Gannon began to move.

Neither of them said anything as Gannon began to fuck him, slowly at first, then faster. Gannon's cock brushed sensitive nerve endings, caressing that spot that had Cam seeing stars. Over and over, Gannon's lean body moved with him, forcing him to take every powerful inch, pounding away as sweat dripped down from his face onto Cam's stomach.

"So beautiful," Gannon huffed. "So fucking beautiful."

Cam didn't want it to ever end, he wanted to feel Gannon inside him forever, but he was quickly ascending to the point of no return, overcome with pleasure and a desperate need to come. He'd waited too long for this. Feeling Gannon inside him... It was better than he'd anticipated, better than he'd dreamed it would be.

Gannon gripped Cam's cock firmly, stroking him as he scooted closer, his dick sliding in and out of Cam's ass with every urgent jerk of his hips.

"Fuck, Cam. You feel so damn good. I don't wanna stop."

Cam closed his eyes, breathing hard, melting into the cushion. Delirious with pleasure as the thick head of Gannon's dick stroked Cam's prostate every so often, Cam tried to hold on. It wasn't until he felt Gannon shift again that Cam opened his eyes.

Gannon toppled over, forcing Cam's left leg across his body as he shifted positions, twisting Cam's hips so that he was partially on his side. Gannon lay spooned behind him, holding him tight, still lodged deep in Cam's ass, continuing to impale him, driving him higher, higher still. It was as though they were made to fit together. Cam couldn't get enough. Gannon continued to stroke Cam's cock while he buried himself deep, keeping a steady rhythm that coincided with the pounding of Cam's heart.

He had no idea how long they went at it, but Cam was racing toward the breaking point when Gannon suddenly stopped rocking his hips. He turned Cam's face back toward him, finding Cam's mouth with his own, Gannon's tongue delving inside in a kiss so hot it sucked the oxygen right out of his lungs.

"Turn over," Gannon urged, rolling Cam beneath him, never dislodging from his ass.

When Cam was on his knees, Gannon's arms came around him, his mouth on Cam's back, teeth nipping his skin as Gannon began driving into him again, filling him with more pleasure than he'd ever thought existed.

A strong hand gripped Cam's hip, jerking him back against the thick cock that tunneled in and out of his ass over and over. Then Gannon's strong hand came to rest on Cam's shoulder, keeping him firmly in place while he picked up his pace, slamming into him until the telltale tingle at the base of Cam's spine ignited, warning he wasn't going to last.

"Gannon," he groaned. "Gonna come... Oh, fuck."

"Come for me, baby. Come while I'm buried in your ass."

Those few words, as well as the endearment he hadn't expected, ignited the fuse, and as Gannon pounded away, driving deeper and deeper, harder, faster, Cam's orgasm slammed into him, his cock jerking in his hand as he came in a rush.

In a flash, Cam was once again on his back, Gannon coming down over him, guiding himself inside his ass once more, their mouths melding, tongues lashing as Gannon rolled his hips forward, back.

"Can't get enough," Gannon said through clenched teeth. "Feels so good."

Cam wrapped his arms around Gannon, holding him to him as Gannon continued to glide in and out of his body, their sweat-drenched skin sliding together. Cupping the back of Gannon's head, Cam released his mouth, their heavy breaths colliding as Gannon didn't hold back.

"Want you to come," Cam urged, his hand sliding down to cradle the back of Gannon's neck as he braced his knees against Gannon's hips. "Need to feel your dick pulse in my ass."

A few panting breaths escaped Gannon as the beautiful man stared down at him, his eyes closing briefly, pleasure distorting his near-perfect features.

"That's it," Cam said, rolling his hips back to give Gannon better access.

Gannon sat up, his hands pressed against the back of Cam's thighs as he bent him over, his hips driving down, cock buried to the hilt.

"Come for me," Cam whispered.

"Fuck, yes," Gannon cried out, the muscles in his arms standing out in stark relief as his hips slammed into Cam one last time, his cock pulsing inside Cam's ass. "Coming. Ahh! Fuck!"

Cam watched, enamored by the sight of Gannon in the throes of an orgasm. It was honestly the most beautiful thing he'd ever seen. And though he was exhausted, Cam couldn't help but wonder when he'd get to see it again.

Because whenever that would be suddenly felt like a long damn time.

GANNON FOUGHT TO fill his lungs with air as he flopped down beside Cam, wrapping him in his arms and holding him close. That had been the single most intense thing he'd ever experienced in his life. Being inside Cam, one with the man who'd filled his days with more happiness in the last three weeks had been better, and far more powerful, than he'd ever expected.

Hell, he hadn't wanted it to end.

"You okay?" Gannon asked when he could finally speak a few minutes later.

"Good," Cam murmured, shifting so that he could pull Gannon toward him.

Resting his head in the crook of Cam's arm, he welcomed the security he felt there. For whatever reason, when he was with Cam, Gannon didn't ever want to let him go. How he'd gotten to this point, he didn't know, but he wouldn't change a single thing about this moment, even if he could.

Reckless

Long minutes passed as they lay on the cushion beneath the stars, his sweat-drenched body cooling in the breeze. Gannon trailed his finger over the bold script inked across Cam's chest. Reckless. For some reason, that suited Cam. The man was certainly wild, untamed. And maybe that was what Gannon liked most about him, that sense of freedom. Anyone who knew him knew that Gannon was definitely not reckless. He was probably too cautious, too controlling, too buttoned up as Cam had once called him. But he didn't feel that way when he was with Cam. He felt … free.

Once his breathing was normal again, Gannon shifted so that he was on his back, Cam's muscled arm still beneath his head. "So, what made you want to get your dick pierced?"

He felt Cam shrug beneath him. "Don't know. Seemed like the thing to do at the time."

"Getting your dick pierced? Since I can't imagine a needle coming anywhere near my dick, I would think you had to have given it some thought."

Cam chuckled but didn't say anything.

"How old were you?"

"Twenty-two."

"How old were you when you got your first tattoo?" Gannon inquired.

"Eighteen."

"What was it?"

Cam shifted, his hand sliding down to the tattoo that ran vertically up his side. Gannon moved, looked down to read it. *This moment is all we have.* He nodded, understanding. Cam lived in the moment, there no doubt about that. He feared the future and ran from his past. And Gannon understood why.

"How many do you have?" he asked.

"At last count, it was something like thirty-five. At that point, I stopped counting."

"And the other piercings?" Gannon found everything about Cam sexy, and he wanted to know the driving reason behind why the man did the things he did.

"What about them?"

"What made you want them?"

"I got my tongue pierced because I wondered what it would feel like."

"Did it hurt?"

"Surprisingly, no," Cam said with a chuckle. "Swelled up for about a week after, but no pain."

"And your nipples?"

"That took a little more coaxing, and I probably wouldn't have done it if Dare hadn't dared me. Hurt like a motherfucker. But I got the pleasure of watching Dare squirm when they pierced his nipples, so it was worth it."

Gannon smiled. "Plans for more?"

"Tats, yes. Piercings, probably not. What about you?"

"Never walked on the wild side," Gannon admitted.

Cam's bicep flexed beneath his head, the movement forcing Gannon to turn toward him. He opened his eyes to find Cam looking at him. "I happen to think you'd look sexy as fuck with a tattoo."

"Yeah?" Gannon wasn't so sure about that, but he liked that Cam thought so. "Like what?"

Cam shrugged. "Something that reflects how strong you are."

Gannon knew he wasn't talking physically. "Who knows? Maybe some day."

Cam's lips brushed Gannon's forehead and he fought the urge to sigh against him. He liked this, the easiness between them. It was a nice change of pace for Gannon.

But as much as he wanted to simply enjoy it, he knew himself. If he wasn't careful, he'd start trying to map out the future, figure out where this was going and how they were going to get there. After all, he was a type A. He didn't know how to live in the moment, was always wanting to try to control the outcome.

It was his nature, the way he was programmed.

And he only hoped he could keep it under wraps or he feared he'd lose the best damn thing that had ever happened to him.

"WHAT'RE YOU DOIN' out here?"

Roan looked up to see Teague strolling toward him down the pier.

"Just chillin'," Roan said. Although he was doing a hell of a lot more than that.

For the past hour, ever since Cam had darted out of the office like his ass was on fire, Roan had been thinking about where Cam was going, what he was doing. When he would be back.

It didn't take a rocket scientist to know that Cam had gone to see Gannon. But despite knowing better, Roan couldn't seem to stop thinking about the two of them. And not in a way that made him feel good, either.

"Mind if I sit?"

It wasn't like Teague to ask permission for anything, but Roan grunted an affirmation anyway.

Roan passed over a beer.

"Thanks."

"Somethin' wrong?" Roan wasn't sure Teague would open up to him, that was something Teague rarely did, but it seemed as though something was on his mind.

"You see that guy Hudson went out with?"

Ah. Well, that explained it.

Roan nodded, but neither of them said anything more. Yeah, he'd seen Hudson leave with the hot guy who'd stopped in to see him again today. Third time that week Roan had seen Hudson with that guy, in fact. No one seemed to know who he was.

"Cam go to Gannon's?" Teague asked a few minutes later.

"Yep." And this time, he doubted Cam would be back tonight. He knew Cam and Gannon had been seeing each other for about three weeks, which was a record for Cam. At least for the past few years. And though they appeared to be having a rocky go of things, Roan still hadn't seen Cam quite as caught up with anyone the way he seemed to be with Gannon.

Roan fucking hated every second of it. Hated that he cared, hated that it bothered him. He was still battling these strange emotions, wondering why they'd crept up on him now. Sure, he'd had some crazy thoughts about Cam over the years, but the more he thought about it, the more he realized he'd never said anything because he thought it would never matter. Cam hadn't found a serious relationship, nor had Roan. That had been his hope.

Stupid as it was.

"How many beers you got over there?" Teague asked, pulling Roan back from his derailed thoughts.

"A few, why?"

"Think we're gonna need more than a few."

Roan nodded, understanding just what Teague was thinking. The best thing to do right now was to drown his thoughts with alcohol.

At least then it wouldn't hurt as much. Maybe.

Twenty-Four

RELEASING A CONTENTED sigh, Cam woke when a warm body flattened up against his back, strong fingers sliding up his chest, gliding over the steel bars in his nipples. He could see the light coming in the window from behind his eyelids, and he fought to keep his eyes closed, not wanting to get up just yet.

"Mornin'." Gannon's sleep-roughened voice caressed his ear while his fingers tweaked the barbells, sending bolts of electricity shooting from his nipples to his dick.

God, he loved when Gannon played with his nipples. It made the pain of getting them all those years ago so worth it.

"Mornin'," Cam responded, pressing back against the insistent hard-on grinding against his ass. "You gonna put that thing to work? Or is it just plannin' to wave hello?"

Gannon grumbled, a deep, raw sound that had the hairs on the back of Cam's neck lifting from the sensuality of it all. The next thing he knew, he was on his stomach, a warm, heavy weight crushing him into the mattress.

Gannon nipped Cam's earlobe. "You ready for me? Or you need me to play with you?"

Well, this was one hell of a way to wake up.

"Ready," Cam grunted, smiling into the pillow. "So fucking ready."

He'd been ready all damn night. After Gannon had driven him out of his fucking mind on the back deck, he'd been counting down the seconds for the next time. They'd both been too tired to have another go at it, having fallen asleep outside for a couple of hours. Gannon had finally convinced him to come inside, and after they had cleaned up, they'd crashed as soon as they'd hit Gannon's pillows.

But now ... Cam was wide awake. Every single part of him.

Gannon's weight disappeared briefly, but before the disappointment could set in, he was straddling Cam's thighs, squirting lube along his crack, then urging his dick against Cam's asshole. After sliding his cock through the slickness several times, Gannon pressed forward, slipping in deep, drawing a breathless moan from Cam. And then his weight was back.

"You feel so good," Gannon mumbled, his lips sliding along Cam's neck. "So hot, so fucking tight."

In the position he was in, trapped beneath Gannon, Cam couldn't get the momentum he needed to increase the friction he craved, but he soon learned that was Gannon's plan when he attempted to thrust back against him.

"Still," Gannon barked softly. "Need this right now."

Cam didn't argue; he merely gripped Gannon's thighs with his hands, holding on while Gannon rocked into him, tormenting him with just enough pressure to make him desperate for more. Gannon's weight shifted, his hand firmly planted in the center of Cam's back as he rolled his hips forward.

The forcefulness of it all was so fucking erotic. Though last night had given him an idea of how giving Gannon was, Cam found it arousing that the man would take what he wanted, as well.

"I could get used to this," Gannon whispered, leaning forward again, his tongue trailing over Cam's shoulder. "Waking up, burying my dick in your ass."

Cam could get used to it, too, but he didn't say as much, enjoying the gentle glide of Gannon's dick in his ass, the tingles Gannon's mouth left on his skin.

Long minutes passed as Gannon ratcheted up Cam's need by trailing his teeth over his shoulders and neck, his thick dick thrusting inside him, slow and deep, filling him completely. Cam's cock was rock hard and trapped between him and the mattress, but even that friction wasn't enough.

"I've been watching you sleep." Gannon's warm breath fanned Cam's cheek. "Stroking my cock and waiting for you to wake up."

"I'm awake now," Cam grunted, needing to move, needing more friction in his ass.

"I can see that," Gannon said with a chuckle. "On your knees."

Cam didn't waste a second, shifting to his knees when Gannon gripped his hips and jerked his ass back. The position allowed Gannon to go deeper, hitting that spot that made flashes of light dance behind Cam's closed eyelids.

"Love your ass," Gannon growled, pressing down against Cam's back, forcing his chest flat, his face once again crushed against the pillow, ass up. "So fucking tight."

Cam was almost positive it was possible to come from the sound of Gannon's voice alone. The deep, rough baritone mixed with the dirty talk... Cam fucking loved it.

Gannon groaned long and loud, pounding Cam's ass harder. The sensation was incredible, Gannon's dick tunneling in and out of him, overwhelming him with pleasure.

Without warning, Gannon moved, roughly forcing Cam onto his back, flipping him, then slamming his dick back in as though he couldn't get enough.

"Fuck," Cam cried out, his back arching, head digging into the pillow as Gannon's dick surged deep and hard.

Lifting his legs, Cam held his knees close to his chest, changing the angle once again. Gannon took advantage of the position, shifting to his feet so that he was crouching over Cam, driving his cock straight down into Cam, thrusting deeper, harder, faster.

The man was insatiable—not to mention incredibly flexible—and Cam reveled in watching him.

"Stroke your dick," Gannon ordered. "Wanna watch you come."

He wrapped one hand around his dick, grazing the shaft, but it was too dry. Rather than spit in his hand as he normally would, Cam fumbled around, feeling for the bottle of lube he knew Gannon had tossed on the bed. Once he gripped it, he squeezed a generous amount into his open palm, then wrapped his hand around his dick, jerking roughly, fingering the metal piercings, adding that touch of pain he craved. All while keeping his eyes locked on Gannon, who was still impaling him from above. Gannon lowered to one knee, thrusting into him as he held Cam's legs wide.

He was watching Cam jerk off, and the sight of it was so fucking hot Cam knew he wasn't going to last.

"Fuck me," Cam groaned. "Goddamn, it feels good." The powerful thrusts of Gannon's hips rocked his entire body, but he didn't care. "Gonna come, Gan… Fuck, gonna … make … me … come."

Gannon's roar split the air, and Cam's dick twitched and pulsed, shooting over his chest and stomach while Gannon grunted his release. For a split second, he was light-headed, and he wondered if it was possible to black out from an orgasm.

Perhaps, if it was, he might one day find out. Especially if Gannon continued to fuck him like that.

"WHAT TIME IS it?" Cam asked when Gannon's heart rate finally resumed a normal beat. Hell, there for a minute, he'd thought he was having a heart attack.

"Six thirty," Gannon told him, rolling off the bed and getting to his feet. He went straight for the bathroom, tossing the condom into the trash can and turning on the shower.

A few minutes later, while he was soaping up his body, he heard the sound of the glass door open and knew Cam had decided to join him.

"I used your toothbrush," Cam said, stalking Gannon as he filled the oversized shower stall with his presence.

"Did you?" Gannon smirked, backing up as Cam moved closer.

"I did."

Reckless

Cam stopped when there was nowhere for Gannon to go, but before Gannon could reach for him, Cam had their fingers linked and Gannon's hands flattened against the wall on each side of his head. He had a split second to inhale before Cam's mouth slammed down on his, bruising his lips with the sheer force. And though he'd just come harder than he'd ever come in his life, Gannon's dick twitched to life.

"Mmm," Cam groaned against his mouth, lifting Gannon's arms above his head, then gripping Gannon's wrists with one big hand. "Have I mentioned how much I like when you're aggressive?"

Gannon didn't respond, sliding his body against Cam's, feeling the metal bars in Cam's nipples against his chest.

Cam pulled back and stared at Gannon. "But you know it won't always be like that, don't you?"

Gannon wanted to argue, but words escaped him when Cam gripped the back of Gannon's knee and lifted it, holding his leg close to his hip. Gannon felt Cam's rough hand slide down the back of his thigh.

"Aw, fuck," Gannon cried out when Cam's fingers kneaded his balls from underneath. But when Cam's wet finger found his asshole, Gannon nearly came undone.

"I look forward to burying my dick in your ass," Cam said, his lips closer to Gannon's.

Gannon could see Cam's eyes as they trailed over his face, likely watching to see Gannon's reaction. He couldn't hide it, not even if he'd wanted to. He'd imagined what it would feel like to take Cam's dick, to feel those piercings inside him.

Cam's finger slid in deeper, gently thrusting into him, making him ache for more.

"Do you have a problem with that?" Cam whispered.

"No." Gannon didn't have a problem with that. Though he didn't usually bottom, at the mere thought of Cam taking him, claiming him, he felt more blood rush to the head of his dick. "No problem."

"Good." Cam's lips brushed his once again. "Because that seat over there…" Cam nudged his chin toward the tiled bench seat in the shower. "One of these days I'm gonna sit there while you ride my dick."

"Fuck." Gannon's dick jerked as Cam inserted two fingers into his ass.

The sound of the water and the rapid thump of his heart beating against his chest were the only things Gannon heard as Cam continued to finger fuck his asshole. He didn't think he could come again, but if Cam kept doing that…

But before he could reach the pinnacle, Cam stopped, his fingers sliding out of him and leaving him feeling empty.

He opened his eyes to see Cam smiling.

Gannon fought to get his bearings as he allowed the tiled wall to keep him upright, his gaze following Cam's hands as they moved over his thickly muscled chest, then lower. He knew Cam wasn't doing anything more than washing up, but the sight of all those tattoos and piercings, the bronzed skin over thick, rippling muscle… Fuck. Gannon could've watched him all day long.

"When will I see you again?" Cam asked after he'd washed his entire body and shampooed his hair, stepping beneath the spray to rinse off.

"Soon," Gannon told him. He wasn't sure he'd be able to stay away at this point, though he kept that to himself.

"Good." Cam smirked, leaning in and kissing Gannon on the mouth. "And when I do, I'll finish you off." Cam glanced down at Gannon's erection. "So keep that in mind."

Gannon laughed. He wanted to ask Cam to finish him off now, but he didn't.

Cam smiled. "I've gotta get back to the marina."

Gannon locked his gaze with Cam's, willing him to see how much he wanted him, how he fully intended to pursue this. He could tell that Cam was trying to distance himself at the moment, and maybe that was a defense mechanism; he couldn't be sure.

When Cam's mouth brushed his once more, Gannon gripped the back of Cam's neck, holding him so Gannon could explore his mouth, teasing, tasting, trying to get his fill so that he could last the day without being with this man. Cam's hands gripped Gannon's hips, and they felt so good on his naked skin he fought back a groan.

"Call me later," Cam said when he broke the kiss.

Gannon nodded, still watching Cam's face closely.

A smile formed and Gannon felt a flood of relief fill him.

"I'll let myself out," Cam said, moving toward the shower door. "Thanks for dinner last night."

Gannon smiled. "Any time."

Something flitted across Cam's face, an emotion Gannon didn't recognize. "I may just take you up on that."

And with that, Cam stepped out, leaving Gannon alone with his thoughts and his now aching dick.

Twenty-Five

CAM MADE IT back to the marina before anyone else showed up, which was surprising considering it was after eight when he stepped into the office. He started a pot of coffee, skimmed the appointment book, and prepared himself for the ass chewing he would likely receive from Roan once he came down. There was no way his buddy hadn't noticed that Cam's truck hadn't been in the parking lot last night, which meant he was going to hear about it this morning.

Just as he'd predicted, Roan appeared a little after eight thirty, dark circles beneath his eyes as though he hadn't slept last night.

"You all right?" Cam asked, concerned, watching Roan closely.

"Yeah," Roan said on a slow exhale, wiping his hand over his face. "Had to go pick up my sister last night."

Cam stood up straight. "Everything okay with her?"

Roan grabbed the carafe and poured a cup of coffee, wiping his hand over his hair, brushing down the spikey strands. "No."

Reckless

The finality of that one word surprised Cam. Roan's sister had been in and out of drug rehab for the last three years. While Roan's family—all except Roan's mother, who'd abandoned the family when Roan was a teenager—and friends banded together in an effort to help her get clean, she hadn't been as on board with the plan as everyone else. And now, it appeared she'd relapsed. Again.

"Where is she?"

"My dad's house." Roan sipped his coffee and leaned back against the counter. "I told her I'd stop by later today to talk. She's pretty fucked up."

Cam was close to Roan's family because he and Roan had been best friends since elementary school. He'd known Roan's sister, Cassie, almost her entire life. She was four years younger than Roan, the youngest of three children, the baby of the family.

Cassie had taken it hard when their mother had bailed on them, blaming Roan for her inability to remain in a house where the devil lived. The devil being Roan because he was gay. Cam still remembered that day, the day she had packed a suitcase and walked out, telling Roan and Cam that they'd burn in hell for their sins.

The only thing they could figure was that she'd been eavesdropping on their conversations. At the time, Roan had been interested in a guy at school, and they'd talked about it a few times.

Apparently she hadn't been exaggerating, because she'd left and she'd never come back.

Although Cam had known her leaving had hurt Roan, he hadn't been sorry to see her leave.

"Want me to go with you?" Cam offered.

"Not this time. She doesn't want anyone to see her this way, and I can't say I blame her."

Cam understood. "Well, if you change your mind, just let me know."

Roan nodded, then pushed away from the counter, once again running his hand over his short hair. "You stay with Burgess last night?"

"Gannon," Cam corrected. For some reason, he didn't like the way Roan used Gannon's last name. It seemed oddly impersonal. "And yes, I stayed with him."

Roan turned to look at him, and Cam saw the worry in Roan's golden eyes. "Y'all gonna make a go of this?"

Cam shrugged. "One day at a time." He hoped like hell things continued the way they had been going, but he'd long ago stopped trying to predict the future. In turn, he'd also stopped getting his hopes up, because it never seemed to work out in his favor.

As far as he was concerned, they would continue to take things slow. Although slow at this point was relative. It was still to be seen where this was going, because Cam still worried that their differences would eventually interfere and they'd be forced to look at things a little more rationally. Right now, the sex was going to steal the show, and though they'd probably be able to ride the tide of sexual attraction for a while, there was no guarantee that it would last.

Always the pessimist, Cam thought.

"For what it's worth…" Roan turned to face him fully. "I'm happy for you."

Cam wasn't sure if there was something else Roan wanted to say, but when he left it at that, Cam offered a smile. "Thanks."

"If you don't mind, I'm gonna pass off one of my afternoon appointments to Teague," Roan said, holding his coffee cup in both hands. "I'm exhausted and I'm sure tonight's gonna be another long night. I think my stepmother is hoping for an intervention. I figured I'd catch a nap in a bit if I can."

"No worries. And if Teague can't get it, I'll cover for you."

Roan nodded, then, with coffee cup in hand, headed toward the back door. "I'm gonna go check on Hudson. Be back later."

Cam watched his friend walk out, saw the tense set of his shoulders, and wondered what else was bothering Roan. For the past few weeks, he'd been acting strangely. Though strange for Roan wasn't exactly foreign. However, the guy who was usually quick-witted and even quicker to laugh now seemed to be weighed down by something. Whether or not it was his sister, Cam couldn't say.

He only hoped that Roan would talk to him if he needed to. They'd always been close, but now that he thought about it, that relationship had been a little strained in recent weeks.

The reason for that … Cam had absolutely no idea.
But now he couldn't stop thinking about it.

ROAN FORCED HIMSELF to walk away, not to look back at Cam.

His heart was in his throat, his chest aching.

He hoped that he had managed to mask his true feelings back there, but he was so damn tired he wasn't sure. Between his family problems and Cam sleeping with Burgess...

Roan groaned, thrust his hands through his hair once more.

Having to deal with his sister, his family... It wasn't easy, but it never had been. Last night, he'd been content to sit on the pier and drink himself stupid with Teague, but before he could do that, his phone had rung. His stepmother had called, insisting that Roan come over to talk to Cassie.

So he had. He'd pushed aside his own issues and made it his mission to deal with Cassie and her problems.

And now, he felt as though he had to do it without his best friend. The only thing he wanted to do was to walk into Cam's arms and let him hold him for a few minutes, to tell him everything would be all right.

Not that he'd ever done that before, but it wasn't the first time he'd thought about it.

And now he might never have the chance. Cam was with Gannon, and with every passing day, the more they spent time together, the happier Cam seemed to be. Sure, it looked as though Cam was attempting to play it safe, but Roan could tell Cam was falling—hell, he could already have fallen—in love with Gannon.

Not that he was surprised. From what Roan knew of him, Gannon seemed to be a good guy. It was evident he cared about Cam, and Roan couldn't fault him for it. As much as he wanted to interfere, he couldn't bring himself to do it. His thoughts were a jumbled mess. One minute, he felt as though his heart might shatter in his chest; the next, he was scolding himself because he couldn't really be in love with his best friend—or so he wanted to believe.

Yep, he was confused.

Above all else, he truly wanted his friend to be happy. Roan was the idiot who'd kept his feelings to himself. All these years, he'd feared ruining their friendship, making Cam hate him. Keeping his mouth shut had been the only way Roan knew to make sure things didn't end up awkward between them. Had they made a run at it and things didn't work out, Roan couldn't have lived without that friendship.

So maybe it was better this way.

Cam was happy and Roan would eventually move on.

Maybe.

"WHAT ARE YOU doing?" Milly asked, closing the door when she stepped into Gannon's office.

Gannon stopped pacing. "Nothing. Why?"

"Because you're making me dizzy with all this back-and-forth. And you're making the guys nervous. What's wrong?"

Gannon sighed, then moved around his desk and stood beside his chair, gripping the headrest to keep from pacing again. "I need to remind Cam that I'm going to Singapore on Friday."

"Why? Well, other than the obvious and it's nice when one boyfriend tells the other boyfriend his plans." Milly smiled.

Gannon wanted to smile, but he couldn't. "He freaked when I went to California," he reminded her.

"Yes, but you came back safe and sound."

That wasn't the point, but Gannon didn't feel right sharing Cam's deepest, darkest secrets with anyone. Not even Milly. He was honored that Cam had shared them with him. Telling Milly... Well, that would be like betraying that confidence even if she was Gannon's closest friend.

"I don't think it's that simple for him," Gannon muttered.

"What's not that simple? Is he worried you'll cheat?"

"No," Gannon said defensively.

"Good. Then at least he trusts you."

Trusting Gannon didn't seem to be Cam's issue. Trusting the universe ... now that was a different story.

"Well, why don't you surprise him? Show up at his place, bring dinner, watch ... whatever it is you guys watch on TV. And after your smexy time, you can tell him."

"*Smexy* time?" Gannon tilted his head and peered at her over his glasses.

Milly simply smiled. "Yep. And in the glow of an orgasm, he'll take it in stride."

Gannon doubted that, but he kept that to himself. "Is that some sort of hetero manipulation technique?"

"No, it's a technique that works on *all* men. Gay or straight. Y'all are easy like that," Milly said, but he could tell she was teasing, probably attempting to lighten the mood. "But seriously, you're gonna give the guys ulcers if you keep this up. They've never seen you like this."

It was true, Gannon usually managed to keep his personal life—what little of one he'd had—out of the office. It only went to prove how important Cam had become in Gannon's life in recent weeks that he was allowing this to interfere with work.

"You're right," he told her, lowering himself into his desk chair.

"So, you'll do what I said?"

Gannon lifted an eyebrow in question.

"Romantic dinner, smexy time, orgasm … boom. Reminder."

Shaking his head, Gannon didn't reply as Milly sauntered out of his office.

He watched as she stopped a few feet from his door, her back to him.

"Don't worry, y'all," she called out, drawing the attention of everyone in the room. "Gannon's not freaked out about the game release."

He could practically hear the sighs of relief from the others.

"He's just in love," Milly tacked on after a dramatic pause.

Dropping his head to his desk with a painful thud, Gannon closed his eyes and prayed like hell that hadn't just happened. But the chorus of applause that sounded told him it had.

"Don't worry, boss," Milly said a moment later, her voice lower this time, "At least now you won't think about your problem because you're dealing with your public humiliation."

"Thanks," he muttered, not bothering to look up.

"You're welcome. That's what I'm here for."

Shaking his head—rolling his forehead on his desk— Gannon sighed.

That woman.

Twenty-Six

CAM WAS SITTING on his sofa, a baseball game on the television, when a knock on his door surprised him. Figuring it was Roan or Dare coming by to hang out, he hollered to let his friend know the door was unlocked.

But when the door opened, it wasn't Roan's or Dare's face staring back at him.

Cam couldn't contain the smile that lit from within him, working its way through his entire body and finally making its way to his face.

"Hey," Cam greeted Gannon. "What're you doin' here?"

Gannon returned the smile, stepping inside and closing the door behind him. Holding up a bag, he said, "I brought dinner."

Cam glanced down at the bag. "Don't tell me it's a frozen pizza again? I still have the last one you brought."

"No frozen pizza," Gannon confirmed, turning the bag around.

"Chinese?"

"Thought we'd do somethin' different."

"Works for me." Cam sat up, dropping his feet to the floor and moving over to make room for Gannon. "Sit."

Gannon glanced over at the television as he came to sit beside Cam. "I've never understood why people like this sport."

"Well, I've never understood how people can spend countless hours playing video games, so we're even."

Chuckling, Gannon retrieved the cartons from the plastic bag. And when he handed Cam a plastic fork, Cam reached over and pulled Gannon to him. Without hesitation, he kissed him. Sweet, simple, but it was enough to have Cam's dick hardening. He'd been thinking about Gannon for the past couple of days, wanting to see him again. Rather than be too forward and push himself on Gannon, he'd been waiting for Gannon to make the next move.

Needless to say, he had, and Cam couldn't have been happier than he was right then.

"Eat," Gannon whispered, his hand resting on Cam's thigh.

"What if I'm not hungry for food?" Cam mumbled against Gannon's mouth, unable to resist touching him.

"What *are* you hungry for?"

"Hmm," Cam groaned, sliding his mouth down Gannon's jaw. "You smell good." So fucking good.

Although the food smelled delicious, Cam couldn't focus on anything other than the rich, spicy scent emanating from Gannon. He'd missed him the last couple of days, eager to pick up where they'd left off in Gannon's shower.

"I'm glad you're here," he told Gannon. And now that he was there, Cam knew there was no way he could focus on food right now.

Sliding his hands beneath Gannon's shirt, Cam forced it higher until he was insistently maneuvering it over Gannon's head. The beast within him, the one that had been caged for these past few weeks, was ready to get free, desperate to feel more of Gannon.

"Ah," Gannon moaned when Cam nipped his shoulder, forcing him down onto his back.

Cam easily worked his way over Gannon, one knee between his legs, his other foot on the floor, holding him above him.

"I've been thinking about you," Cam admitted, keeping his voice low as he kissed Gannon's neck.

"That right?"

"Mm hmm. A lot."

"What about?"

Cam continued trailing kisses over Gannon's warm skin, then stopped briefly to meet Gannon's eyes. "About all the things I want to do to you."

"I like the way you think," Gannon said, a smile flirting with his mouth.

"I thought you might." Cam reached down and worked the button on Gannon's jeans free. "Need to taste you."

"This wasn't what I had in mind when I came over," Gannon said, his tone raspy with arousal.

"No?" Cam looked down into Gannon's eyes.

"Not that I'm complaining," Gannon reassured him, making Cam laugh.

"Good." Cam continued to work Gannon's jeans down his legs, stopping long enough to pull off Gannon's loafers and toss them to the floor.

Loafers.

As nerdy as that was, it didn't dim the raging lust that coursed through him. Everything about Gannon—nerdy or not—turned him on.

Everything.

Rather than start at Gannon's mouth, Cam began trailing kisses up Gannon's legs once he'd relieved him of his clothing. He didn't rush, making sure to linger on all the sensitive spots, cataloging them whenever Gannon would moan. He wanted to make him crazy. As crazy as Cam was.

Cam forced one of Gannon's legs up, resting it along the back cushion of the couch, then positioned himself between Gannon's legs. Brushing his lips over the insides of Gannon's thighs, he continued to watch him, enjoying that bewildered expression.

"Cam," Gannon groaned when Cam licked him, sliding the flat of his tongue across Gannon's balls as he worked his way to Gannon's other thigh.

"Hmm?"

"Love your mouth on me."

Yeah, well, Gannon wasn't the only one. Cam loved exploring every inch of Gannon's delectable body, the intoxicating scent, the warmth of smooth skin over sleek muscle, the salty taste of him. If Gannon would allow it, Cam could do this all damn day.

Gannon's back bowed when Cam laved his balls once more, licking, sucking.

"You're gonna kill me," Gannon groaned.

"Want me to stop?" Cam asked with a chuckle.

"Fuck no. Never."

Cam resumed feasting on him, teasing him but not touching his thick cock, currently standing eager and proud. When Gannon reached for Cam's head, he pushed his hand away.

"No touching," Cam warned. "Put your hands behind your head."

The annoyed glare that Gannon shot him made Cam grin, but he continued to torture him, watching the way Gannon's dark eyes turned nearly black with arousal.

Needless to say, dinner was going to have to wait.

At least until Cam had dessert first.

GANNON WASN'T SURE how he was going to make it through this unscathed.

Honestly, he hadn't been thinking about sex on the drive over. Not entirely, anyway. He'd really come to have dinner with Cam, spend a couple of hours with him.

But like he'd told Cam, he definitely wasn't complaining.

Cam hadn't done anything more than use that wicked tongue and those delicious lips, and Gannon was ready to explode. When Cam ordered him to put his hands behind his head, somehow he managed to obey. Watching Cam as he explored, his damp hair—obviously from his shower—tickling the insides of Gannon's thighs ... it made him want to beg and plead for Cam to put him out of his misery.

Yet he kept his mouth closed, save for the few grunts and groans that drifted up from his chest, rumbling out of him as his blood heated from the sinful seduction. He couldn't look away, mesmerized by the promise in Cam's blue eyes, the insistence of his tongue.

And here he'd thought they'd have dinner together and then...

"Fuck," Gannon cried out when Cam's tongue lightly grazed Gannon's dick as he moved upward. He was barely hanging on, and that slight caress... It was almost more than he could take.

Much to his dismay, Cam didn't linger, didn't take Gannon's aching cock into his mouth. As he worked his way upward, licking across the sensitive skin beneath his navel, Gannon sucked in a breath, willing Cam back down.

It didn't do any good, because Cam continued to kiss his stomach, making his abs flex from the soft press of his lips. As he moved higher, Gannon was tempted to move his hands, but he clutched his own hair instead, forcing himself to endure the sensual torment.

"Mmm." The vibration from Cam's mouth against Gannon's nipple had his dick jumping, pressing demandingly between their bodies.

Gannon forced his eyes to remain open, watching as Cam flicked his tongue over his nipple, using his teeth to provoke the small brown disc until it hardened against Cam's lips. He quickly learned that the torture wasn't over. Cam moved to Gannon's other nipple, then moved higher, nipping Gannon's skin along the way, never stopping, even as he worked his way past Gannon's armpit to the sensitive skin on the underside of Gannon's arms.

The persistent nudge of Cam's cock—still clothed behind his shorts—against his own had him gritting his teeth, desperate for more. Only Gannon didn't know what he wanted. Not exactly, at least. He was torn. He wanted Cam naked, so he could feel him skin to skin, but he didn't want Cam to stop doing what he was doing. He wanted to return the favor, to explore every inch of Cam with his tongue, but he didn't want Cam to stop. He wanted to wrap his lips around Cam's thick erection, sucking him into his mouth, but he wanted Cam to wrap those sweet, soft lips around the head of his cock and tease him with his tongue. He wanted to bend Cam over, slide his aching dick into the heated recesses of Cam's body, but he wanted Cam to fold him in half and impale him, fucking him until only one syllable existed in Gannon's vocabulary: Cam.

"Too many clothes," Gannon muttered.

Cam lifted his head and smiled. "I can fix that."

As he lay there, body humming, Gannon watched Cam undress. His shirt coming off first, then his shorts. No underwear. Huh.

Gannon liked that. A lot.

Before he could say anything, Cam resumed his position above him, the sweet torment returning.

Gannon was coming undone, probably what Cam had wanted when he'd started this a short time ago. But now, as he lay there on the couch, enduring the exquisite torment, there was nothing more that he could do except enjoy it and pray that Cam didn't stop.

When Cam's lips brushed his, Gannon sucked Cam's bottom lip into his mouth, drawing a hiss from Cam. Cam's hips rocked, his cock sliding against Gannon's, and he thought for a moment that he would come just like that.

"Cam," Gannon sputtered in warning.

"Mmm. Close?" Cam questioned, sucking the sensitive skin of Gannon's neck.

"Need more," he urged.

"You wanna feel me inside you?"

Gannon nodded.

"Tell me," Cam ordered, propping himself up on his elbows and staring down at Gannon. "Tell me you wanna feel me buried deep inside you."

"God, yes."

"Say it."

"Fuck me, Cam," he pleaded. "Wanna feel you."

"Skin to skin?"

Gannon locked his eyes with Cam's, understanding just what he was saying. A wave of heat so powerful, so overwhelming tore through him, making him tremble. The thought of Cam bare … inside him. It was something he'd thought about, sure, but hadn't expected. Not yet, anyway.

Again, not complaining.

Cam must've thought he was hesitating, because he said, "Trust me?"

There was so much hope in those liquid blue depths Gannon's heart shuddered in his chest. Condoms had always been a requirement for Gannon—giving or receiving. He'd never been in a relationship that had made it far enough to consider not using one.

But with Cam…

"I'm clean," Gannon blurted, as though he'd been the one to make the suggestion.

"Me, too," Cam whispered, pressing his lips to Gannon's briefly. "This'll be my first time without one."

Gannon nodded, his mind reeling. "Me, too. I've never… Not without one."

"You sure you're okay with this?"

Gannon liked that they were having this conversation. Oddly it wasn't weird. And they were obviously on the same page here.

The mere notion of being Cam's first … anything… It caused an even stronger tremor to work its way through his body. "Yes."

"Bed," Cam barked. "Need more room."

Before Gannon could process the words, Cam was on his feet, pulling Gannon up with him. They fumbled their way over to the big bed, hands gliding over warm skin, mouth to mouth, tongue to tongue. Gannon didn't even flinch when he fell onto the bed, dragging Cam down with him, wrapping his legs around Cam's lean hips, trying to bring him closer.

Cam didn't remain where Gannon wanted him for long, sliding back down Gannon's body, his lips lightly brushing over his dick again, a tortured cry erupting from him as the sensitive head throbbed.

Strong hands eased beneath Gannon's thighs, and he found himself folded over, Cam's dark head bent between his legs.

"Ahh … fuck … Cam." Gannon was blinded by pleasure when Cam's tongue slid against the sensitive tissue, gently probing Gannon's asshole.

This time, Gannon did reach down, twining his fingers in Cam's silky hair, holding him to him as Cam rimmed him roughly. Gannon rocked his hips, trying to increase the friction, wanting to feel Cam's tongue inside him, fucking him.

"More," Gannon pleaded.

"Hold that thought," Cam said, pulling away from Gannon.

Reckless

Lying there, his heart in his throat, body ablaze, Gannon watched as Cam retrieved lube from the nightstand drawer. He never looked away as Cam squeezed a generous amount into his hand, then stroked his cock, leaving the thick shaft glistening.

Cam probed Gannon's ass with a finger, slowly, gently. Another finger joined the first, and Gannon forced himself to relax.

"Hurt?"

Gannon shook his head, sighing when Cam twisted his fingers, stroking Gannon's prostate. "Ah, fuck," he groaned, the pleasure intensifying.

Then he felt Cam add a third finger, scissoring them, working him open, preparing him to take his cock. It was too much but not enough. "Need to … feel you."

"Legs around me," Cam ordered, resuming his position above Gannon.

Gannon wrapped his legs around Cam, trying to pull him closer, but Cam kept a small amount of space between them, his hand reaching down to guide the thick crown of his cock against Gannon's anus.

When the head touched Gannon's ass, he held his breath. It'd been a long damn time since he'd bottomed. And though he wanted this more than he wanted anything else, he feared the pain. He felt the piercing first, the chill of the metal against his sensitive tissue.

"You're in control," Cam whispered softly, leaning forward, his warm breath caressing Gannon's ear. "It's all about you."

Gannon reached up, grabbing Cam's head and pulling his mouth down. Sliding his tongue inside, he explored slowly, forcing himself to relax. Within minutes, the tension was building once again, but this time, only the feel of Cam lodged deep inside him would be able to quench the thirst. Only Cam seemed to be holding back.

Gannon shifted and the head of Cam's cock breached him.

While Cam kissed him, Gannon pulled Cam's hips forward, allowing Gannon to take more of him. It still wasn't enough. Gannon tried to move, hoping to encourage Cam deeper, but it didn't help. Breaking the kiss, Gannon pushed Cam's chest, forcing him up so that Gannon could see him. That was when he noticed the pained expression on Cam's face.

"So fucking tight," Cam growled, opening his eyes to meet Gannon's. "Never felt … anything like it."

"Deeper," Gannon urged.

Cam's hips shifted slightly and Gannon felt more of him press inside. He wasn't sure he could take all of Cam. He was too big, too thick.

"You're gonna feel the piercings," Cam warned.

Gannon prepared for the pain, but it didn't come. He felt the slide of the metal balls, but it didn't hurt. Different, yes.

"Okay?" Cam asked.

Gannon nodded. "Need all of you. You won't hurt me."

Cam's eyes widened and a flash of heat ignited. That was when Gannon knew that he'd triggered the beast within.

Reckless

Cam's big hands gripped Gannon's knees, forcing his legs close to Gannon's body as he pushed his hips forward, feeding inch after inch into Gannon's body until Gannon was so full it hurt. Not so much that he wanted Cam to stop but enough that he was aware of every inch penetrating him.

Cam retreated slowly, but even at that pace, Gannon felt the piercings inside him. They still didn't necessarily hurt, but it was a different feeling. Something he hadn't anticipated.

And just when he caught his breath, ready for more, Cam gave it to him.

Hard.

"Oh, fuck," Gannon cried out as Cam began impaling him, deep and hard, over and over.

Strong hands tightened on his knees, forcing him into the mattress as Cam's big, beautiful body powered into him, fucking him hard, fast, deep. The pain receded, and the only thing left was glorious pleasure, filling him, stretching him, those piercings making him very aware of how deep Cam was inside him.

Droplets of sweat trickled down Cam's face, but he never slowed, and Gannon took everything he offered, yanking his cock firmly, desperate for release.

Time receded and nothing mattered except for the way their bodies were joined, the sweet friction of Cam in his ass, of his own hand furiously jacking his cock. Gannon was ablaze with sensation, overcome with a desire so strong, so fierce he knew he couldn't outrun it.

His groans were punctuated with every driving thrust, mingling with the groans of pleasure coming from Cam, who still hovered above him, watching the place where their bodies were joined.

Cam's eyes slid up to meet Gannon's briefly, and he knew that Cam was trying to hold back.

"Come ... for ... me..." Gannon could hardly get the words out as Cam continued to fuck him hard and fast, stretching him wider, going deeper with every thrust of his hips.

A rumble started in Cam's chest, but it quickly graduated to a roar as Cam slammed into him, once, twice, stilling on the third brutal thrust. Gannon fisted his cock, jerking himself harder as Cam's dick pulsed in his ass. And the thought of what they'd done, coming together like that— skin to skin—had Gannon's release erupting, his cock jerking as he came, his eyes locked on Cam's the entire time.

"Oh, yeah. Beautiful," Cam mumbled, watching Gannon's dick spurt over his stomach and chest.

Gannon knew in that moment that he'd fallen for Cam, given himself over to him completely. And not just his body. His heart, his soul. Every piece of him.

And he could only hope that Cam felt the same, because what he had to tell him next wasn't going to be nearly as pleasant as what they'd just done.

Twenty-Seven

AFTER A QUICK shower with Gannon, Cam pulled on a pair of shorts and returned to the couch, where they'd originally started out. His mind was whirling with thoughts of what they'd just done. More accurately, of how amazing that had been. Cam had never felt anything like that. Then again, he'd never felt anything like what he felt when he was with Gannon period. He knew that this was more than sex, more than a casual acquaintance combined with intense sex.

Hell, it couldn't be casual. They'd just had sex without barriers, without a condom. Something Cam had never considered until Gannon. Definitely not casual.

No, this was…

"I'm flying to Singapore tomorrow."

Staring blankly up at Gannon, who was standing in front of him, Cam processed what he was saying. And just like that, those few words numbed him completely.

Flying.

Singapore.

Gone.

Gone was the incredible high from making love to Gannon in a way Cam had never done before. Gone was that strange stirring in his chest that caused his heart to feel so full he thought it might burst. And gone Gannon would be tomorrow.

There was a feeling there, though. This was a tightening in his chest that cut off the oxygen to his brain. Cam felt that invisible band tighten, constricting his lungs, as he sat motionless on the couch, the container of food in his hand, fork halfway to his mouth.

He suddenly wasn't hungry.

Slowly, he set the container on the table, placed the fork neatly beside it, and looked at the television. He couldn't bring himself to look at Gannon again.

"I'll be gone for a week," Gannon explained.

Cam barely heard the words, though. His pulse was pounding in his ears. He could feel sweat trickling down by his ear, his hands were shaking, and his stomach flipped.

"Cam? Talk to me."

He couldn't. That deeply ingrained fear had taken root, stealing his breath and his voice. They were all symptoms of a panic attack, something that he'd battled for years and years. He'd purposely distanced himself from people whose lives revolved around travel because it was too hard for him.

Rational or not, he couldn't stop it.

What he should've done was tell Gannon to be careful, to call him every day while he was gone. Let him know that Cam loved him, wanted to be with him, couldn't wait for him to get back so they could do what they'd done a few minutes ago again and again.

Instead, he could only think about what his life would be like if Gannon never came back from this trip.

What they'd just shared … even he wasn't naïve enough to think that was just lust and hormones. The entire time he'd been buried inside Gannon—without a fucking condom because he'd wanted to feel *all* of him—Cam had felt a pleasure unlike anything he'd ever known. But it had been more than that. So much more.

So, now, the thought of losing Gannon... It was more than he could bear.

He saw Gannon take a step closer. "Cam, we—"

"You should go," Cam blurted, his heart racing, his stomach churning.

Forcing himself to look over, he felt his heart seize in his chest when he saw the devastation that transformed Gannon's handsome features. He watched as Gannon swallowed hard, his throat working, and Cam suddenly felt sick.

But forcing Gannon away now, that wasn't nearly as hard as losing him forever would be.

At least that was what he told himself.

"Is that what you really want?" Gannon asked, his voice rough.

"Yeah," Cam lied. "I want you to go."

"I'm sorry," Gannon said, taking a step back. "I know what you've been through..."

"You don't know," Cam yelled. "You don't fucking know what it feels like." No one knew. "I can't go through that again. It's over, Gannon. We're done."

Gannon's dark eyes narrowed on his face. "See," Gannon choked out, pointing at him, fury creasing his brow, "I thought we could get past this. I just wish I'd known before..."

"Before *what*?" Cam snapped.

"Before I went and fucking fell in love with you."

It was Cam's turn to swallow hard, shock settling inside him as he watched Gannon spin away from him and go for the door. Before Cam could call him back—if he'd even wanted to—Gannon was gone, the door slamming behind him.

For the second time in his life, that devastating loss settled over him, choking him, singeing every nerve ending with horrific, overwhelming pain. And when Cam rolled onto his side, staring at the muted television, he realized he couldn't see the screen through the blurry haze.

Because now, for the first time since that dreadful day when he'd learned his mother would never be coming home, he was crying.

Sometime later, a knock on his door had Cam bolting upright once again, wiping the moisture from his face. He waited, praying that the person on the other side of his door wasn't Gannon. He didn't want Gannon to see him like this.

"Cam? You okay?"

Roan.

Wiping his eyes with the heels of his hands, he took a deep breath, exhaled, and pretended he hadn't just been crying like a fucking girl. Pretended that he wasn't disappointed that Gannon hadn't come back for him.

Not that he deserved it.

"Come in."

When his best friend opened the door, glancing around slowly, Cam wondered what Roan saw. What he was looking for.

"You all right?" Roan asked again, closing the door behind him and making his way over to the couch. "I heard yelling. Then the door slam."

"Perfect," he choked out, hating the hoarseness of his voice.

"You sure? I saw Gannon leave a few minutes ago and he didn't look happy."

Cam doubted that he was, but he wasn't going to tell Roan that. "I'm cool," he told his friend, keeping his eyes on the television.

"What happened?"

"Nothing," Cam lied. He didn't want to get into this. Not now. Not ever. "It's over between me and Gannon."

Was it his imagination or did Roan's body go completely still?

"Y'all broke up?"

Cam nodded as he fell into the cushions, placing his hands on his stomach. As far as Cam was concerned, no matter how much he wanted them to, things between him and Gannon wouldn't work. He'd spent years trying to get over his fears, and no amount of talking about it had ever helped, but he'd managed to deal with it, to surround himself with people who weren't planning to go off and leave him.

Selfish? Maybe.

Something he could change? No.

"You want me to stay?" Roan offered.

"No." Cam just wanted to be alone.

Roan nodded, then got to his feet. "If you need anything, I'm across the hall."

"Thanks." Cam didn't bother to look at his friend.

And when the door clicked shut behind Roan, Cam once again fell over onto the couch and closed his eyes. Praying for no more tears and for at least a measure of peace, because the pain in his chest was overwhelming.

When someone suffered from a broken heart, did it actually hurt?

Cam rubbed his chest. He wasn't sure what the answer was, but based on the pains he was experiencing, he was beginning to think that was the case.

AS GANNON DROVE back home, he fought the nausea roiling in his gut. After what had happened between him and Cam … well, Gannon felt violently ill. But he managed to keep breathing as he drove, turning the AC on full blast, but it hadn't helped. His head was spinning, and his stomach actually hurt. Never mind the pain in his chest. If he didn't know better, he would've thought he was having a heart attack.

Maybe he was in shock. That could happen, right? After all, his world had just been flipped on its axis. Fucking rainbows and glitter one minute and the next … poof! All gone.

He still wasn't sure how it'd all happened. He hadn't actually intended for things to work out that way. Yeah, maybe he'd taken some of Milly's advice, but the truth was, he hadn't expected anything to happen between him and Cam tonight. He'd been surprised when things had escalated so rapidly, but he couldn't—wouldn't—have stopped it. Being with Cam… For Gannon, it was the only thing that felt right at this point.

And now it was over.

Just like that.

As he was turning into his neighborhood, his phone rang. He stabbed the button to answer it, wishing it was Cam but knowing it wasn't. "Hello?"

"Hey." Milly's voice was soft, concerned. Clearly she had listened to the voice mail Gannon had left her nearly an hour ago. "I'm on my way over. Are you home yet?"

"About to be," he told her, his voice rough with the emotion clogging his throat.

"Okay. Leave the door unlocked. I'll be there in a few."

Gannon disconnected the call, then pressed the button to open his garage door, pulling inside faster than he should have. He slammed on the brakes to keep from going through the wall, shoved the gear in park, turned off the ignition, and dropped his head onto the steering wheel. The dry sobs tore at him, making his chest hurt, but he refused to cry because someone else had kicked him to the curb.

He should've known this would happen. Hell, maybe part of him had, but he'd cared so much about Cam that he'd convinced himself they could work through this.

"This can't be happening," he muttered, closing his eyes.

He had no idea how long he sat like that, but it must've been a while, because that was exactly how Milly found him. When she opened the driver's door, he jumped.

"What're you doing in your car?" she asked, reaching in and pulling on his arm.

Gannon didn't say anything, forcing his stiff legs out.

"At least you had the good sense to turn off the engine and leave the garage door open."

Well, he wasn't suicidal. Just heartbroken.

"Come on," she urged, closing the door and nudging him toward the house. "What the hell happened? I damn near wrecked my car when I heard your voice mail."

Without feeling his legs, Gannon made it inside with Milly pushing him from behind. Not bothering to turn on lights, he trudged over to the sofa and flopped down. "I reminded Cam that I was going to Singapore."

"So? We'll be back in a week."

"He told me to leave."

Milly lowered herself to the cushion beside him, her expression softened. "He broke up with you?"

276

That was one way to look at it, yes. Gannon's stomach lurched, and more pain erupted in his chest as he nodded.

"What a prick," she hissed.

"He's not a prick," Gannon said defensively.

"In my book he is. What? Does he think you can stop the world and stop running your business just because y'all are together? That's not how relationships work. What does he think you're gonna do there? Did you tell him it's work? That you have no choice?"

Gannon stared back at Milly. As much of a betrayal as it might be, telling her was the only thing he could do. He needed her support right now. Probably more than ever.

"*What?* Talk to me, Gan. What is it?"

Giving in, Gannon relayed the harsh details to her, watching her eyes widen as he explained how Cam's mother had been away on a business trip when she'd died.

"Oh, the poor guy."

"I thought he was a prick?" Gannon mused, sitting up and putting his elbows on his knees.

"So you asked him about his mother?"

"No. He told me."

"Did you tell him about *your* parents?"

That was the worst part of it all. Gannon *had* told Cam about how he'd been disowned by his parents, kicked to the curb because he couldn't live up to their expectations, wasn't who they wanted him to be. Much in the same way Cam had kicked him out tonight. But still, here he was.

"Yeah," he admitted.

"What a prick," she muttered.

Gannon's lips tried to turn up into a smile, but halfway there, they gave out.

"Don't move," Milly said, patting his knee. "I'll get you a drink."

Reckless

He didn't need a drink, but he didn't say as much. He needed a new heart, for someone to take the broken one out of his chest and replace it with one that was a hell of a lot less fragile. Indestructible would be nice.

Milly returned a few minutes later with a tumbler of scotch. "Have you packed?"

Yeah, he'd packed. He was all set for their flight out tomorrow morning.

Physically, anyway.

Mentally, he wasn't sure he'd be able to go.

Twenty-Eight

THE NEXT MORNING, Cam found himself standing on the dock just before sunrise. He hadn't slept for shit, tossing and turning, waking up from a nightmare that reminded him so much of the day the cops had shown up to tell Cam's father that Cam's mother wouldn't be coming home ever again.

Only, in his dream, the cops had come to talk to *him*. And the person they'd said wouldn't be coming home was Gannon.

"Hey, man. What's kickin'?"

Cam glanced over to see Dare approaching, his feet bare, ball cap on backwards, wearing a white tank top and shorts. He looked as though he didn't have a care in the world, and Cam envied him.

Turning his attention back to the water, Cam sipped from his coffee cup.

"Did Gannon leave for Singapore today?"

Cam nodded, the coffee burning down his throat, feeling like acid as it settled in his stomach. He wasn't sure how Dare knew that Gannon was leaving, but he didn't have it in him to ask. Maybe he'd said something, maybe Gannon had. Who knew? Who cared? The fact of the matter was, Gannon was on a plane to Singapore.

Dare came to stand beside him, hands in his pockets as he stared out at the water.

"He's gonna be fine, you know."

No, Cam didn't know, but he appreciated the sentiment. It was what he'd expected last night from Roan, but Cam got the impression Roan had actually been relieved that he'd broken up with Gannon. When he hadn't been thinking about Gannon, worrying that he would be found dead in some hotel room, worried that he would never, ever get over the man he'd fallen in love with, Cam had tried to figure out why Roan wouldn't have been more supportive.

"I broke up with him," Cam muttered.

"What?" Dare turned toward him, adjusting his ball cap as he stared at Cam, frowning. "Are you fucking crazy?"

Yeah, he was pretty sure he was.

"Dude, seriously," Dare huffed. "Please don't tell me you sent him packing because you're scared."

Cam glared at his friend.

"What? Someone has to call you on this shit, bro. I could rub your ass and make you feel better, but that won't help. Roan's been doing that for too long."

Cam frowned. *Rub his ass?*

"I'm just sayin'," Dare continued. "I only want you to be happy, and to be honest, Gannon's the best thing that's happened to you in a long damn time. Sure, he's a nerd"— Dare raised his hands in his *I surrender* move when Cam narrowed his eyes—"but that seems to work for him. And you…"

"What about me?" Cam asked.

"You're different when you're with him. Not quite so … reckless."

"And that's a good thing?"

"I didn't say it was good or bad. But seriously, bro, you're willin' to bungee jump off the Macau Tower, but you can't take a fucking leap and fall in love with some guy who obviously makes you feel more alive than any of that crazy shit you do."

"Whatever." The way Dare made it sound, Cam was using his fear as an excuse. He was *not* using this as an excuse. The panic attack was proof.

"Last I checked, there was like a one in fifteen million chance that you'll die in a plane crash. Now, I don't have a clue what the statistic is for … you know … but I do know that the chances are slim. How many times has Gannon gone to Singapore?"

Cam shrugged. He didn't know. Hadn't bothered to ask.

"Well, I'm sure it's more than this one time. And he's come back every time. Wasn't he in Cali a couple of weeks ago?"

Cam didn't answer. He didn't like where Dare was going with this.

"Man, I love you and all, but seriously. You're your own worst enemy. Give the guy a chance."

"Why didn't Roan give me this encouragement?" he mused aloud.

"Are you fucking serious?" Dare's voice was low. "The guy can't see past his own love for you."

"*What?*" Cam froze, turning to look at Dare. "What the hell are you talking about?"

"Ah, hell. I forgot. You can't see it, either. He's so fucking in love with you—or at least he *thinks* he is—it's awkward to be in the same room with the two of you together."

Cam had no idea what Dare was talking about. Roan wasn't in love with him. That was fucking absurd. "Bullshit."

"Call it what you want," Dare said with a shrug. "I call it as I see it."

Cam turned away, his mind spinning with all the information Dare had just thrown at him.

"Well," Dare said, clicking his tongue, "it's been romantic as hell watchin' the sun rise with you and all, but quite frankly, you're just not my type. I'll see you in the office later. Cool?"

Cam nodded, not bothering to watch Dare as he walked away.

Roan was in love with him?

There was no way that was true. He would've realized it, wouldn't he? They'd been friends for... Christ. They'd been friends for twenty-five years. Ever since they were seven years old. Never once in all that time had he gotten the impression Roan felt anything for him.

Not that it mattered. Cam didn't have those feelings for Roan. No, he couldn't imagine his life without the guy, but he also couldn't imagine... A chill raced down his spine as he thought about kissing Roan. It would be like kissing his brother.

Not cool.

As he stood there, trying to assemble all of his jumbled thoughts, his phone vibrated in his pocket. Retrieving it, he checked the screen to see a text message. Well, more like a text *novel*.

This is Milly. Remember me? We're on the plane getting ready to leave Austin. I've spent the last few hours thinking about what I wanted to say to you. And though I think you're being a douche, I kinda get it. I don't approve, but I get it. But that's not why I'm texting you. I'm sending you this because it's the first of many you'll get from me for the next week. I'm gonna walk you through this. I'm gonna show you that Gannon's okay. If I have to send you a million texts a day just to get through that thick skull of yours, I will. Because he's my friend and what you did to him last night... You broke his heart, which is not cool. Now, you can't tell him I told you that cuz he'll kill me, but still, it's true. So, be expecting me to blow up your phone. And I want you to do me a huge favor while we're gone. Think about Gannon. Think about what you have with him. Because if you let him walk out of your life, you're not only a douche, but you're also stupid. TTYL.

Cam stared at his phone for long minutes, rereading the text message again and again. He was running through it again when another message came in.

Oh, and it'd be really awesome if you'd respond so I know you got this.

Unable to hold back, Cam smiled. This woman... She was something else. She was the female version of Dare. That's what she was.

Thumbing the buttons on the screen, Cam responded with: *I heard you. Loud and clear.*

Good. Now quit being a douche.

Dropping his phone into his pocket, Cam turned to stare out at the water again. The tightness in his chest was still there, but he felt a measure of relief. Whether it was Dare's not-so-subtle way of putting him in his place or Milly's ... one way or another, his eyes were open this morning.

And he was seeing things he hadn't seen before. Not that he knew what exactly that meant yet.

PLANES WEREN'T HER thing, but Milly had learned to get over that fear. Having worked for Gannon for ten years, she'd done it enough times at this point. It seemed they were going one place or another every other week. Usually at this point, she would've been meditating while the crew members prepared for take off.

But for this trip, she had other things to worry about.

Like the fact that her best friend was moping around as though someone had run over his dog.

Poor Gannon.

She did feel bad for him. Which was why she'd sent the text to Cam. The idea had come to her last night after she'd forced Gannon to go to bed and made herself at home in his guest room. As she was lying there, trying to figure out how she could fix this, or at least try, it'd hit her. So, she'd snuck back downstairs, found Gannon's phone, broken into it using the password he didn't think she knew—seriously, the code was her birthday, how could she not know?—and jotted down Cam's number.

Being Gannon's friend, it was her responsibility to take matters into her own hands when he was too upset to do so. And since Cam was obviously in no shape to figure this out on his own, Milly was helping him, too.

"Would you like something to drink before we take off?" the first-class attendant asked her, leaning in and smiling.

Milly glanced at Gannon. He shook his head. "We're good for now, thanks."

When the woman moved to the people on the other side of the aisle, Milly turned her phone so that the camera faced Gannon, then hit the button to take a picture.

"What are you doing?" Gannon asked, frowning over at her.

Milly smiled. "Nothing."

A few seconds later, she'd sent the picture to Cam with the caption: *I think the frown is permanent.*

She wasn't above making Cam feel bad for what he'd done. Sure, she felt some sympathy for him. What he'd gone through couldn't have been easy. Gannon had filled her in on the sad details after he'd had a couple of drinks, and the more he'd talked, the more upset she'd gotten.

But still, these two men were meant to be together. Milly had known Gannon for a long time, and not once in all those years had she ever seen him as happy, as carefree as he'd been for the past few weeks. Cam had lit something inside him, and Milly hated to see that flame die because these two stubborn men were too blind to see it.

So, when she'd woken up that morning, she'd made a vow to do something to help them both. Sure, Gannon would probably be a little peeved when he found out she'd interfered, but if it helped them to see what they'd be losing by giving up at this point, then it would be totally worth it.

Twenty-Nine

One week later—Thursday (Hong Kong)

"WHAT ARE YOU doing?" Gannon asked Milly as she was typing away on her phone. They'd just boarded the plane in Hong Kong after a four-hour flight from Singapore. Only eighteen more hours and they'd finally be home.

"Nothing," she said, looking up at him, a twinkle in her clear blue eyes. "What are *you* doing?"

Studying her momentarily, he tried to figure out if she was hiding something. Knowing Milly, she was; he just didn't know what. For the past week, she'd been acting strange, taking pictures of him when she didn't think he saw her, texting all the time, day and night.

"Who're you texting?" he asked, glancing down at her phone.

"None of your business," she muttered, turning her phone screen so that he couldn't see it.

Any other day, Gannon would've dug deeper, tried to get her to tell him, but he didn't have the energy. He was waiting for the attendants to close the door so he could relax and hopefully get some sleep.

He hadn't slept for shit all week. Every night, it had been around three o'clock before he finally managed to close his eyes, but at that point, the only thing he could do was relive the moments he'd shared with Cam. Every single one, starting back to the day he'd walked into that marina and gotten his first look at the man who would so easily steal his heart, then crush it into oblivion.

And a week apart hadn't helped him at all. He still thought about Cam every waking moment, still dreamed about him during the few hours he managed to pass out. But now that he was heading back to Texas, he wasn't sure how he was going to survive knowing Cam was only a short drive away. It had been relatively easy while he'd been in Singapore. With the time difference, not to mention the miles between them ... Gannon had focused on work, because that was the reason he'd been there.

He feared that once he was home, he wouldn't be as strong.

If only he could harden his heart, forget about Cam, forget about the amazing four weeks they'd shared. Sure, there had been ups and downs, but that was expected. It had been emotional on so many levels. Unfortunately, Gannon was too invested at this point, and the breakup was brutal. He feared he would suffer for a long time to come.

Thankfully, he'd had Milly around to keep his mind off things, even if she'd been acting strange. He was never bored with her around, and since she'd known he was devastated, she'd doubled her efforts to keep him in a good mood. Over the years, he'd learned to fake it, and this trip had been no different. The last thing Gannon would do was let people know he'd been hurt. It was easier to pretend he wasn't human than to cut himself open and bleed for people.

But now he had eighteen hours to prepare himself for the inevitable.

Only he wasn't sure that was enough time.

Eighteen hours later—Friday morning

The ding of the seat belt warning had Gannon looking up. A second later, the flight attendant's voice came over the speaker, announcing they were preparing to land.

Finally.

Gannon was back in Texas—*technically*, although still thirty thousand feet in the air. According to the disembodied voice, they were preparing to land in the next half hour, and he couldn't wait. He was antsy and fidgety, something that was completely foreign to him. He'd spent the better part of the flight from Hong Kong to Dallas taking care of business, sending emails to get everything set up for the new operations director he'd hired while in Singapore, but now that he was almost home, he couldn't focus long enough to do anything more.

From the moment he'd stepped onto the plane in Austin eight days ago, preparing to go overseas, he'd been plagued by thoughts of Cam, trying to figure out how things had gone so very wrong. Not a minute went by when he hadn't wished he was back in Texas so he could… He didn't even know what he'd wanted to do. It wasn't as though he could simply walk up to Cam and insist that the man love him back.

Unfortunately, it didn't work that way.

Gannon knew that Cam didn't like the fact that he traveled, and he knew why. Hell, he even *understood* why. He sympathized with Cam, understood how Cam felt, how tragic it was that his mother had died while she'd been away on a business trip, but surely other people in Cam's life had traveled since then. The fact that they continued to come back should've reassured him, but that didn't seem to be the case.

But in the same sense, Cam knew what had happened to Gannon, yet he'd had no issues kicking him to the curb. Not once during the entire trip had he heard from Cam. Not one single time. Then again, he hadn't tried to reach out, either. The thirteen-hour time difference had helped in that regard, making it so that they weren't even awake at the same time.

So, instead of reaching out, Gannon had done a lot of thinking. Mainly about the night that had changed Gannon's life forever. The night they'd made love and Gannon had gone and ruined it by reminding Cam he was flying to Singapore. Not that he could've done it differently. It would've been wrong of him to simply disappear for a week.

Then again, maybe that would've been better than having Cam break up with him.

Although Gannon had forced himself to walk away, his stomach churning with every step, he'd since realized that giving up on Cam wasn't an option. He couldn't simply walk out of Cam's life and never look back. He loved him.

Reckless

So he'd made a promise to himself that once he got back, he would confront Cam, get to the root of the matter, and figure out a way to make it work between them. There was no doubt in Gannon's mind that Cam was trying to protect himself emotionally. They'd ventured to that next level, and when they were having sex, Cam was more open than Gannon had ever seen him. It was amazing.

But this rift between them... There had to be a way to fix it. It was the only option.

He needed to talk to Cam, settle his fears, assure him that he would be fine. Then again, Gannon wasn't sure he could promise that. And he'd never made a promise he couldn't keep.

Being that he was used to being in control, running a multimillion-dollar company, taking risks regarding innovation and design in an industry that was consistently evolving and changing, never sitting still, Gannon had a hard time not being able to predict the future. However, where his company was concerned, Gannon had people in place who managed those things, gave him reports, anticipated problems, identified areas of improvement. There was some semblance of control there.

Where his relationship with Cam was concerned, Gannon felt so out of control. To the point it scared the hell out of him most of the time.

Gripping the armrests, Gannon closed his eyes as the plane made its descent into ABIA. He thought about Cam, about seeing his face for the first time in a week.

And he realized that everything that would happen going forward was outside of his control, hard as that was to grasp. Now, as he was used to doing with his business, he merely needed to figure out how to acclimate.

CAM WAS SO fucking nervous.

No, nervous was an understatement. More like terrified.

Standing near the baggage claim area at Austin-Bergstrom International Airport, he wiped his hands on his shorts for the millionth time. His palms were sweaty, his heart beating as though he'd just jumped out of an airplane and his parachute wasn't opening. He'd done a lot of reckless things in his life, crazy things, but this...

By far the craziest risk he'd ever taken.

His phone vibrated in his pocket and Cam jumped.

Shit, at this rate, the TSA was going to sit him down and have a chat, thinking he was up to no good.

We're about to deplane.

Cam's fingers shook too much to type a response to Milly, so he didn't bother. He didn't know what to say, anyway.

Her instructions had been for him to man up, to do something to salvage what he and Gannon had. For a solid week, Cam had endured endless texts from her, dozens of pictures of Gannon sent to his phone, all because Milly wanted to reassure him that Gannon was okay.

It might've helped.

That didn't mean he hadn't spent the week panicked, scared that something bad would happen and he wouldn't get any more texts or pictures. He'd started to look forward to them, eagerly anticipating every update until he knew he was a basket case, staring at his phone all the time, willing another text message to come in.

But Milly had come through, just as she'd said she would, and now it was Cam's turn to come through for her. For Gannon.

Coming down the escalators.

Reading the text, Cam's heart punched hard against his ribs as he looked up from his phone, peering past the huge guitar that sat atop one of the baggage carousels toward the escalators.

Sure enough...

Cam's breath lodged in his throat when he caught a glimpse of Gannon, who was looking over his shoulder at Milly. She seemed to be chatting endlessly, keeping Gannon's attention as they stepped off the escalator, walking side by side until they were only a few feet from him.

Milly stopped and Gannon did, too. Then she nodded toward Cam.

When Gannon looked up in Cam's direction, Cam stood motionless, watching as that beautiful face realized he was standing there.

"Cam."

Swallowing hard, he choked out, "Hey."

"What are...?" Gannon's head swiveled to look at Milly.

"Gotta run," she said cheerfully, offering Gannon a small wave.

"Wait, what about...?" Gannon's eyes landed on Cam again, then back to Milly, still looking dazed and confused.

"My stepbrother's picking me up," Milly said, smiling as she headed toward the baggage carousel. "You two have fun."

Cam never took his eyes off Gannon, fear and trepidation forming a toxic cocktail in his gut as he waited to see if Gannon would send him away.

"What are you doing here?" Gannon blinked once, as though he didn't believe Cam was standing there.

"I heard you needed a ride home."

Gannon's head snapped over to the baggage area, then back to him. "You're the one she's been texting?"

Cam nodded, the dizzy feeling making him sway slightly. He planted his feet firmly on the floor, shored his nerves. He could do this. "Can I take you home?"

"I... I don't... Yeah," Gannon said with a sigh. "I'd like that."

Cam exhaled, realizing he'd been holding his breath. Which explained why he was light-headed.

"Got any bags?"

Gannon nodded.

Scared to reach for him, Cam nodded toward the carousel, then started walking, hoping Gannon would follow.

He did.

A few minutes later, they'd retrieved the one suitcase Gannon had. Cam wheeled it toward the door, where a man in a suit was standing.

"Are you ready, sir?" he asked Cam.

"Yes. Thanks."

The guy took Gannon's suitcase, and Cam felt Gannon's eyes on him as they walked out the door toward the limousine waiting for them.

Cam had thought about bringing his truck, but this seemed the more logical way to travel. With someone else driving, it would give Cam a chance to talk to Gannon, to explain. To apologize.

After confirming for the man where they were going while he placed Gannon's luggage in the trunk, Cam opened the door for Gannon, then climbed in after him. The window between the front and the back was closed, exactly as Cam had requested.

"I don't understand what's—"

Before Gannon could say more, Cam reached for him, cupping his head and pulling him forward so that Cam could kiss him.

And kiss him he did.

He knew he had a lot of explaining and apologizing to do, but he needed this right now. Kissing Gannon, feeling that electrical charge ignite between them, it calmed Cam's rioting nerves.

Kind of.

"Cam. Oh, God, Cam."

Cam wrapped his arms tightly around Gannon, holding him close as he thrust his tongue into Gannon's mouth, feeling the moment Gannon gave in, his body molding to Cam's. A sweet assault ensued, and for a while, Cam forgot where they were. The only thing that mattered was Gannon's lips on his, his hands roaming over Cam's back.

"I missed you," Cam whispered, cupping Gannon's head, separating their mouths. "So fucking much."

Gannon's eyes appeared glassy, but Cam wasn't sure if that was lust or some other emotion.

As much as Cam wanted to heat the car up for the entire ride to Gannon's, he knew they needed to talk first. The sex … yeah, Cam had missed that too, but more than that, he'd missed Gannon, and until he could assure himself that they could move forward—permanently this time—that Gannon could forgive him for being a royal ass, he had to put a halt to this.

Taking Gannon's hand in his, he took a deep breath.

And before he could say anything more, the driver alerted them that they'd arrived at their destination.

Damn. That was fast.

Thirty

GANNON WAS PRETTY sure he was dreaming. There was no way this could be real. Life simply hadn't been that good to him, so for Cam to show up out of the blue … it was surreal. The only thing that made him believe it could be real … in his dreams, Cam didn't kiss like that. Sure, it was good, but *nothing* compared to the real thing.

"Sirs, we've arrived," came the disembodied voice from a speaker behind them.

Unable to look away from Cam, Gannon remained where he was, fingers linked with Cam's, still trying to convince his overtaxed brain that this was really happening, that Cam was really there.

That Cam had actually come to the airport to pick him up.

That Cam had made the first move to fix this.

Please, God, let it be real.

The back door opened, sunlight spilling in, and Gannon managed to regain some of his faculties. Releasing Cam's hand, he grabbed his carry-on, then forced his legs to move. Outside the limo, he walked around to the back in time to see Cam passing the man a tip and taking Gannon's luggage. That was when Gannon noticed Cam's truck parked in his driveway.

Surely he wasn't dreaming that, right?

"Come on," Cam urged. "I'll make us some lunch and we can talk."

"*You'll* make lunch?" The words were out before Gannon could stop them.

Cam's lips curled up at the corner, reigniting that spark in Gannon's stomach. "Nothing fancy. I picked up a couple of cans of SpaghettiOs on my way over."

Gannon laughed, relaxing for the first time since he'd seen Cam standing in the airport waiting for him.

Once they made it inside and Gannon dumped his luggage in his bedroom, he returned to the kitchen to find Cam peering into the freezer.

Cam glanced over at him. "I'm disappointed in you, Gannon. I thought for sure you'd been lying about not cooking frozen meals."

Gannon unbuttoned his cuffs, then rolled up his sleeves as he stared at Cam, not sure what to say to that.

"But don't worry," Cam continued. "I'll find something."

Before Cam could open the refrigerator and resume his search, Gannon moved closer until there wasn't a breath between them. Cam's hard chest pressed against his own, his body heat infusing Gannon.

"I don't want food," Gannon whispered, reaching up and cupping the back of Cam's neck. Cam was tense; he could feel the tight muscles beneath his fingers.

"I need to apologize," Cam said quickly, his hands fisting into Gannon's shirt, as though he were holding on for dear life. "What I did... I was ... wrong. It's just..."

"You were scared," Gannon filled in for him.

"Petrified."

"I know the feeling." Gannon brushed his thumb along Cam's cheek. "And I'm not talking about what you've been through. I won't pretend to know how that feels, but I do understand the fear, the pain."

Hell, he'd endured the pain of losing the most important thing in his life for a solid week. It was a wonder he was still standing, still capable of breathing when there'd been moments he'd felt as though his chest had been filled with jagged shards of glass. The pain unbearable. Truth was, he'd never thought he'd see Cam again, never believed he'd feel the overwhelming surge of emotion that filled his soul right now as he stared at the man he loved.

"I thought by pushing you away… It seemed an easier decision than having you taken from me."

Gannon met Cam's gaze. "You won't lose me, Cam. Not if I have anything to say about it."

"I wish it were that simple," Cam said, placing his hand on Gannon's mouth before he could argue. "Regardless, while you were gone, I realized something."

Gannon waited patiently for Cam to continue, his heart pounding in his chest.

"It dawned on me that either way, whether I broke up with you or … you know … I wouldn't have you in my life. And only in one of those scenarios do I actually have control."

Control. Something Gannon felt he had so little of when it came to Cam.

"The past week was brutal," Gannon admitted.

"I know." Cam took a deep breath. "Milly kept me afloat the entire time."

Gannon wasn't as shocked by that as he should've been. He knew she'd been up to something, and he should've suspected she would stick her cute little nose in the middle of his business. She was his friend, she cared about him, and he loved her for it. Even if she had been meddling.

Cam smiled. "She loves you."

"I know. I love her, too. And that's what friends do."

There was a strange flicker in the cobalt-blue orbs staring back at him, but Gannon didn't get a chance to ask before Cam's eyes widened and he said, "I'm sorry that I hurt you. It's just…"

"You're safe with me," Gannon whispered, tightening his grip on Cam's neck. "Those are the words you told me that day when I went into the water after you. Remember?"

Cam nodded.

"I don't like water. No, actually, I detest it," Gannon told Cam. "Not because of a traumatic experience. I just don't like it. But when you told me to trust you, I did. And when we made love…" Gannon watched Cam's face. "When you asked me if I trusted you, I wasn't lying when I said I did. I still do. But I need you to trust *me*."

"It's not about trust," Cam said. "I *do* trust you. It's the fear…"

"Of losing me?"

Again, Cam nodded.

"Maybe this didn't go as slow as we'd planned, or maybe it did. I don't know. Regardless, I fell in love with you somewhere along the way. It wasn't until you sent me away that I realized I couldn't control everything; I couldn't predict the future. But that's okay. As long as I have you, I don't need to know what tomorrow will bring. I just need you beside me."

Cam pulled Gannon forward. "You really love me? I mean … I know you said it that day … but…"

"Yes. I love you. With every breath I take," Gannon whispered.

"I love you, too. And that's not easy for me to say."

"Trust me, I know." Aside from Milly, Gannon hadn't loved anyone else since his parents had so selfishly tossed him aside years ago. He'd been scared to love anyone, for fear of being rejected.

Cam wrapped his arms around Gannon's back, pulling him even closer. "I can't promise it'll be easy. In case you haven't noticed, I'm a little fucked up."

"Aren't we all," Gannon teased.

Cam smiled, his eyes raking over Gannon's face. "Tell me you forgive me."

"That's part of loving someone, Cam. You accept them for who they are, faults and all. And you forgive them."

They stood like that for several heartbeats, holding one another. And every second that passed, Gannon felt as though his heart was mending, the jagged edges not quite so sharp.

"God, I missed you," Cam muttered just before he slid his hands behind Gannon's head, pulling him down.

Their mouths met, and Gannon gave in to the overwhelming heat that had suffused him from that very first kiss they'd shared right here in his kitchen. He honestly loved this man. It was scary how much he cared for Cam.

"So what do we do now?" Gannon asked, planting kisses over Cam's lips, his chin.

"Bedroom?" Cam mumbled, kissing him back.

Pulling back so he could meet Cam's beautiful gaze, Gannon smirked. "I was thinking shower."

"I like where you're going with that."

Gannon leaned in, brushing his mouth across Cam's jaw. "Only this time, I'll be sitting on that tiled ledge..." Gannon nipped Cam's earlobe. "And you'll be riding my dick." He absorbed the shudder that raced through Cam, holding him close. "And if you're lucky," Gannon continued. "Maybe I'll let you return the favor."

With that, Gannon released Cam and then turned and walked away, smiling.

CAM WATCHED GANNON walk away, taking deep breaths to calm himself. He couldn't believe this was really happening. A second chance with Gannon ... one he wasn't sure he even deserved. Someone was definitely looking out for him.

"Cam?" Gannon called out from the living room.

"Yeah?"

"Shower. Now."

Ah, hell.

Trying not to run, Cam followed after Gannon, coming to a stop in the bathroom, watching in the mirror as Gannon undressed, unbuttoning his shirt slowly before allowing it to slide down his arms.

He was beautiful. So damn beautiful.

How he could've been so stupid to think he could live without him after spending four weeks falling deeper and deeper... Cam released a breath. Relief washed over him as it really sank in that this wasn't over, that he hadn't done too much damage.

Gannon crooked a finger, urging Cam toward him.

Before he knew it, he was closing the distance between them, his hands coming to rest on Gannon's chest, fingers sliding through the soft hair there. He watched Gannon's face as he reached up and pulled Gannon's glasses off, setting them on the counter behind him.

Gannon took Cam's hands, forced them down to his sides as he turned Cam to face the mirror. Cam never took his eyes off Gannon as he moved behind him, his hands coming to rest on Cam's hips, his mouth brushing the sensitive skin of his neck.

"Tell me you trust me," Gannon said, his voice strong, urgent.

Cam nodded. "I trust you." More than he wanted to. More than he'd ever trusted anyone.

"Tell me you love me." Gannon met his eyes in the mirror.

"I love you," Cam told him, not breaking the eye contact.

Gannon's hands slid beneath the hem of Cam's T-shirt, forcing it up his torso, then over his head in one quick move that had Cam sucking in a breath. When Gannon's chest pressed against Cam's bare back, he drew in a breath. Skin to skin.

Watching intently, he followed the path that Gannon's hands made as they leisurely caressed his stomach, gliding up, up, until his fingers rested on the metal piercings in Cam's nipples. When Gannon tweaked them, at the same time gently sucking on his neck, Cam's legs swayed beneath him. Gannon's arms banded tightly around him, holding him in place as their eyes met in the mirror.

Reckless

They remained like that for long minutes while Gannon managed to undress Cam completely. And while he stood naked before Gannon, his cock rock hard and aching for Gannon's touch, Cam felt as though he were in a trance, mesmerized by the smooth way Gannon maintained control of his body, his pleasure.

"Screw the shower," Gannon bit out, stepping from behind Cam as he disrobed.

Cam didn't try to hide the fact that he was watching. He admired the long, lean lines and smooth, rigid contours as Gannon unveiled himself, forcing his slacks down his legs, followed by his boxers. He was rooted in place, unable to take his eyes off Gannon, so when Gannon grabbed his hand and pulled him toward his bedroom, Cam stumbled behind him, trusting that he knew what he was doing, because Cam damn sure didn't.

The next thing Cam knew, Gannon was on the giant four-poster bed, propped up on a pillow, tugging Cam's hand, urging him to join him. Thinking ahead for the first time since he'd walked into Gannon's house, Cam grabbed the lube from the nightstand, then joined him.

He was tempted to use his mouth to drive Gannon wild, but Gannon clearly had other plans, pulling him down on top of him.

"I missed you," Gannon whispered, pulling Cam's mouth to his.

Cam would never tire of hearing that.

Their tongues melded together, dueling as the urgency built, the need to feel Gannon inside him, claiming him... It became too much. At the same time, he never wanted it to end, loving the feel of Gannon's smooth hands caressing his back, his ass. The way Gannon's lips pressed against his while his tongue thrust into Cam's mouth, a kiss that proved how much they both needed this.

"Lube," Gannon mumbled.

Straddling Gannon's legs, Cam grabbed the tube, squeezed a generous amount into his hand. While he stroked Gannon, lubing him, loving the way he hissed and moaned, Cam continued to watch him, those dark eyes nearly black with desire. He really was the most beautiful man Cam had ever met. Inside and out.

"Ride me, baby," Gannon breathed out roughly. "Let me feel you. I need to feel you."

Cam scooted forward, reaching behind him and guiding Gannon's steely length to his entrance.

"God, yes," Gannon groaned as Cam took the wide head inside him. "Fuck."

Cam watched Gannon's face, wondered if he felt the same thing Cam had when he'd taken him bare just a week ago. This would be Gannon's first time, skin to skin. And that meant everything to Cam.

Gannon didn't move, allowing Cam to control how much he took, how deep, how slow, how fast. It wasn't long before Cam was ablaze with sensation, Gannon's girth filling him. Only when Cam had taken him all the way did Gannon reach for him, pulling him forward, taking control.

"Cam. Fuck." Gannon's breath fanned Cam's face, his hands gripping Cam's hips, holding him still while he rocked his hips, driving up into him. "Hot. Tight. Never felt anything … this good."

Resting his elbows beside Gannon's head, Cam watched him, needing this moment, needing to feel one with this man. The man who'd waltzed into his world and stolen his heart when he wasn't looking. The emotions confused him. Pleasure, pain, love, fear. It all melded together, churning inside him, making his chest expand and contract, his heart beating hard as he tried to wrap his mind around all that he was feeling.

"Love me, Cam," Gannon insisted, still holding Cam's hips. "And let me love you."

Cam nodded, unsure what he was supposed to say. Scared that the emotion was going to burst free, he buried his face in Gannon's neck, allowing the pleasure to consume him.

Gannon's hand slid up to his neck, gently holding him there, his other hand gripping his hip as he continued to make love to him, filling him, stretching him. Cam rode the waves of pleasure, never wanting it to end.

Again, Gannon had other plans. As though he weighed nothing, Gannon flipped them so that Cam was on his back. He didn't have time to shift into position before Gannon was straddling his hips, lubing Cam's cock roughly before sliding down onto him.

"Oh, fuck," Cam cried out, the heat of Gannon's body strangling his dick, sucking the air from his lungs from the sheer ecstasy of it.

"Fuck me," Gannon pleaded, leaning forward.

Cam thrust his hips upward, lodging himself to the hilt inside Gannon, drawing a ragged moan from them both.

"Harder, Cam."

Holding Gannon's hips, Cam controlled the pace, slamming into Gannon, then slowing. He repeated, maintaining a steady, alternating rhythm until they were both covered in sweat.

Again, Gannon changed positions, Cam's cock slipping from Gannon's ass as he moved, forcing Cam's leg across his body before he was once again filled by Gannon.

"Fuck me," Cam begged, fisting his hands in the sheets as Gannon fucked his ass, refusing to touch himself, knowing he could come from this alone. "Gonna come, Gan. Make me come."

Gannon's hips resumed a rapid pace, slamming into him, his cock driving deeper than Cam thought possible. Grunts and groans echoed in the room, mixed with their desperate attempts to inhale as the pleasure intensified. The tingle that had started at the base of his spine strengthened, sending sparks along every nerve ending in his entire body.

"Fuck," Cam groaned, absorbing the impact as Gannon fucked him into oblivion.

"Gonna … come… Oh, fuck, Cam." Gannon's labored breaths sounded closer when he leaned over Cam, their faces nearly touching. "Come for me, Cam. Oh, God, baby. I…"

Cam wrapped his arms around Gannon, holding him close as he gave in to the rush, the soul-shattering orgasm that detonated inside him. He growled as his release took control of his body, locking his muscles as his dick jerked between them.

"Oh, yeah," Gannon roared, slamming into Cam one last time, his cock pulsing deep inside him. "Perfect. So fucking perfect."

Cam's thoughts exactly.

Thirty-One

"WHAT ARE YOU doing out here?" Gannon asked as he joined Cam out on the back deck.

It was two o'clock in the morning.

"Just thinking," Cam told him, peering back at Gannon over his shoulder.

"About?" Gannon took a seat in the chair beside Cam.

"You. Me. Us."

That surprised Gannon, but he tried not to show it.

"I think I need to get back into counseling," Cam said, his voice softer than before.

Gannon swallowed hard.

"I know that you have to travel, and the last thing I want is for that to come between us. It's not fair to you."

"Or you," Gannon told him.

"True. And I was wondering…" Cam paused, looked over at him. "Would you consider going with me?"

"To counseling?"

Cam nodded.

"Of course." He'd be honored to go with Cam.

"Good."

Good? That was it? Gannon wasn't sure what to say, so he didn't say anything at all.

"What if they can't fix me? What if I'm permanently fucked up?"

The fear in Cam's voice told Gannon he was serious.

"We'll get through it, Cam." He wasn't sure how, but Gannon was willing to do whatever it took.

"I really am sorry. You didn't deserve what I did to you."

"It's over now," Gannon said, leaning forward and resting his elbows on his knees while he looked over at Cam. "One thing I've learned, you can't live in the past. One day at a time. One *breath* at a time."

"I love you, you know?" Cam smiled.

"I love you, too."

"This won't be easy."

"Probably not," Gannon agreed. "But it'll be worth it."

Cam nodded, then turned back to peer out at the trees.

"You hungry?" Gannon asked. They hadn't bothered to eat after they'd gotten back to the house, choosing instead to spend their time in bed, then moving to the shower shortly thereafter.

"I'd cook, but your freezer's empty," Cam replied.

"I'm sure I can come up with something." Getting to his feet, he stared down at Cam. "Give me a few minutes. I'll let you know when it's ready."

Another nod from Cam and Gannon headed inside to cook.

Reckless

Half an hour later, just as he was finishing the stir-fry he'd tossed together from the frozen chicken strips and the bag of frozen vegetables he'd had—which, according to Cam, had equated to nothing in the freezer—Cam came back inside to join him. They ate in comfortable silence, then cleaned up the kitchen together. Without a word, Cam took Gannon's hand and led him back to the bedroom.

As though they'd done it a million times before, Cam crawled into bed, and Gannon climbed in after him, spooning against him.

Holding Cam, feeling the slow rise and fall of his chest, hearing him breathe... It was truly the best feeling in the world.

Well, aside from making love to him.

But this was good, too. Different good.

And for the first time in a week, Gannon slept.

CAM OPENED HIS eyes to see the first rays of the sun slipping between the wood blinds in Gannon's bedroom. Sleep hadn't come quite as quickly as Cam had thought it would, although he'd been pleasantly exhausted, but only because he hadn't wanted to close his eyes.

He didn't know how long he'd stayed like that, but at some point, he must've fallen asleep, because now he was awake, the sun was coming up, and Gannon's arms were still around him.

And just as it had been last night before he'd drifted off, his mind was spinning from everything that had happened since yesterday when he'd gone to the airport to pick Gannon up.

What it all meant.

Cam was overwhelmed by so many things. There was so much Cam wanted to tell Gannon, but he didn't even know how. Only because he didn't think there were words that could describe the magnitude of what he felt for the man. Hell, it was crazy.

For the first time in his life, Cam was ready to introduce someone to his father.

It felt strange, complex even. As though he couldn't contain everything he was feeling.

And today, moving forward felt different, too.

While he'd been sitting outside last night, Cam had actually thought about getting married.

Freaking married.

Never in his life had he considered that, but he'd gone so far as to imagine picking out a ring, getting down on one knee, and proposing to Gannon. Hell, he'd even thought about the wedding.

Yep, definitely crazy. That's exactly what it was.

They'd been going slow this entire time, and suddenly Cam felt as though he was trying to fast-track things.

Did Gannon even want to get married? That was something Cam didn't know about him.

"Mmm."

Cam smiled when he felt Gannon's breath on his shoulder, his erection pressing against his ass.

"You're insatiable, you know that?" Cam muttered, tightening his hold on Gannon's arm, which was still tossed over Cam's stomach.

"I blame you," Gannon whispered, his voice rough from sleep. "What about you?"

"What *about* me?" Cam rolled to his back, turning his head so he could see Gannon.

Gannon's hand slid lower, wrapping around Cam's dick.

"Looks like you're insatiable, too."

Before Cam could answer, Gannon's head disappeared beneath the blanket.

"Ah, fuck," Cam hissed when Gannon's smooth lips wrapped around the head of his dick. Not wanting to miss the show, Cam forced the blankets off, revealing Gannon, who was lying on his side facing Cam, knees up by Cam's chest, propped up on one elbow as he sucked him.

Placing an arm over Gannon's hip, Cam caressed the smooth skin there as Gannon slowly sucked him, their eyes locked together. It was so hot to watch him, to see how much he enjoyed doing that. Cam knew the feeling because he loved it just as much.

Which gave him an idea.

"Roll onto your back," Cam instructed, turning onto his side.

When Gannon was on his back, Cam crawled over him, straddling Gannon's head, while Cam's mouth hovered above the heavy length of Gannon's erection.

"Perfect position," he said softly, fisting Gannon's cock and guiding it into his mouth.

The sixty-nine position wasn't an easy position. Sure, doing it was easy, but maintaining focus was far more difficult. With so much pleasure assaulting him, the heat of Gannon's mouth working over his cock, Gannon's fingers teasing his balls, Cam found it difficult to focus on returning the pleasure.

He tried.

He really, really did.

But it seemed that Gannon was hell-bent on driving Cam completely out of his mind. Minutes later, Cam was on his back once more, and this time Gannon was between his legs, bent over and sucking Cam for all he was worth.

Cam didn't look away, sliding his fingers gently through Gannon's hair, doing his best not to pull him closer, not to shove his dick as deep into Gannon's mouth as it would go.

"Damn," Cam mumbled. "You want me to come in your mouth?"

Gannon didn't say a word, just met Cam's gaze and sucked harder, faster, using his fist to stroke Cam right over the edge.

"I'm gonna come," Cam warned. "Take all of me. Everything."

Gannon didn't stop, bobbing up and down, taking Cam as far as he could until Cam passed the breaking point, sputtering nonsense as he came, erupting into Gannon's mouth, eyes still locked on him.

Yeah, if he'd thought he was attempting to fast-track things before…

This certainly hadn't helped.

But right now it didn't matter, because it was time to return the favor.

Thirty-Two

THE LAST TWO days had gone by in a blur. For nearly seventy-two hours, Gannon had had Cam all to himself. Not once had they left his house. Hell, they'd rarely left his bedroom.

It had been incredible.

Now, as Gannon sat at his desk, reviewing one of the reports his operations manager had provided him, he could hardly focus. He knew he needed to, but thoughts of Cam continued to interfere with his good intentions.

"Hey."

Gannon looked up to see Milly stepping into his office, a huge smile on her face. "Hey."

"Have a good weekend?" Her tone said she already knew the answer to that question.

Gannon leaned back in his chair, smiling at her.

Milly quickly turned and closed his office door, then lowered her voice to a conspiratorial whisper. "How'd it go? Did y'all work it out?"

"We did, but I'm sure you already knew that."

"Since I didn't get a phone call, I assumed." Taking a seat across from him, Milly regarded him steadily. "If you expect me to apologize, I'm not gonna do it."

Gannon laughed, leaning forward and resting his arms on his desk. "I didn't figure you would."

"But it worked, didn't it?"

"What? You sticking your nose in my business?"

Another smile, this one had her cheeks turning pink. "You would've done the same for me."

Maybe. Gannon tried not to interfere in other people's business, but he had to admit, Milly was probably the one who'd salvaged the most important relationship Gannon had ever had.

"Did he stay the weekend?" she asked, curiosity making her crystal blue eyes sparkle.

"He did."

"You're not gonna tell me the details, are you?" Milly's smile turned into a frown.

"Nope."

"At least tell me when the wedding is."

Gannon choked and spurted, sitting up straight and trying to catch his breath. "No wedding."

"Not yet, you mean."

He didn't know what he meant. At this point, he was simply content to continue moving forward with Cam. They'd been through a lot, and because Gannon would continue to travel, he knew that they had a long road ahead of them. Milly might've saved the day this time with her quick thinking, but she wouldn't be able to do it going forward. Not every time, anyway.

Counseling would probably do them good. No matter what, Gannon was willing to give it a shot. Anything to help Cam, because he'd seen it firsthand when he'd mentioned Singapore. The mere thought of someone going away sent Cam spiraling into a panic attack.

"You think it'll get easier for him?" she asked.

"What?"

"The traveling?"

Gannon shrugged. He didn't know how things would go in that regard. He wanted to believe that Cam could eventually come to grips with it, but even he knew it wasn't that simple. And like Cam, Gannon still had his own fears, as well, knew they could get out of hand with little effort. He'd merely managed to keep them contained all these years, tucked away in a box. Out of sight, out of mind.

He'd done a pretty good job of dealing with them until that night when Cam had broken up with him. They might've worked things out this time, but he still worried. What if Cam did it again? What if they couldn't get past the fact that Gannon had to travel to keep his company running smoothly?

Those were questions Gannon wouldn't have answers for until the next time. Or the time after that. All in all, his love for Cam still scared him, still made him wary.

That didn't mean he wasn't willing to go the distance. To persevere.

"Y'all are good for each other," Milly told him, brushing her long blonde hair over her shoulder. "Don't let him screw it up."

"*Him?* What about me?"

"Well, if you fuck it up, I'll just kick your ass. But you're my best friend. I can do that."

Gannon chuckled. "I appreciate what you did, by the way."

Milly's smile lit up her entire face. "I figured you'd be pissed."

He'd wanted to be, but she'd saved his relationship, convinced Cam to give him another chance. So he couldn't be too upset. "Just don't do it again."

Holding up her hands, fingers crossed, Milly said, "I promise."

Of course she did. That was Milly.

"But you have to promise me something in return," she prompted.

"What's that?"

"I want to be the maid of honor at the wedding."

Gannon felt his face flame from embarrassment. As much as he liked the idea of marrying Cam, spending the rest of his life with the man, they had a long road ahead of them. They'd made it this far, but it had been rocky to say the least. Being optimistic was one thing, but jumping into something that he still had doubts about was something else entirely.

He loved Cam. There was no doubt about that. He wanted to spend every waking moment with the man.

However, he had a feeling that loving Cam might possibly be the hardest thing he'd ever done.

"WHAT'S UP, PART timer?" Dare greeted when Cam walked into the office.

Cam gave his friend the finger, smiling as he did. Even Dare's taunting couldn't affect Cam's good mood. He'd just spent an entire weekend with Gannon. Practically three entire days they'd been together, and from the minute he stepped out of Gannon's front door that morning, he'd been ready to go back.

Dare clutched his chest dramatically. "Ouch. I'm hurt, man."

"Thanks for fillin' in for me," Cam told his friend, grabbing the coffee carafe.

"No problem. Just remember my generosity in the future when I need to run away for the weekend."

Cam looked away, his neck heating as he thought about how he'd spent the last three days with Gannon. And it had been the best damn weekend of his life.

"How was it, anyway?" Cam cast a sideways glance at Dare.

"No problems on this end. Teague took one of my appointments, but that's it. Honestly, it was kinda slow."

Reaching for the appointment book after pouring himself a cup of coffee, Cam looked up to see Roan heading toward the door.

"That's my cue to jet," Dare whispered loudly, then bolted out the back, mumbling as he went. "Do *not* want to see the fiery crash this morning."

Cam glanced over his shoulder, then returned his attention to the door when the alarm sounded. Because of the chime delay his friend had already entered the building, so Cam studied him briefly, noticing he hadn't shaved in a couple of days. His hair was mussed as though he hadn't bothered to brush it. And to go along with the scraggly appearance, Roan did not look happy.

"Mornin'," Cam greeted, watching him.

"Yeah," Roan replied, not looking at Cam.

Shit.

He couldn't say he hadn't expected Roan to be pissed at him for taking a few days off without talking to him first. If he had to guess, Roan had been surprised since Cam rarely took time off, and never did he take more than one day off at a time.

Nor did he spend the weekend with a guy. But in his defense, Gannon wasn't just any guy.

Cam decided to extend the olive branch, not wanting the tension between him and Roan. "How's your sister?"

Roan glared at him. "Fine."

"She go to rehab?"

Roan stopped a few feet away, staring at Cam as though he didn't know him. "What the fuck do you care?"

Cam felt as though he'd been slapped. He didn't know what to say to that, didn't know if he should even attempt to smooth things over with Roan or merely give him some space. Had something happened to Cassie? Or was Roan seriously pissed at Cam?

Then he remembered his conversation with Dare.

Why didn't Roan give me this encouragement?

Are you fucking serious? The guy can't see past his own love for you.

What? *What the hell are you talking about?*

Ah, hell. I forgot. You can't see it, either. He's so fucking in love with you—or thinks *he is—it's awkward to be in the same room with the two of you together.*

Cam still didn't believe it. There was no way Roan had feelings for him. No matter what Dare said.

Only, standing there now, it looked as though Roan's anger was directed at him. Since Cam had called Dare and asked him to fill in, he couldn't imagine that Roan had been inconvenienced by his absence.

Could it be true?

Was Roan jealous? Of Gannon? Or was something else bothering him?

"I care," Cam retorted. "She's like family."

"Then I guess you shoulda been here," Roan snapped.

"What the fuck is your problem?" Cam spat, angry that Roan would treat him this way. They'd been friends for too long for Roan to act like this.

"Not a goddamn thing," Roan yelled. "Why don't you go back to your *boyfriend* and leave me the fuck alone?"

No.

God, no. It couldn't be true.

Reckless

Cam didn't say a word, didn't know how to address this in a civil manner. Not to mention, he didn't want to jump to conclusions. Accusing Roan of being jealous—when there wasn't anything to be jealous about because their relationship wasn't like that—would only piss him off more.

Roan held his stare for another few seconds, then spun around and hauled ass out the front door, not looking back.

Cam remained where he was, confusion and, yes, anger replacing the giddiness he'd felt that morning when he'd woken up beside Gannon.

Just when he'd thought he had overcome the toughest hurdles this relationship had brought thus far, Roan had to go and do this.

Thirty-Three

AT SEVEN O'CLOCK that night, Gannon stepped into the marina office, hoping to find Cam, but a quick perusal told him that Cam wasn't there.

But Dare was.

The man's head lifted from the magazine he'd been reading, hazel eyes leveling on him. "Hey."

"Hey." Gannon glanced around, trying to appear casual. "Cam around?"

Dare leaned back in his chair, flipping his ball cap around backwards. Gannon noticed, unlike most of the other times he'd encountered Dare, the man was shirtless. It was hard to miss the muscles in his chest flexing as he crossed his arms. "Everything cool?"

Gannon wasn't sure at this point. He'd texted Cam several times throughout the day, letting him know he'd be stopping by if Cam was up for company. Never heard from him. Then, when he'd left work, before he'd pulled out of the parking lot, Gannon had shot off another text, letting him know he was on his way. And when he still didn't get an answer, he had attempted to call only to get Cam's voice mail.

It appeared as though Cam was avoiding him. Or perhaps that was his own insecurities talking. It was possible that Cam was just incredibly busy, making up for taking off the weekend to spend with Gannon.

"Yeah," Gannon said. "Just wanted to see him."

"How's work?" Dare asked, getting to his feet and moving to the counter.

"Good. Busy."

"Any upcoming trips?"

Dare seemed oddly curious, but Gannon didn't mind. Considering he knew that Cam was close to them all, he welcomed the casual conversation.

"Yeah. Gotta go back to California in a couple of weeks."

"The travelin' thing…" Dare said, resting his arms on the counter. "It's not easy for Cam."

He knew that already, but still, Dare's blunt assessment of the situation sparked Gannon's curiosity. He knew he shouldn't encourage Dare because it was an invasion of Cam's privacy, but he couldn't help himself. The words simply came out. "I know. It's been tough, but I think we'll make it work."

"Think?"

Gannon swallowed hard, trying to figure out what Dare expected from him. What was he supposed to say?

Dare continued to study him. Gannon fought the urge to fidget.

"You're good for him, you know."

Well, that wasn't the direction he'd expected the conversation to go, but it did help to alleviate some of the tension. "Thanks."

"It'll take him some time, I'm sure. But don't give up on him."

He hadn't planned on it, but still, something seemed off about this conversation. "Is there something I need to know?"

Dare glanced behind him, then met Gannon's gaze again. "Do you love him?"

Gannon didn't feel comfortable telling Dare how he felt about Cam, so he lifted his eyebrows in question.

Dare smiled. "Fine. Not my business. But if you do, just fight for him. That's all I'm sayin'."

Fight for him?

Gannon forced his jaw to remain closed, although he was sure he looked as confused as he felt. He wanted to know what Dare meant by that, but he couldn't bring himself to ask. Nodding, as though he understood completely, he looked around again. "So, is he here?"

"Out in the shed. He's been runnin' around like crazy today. I think he's helpin' Roan put some stuff up."

The door chimed and Gannon looked back to see a young couple coming in.

Dare smacked the counter, nodded at Gannon, then greeted them with a smile.

Gannon gave a curt, two-finger wave and then headed outside. He needed to talk to Cam.

Making his way down the pier, he noticed that the doors to the shed were open, so he figured Cam and Roan were still inside. He didn't want to surprise Cam, but he didn't know what else to do. Maybe Dare was right and they'd just been busy, which was why Cam hadn't answered him.

But if not, and Cam had once again gotten cold feet, Gannon knew he needed to address it before they took two steps back and ended up right where they'd started.

Considering how much work it'd required to make it this far, Gannon damn sure wasn't about to let that happen.

CAM HAD FOLLOWED Roan out to the shed, wanting to get him to talk. After the way they'd left things that morning, he couldn't sit by and allow this rift between them to grow. If he didn't address it now, he risked losing Roan completely. And that wasn't something Cam was willing to do.

Clearly something was bothering Roan, and Cam needed to get to the bottom of it, even if he didn't want to know. And if Roan's issue had to do with Cam and Gannon, he *definitely* didn't want to know.

For weeks now, Roan hadn't been himself. Every time Cam attempted to talk to him, he found himself shut out. At first, he'd thought it was just the summer months arriving and work increasing. Then, he'd figured it had to do with Roan's sister and her relapse.

Now, he wasn't so sure it had anything to do with those things.

They'd been friends for so long, and Roan had always talked to him when he had a problem, and now it seemed as though his best friend was purposely avoiding him. Which made Cam think that Dare might be right.

Although he hoped that wasn't the case.

He *really* hoped that wasn't the case.

"Hey," Cam called out to Roan when he stepped into the shadows inside the large shed they used to house tools and extra equipment. He'd expected to see Roan moving things around or getting supplies.

That definitely wasn't what Roan was doing. "What's wrong?"

Roan's head jerked up, his hands sliding up to wipe what looked a hell of a lot like tears from his face.

"Is your sister okay?" Cam asked, immediately assuming something had happened to her.

Dare had filled him in earlier after Cam's failed attempt to get Roan to talk. According to him, Roan's family had attempted to get her into rehab, but she'd refused to go. Dare hadn't expanded on the details, probably because he didn't know the details, but Cam knew how hard that must've been on everyone.

And Roan was right about one thing, Cam hadn't been around much lately. He should've asked about her more often, offered to go with Roan to see her even though Roan had shot him down the first time.

"Yeah," Roan said gruffly, getting to his feet, turning his back on Cam.

"Then what's wrong?" Cam asked, placing his hands on his hips and watching Roan closely.

"Nothin'." Roan moved toward the opposite wall, messing with one of the life jackets hanging there.

Cam studied him momentarily. As he saw it, he had two choices. He could either walk away, accept that Roan was pissed at him, and leave this thing between them unsettled, or he could confront Roan by pissing him off and forcing him to address the issue.

Cam decided to go with option two. "Bullshit. If nothin's wrong, then why are you hidin' in here?"

Roan's body twisted around, his golden eyes pausing on Cam's face. "I'm not hiding."

"Sure looks like it to me." And now that he'd gotten Roan's attention, Cam didn't want to argue. Lowering his voice, he added, "Talk to me, man. What's bothering you?"

He fucking hated this silent treatment.

"Something's obviously wrong, Roan. And I'm pretty sure you're pissed at me. I deserve to know why."

"Nothin' to talk about," Roan said and Cam knew he was lying.

"So you're in here having a breakdown for no fucking reason?"

"Fuck you," Roan bit out.

Cam held his ground when Roan moved toward him, hands balled into fists. Maybe he was a little masochistic, but he definitely preferred Roan pissed than seeing him falling apart. That was so unlike him Cam didn't even know how to approach the issue.

"Talk to me," Cam said, keeping his voice low, even.

Roan's gaze remained locked on Cam's face, and he fought the urge to squirm. Something was definitely up, but he couldn't, for the life of him, figure it out.

"Where's Burgess?" Roan asked.

"His name's Gannon," Cam corrected. Again. No matter how many times he did, Roan still insisted on calling Gannon by his last name.

"Where is he?"

Cam shrugged. He figured Gannon was at work. He hadn't talked to him all day. Since he hadn't charged his phone all weekend, the damn thing had died on him, and he'd hooked it up in his apartment earlier, figuring he wouldn't need it.

"He back from his trip?"

Roan already knew the answer to that. Cam wouldn't have been gone all weekend otherwise. Still, he answered, "Yeah. He got back on Friday."

"Is that where you were all weekend?"

Cam nodded.

"I thought y'all broke up."

Cam didn't want to go into the details of his relationship with Gannon. "We worked things out."

"So you're not gonna freak the next time he goes on a trip?"

Cam narrowed his eyes at his friend. Roan was baiting him, he could tell. And he didn't fucking like it one bit. Roan knew Cam better than anyone. He knew how hard it was for Cam. Hell, when Holly and Keith had gone on their honeymoon, Cam had been a basket case. His father had had to sedate him to keep him under control.

And that same terrifying panic had returned when Gannon had left.

But they were working through it. Because Cam loved Gannon.

Cam met Roan's eyes, confused by the antagonizing tone. Frowning, he tried to figure out if Roan wanted that to be the case, for Cam not to be able to deal with Gannon traveling. "Why would you ask that?"

Roan shrugged. "It just seems like he doesn't care that it bothers you."

"It's his job," Cam countered.

"Yeah? And his job's more important than you are?" Roan rolled his eyes. "Doesn't sound like a stable relationship to me."

Cam took a deep breath, trying to contain the anger that threatened to erupt. Before he could say anything, Roan spoke again.

"Look, I'm sorry." Roan's tone had softened, his eyes pleading.

Cam took a step back, baffled by Roan's complete one-eighty. One second he'd been provoking Cam, the next he was apologizing.

None of it made sense. His best friend was acting really strange.

"Cam…"

Reckless

The hair on the back of his neck stood up in warning. That tone of voice... He'd never heard Roan talk like that, and if he wasn't mistaken...

"I need to tell you something."

Cam lifted an eyebrow, forced himself to stand in place when Roan took another step closer.

"Ever since you and Gannon started goin' out..."

Cam waited, not breathing. Praying that Dare wasn't right. That Roan wasn't going to say something now that could alter their friendship forever.

"It's been hard for me."

"What?" Cam asked, confused. "What's been hard for you?"

When Roan's eyes dropped to Cam's mouth, it all became very, very clear. The uncomfortable silence thickened, making it impossible to breathe. His best friend could not possibly be saying...

"I'm in love with you."

Someone cleared their throat, and Cam's head snapped over to see Gannon standing in the doorway, his eyes wide as he stared between Cam and Roan.

Holy fuck. Had he heard Roan's admission?

Roan took a step back instantly and Cam did, too. It was as though they'd been busted doing something they shouldn't have been doing. And the heartbreaking look on Gannon's face made Cam's stomach churn.

"Sorry," Gannon said softly as he turned to walk away. "Didn't mean to interrupt."

"No, wait," Cam called after him, starting toward the door to follow. He would've given chase except Roan grabbed his arm.

"Cam. Don't leave me hangin' here."

Cam stared at Roan. "I... I don't..." Glancing at the door, Cam realized he needed to go after Gannon. He had to settle that first, then he could talk to Roan.

Maybe.

"I have to talk to Gannon," he blurted, pulling out of Roan's grasp and lunging for the door, not bothering to look back at his friend.

His best friend had just told him he was in love with him. How could that be? And if that was the case, why the fuck hadn't Roan said something before now? Not that it would've made a damn bit of difference. Cam didn't have those feelings for Roan. He never had. Sure, they were friends, and Cam would do anything for Roan, but there was no chemistry there. As far as Cam was concerned, Roan was like his brother.

"Gannon, wait!" Cam called after him when he reached the pier, but Gannon seemed to pick up the pace.

When Gannon practically broke into a jog across the parking lot, Cam took off after him, running full out. He didn't stop until he nearly tackled Gannon against his car.

"When'd you get here?" Cam asked, winded from the short run.

Gannon's eyes widened as he stared back at Cam, but he didn't say anything.

"I didn't know you were coming," he added.

"Obviously." Gannon's eyes narrowed; the pain Cam saw there broke his heart all over again. "I didn't mean to interrupt."

"You didn't," Cam told him, reaching out for Gannon's hand, unable to help himself.

But Gannon pulled back from him instantly.

When he reached for the door handle, Cam put a hand out to stop him. "Don't leave. We need to talk."

Gannon shook his head, not bothering to look at Cam.

Cam tried to see the situation from Gannon's point of view. He could understand why he was upset, but he definitely didn't want Gannon to get the wrong impression. "It wasn't what it looked like."

The hurt look on Gannon's face disappeared, replaced by something Cam had never seen before.

Anger.

Disappointment.

And the strange pinch in his chest made it hard to breathe.

Just when he'd thought they were making progress. Working through their issues. It looked as though they'd only circled back to where they'd been before, back to when they'd been guarding themselves from one another, fearing the worst.

Now, it looked as though that tension had the chance to escalate into something Cam wasn't sure he could handle.

There was no way he could let Gannon walk away from him now.

Cam didn't think he'd survive it again.

Thirty-Four

GANNON COULDN'T FEEL his hands. Hell, he couldn't feel anything at all. He was numb all over.

From the moment he'd stepped inside that shed, seeing Roan and Cam standing so close, he'd had a hard time breathing. But when Roan had admitted to Cam that he was in love with him…

Did this remind anyone of a movie? *My Best Friend's Wedding*, maybe?

Uggh!

Gannon's heart was breaking all over again. The fear he'd experienced throughout the day had eased somewhat after he'd talked to Dare in the office, but now … it was back full force, threatening to pull him under again. And now that he was standing face-to-face with Cam, he couldn't stop thinking about what he'd seen.

Was that why Cam was ignoring him? Had something happened with Roan today? Or had it been building for a while? The thought of Cam and Roan together… It made Gannon's stomach lurch.

"Is that why you haven't answered your phone today?" Gannon asked bluntly, pointing in the direction they'd just come from.

"What?" Cam frowned. "No. My… Shit. My phone's in my apartment charging. The battery died this morning."

Well, that made sense. Sort of.

"Please talk to me," Cam said, his voice low, his hand coming to rest on Gannon's arm. "Let's go up to my apartment and talk."

"Not sure there's anything to talk about," Gannon rasped. He could hardly breathe. The pain was unbearable. Worse than that, it had felt like a sucker punch. So totally and completely unexpected...

"There's actually a *lot* to talk about."

Oh, shit. Gannon did not like the sound of that.

Was Cam about to break up with him again?

Gannon did not like this flip-flopping emotion. Love, fear, elation, fear. It was making him crazy. The two of them seemed to be riding a tidal wave. When one crested, another picked them up and carried them farther, only to crash once again.

Gannon was trying to come up with a reason to leave, but he didn't get the words out before Cam was stepping closer, erasing the distance between them completely. Cam's warm hands came up to cup Gannon's face, forcing him to look into those stormy blue eyes.

"Don't walk away, Gannon. Trust me, remember?"

The edge in Cam's tone reflected the same trepidation Gannon felt. As though he was letting Gannon know that if he did, they'd be finished. Part of him wanted to tell him to go to hell, to turn and get into his car, drive away, and never look back.

But the other part of him loved this man.

Loved.

Him.

And walking away again would likely break him.

"Should you go talk to Roan?" Gannon asked, trying to calm himself enough that they could have a civil conversation.

"I will. Later. He's my friend, and I have to address the issue with him, but you're more important."

Did Cam mean right now? Or always?

Gannon wasn't sure he wanted to know the answer to that. Since he couldn't come up with a rebuttal, he simply nodded his head, allowing Cam to lead him away from his car, toward the stairs on the side of the building.

With leaden feet, he followed Cam up, then down the hall and into Cam's apartment. Once inside, with the door closed behind him, Gannon's stomach did a strange, painful flip. He didn't know what was about to happen, but he knew without a doubt that he was in love with this man. And the mere thought of losing him...

Gannon wasn't sure he'd be strong enough to handle that. Not again.

OKAY, SO ROAN didn't feel the amount of relief he'd thought he would. When he'd admitted to Cam that he loved him ... the words hadn't felt right. He'd thought that getting it out in the open would clear the air, possibly help clear his head, but instead, he was only more confused now.

Didn't mean he wasn't pissed. Cam had walked away from him.

Roan stormed into the marina office in time to see Cam leading Gannon toward the stairs up to his apartment. He had an overwhelming urge to stop them, to force Cam to hear him out. Before he knew it, he was lunging for the door, but before he could skirt the counter, Dare was grabbing his arm, pulling him back.

"No fucking way," Dare snapped. "You're not goin' out there."

Roan spun around to face his friend. "Fuck you. Stay the hell outta my business."

Dare pointed toward the door, his eyes shooting fire. "That's *not* your fucking business."

"The hell it ain't." Roan couldn't let Cam turn his back. He needed Cam to understand how he felt, that he'd be the man who could make him happy.

"Roan!" Dare yelled. "Get a grip, man."

"I need to *talk* to him," Roan declared, peering out the door in time to see Gannon and Cam slip out of sight. "Need to explain."

"No," Dare roared. "You don't."

Turning to face Dare, Roan let his anger build.

"Hit me if you want," Dare told him. "But I'm not gonna sit back and let you fuck this up for him."

"Me? I didn't fuck this up for anyone."

"He's your best friend, bro. You're *not* in love with him."

How the hell did Dare know? And who was he to say how Roan felt?

"Cam's happy, man. Seriously. Have you looked at him lately? Have you ever seen him that fucking happy?"

"Happy? How the fuck is he happy when the man he's dating runs off and leaves him?"

"Gannon didn't leave him. He went on a business trip."

"And you know how that hurts Cam. He can't deal with that shit."

"Have you ever thought that he needs this? He needs someone who forces him out of his comfort zone?"

Roan didn't want to hear this. Jerking away from Dare, he stalked toward the back door.

"Roan, I'm serious. You need to think this through. You want to lose Cam forever? Fuck this up for him and he'll never forgive you."

Roan stopped walking but didn't turn around. "You don't know how I feel."

"I know that for the first time in years, things are changing around here, and that bothers you. Cam met this guy who makes him happy. He deserves to be happy."

"*I* can make him happy," Roan snapped, even though he didn't really believe that. Not anymore. Not after he'd professed his love and ended up feeling … awkward, selfish even.

Dare was behind him. "Yeah? Then why the fuck didn't you lay this shit on him when he was single? Why now, huh?"

"Because…" Roan didn't have a retort. It was the same question he'd been asking himself all along. It hadn't been until Gannon Burgess had made an appearance in Cam's world that Roan had felt threatened. As though he were running out of time.

Roan turned to face Dare.

"When did you start feeling this way about him?" Dare asked, not an ounce of condescension in his tone.

"I don't know." It was the truth. He didn't know when he'd fallen in love with Cam, or even if that was real. Something was definitely off. The only thing he knew … he didn't want to lose the chance. If Cam wasn't with Gannon, then Roan would still have a chance.

"You aren't in love with him," Dare repeated. "You're scared that Gannon will come between you and Cam. That you'll lose that friendship."

"How the hell do you know how I feel?" Roan countered, hating that Dare could even possibly be right.

Roan hadn't been able to untangle his thoughts for days, weeks. But Dare was right, this hadn't started until Gannon had come into the picture. Until Cam had...

Oh, fuck.

Dare's voice pulled him up short. "Because I've been there."

Roan's gaze swung to Dare's. The lighthearted, carefree playboy had never looked as serious as he did right then. And that was when it hit Roan ... someone had broken Dare's heart before.

Dare cleared his throat. "If you want to interfere, I won't always be here to stop you. But I can tell you one thing. If you fuck this up for him, Cam will never forgive you. Do you really want to lose your best friend because you're insecure?"

Roan stared at Dare, fighting the burning sensation behind his eyes. "No," he said roughly. "I don't."

"Then let's take a walk. Give them some time to work this out."

Roan allowed Dare to turn him toward the back door again.

"And later, you can apologize," Dare noted. "To both of them."

Thirty-Five

IT HADN'T BEEN until he was up the stairs and through the door that Cam realized what he wanted to say to Gannon. He hated the fact that Gannon had witnessed that, and he fully intended to explain to Gannon that whatever Roan felt for Cam, it wasn't reciprocated.

Sure, Cam knew he needed to talk to Roan, as well. He hated that he'd left things up in the air with him, but he'd been telling Gannon the truth when he'd said he was more important. Roan was definitely important, but Gannon… Gannon was Cam's everything. So, he would talk to Roan in a bit.

But first…

When Gannon closed the door to the apartment, Cam turned to face him. Without hesitation, he took a step closer, coming face-to-face with the man he loved. Cam was tempted to reach up and smooth the worry line creasing Gannon's forehead. He hated that he'd been the one to put that there. What Gannon had seen… It had been a case of bad timing; that was it.

Gannon's eyes searched Cam's face, and he briefly wondered what was going through that beautiful mind of his. After the weekend they'd just spent together, Cam hated that this shit had happened. They were making progress, and there was no way Cam would allow this misunderstanding to come between them.

When Gannon's eyes lifted to meet his, Cam held his gaze. "I love you." Holding up a hand to stop Gannon from saying anything, Cam continued, "Roan's my friend. I love him, but he's like a brother to me. Always has been, always will be. I'm not sure what's goin' on with him, but I know he's confused. Roan doesn't love me. Not like that. He might think he does, but I assure you, even if that's the case, it's not reciprocated."

Gannon didn't make a sound, so Cam continued.

"When I tell you I love you, that's not easy for me. I've never said those words to anyone. Not the way that I mean them toward you. This thing between us, it's real. It might be a little rocky, but it's real. And I'm not willing to lose you, Gannon."

"I—"

Cam cut him off before he could speak. He wanted to say something else, needed Gannon to understand.

As he stared back at Gannon, his heart leapt into his throat, his nerves rioting from what he was about to say, what he was about to do.

But it was time.

Slowly, very, very, slowly, Cam took a small step back and then lowered himself to one knee in front of Gannon, keeping his eyes locked with Gannon's the entire time.

Gannon's eyes widened, his mouth opening slightly.

"Gannon Burgess," Cam said confidently, his heart pounding in his throat, "I've never loved anyone the way that I love you. The thought of losing you, not having the opportunity to spend the rest of my life with you... I can't bear it."

"Cam, no," Gannon whispered.

For a second, Cam doubted himself, but then he shored up his nerve. He wasn't going to be deterred, regardless of what the outcome might be.

"I love you," Cam repeated. "And I want to spend the rest of my life with you, Gannon. I can't help how I feel. This is real for me. Confusing, sure." He offered a small smile. "But real." Cam paused for a moment, still looking up at Gannon. "I don't have a fancy ring to offer right now, but I'll rectify that as soon as possible. Marry me, Gannon. Agree to spend the rest of your life with me."

The silence in the room was deafening. Cam could hear his heart thundering, feel the painful thump in his chest as he waited for Gannon to say something. He *needed* Gannon to say something.

Hell, anything, at this point, to let Cam know he'd heard him.

"Gan—" Cam didn't get any further, because Gannon quieted him by placing his hand over his mouth.

"Quiet," Gannon said softly, firmly. "Let me think."

"You need to think about this?" Cam asked, but the words were unintelligible, muffled by Gannon's hand.

"Yes," Gannon finally said, his eyes softening. "Of course I want to spend the rest of my life with you."

"So you'll marry me?"

"One day," Gannon assured him. "Yes." Gannon smiled. "But I reserve the right to be the one to propose officially."

Cam could live with that.

He could *definitely* live with that.

GANNON'S HEAD WAS spinning, his mind racing with so many questions. But the most pressing one of all...

Was this real? Was Cam *really* asking him to marry him?

Based on the fact that Cam was kneeling before him, he had to think that was the case, but still.

Not that it would change his answer. He wanted to spend the rest of his life with Cam, yes. Not that he necessarily wanted to get married any time in the near future, but one day, yes.

Hell, Gannon intended to meet Cam's father and sister first.

After Milly had mentioned a wedding that morning, Gannon had thought about it throughout the day. He'd even gone so far as to pull up jewelers on the Internet to check out rings.

No, he hadn't bought anything, but that was because he wanted them to pick out their rings together. They would be the symbols of their everlasting love; he wasn't going to jump the gun there. But he was serious when he'd said he wanted to meet Cam's family.

Staring back at Cam now, Gannon knew they would spend the rest of their lives together. It was inevitable, but that was what happened when soul mates finally met, when they finally realized that their match was waiting for them.

Cam was his soul mate.

The love of his life.

The man Gannon would forever give his heart, body, and soul to.

Still, Gannon had one question... "What happened to taking things slow?"

Cam's smile was radiant, and Gannon couldn't look away as Cam got to his feet. "Eh. Who's got time for that shit?"

Gannon smiled, his heart warming, the thin layer of ice that had formed around it a short while ago melting away.

"But I'm serious," Cam told him. "I want to marry you. Maybe not tomorrow or next week or next month. But it will happen."

"I know," Gannon assured him.

And he did know. They would get through the rough patches together. They'd proven they could do it already, and Gannon had no doubt that their love for one another was strong enough to endure.

"I think you need to go talk to Roan," he suggested to Cam. "He needs to know how you feel. But more importantly, I think he needs to understand that I'm not here to interfere with your relationship with him. Y'all are friends and that can be a fragile thing sometimes. Especially when someone comes along to shake things up."

"I really don't think he's in love with me," Cam stated, the conviction in his tone reassuring. "That was the first time he's ever said anything. I've known him for twenty-five years. Why now?"

That was a question only Roan could answer.

"Do you think he's in love with me?" Cam asked, frowning.

Gannon had thought about that when he'd seen the two of them together, heard the things Roan had said. "No, I don't think he is, but I think he thinks he is."

Cam's eyebrow lifted, a lopsided grin emerging. "English, Gannon."

Gannon smiled back. "I love you. Now more than ever."

"I see a but in there," Cam replied, eyes narrowing.

"No but. My love's definitely unconditional. But..." Gannon laughed. "Okay, so there's a but."

Cam's eyebrows lifted.

"I want to meet your father. Your sister and her husband. Your nieces and nephews. You've met the only family I have. Milly. Now it's time that I meet yours."

"Right now?" Cam's eyes sparkled mischievously.

"No. Right now, you need to go talk to Roan."

Cam nodded. "I want you to go with me."

Gannon shook his head. Although he would give anything to be a fly on the wall, this was something Cam needed to do on his own. Roan would feel as though they'd ganged up on him, and that wasn't fair to the friendship they'd built through the years. "Why don't I figure out dinner while you go talk to him?"

Cam took a deep breath, let it out. "All right. But you have to promise me one thing."

"What's that?"

"I want you to stay the night with me tonight."

Gannon pretended to consider that for a moment, then laughed when Cam grabbed his face and pressed a loud, sloppy kiss on his mouth.

"Okay," Gannon said, pushing Cam back. "I'll stay."

"Good." Cam grabbed his cell phone from the charger on the counter, then took a step back. "Now wish me luck."

"I was thinking you should wish *me* luck," Gannon retorted. "I've seen what's in your refrigerator. Or rather, what's *not.*"

Thirty-Six

CAM HATED LEAVING Gannon behind in his apartment. He would've preferred to stay there with him, get naked, and have some hot, sweaty makeup sex.

After all, what was the point of arguing if you couldn't have makeup sex?

Instead, Cam was going to have one of the most difficult conversations of his life. With his best friend.

As he made his way down the stairs, he grabbed his phone from his pocket. It took a second to pull up Roan's number and hit the call button. Another second and Roan answered.

"Hey," Cam greeted. "Can we talk?" Noticing Roan's SUV in the parking lot, he added, "Where are you?"

"Down on the dock."

"I'll be there in a second. Cool?"

"Yeah."

Cam hung up the phone, made his way across the gravel parking lot in front of the marina office, past the security gate, then to the private pier that led down to the water. He slowed when he noticed Dare walking toward him.

"He okay?" Cam asked, stopping in front of Dare.

Dare turned to look back down the pier. "He will be. He's confused, yeah."

"I swear to God I had no idea," Cam blurted.

"I know. And he knows that, too." Dare shoved his hands in the pockets of his shorts. "I think he's worried that your friendship's at risk."

"That's what Gannon said."

Dare smiled. "Gannon's a good guy. I like him. And I like him for you. Y'all figure it out?"

"Yeah." Cam couldn't contain the smile when he thought about how he'd proposed. Dropping his head and staring down at his feet, Cam added, "I'm gonna get back into counseling. He's gonna go with me."

"I think that's smart," Dare said when Cam met his gaze. "Love's not easy, man. But when you find that person … it's worth it."

Cam sensed that there was something Dare wasn't saying. They'd been friends for a long time. Not nearly as long as Cam had been friends with Roan, but fourteen years was a long damn time. In all that time, Cam had never known Dare to have a serious relationship. But he wondered if there hadn't been someone at some point.

"I'll get outta your hair. Go talk to him," Dare said, shrugging his shoulder toward the lake. "See ya tomorrow."

"Later." Cam remained where he was as Dare headed back toward the office.

After a few deep breaths, he forced his feet to carry him down the pier toward the lake. He found Roan sitting on the edge, feet dangling in the water, a beer in his hand.

"Hey," he greeted, dropping down onto the wood beside Roan.

"Man, look," Roan began, but Cam cut him off.

"If you're gonna apologize, I'm gonna punch you."

Roan's eyes slammed into his. Cam smiled.

"I owe you an apology," Roan stated defensively.

"No, you owe me a beer," he countered, nodding toward the cooler beside Roan.

Roan handed over a beer.

"We haven't talked much in the last few weeks," Cam said, twisting off the lid. "And I'm sorry about that. This thing with Gannon…"

"You love him."

Cam noticed it wasn't a question.

"I love him," Cam confirmed. "I plan to marry him and spend the rest of my life with him, Roan."

Roan's eyes widened, but he didn't speak.

Cam continued, "But I want you to know that our friendship—yours and mine—it means everything to me. And Gannon knows that. Hell, I asked him to come down here with me, and he told me that this was something you and I needed to work out. He doesn't want to come between us."

Roan released a breath. "I don't know what I've been thinkin'. When I told you I was in love with you, I thought it made sense. In my head, it did, but when the words came out … it just felt weird."

Maybe Dare and Gannon were right, Roan wasn't in love with him; he was simply worried about the friendship.

Roan continued, "Doesn't mean it's real. But it's confusing, nonetheless. Regardless, I want you to be happy, man. And I can see Gannon does that. He makes you happy."

"He does," Cam agreed. "Doesn't mean things are easy with us, but no one's perfect. The shit we've been through—before we ever met—that plays a huge role in our relationship. But I love him enough to move past it."

"How do you do that?" Roan asked, turning and peering out at the water. "He travels and that shit freaks you out."

Roan sounded genuinely curious, so Cam answered. "I'm gonna go back to counseling. He's gonna go with me. It might not be easy, but we'll get through it."

"*Can* you get past it?"

"Maybe." Cam didn't know the answer to that, but he was willing to do whatever it took to keep Gannon in his life.

Neither of them spoke for a few minutes. Cam watched the sun slowly slide past the horizon, drinking his beer and enjoying the peace and quiet.

"I don't want this to fuck up our friendship," Roan finally said.

"It won't." Cam nudged him with his shoulder. "Just as long as you don't try to fucking kiss me, man. It'd be like kissin' my sister. Not cool at all."

Roan laughed, and Cam was glad he could see the humor in that. "Are you comparing me to your sister?"

"No." Cam smirked. "Don't tell her I said this, but I think you're prettier."

Roan shoved Cam, making him laugh.

"I'm not pretty," Roan argued.

Cam shrugged. "I don't know about that."

Roan met Cam's gaze, his smile disappearing. "We're cool?"

"We're cool," Cam assured him, finishing off his beer. "I need to get back upstairs. Gannon's makin' dinner, and I have no idea what the hell he's gonna find in that pantry."

Roan laughed. "Whatever he finds, I'm sure it's expired."

"Yeah, me, too." Cam got to his feet. "You need anything?"

"Nah," Roan said, looking up at him briefly. "I'm just gonna chill for a while."

Cam turned to walk away.

"But hey," Roan called out.

Cam stopped, turned back toward him.

"I'm gonna have to come upstairs at some point, so could you keep all that moaning and shit to a minimum?"

Cam laughed, grateful it was dark so Roan didn't see him blush. "I'll do my best to keep Gannon quiet."

"Not him," Roan said, chuckling. "You. You're the screamer."

Cam shook his head, then turned back toward the marina office.

GANNON HAD JUST set everything out on the table when Cam returned. He hadn't known how long Cam would be gone, but he'd wanted to be prepared, so he'd heated up the oven and tossed the frozen pizza in, figuring he could microwave it if necessary.

Cam stepped into the apartment, and Gannon looked him over. "You okay?"

No fresh bruises. No tears. That was a good sign.

Cam came over to the table, placing his hands on the back of one of the two chairs. "We're good."

"Glad to hear it. Hungry?"

"Depends," Cam said, glancing around the small kitchen. "What's bein' offered?"

"Sit," Gannon told him, then returned to the microwave, where he'd stashed the pizza to keep it warm for a few minutes. He returned, placing it in front of Cam. Back to the kitchen once more, he returned with the bowl of soup he'd prepared for himself.

Cam laughed, making Gannon chuckle.

"I think it's safe to say I'll be in charge of the grocery shopping," Gannon told him, retrieving his spoon.

"Mmm. You're gonna cook for me?"

"If I want to eat, I'm thinkin' that might be my only choice."

"We could always have burgers," Cam said, his eyes dancing with amusement.

"True. Now eat."

Twenty minutes later, they'd downed what little food they'd had and hand-washed the few dishes they'd used, leaving the kitchen just as Gannon had found it. Spotless, with even less food than before. Gannon was sure he'd be hungry in a little while, but for now, it would tide him over.

Considering what he was hungry for wasn't food, anyway.

"Am I a screamer?" Cam blurted, his eyebrows downturned as he walked over to the couch that separated the kitchen area from the small living area.

Gannon choked on a laugh, watching to see if Cam was serious.

Cam didn't appear at all amused by Gannon's reaction, which only made Gannon laugh harder.

"Maybe we should find out," Gannon suggested.

"So I'm *not*?" Cam confirmed.

Gannon grinned, crossing his ankles as he leaned against the kitchen counter. "Not yet, no."

"Why're you lookin' at me like that?" Cam asked, his dark blue eyes turning molten.

Gannon admired him as he leaned against the back of the sofa, crossing his arms over his chest as he stared back at Gannon. "How am I looking at you?"

"Like I'm dessert."

"Mmm. Dessert. I like that idea." Gannon moved toward him, loving the way Cam opened his arms when he approached.

Stepping closer, Gannon pressed his lips to Cam's, lowering his voice. "I like that I can make you scream when you come."

Cam watched him and Gannon waited to see what he'd do. The hard lines on Cam's face softened, as did his smile. That only lasted a second before a delightfully mischievous sparkle ignited in the cobalt-blue orbs peering back at him. "How much do you like it?"

"A lot."

Another twinkle in Cam's eyes. "Care to show me?"

"How much I like it? Or how loud I can make you scream?" Gannon had an idea of his own, but he wanted to hear Cam's version.

Cam didn't disappoint, taking a step closer and erasing the space between them. "Both. Right here. Right now."

"Is that a dare?" Gannon retorted.

"Depends," Cam said.

"On?"

"On whether or not you're feelin' reckless."

Reaching out and grabbing Cam's hips, jerking him forward, Gannon stared deep into those beautiful eyes. "*Now* I'm feelin' reckless."

"Hopefully you intend to feel a whole helluva lot more than that."

"Oh, I do. I definitely do."

Gannon heard Cam's sharp intake of breath, his eyes widening.

Now that things had been settled between him and Cam, as well as between Cam and Roan, Gannon couldn't resist the temptation, the deep, driving need to touch Cam, to hold him, to feel the warmth of his body wrapped around him in every way possible.

And he didn't care how they made that happen, as long as they did.

Luckily, Gannon didn't have to wait long. Cam's firm, soft lips came to rest over his, his warm breath fanning over Gannon's mouth. It was sweet and reassuring, but after all the events of the day, Gannon suddenly didn't want sweet and reassuring.

He needed to possess Cam, to claim him in the only way he knew how.

"Turn around," Gannon ordered softly.

Yeah, he knew his tone was gruff, commanding, but Cam didn't seem to mind. In fact, it looked as though Cam was just as excited about the turn of events as he was. With one last long look between them, Cam turned slowly so that he was facing the back of the couch.

Gannon moved behind him, the warmth of Cam's body reassuring as Gannon leaned into him. Anticipation fizzed in his veins.

"You like when I take control?" Gannon asked, pressing his mouth to the back of Cam's neck.

"You have no idea," Cam sighed, leaning into him. "No fucking idea."

Gannon nipped the sensitive skin there, inhaling Cam. He smelled like sunshine. Warm and intoxicating.

Cam didn't put up a fight when Gannon arranged his body the way he wanted it, placing Cam's hands on the back of the couch before pushing his shirt up and over his head. Cam tossed it aside, then returned his hands to their original position while Gannon pressed kisses along Cam's muscled back, loving the way the smooth skin moved against his lips when Cam shifted.

The man was beautiful. All sleek lines. Powerful and so fucking sexy, and now Gannon couldn't keep his hands off of him. Reaching around, Gannon untied the string that held Cam's shorts up. As he continued to run his mouth over every delectable inch of Cam's back, licking down his spine, he worked the shorts down Cam's hips, allowing them to pool on the floor.

Cam stepped out of them, kicking them off to the side before resuming his position, this time spreading his legs wide.

Gannon took the opportunity presented to him, sliding his hand between Cam's legs and cupping his balls, kneading them with his fingers as he leaned against Cam.

"Ah, fuck," Cam hissed softly.

Teasing Cam was a pleasure Gannon would enjoy for years to come. Watching the muscles in his shoulders and back tense as Cam sucked in air, shifting his hips in an attempt to encourage Gannon to do as he wanted... So fucking beautiful.

Gannon managed to work the button on his jeans free while he stroked Cam's smooth, rigid cock, enjoying the rumbling groans. In an effort to throw him off, Gannon released him, then turned and headed for the shower. "Join me, Cam."

It wasn't a request, and he caught Cam's smirk as he released the couch and followed.

Several minutes later, once the water had heated and Gannon had stripped, they stood beneath the hot spray, their chests sliding together as their mouths fused. Gannon didn't rush, instead allowing his tongue to linger, gliding over Cam's lips, then inside his mouth while he used his hands to smooth over the hard muscles of Cam's back and ass.

Taking a step back, he grabbed the soap, then proceeded to wash Cam from head to toe, leaving not an inch untouched. While he did, he watched Cam watch him. The way his eyes glowed as they tracked him, it sent a shiver racing down Gannon's spine.

"My turn," Cam said when Gannon finished, taking the sprayer from the wall and rinsing all the suds away.

Gannon traded places with Cam, humming his approval as Cam did the same thing to Gannon, gliding the soap over his chest, his stomach, then lower. Cam used his hands, stroking Gannon until he was so hard he hurt. Somehow Gannon managed to remain still until Cam was finished.

"Turn around," Gannon ordered after Cam had rinsed the soap from his skin. "Hands on the wall."

Cam didn't hesitate, assuming the position. When he did, Gannon licked and kissed Cam's back, down, down. When he reached the indent above Cam's ass, Gannon dropped to his haunches, spread Cam's butt cheeks, and used his tongue to tease and torment until Cam was begging for more.

Truth was, Gannon had intended to play with him for a while, but his cock was like a steel rod, aching and desperate to feel the warmth of Cam's body. Getting his feet, he snatched the lubricant from the porcelain shelf, squeezing a generous amount into his hand and coating his dick while inserting two fingers into Cam's ass.

Cam grunted, pushing his hips back against the intruding fingers. Placing a hand on the center of Cam's back, Gannon forced him forward, the new position giving him better access.

"You ready for me?" Gannon asked, sliding his dick through the crack of Cam's ass.

"Always," Cam groaned.

"Good. 'Cause you better hold on."

Gannon teased a little more, forcing the head of his dick into Cam's ass and retreating. He worked him open that way until neither of them could stand the sensual torture any longer.

Moving closer, Gannon gripped Cam's shoulders, then slammed his hips forward, impaling Cam.

"Ah, fuck," Cam groaned, one hand slipping on the tiled wall but then returning instantly. "Fuck me, Gannon. Ah, God, yes. Fuck me hard."

Gannon rocked his hips forward, back, forward, back. His dick tunneling into Cam, slow and deep, then faster until he was fucking him harder and harder. Their combined groans echoed in the small space as Gannon found a rhythm that stole his breath and made Cam beg louder.

"More?" Gannon asked, the word coming out in a rush.

"Fuck yes." Cam shifted, placing his right foot on the edge of the tub.

"Oh, yeah," Gannon growled, sinking in as deep as he could go.

Blinded by pleasure and an intense need to claim Cam in the most primal way possible, Gannon continued to fuck him, possessing him until his thighs burned from exertion and his cock was throbbing with the need for release.

Keeping one hand on Cam's shoulder, Gannon reached around and gripped Cam's cock, jerking roughly as he drove his hips forward and back.

A rough growl escaped Cam. "Gonna make me come," Cam said through clenched teeth.

"That's the idea," Gannon panted. "And when you do, I want to hear you say my name."

"Ah, fuck," Cam groaned, his head falling back on his shoulders. "Ah, damn. It's too good."

That it was. Being buried inside Cam, possessing him like this was the most incredible feeling in the world.

"Gannon!" Cam yelled as he gripped Gannon's hand over his cock, forcing his grip tighter.

Gannon continued to fuck him and allowed Cam to guide his hand along Cam's thick shaft. He was hanging on by a thread when, finally, Cam yelled his name again.

"That's it, baby," Gannon urged. "Come for me."

And when Cam's body tensed, Gannon let go.

Thirty-Seven

THE FOLLOWING MORNING, after spending the night curled up against Gannon, Cam headed down to the marina office to open up, leaving Gannon asleep in his bed. After making a pot of coffee and checking the appointment book, Cam grabbed his cell phone.

He wanted to get the call out of the way before anything could disrupt the plans he had.

"Mornin', Pop," he greeted his father when Michael answered. "Did I wake you?"

"Nope. Just sittin' here watchin' TV. Everything okay?"

It was better than okay, but Cam didn't tell his father that. Instead, he hummed an affirmation and followed with, "You doin' anything today?"

"No, why? Need some help?"

"Not exactly," Cam told him. "I was wonderin' if I could stop by for lunch."

"Yeah," Michael answered. "I didn't have nothin' planned, 'cept maybe to work on the car today."

Cam took a deep breath. "There's someone I want you to meet."

His revelation was met with silence and Cam's gut tightened.

"Well, then I'll plan to have somethin' made for lunch. Look forward to seein' you both." There was a smile in his father's voice, and Cam released the breath he'd been holding.

"Perfect," he said, hoping his father didn't notice the relief in his tone. "Need me to bring anything?"

"Nope. Looks like you've already got that part covered."

Cam smiled. "See you at eleven?"

"Sounds like a plan."

With that, Cam disconnected the call, stared down at his phone, and smiled. He'd never brought a guy home to meet his father. Sure, he'd told his dad about a few of the guys he'd dated, but never had he felt the urge to introduce them. He'd always considered that to be a step for something that was long-term, with a future potential. He'd never had that.

Until Gannon.

And this … this was the final step.

Funny how he and Gannon had met six weeks ago, and now, after attempting to take things slow, Cam was ready to plow forward at full speed. Truth was, he wanted to spend his time with Gannon, to see him all the time, to spend every night with Gannon.

And the three hours that he had to wait until lunch… Those would probably be the longest three hours of his life.

"Dude, you got laid last night."

Cam jerked his head up to see Dare standing in the office, and only then did the damn alarm on the door sound. Worthless piece of shit. It was supposed to alert them when people were coming *in*, not when they were already *there*.

"Whatever," Cam muttered.

"That's one helluva smile on your face," Dare teased, tipping his Monster Energy drink to his lips. "Only sex can make a man smile like that."

Sex and love, yes. Not that Cam was going to say as much, because he'd been teased enough by Dare already. No reason to give him more fuel for the fire.

"Speaking of," Dare said, looking around. "Where is lover boy?"

"Sleeping." Cam rested his elbows on the counter. "Would you mind watching things for a couple of hours today? I'm gonna have lunch with my dad."

"Sure. You takin' the boyfriend this time?" Dare leaned against the counter, studying Cam briefly.

"Yeah," he admitted, unable to hide the smile. Boyfriend. He liked the sound of that.

Dare nodded his head as though considering something. "Yep, I was right. I knew there was a wedding in the future, and it damn sure ain't gonna be mine."

Cam glared at his friend, but again, the smile broke free. There would be a wedding, Cam had no doubt about that. When, Cam didn't know yet. But he was okay with that.

"You seen Roan this mornin'?" Cam asked, standing straight once more.

"No," Dare said, glancing out at the parking lot. "I was gonna ask you the same thing. The Tahoe is gone."

Cam looked out the window. Sure enough, Roan's Tahoe wasn't parked in the lot.

"Maybe he went to check on Cassie," Cam said, continuing to look at the empty parking space.

Last night, when he'd talked to Roan, he'd seemed fine. Surely his absence didn't have anything to do with Cam or the discussion they'd had. Not that he wanted there to be a problem with Roan's sister, but it would be an explanation, at least.

"Well, if you hear from him, let me know," Dare said, tossing back the rest of his drink and crumpling the can in his hand.

"Will do. And I'll be out of here before eleven."

"I'll make sure I'm around," Dare said with a smile.

WHEN CAM HAD woken him up to let him know that they had plans to have lunch with Cam's dad, Gannon had been both excited and nervous. He liked the idea of meeting Cam's father. It made this thing between him and Cam seem all the more real.

Strange.

Gannon had never met anyone's parents before. He'd never been in a relationship for long enough that they'd made it to that step. And he didn't have any parents to introduce anyone to, so he honestly wasn't sure what to expect.

They arrived at Cam's father's house a little after eleven, and as they were walking to the door, Gannon felt his stomach plummet to his feet. He was pretty damn sure he'd never been this nervous in his life. Not even when a new game released and he waited to hear what the world thought.

As they made their way up the stairs, Gannon noticed Cam glancing sideways at him, grinning from ear to ear.

"Are you making fun of me?" Gannon whispered.

"Maybe a little."

"Figures."

Reckless

Cam rapped his knuckles on the wood door twice before opening it and stepping inside. They were greeted by a darkened living room with a small lamp in the corner. The curtains were closed, and on the huge television, a baseball game was playing. At least Gannon knew where Cam had gotten his love for the game.

"Pop? Where're you at?" Cam called out, taking Gannon's hand and pulling him through the room.

They stepped into a bright, updated kitchen. The stainless steel appliances glowed from the sun shining in through the floor-to-ceiling windows that looked out at the water. From where he stood, Gannon could see a boat ramp, a pier, and two chairs. Looked as though Cam's father spent a lot of time down there.

This was the type of house Cam needed. One that was right on the water, giving him access to the lake whenever he wanted it. Not that he didn't have access from the marina, but this... It was private, and Gannon liked the idea of a place like this, one that would give Cam what he enjoyed most.

A throat cleared from behind them, and Gannon turned to see Cam's father, a man he vaguely remembered seeing in the marina office the very first time he'd come to rent a boat with Milly.

The man was tall, closer to Gannon's height. And there was an air of authority that surrounded him. He was a man people respected, that was clear.

"This the one?" Cam's father asked, the imposing tone making Gannon's insides churn.

Gannon glanced over at Cam to see him still smiling.

"Be nice, Pop." Cam laughed, then took a step closer, still holding Gannon's hand. "Gannon, this is my father, Michael Strickland. Pop, this is Gannon Burgess."

Michael held out his hand, and Gannon shook it in return, praying his palms weren't as sweaty as he thought they were.

"I remember seein' you," Michael said, his dark blue eyes—very similar to Cam's—studying him intently. "Over at the marina, right?"

"Yes, sir," Gannon replied. "You were leaving when I was coming in."

"What's for lunch, Pop? I'm starvin'," Cam said, drawing Michael's attention away.

"Hamburgers," Michael said with a smile, peering from Cam back to Gannon. "But don't worry. I've got the real deal. Not the flat patties you get over at the marina grill. Come on. We'll eat outside."

Michael passed by them, then out through the sliding glass door to the deck. Gannon started to follow, but Cam pulled him up short. He turned to face Cam, noting the smile still plastered on his face.

"He likes you," Cam said softly, leaning in and kissing Gannon briefly.

"How can you tell?" Gannon whispered, running the events of the last few minutes through his head. Nothing in that time made Gannon think Mr. Strickland liked him.

"He didn't interrogate you," Cam told him.

"I heard that!" Michael yelled from outside. "Lunch ain't over yet, boy."

Gannon laughed, feeling the tension that had coiled him into a knot ease.

It wasn't a given that Cam's father would like him, but if Gannon expected to spend the rest of his life with Cam—which he did—then he was just going to have to make sure that he did.

Straightening his shoulders, Gannon squeezed Cam's hand, then headed toward the back door. He was up for the challenge, there was no doubt about it. And before he left that house, he would make sure Michael Strickland knew that he intended to love Cam for the rest of his life.

Cam chuckled from behind him. "Who's the reckless one now?"

An hour and a half later, while Cam was inside cleaning up, Michael was giving Gannon a tour of his garage. More like a workshop, actually. There were two cars inside, one a '69 Barracuda, the other a '67 Mustang that he was restoring. Both still needed a lot of work.

"So, you travel a lot for your job?" Michael asked, turning to face Gannon and leaning against the wooden shelf that held a wealth of tools.

Gannon stopped moving. "Yes, sir."

They'd discussed what Gannon did for a living over lunch. Although Cam's father had insisted he wasn't interrogating Gannon, he'd answered more questions in that hour and a half than he had in his entire life. Or it felt like it.

"I take it Cam's told you about his mother."

"Yes, sir. We've dealt with a few things."

Michael nodded. "I'm glad he's getting into counseling again. I think it'll be good for him."

Figuring he needed to be candid, Gannon moved to stand beside Michael, leaning against the shelf and staring over at the cars. "I love him, sir. He means the world to me, and I'm willing to go the distance with him. I know it won't always be easy, but I'm willing to give it everything I've got."

"I knew you were important to him," Michael said. "I've never met one of his boyfriends. Not that he's had many. At least not that I know of. But not once has he brought one home to meet me. What do your parents think about all this?"

Gannon swallowed hard. "I haven't seen them since I was seventeen," he admitted. "They weren't very supportive of me being gay."

He could feel Michael's eyes on him, and he was prepared to hear a reprimand. He'd heard plenty over the years, people telling him he needed to make amends, that he needed to make things right with his parents, no matter what it took.

"Well, it's their loss, then, son. As far as I'm concerned, a parent's one and only job is to love their child, regardless. It's not so hard, I don't think."

Gannon smiled. "Thank you for that."

"Anytime."

Gannon turned to face Michael. "I know I've just met you and all, but…"

Michael stood up straight, his hands dropping to his sides.

"I plan to marry your son one day. Hopefully one day in the near future. I know it's a little presumptuous of me to ask this now, since you don't know me very well, but I'd like to have your blessing."

Michael grinned. "Yeah, Cam was right."

"About?"

"You're good enough for my boy."

Gannon was going to take that as a yes.

"Come on," Michael said, clapping Gannon on the back and steering him toward the door. "Let's go see what that boy's gettin' himself into."

Thirty-Eight

"SO..." CAM SAID, drawing Milly's attention toward him. "You still seein' that Gary guy?"

Milly rolled her eyes, then tilted her beer to her lips. "Not anymore, no."

Cam knew that dinner had been a disaster, but he never claimed to understand the inner workings of a woman's mind, so he hadn't made any assumptions. "What happened?"

"Oh, you know ... I realized I'm a grown woman and ... he's a child."

Cam laughed.

"I know a guy you'd get along with," Dare said but didn't elaborate.

Cam looked up at his friend. They were all sitting along the dock, drinking beer and watching the sun set. It had been a long day, but after he and Gannon had lunch with his father, Cam had come back to work, and Gannon had pitched in. When Milly had called, Cam had told him to invite her down, to hang out. It hadn't been hard to convince her.

And here they were.

"Hey, you got a minute?" Gannon asked, turning to Roan, who was sitting beside him.

Cam watched the interaction, noticed Roan look over at Cam as though asking what this was about. Cam offered a shrug. He honestly had no idea.

"Yeah, sure," Roan finally said, getting to his feet and following Gannon as they headed back toward the marina office.

"Where're they goin'?" Teague asked.

"Oh, I'm sure Gannon's gonna ask Roan if he wants to be a beta tester for the new game."

"No shit?" Teague leaned forward. "Why not me?"

"You don't play video games," Dare told him, tilting his beer to his lips.

"So?" Teague leaned back and crossed his arms over his chest. "What if I want to?"

Milly laughed, as did Cam and Dare.

"Well, we'll get you set up with Super Mario Brothers," Dare said. "That's a good start for you."

"Fuck off," Teague said, a grin forming on his face.

"So, how'd lunch with your dad go today?" Milly asked.

Dare and Teague instantly quieted, their full attention on Cam.

"Good."

"When're you gonna introduce him to your sister?" Dare asked.

"Already done," Cam told him. "I should've known my dad couldn't keep his mouth shut. She showed up as I was doing the dishes. She and Keith, along with the kiddos."

"And?" Dare seemed to be hanging on the edge of his seat.

"And nothin'. They met. End of story."

Milly sighed heavily.

"What?" Cam asked, turning to look at her.

Teague and Dare both grunted.

Cam frowned.

"Seriously?" She looked between the three of them. "There's never an abrupt ending to a story like that. Men."

GANNON WALKED ALONGSIDE Roan, leading him back toward the marina office as he did. For the better part of the afternoon, ever since Roan had shown back up when Gannon and Cam had returned from lunch, he'd wanted to talk to him.

"What's up?" Roan asked, glancing over at him.

Gannon stopped walking. "I just wanted to make sure we're cool. You and me."

Roan's gaze dropped to his feet. "I know I owe you an apology."

"You don't actually owe me anything," Gannon countered.

"I do, too. What I did... That was kinda bullshit. I shouldn't've interfered like that."

Gannon waited until Roan looked up at him. "I have no intention of coming between you and Cam," he explained. "I'm actually hoping you and I can get past this one day."

Roan didn't say anything, but Gannon hadn't expected him to.

"I know it's awkward. There've been times when Milly dates someone and brings me along to meet him. Not the coolest thing in the world, to tell you the truth. She's an asshole magnet, and it takes a lot for me to keep my mouth shut."

"Well, you're a lot of things," Roan said, a smile forming on his lips. "But I'm not sure I'd call you an asshole. Not yet, anyway."

Gannon felt the tension ease somewhat. Gannon nodded toward the marina. "I want to show you something."

Roan's eyebrows darted down.

"Cam told me you're a gamer."

Just the mention of video games had Roan's eyes lighting up. That, Gannon had expected.

"Little bit, yeah."

"I've got a new one coming out in a month. Thought maybe you'd want to beta test it."

"You serious?"

"Little bit, yeah," he said, using Roan's words.

Roan laughed. "You know I'm a beta tester for—"

Before Roan could finish his sentence, Gannon cut him off. "Do not say their name," he told him in an exaggerated whisper. "At least not with Milly around."

Roan turned to look behind them, where the others were still sitting by the water.

"She might be small, but she's fierce."

Gannon smiled, and Roan laughed.

"You know, you're not so bad," Roan told him as they started walking again.

"No?"

"Nah." Roan chuckled. "And don't worry, I won't tell Cam that you're bribing me with video games."

"Hey, whatever it takes."

And that was the truth.

As far as Gannon was concerned, his life with Cam was just now starting, and he damn sure wasn't above doing whatever it took to smooth the way.

Especially if it meant bribing Cam's best friend with video games.

Reckless

Epilogue

Ten months later, May

"HOPE YOU DON'T mind me saying, but you look much happier than the last time I saw you," Pete McKinley noted when he joined Cam and Gannon in the small, cozy office.

Cam glanced over at Gannon, then back at Pete. "Things are good."

Pete took a seat in the chair across from them, placing his clipboard on his lap. Cam watched the man's light blue eyes as they studied them both, his lips pursing beneath the salt-and-pepper beard that covered most of his face.

"Wedding plans going well?" Pete asked.

Cam smiled, squeezing Gannon's hand. "We're done. All that's left now is the cryin'."

Gannon bumped his shoulder, making Cam laugh.

"So, it's true, y'all are tying the knot on a boat?" Pete glanced between them again.

"It's true," Gannon confirmed.

"How's Roan?" Pete questioned, his eyes darting between them.

Cam smiled. "He's good, actually. It's no longer weird between us."

"That's good."

Cam nodded, then glanced over at Gannon. "Did I mention that my future husband and my best friend have been spending a lot of time together?"

Pete looked at Gannon.

Gannon shrugged and said, "Video games," as though that explained it all.

And actually, it did. Gannon had brought Roan on as a beta tester at first. And things had only progressed from there. According to Roan and Gannon, Cam wouldn't understand. And they were right. He didn't. Water was his thing, not video games.

"And the house?" Pete asked. "Have y'all moved in yet?"

Ah, the house. Cam loved that house and couldn't wait until it was finished so they could move in together. Back in November, Gannon had convinced Cam to take him out on the lake. He'd known something was up immediately because it was never Gannon's idea to go out on the water, but he'd given in, anyway, because those were the two things he loved most in the world: Gannon and the water.

They'd spent a relaxing afternoon out on the lake, but before Cam had steered them back to the marina, Gannon had pulled out his phone and asked Cam to show him a spot that he'd pulled up on the map. Knowing right where it was, Cam had headed that way. It had been a three-acre plot of land right on the water.

Cam had noticed that Gannon had seemed rather antsy the closer they'd gotten. As though he'd been keeping a secret that was ready to burst out of him. He'd been right, because before they'd even reached the dock, Gannon had admitted that he'd bought the land.

"You bought this?"

"Yeah," Gannon said, seeming somewhat uncertain.

"We're gonna have a house on the water?"

Gannon nodded.

"No more back-and-forth? And living in an apartment above the marina?"

Gannon nodded again, his eyes locked with Cam's.

"What about you? That's a long drive to work every day."

"Milly has informed me that working remote has become a thing."

Cam smiled. He could believe that. Milly was always keeping Gannon up with the times.

"So you'll be working from home?"

"When I can, sure," Gannon replied. "What do you think?"

Cam moved closer to Gannon. "I think I want to strip you naked right here on this boat and have my wicked way with you."

Gannon's eyes lit up, a smile causing that sexy little dimple to appear in his cheek. "No one's stopping you, Reckless. No one at all."

"Not yet," Cam told Pete now, relaxing somewhat. "We did the final walk-through last week. They've got a few things to fix. We'll be movin' in before June, though."

"After the wedding?"

Cam nodded, looking at Pete.

They'd been seeing Pete for nearly ten months. Their sessions had started out twice a week during the hardest part but, over the months, had dwindled down to once a month. Though Cam had come to see him a few extra times when Gannon had been away on business. He still wasn't completely at ease with Gannon's traveling, but it was significantly better. The panic attacks were more like heartburn at this point, but still, Cam had learned that talking to Pete, hearing someone rationalize his fears helped.

"And you?" Pete asked, directing his attention at Gannon. "How are things with you? Still busy?"

"Yeah," Gannon confirmed. "New game launches in the fall, so we're gearing up for a busy summer."

"Any trips coming up?"

"Actually, no," Gannon replied. "I've promoted a couple of people, created a couple of positions that will allow me to slow my travels somewhat."

"But you'll still be going from time to time."

"That's inevitable," Gannon answered, squeezing Cam's hand. "But I think I'm gonna take Cam along with me when he can get away."

"And how do you feel about that?" Pete turned his gaze on Cam.

Cam smiled, looking over at Gannon briefly. "Since there're some things I'd like to check off my bucket list, I think it's a great idea."

"Speaking of bucket list." Pete glanced down at the clipboard on his lap. "If I recall correctly, you were gonna be doing some skydiving." Pete looked up at Cam. "Did that happen?"

Gannon huffed beside him, making Cam laugh.

"Not yet," Cam told Pete. "But it's scheduled."

"And when will that be taking place?" Pete watched the two of them intently.

Cam glanced over at at Gannon and smiled. "During the most reckless adventure of my life."

"Which is?"

Cam never took his eyes off Gannon. "When I finally make this man my husband."

"You're gonna jump out of a plane on your wedding day?" Pete sounded confused by that.

Gannon rolled his eyes and sighed heavily, as he'd done ever since Cam had made the suggestion. But even though he pretended not to like the idea, Cam still noticed that flicker in those dark eyes.

Cam shook his head. "No. *We're* gonna jump out of a plane … on our honeymoon."

♥□□□□♥□□□□♥

I hope you enjoyed Cam and Gannon's story. Reckless is the first book in the Pier 70 series. You can read more about the sexy guys in charge of the marina by checking them out on my website.

Want to see some fun stuff related to the Pier 70 series, you can find extras on my website. Or how about what's coming next? I keep my website updated with the books I'm working on, including the writing progression of what's coming up for the Pier 70 series. www.NicoleEdwardsAuthor.com

If you're interested in keeping up to date on the Pier 70 crew as well as receiving updates on all that I'm working on, you can sign up for my monthly newsletter.

Want a simple, *fast* way to get updates on new releases? You can also sign up for text messaging on my website. I promise not to spam your phone. This is just my way of letting you know what's happening because I know you're busy, but if you're anything like me, you always have your phone on you.

And last but certainly not least, if you want to see what's going on with me each week, sign up for my weekly Hot Sheet! It's a short, entertaining weekly update of things going on in my life and that of the team that supports me. We're a little crazy at times and this is a firsthand account of our antics.

Acknowledgments

I have to thank my family first, for putting up with my craziness. From my sudden outbursts when I think of something that needs to be added or when I question why one of the characters did what they did, to the strange hours that I keep and the days on end when I'm MIA because I'm under deadline or just engrossed in a story... Y'all are incredibly tolerant of me and for that, I am forever grateful. I love you with all that I am.

My street team – The Naughty & Nice Posse. Ladies, your daily pimping and support fills my heart with so much love. You are a blessing to me, each and every one of you.

My beta readers, Chancy and Denise. Ladies, I'm not sure thanks will ever be enough. However, not only are you the ones who catch the weird things and ask the bigger questions, you've both become my friends and you keep me going.

My copyeditor, Amy. Punctuation and grammar... well, that's not my strong suit. But it is yours and you are truly remarkable at what you do. You simply amaze me and I am so glad that I found you.

Nicole Nation 2.0 for the constant support and love. This group of ladies has kept me going for so long, I'm not sure I'd know what to do without them.

And, of course, YOU, the reader. Your emails, messages, posts, comments, tweets… they mean more to me than you can imagine. I thrive on hearing from you, knowing that my characters and my stories have touched you in some way keeps me going. I've been known to shed a tear or two when reading an email because you simply bring so much joy to my life with your support. I thank you for that.

♥••••♥••••♥

About Nicole

New York Times and *USA Today* bestselling author Nicole Edwards lives in Austin, Texas with her husband, their three kids, and four rambunctious dogs. When she's not writing about sexy alpha males, Nicole can often be found with her Kindle in hand or making an attempt to keep the dogs happy. You can find her hanging out on Facebook and interacting with her readers - even when she's supposed to be writing.

Nicole also writes contemporary/new adult romance as Timberlyn Scott.

Website
www.NicoleEdwardsAuthor.com

Facebook
www.facebook.com/Author.Nicole.Edwards

Twitter
@NicoleEAuthor

Also by Nicole Edwards

The Alluring Indulgence Series
Kaleb

Zane

Travis

Holidays with the Walker Brothers

Ethan

Braydon

Sawyer

Brendon

The Club Destiny Series
Conviction

Temptation

Addicted

Seduction

Infatuation

Captivated

Devotion

Perception

Entrusted

Adored

The Dead Heat Ranch Series
Boots Optional

Betting on Grace

Overnight Love

The Devil's Bend Series
Chasing Dreams

Vanishing Dreams

Also by Nicole Edwards (cont.)

The Devil's Playground Series
Without Regret

The Pier 70 Series
Reckless

The Sniper 1 Security Series
Wait for Morning

Never Say Never

The Southern Boy Mafia Series
Beautifully Brutal

Beautifully Loyal

Standalone Novels
A Million Tiny Pieces

Writing as Timberlyn Scott
Unhinged

Unraveling

Chaos

25005442R00212

Made in the USA
San Bernardino, CA
14 October 2015